CINDERELLA'S SECRET ROYAL FLING

JESSICA GILMORE

THEIR INHERITED TRIPLETS

CATHY GILLEN THACKER

MILLS & BOON

First Published in Great Britain 2019
by Mills & Boon, an imprint of HarperCollinsPublishers,
1 London Bridge Street, London, SE1 9GF

Cinderella's Secret Royal Fling © 2019 Jessica Gilmore
Their Inherited Triplets © 2019 Cathy Gillen Thacker

ISBN: 978-0-263-27257-4

0819

MIX
Paper from
responsible sources
FSC™ C007454

This book is produced from independently certified FSC™
paper to ensure responsible forest management.

For more information visit: www.harpercollins.co.uk/green

Printed and bound in Spain
by CPI, Barcelona

CINDERELLA'S
SECRET ROYAL FLING

JESSICA GILMORE

'We've had a beautiful friendship, Diana.
We've never marred it by one quarrel or coolness
or unkind word....'
—*Anne of the Island*

To Sam, a true kindred spirit,
thank you for a beautiful friendship.
I've been so lucky to have you in my life xxx

CHAPTER ONE

The Royal House of Armaria invites you
to a Midsummer Ball
June 21
Time: 7 p.m. until late
Place: Armaria Castle
Dress code: Black tie
RSVP

LAURENT PICKED UP the sample cream and gold heavily embossed card and turned it over. The other side was blank, awaiting a name. Strange to think that in less than a week this card would be one of the hottest tickets in town. No, not just in town, in Europe.

After all, it had been over twenty years since Armaria had hosted one of their famous Midsummer Balls, enough time for the opulent occasions to become part of myth and legend; rumour whispered that anything might happen to those lucky enough to attend. Film stars fell in love with royalty, maids married dukes and unhappy countesses ran away with stable boys. Every Midsummer Ball was filled with wonder, with seduction, with magic.

At least, if you believed the stories they were. The reality was probably a lot more prosaic. After all, if Laurent's plans came to fruition, one day stories might be told about this year's ball, a tale of a midnight proposal and a fairy tale romance. His clasp tightened on the card. Luckily he was too old to believe in fairy tales and he had never dreamt of romance. All a man in his position could do was hope for compatibility and liking.

He turned as the library door opened and his mother entered the book-lined room, relief on her face as she spotted him. Replacing the card onto his desk, he covered it hastily with a blank piece of paper and walked out to meet her in the middle of the vast room.

She held out a regal hand towards him. 'Laurent, I haven't seen you since you returned from England. So this is where you've been hiding yourself.'

'Hardly hiding, Maman,' he protested as he bent to kiss her still unlined cheek. 'My aide knew I was in here. As did the maid who brought me my coffee.' He gestured to the small table set with a coffee service pulled up to one of the sofas dotted around the room. 'It's still hot. May I pour you a cup?'

'Thank you, dear.' The dowager Archduchess took a seat on the antique sofa with her usual unhurried elegance, her feet crossing at the ankle, back ramrod-straight and head tilted. Even when it was just the two of them she didn't allow herself to relax. Her hair was always perfectly styled, her make-up fresh, her clothes smart. The message had been drilled into him since he was a small boy; as a member of the Armarian ruling family—the most prominent and important member—

he was always on display, always representing his country, and even when alone he could not, must not, forget it.

Pouring his mother a cup of the fragrant coffee, Laurent handed it to her and she accepted it with a gracious nod of thanks. 'Thank you, Laurent. But you must know, it's no time to be hiding in the library. The Prime Minister has been looking for you. He's hoping for an answer...'

'No, he's hoping for a different answer. And he won't get one.' With practised effort Laurent kept the anger out of his voice. 'I will not allow him to turn Armaria into some kind of grubby little tax haven. My grandfather and father managed without taking that step; you managed without taking that step. I won't be the one to sell the country out. Our people deserve better.'

'Our people deserve new roads and houses, better hospitals, more schools...'

'Which is why we need a long-term strategy.' It was as if they were two actors rehearsing well known lines. Lines they had been repeating for the three years since Laurent had finished his MBA and his mother had formally ceded her regency of Armaria to him.

'And you have one?' Hope brightened her voice. 'How was your trip to England? Did he say yes?'

She didn't need to specify who *he* was; she knew full well that Laurent had been paying a second under-the-radar visit to Mike Clayton, the tech entrepreneur whose robotic gadgets could be found in households all over the globe. Mike Clayton who was looking for a more sustainable form of energy to manufacture said robots. Energy a small country with a long coastline, windswept hills and mountains and long hours of sun-shine could provide…

Laurent walked over to the tall thin windows, star-ing out at the famous castle gardens full of tourists and sightseers. Tourism was a valuable resource for the small country, but it wasn't enough to make it as pros-perous as it needed to be. 'Not exactly. But he didn't say no either and he's coming out to take a second look at the proposed site and to meet with the university.'

'That's promising. But is it enough? I know the Prime Minister is hoping to have a plan approved by Parliament before the summer break. You need some-thing more concrete than a second visit to offer him.'

'I need nothing. Parliament is merely advisory and the Prime Minister would do very well to remember that.' Laurent inhaled slowly as he turned to face his mother. 'You know that my father was determined not to go down the tax haven route, nor did he want to turn the country into a giant theme park of romanticism and cod medievalism. You worked hard to keep his vision alive and I won't betray his legacy. If we can attract one thriving tech company like Clay Industries then others will be sure to follow. We can turn Armaria into the tech capital of Europe, a Silicon Valley of the north. Create jobs and prosperity without losing our integrity.' He stopped abruptly, aware he sounded like he was giving a prepared speech to Parliament, and his mother smiled with understanding. After all, she had heard variations on the speech many times before.

'It's not me you have to convince, Laurent.'

'No, just Parliament.' Advisory they might be, but

life was infinitely easier with them on side. 'If Clay Industries bite then Parliament will capitulate on the tax haven bill, I know it. I just need that first investment…'

'So you'll find a way to make it happen.' His mother was matter-of-fact. This was what they did. Through ten centuries the Archdukes of Armaria had done whatever they had to, to protect their people from invaders and plagues, wars and famine, bankruptcy and poverty. He would not be the first to fail.

'Yes. I will. Which is why I have suggested that the Claytons are our guests of honour for the newly revived Midsummer Ball. Mike Clayton's sixtieth birthday falls on the same day, and they have yet to decide on the best way to mark it. What better way than for him to celebrate here in Armaria on one of the most iconic nights of the year?'

'Midsummer is always special, but it's less than a month away. And it's been years since we held a grand ball. Not since your father…' Her voice faltered, as it still did whenever she spoke of her late husband. Twenty-one years of widowhood hadn't lessened her grief. Things might have been different if she had been able to move on, but instead Laurent was all too aware that his mother's life had stilled at the moment of her husband's death and she had been trapped into a regency she had neither asked for nor wanted, preserving the small country to hand on to her son. 'There is so much to do, to plan and arrange. The ballroom could do with a lick of paint and a polish, as could half that wing and some of our staterooms.'

'It's a good thing we have a castle full of staff, isn't

it? I know the timing is tight, Maman, but our Midsummer Balls were legendary; reviving them is the kind of gesture we need to show we have faith in Armaria, in our past and traditions as well as in our future. It's the ideal opportunity to make the Claytons fall in love with Armaria, with everything we have to offer. Let Mike Clayton use his heart as well as his head when he chooses us. Speaking of which…' He hesitated. Once he'd said the next words, there would be no going back. He steeled himself. 'I think it's time I got married.'

'Married?' His mother's surprise was almost comical. After all, she had been hinting at this very thing for two years now, drawing up lists of eligible and connected young ladies on a regular basis.

'I *am* twenty-eight, as you keep reminding me. And, as you know, Alex is next in line—how cross would he be if I died without an heir and he had to become Archduke?'

'Dear Alex,' his mother murmured. 'He loves that hospital so much.'

'Which is why I need to settle down and have an heir or two so he doesn't have to worry about hanging up his stethoscope and putting on a crown.'

The dowager Archduchess's eyes narrowed as she assessed her son. 'I didn't know you were seeing anyone.' And, her tone implied, if she didn't know about it, then how could it be happening? 'And you know how it is. You *are* Armaria and you have to do what is right for the whole country, and that includes your marriage. You can't just marry anyone.'

'I wasn't planning on marrying just anyone.' He took

a deep breath. Once the words were said there was no going back. 'Mike Clayton has a daughter. Bella. I'm sure you'll like her. I am considering asking her to be my Archduchess. To strengthen the ties between Armaria and Clay Industries on every level.'

'I see.' His mother blinked and for one moment the formidable regent disappeared, to be replaced with a tearful mother who only wanted her son's happiness. Another blink and the regent returned as if she had never left. 'Oh, Laurent. I do see. And of course it makes sense. The days when we needed to ally ourselves with one of our neighbours through marriage may have gone, but there's always a new generation of buccaneers in town.'

'I haven't said anything to Bella or her parents,' Laurent warned his mother. 'I wanted to discuss it with you first. Obviously, she might have plans for her life that don't include a draughty old castle and living in a strange country.'

'Tell me about her. What makes her laugh? What are her dreams?'

Laurent shifted from one foot to another, uncomfortable with the whimsical question. He was an Archduke. He didn't deal with dreams and laughter; he dealt with facts and figures and if he decided to propose to Bella Clayton and if she accepted then it would be the oldest trade in the book. He had a country in need of investment and her family had that investment to make. A title and a throne for money or influence or protection, just as his forebears had done time and time again.

'As you know, I've stayed with her family twice now

and she seems nice enough.' He didn't need to see his mother wince to realise how far short those words fell. 'She's pretty, possibly even beautiful,' he tried again. 'She loves dogs and horses; we spent most of our time together discussing them.' A mutual love of animals was surely as good a place to start a marriage as any. Many royal couples had less.

'Where was she educated?'

'Nothing to worry about there; she went to an exclusive boarding school and then spent a couple of years at a Swiss finishing school. Since then she has worked for Clay Industries, helping run their charity trust.' Not that she seemed over-burdened with a nine-to-five; her role there seemed more titular, but the charity angle would go down well with the press and was good preparation for many of the duties necessary for an Archduchess.

His mother raised an eyebrow. 'No university? That's a shame. I do think in these uncertain times a girl needs a good education beyond correct knives and the right curtsey—she never knows when she might end up Regent in an absolute monarchy. A good grasp of mathematics and economics can be essential.'

A wave of sympathy swept over Laurent for the young Archduchess his mother had once been, barely thirty, widowed and thrust into a position of responsibility on behalf of her young son. 'Hopefully, it won't come to that. I'm not planning on leaving her to manage alone.'

She glanced up, startled, betrayed into an answering smile when she realised he was teasing her. 'Of course not. But an Archduchess does need a lot of common sense and a thick skin as well as brains. It's not an easy job.'

'No. It's not. But she does seem fully aware of the burdens of her privilege as well as the blessings. And her mother made sure I knew that Bella is descended from the Normans on both sides of her family tree—Mike Clayton informally adopted her when he married her mother, but her natural father was a baron, so her background is good enough for those people who care about such things.'

'Yes, it does sound as if her birth and education will do. Laurent, is this idea yours, or have her parents hinted that the two of you might make a suitable union?'

'All my idea. There has been no pressure from Mike Clayton, no hints that his investment is conditional on such a move. But he is extremely fond of his stepdaughter and very family-orientated. I believe he would welcome our marriage and would want to do his best for the place she eventually calls home.' Bella's mother, Simone, was a different story; she had made several comments linking Laurent and her daughter during his two visits to the family estate and taken every opportunity to throw them together. Laurent had no doubt that she was hoping for exactly this outcome—and that with a proposal would come her complete backing for Clay Industries' investment in Armaria.

'And the young lady herself. Does she seem to like you, Laurent? Will she welcome a proposal after so short an acquaintance? Can you be happy with her?'

They were three very different questions.

'I will be happy watching Armaria prosper,' he said at last. 'As for Bella Clayton… I do not believe a proposal will be either a surprise, or unwelcome. She's twenty-seven and has been raised with an expectation of a place in society. Life here would not be the kind of shock it might be for someone from a different kind of background.'

'Well, then,' his mother said after a pause. 'In that case I look forward to meeting her—and her family. When are you hoping that they will arrive?'

'A few days before the ball.' Walking over to the desk, he unearthed the invitation he had been looking at earlier and handed it to his mother. 'I had this mocked up earlier. Once we're happy with the design we'll get them sent out, so get your secretary to send mine the list of everyone you would like to invite by the end of the week. I know the timing is tight, but this is the first royal ball held at the castle for two decades. I don't think any guests will worry too much about prior plans, do you? And, hopefully, by the end of the summer Armaria will have both new investment and a new Archduchess.'

His mother looked around the library, lips pursed. 'I'll also make a list of all the work that needs doing between now and then. It will have to be all hands on deck if we are going to open the castle up to hundreds of guests.'

'I'm happy to wield a paintbrush if it gets the job done. Thank you. Don't worry about the ball itself, Maman. Simone Clayton has recommended an events planner and, all being well, she should be starting at the weekend.' He hesitated. 'Obviously, I expect to cover all costs, as the host, but the Claytons do have some additions they'd like to make to the traditional plans—and of course they have their own list of guests to invite. As a result, they are insisting on paying for the event planner, their guests and for the cost of any of their extra requirements. I did my best to dissuade them, as you can imagine, but they were adamant.' Laurent's mouth thinned. His country, his castle, his responsibility. But he was supposed to be wooing Mike Clayton—and his daughter—not arguing with them, and in the end gracious capitulation was the only option.

'I see. Are you sure, Laurent? Sure that this girl will make you happy?'

Laurent merely bowed in answer. 'I know exactly what I'm doing, both for myself and for Armaria.'

For Laurent knew there was no real difference. He was the Archduke and with the title came responsibility for every man, woman and child, every meadow and mountain. He had never wasted any time wishing things were different; what was the point? His focus had to be on the future—and now his plans were finally coming to fruition. What was the point of might-have-beens and if-onlys? Bella Clayton was attractive, pleasant, well brought up and well connected—and the heir to a company with the capacity to change Armaria's fortunes. If she was prepared to grant him those assets in return for a title then he was a fortunate man indeed.

Emilia Clayton leaned back in her chair and managed to summon up a professional almost-smile as she regarded her stepmother across the vintage desk.

'You didn't have to make an appointment to see me, Simone.' Only both women knew that was a lie. Emilia did everything she could to avoid her father's family. She was sure they were as relieved as she was when she excused herself from dinners and birthdays. Which was why Simone's presence in her office was such a surprise, and not one of the pleasant variety. Just the sight of her stepmother made it hard for Emilia to be the quiet, controlled professional woman she had grown into, the memory of the rebellious teen with more anger than she could control shuddering through every nerve and vein. She shoved the memories back and maintained her smile.

Simone's almost-smile was as faux genuine as Emilia's own. 'You didn't reply to your father's last texts. An official appointment seemed like the only way to actually guarantee getting hold of you.'

'If I'd known it was so urgent I would have made the time. But I've been busy. As you can see.' Emilia kept her tone light but something in her chest twisted as she spoke. Was her father ill? His texts had been so non-committal, the usual wishy-washy hopes that she was well and that he would see her at some unspecified point soon. The same messages he'd been sending her for the last decade—when he remembered. Nondescript, impersonal, a salve to his conscience.

Probably exactly what she deserved.

'I'd heard you started your own business. This is all very quaint.' Her stepmother looked around the spacious office space, with its soothing tones of white and grey and vibrant pictures and soft furnishings, with an air that strongly hinted that quaint was the most neutral word she could come up with. 'I have to say, Emilia, I was very surprised to hear that *you* were living in Chelsea.' The slight emphasis on 'you' conveyed myriad meanings, each one suggesting that Emilia was not the kind of person who belonged in the once bohemian, now rarefied borough.

'No one was more surprised than me, but this is where our agency is based.' The truth was, Chelsea was the last place Emilia would have chosen if she had had a choice. She hadn't ventured to this part of West London since finally leaving home for good at just sixteen; it was far too close to her father's Kensington apartment and there were unwelcome memories around every corner. But when her colleague and friend, Alexandra, had inherited an old townhouse in a beautiful tree-lined street in the heart of the old Chelsea village, it had been the catalyst for the two of them, along with their friends Amber and Harriet, to quit their day jobs and leave their rented rooms in far flung parts of London for the heart of West London.

'Yes, the Happy Ever After Agency. How whimsical.'

'We guarantee happy clients. Speaking of which, is this a business appointment, Simone, or did you just want to catch up? Only we are rather busy.'

Simone raised one eyebrow ever so slightly, her only comment on Emilia's manners. Emilia had never been able to rile her stepmother, no matter how hard she tried. And she had tried. Truth was, Simone had never cared enough about her for her behaviour to really matter, each act of bad behaviour and rudeness an inconvenience rather than a shock. 'Lady Jane Winspear was highly complimentary about the party you organised for her.'

Emilia kept the half-smile in place to hide her confusion. The party in question had been for a pair of particularly spoiled twins. In her opinion, Bella, her stepsister, was equally spoiled but somewhat past the age of unicorn rides and carousels. 'That's good to hear.'

'So when I needed an event planner with immediate effect, I of course thought of you. My way of helping out your little enterprise. I know you're too proud to accept help but I hope you wouldn't be silly enough to turn down paying work.'

Emilia curled her hands into fists under the desk. She had made it clear years ago that she neither wanted or needed anything from her father or his new family. But, although the Happy Ever After Agency was doing well, turning down work would be a foolish move, especially from people as well connected as her father and stepmother. '*You* want to *hire* me?'

'That's why I am here. I would like you to organise your father's sixtieth birthday ball.'

'My father's…' Emilia swallowed. Of course she was aware that her father's sixtieth was less than a month away. How could she not be when his fiftieth had been the occasion when she had packed her bags and walked out of his family and his life, vowing that this time it was for ever? She had planned to spend his sixtieth as she had every one of his birthdays since then: in denial.

'As I said, we're very busy and it's very short notice. And I can't afford any freebies; this is a new business.' She stopped, slightly appalled by herself as the excuses spilled from her mouth. How did Simone always have this effect on her? It was as if she expected the worst from Emilia and Emilia simply had to oblige her. And the only loser was Emilia herself.

'I'm aware of the short notice. The truth is your father was planning a quiet family birthday.' A family birthday which obviously didn't include Emilia. And that might be partly her choice but it still stung. 'However, he's been invited to be guest of honour at the first Armarian Midsummer Ball to be held in over twenty years.'

This was obviously very impressive news indeed and Emilia did her best to look awed whilst trying to work out where Armaria was. Was it the small country between France and Italy or the small country between Switzerland and Italy? Or was it in the Balkans? 'Congratulations to Dad,' she said and Simone threw her a hard glance.

'Finally your father is getting the recognition he deserves. Of course he will want his friends, family and business partners to attend the ball, and so I offered to supply an event planner to make sure every detail is just how he likes it.' Simone steepled her hands and looked at Emilia, her grey-eyed gaze as hard and piercing as it usually was where her stepdaughter was involved. 'Will you be able to find the time to organise the event of the year or will I need to find another planner? One who *isn't* too busy to accommodate me?'

Emilia's mind whirled as thoughts of palaces and royalty and all the delicious publicity such a job would generate passed swiftly through her mind. How could she turn an opportunity like this down? 'Why me?' she asked bluntly.

Simone's mouth thinned. 'Believe me, Emilia, I thought long and hard about coming here today. I want this ball to be perfect and I haven't forgotten your behaviour at your father's fiftieth—and nor has he. But your reputation as an event planner is very good and I can't believe you'd endanger it because of some long-held teen angst. And, whether you like it or not, you know your father better than any stranger ever could. If you put your mind to it then you can make sure this ball is as special as he is.'

Emilia's fists tightened. 'I see.'

'There's a lot riding on the evening. Not only is it your father's birthday but he is considering moving his European headquarters and new factory to Armaria. We have got to know the Archduke very well over the last few months and he and Bella… Well, I don't want to say too much but I have hopes of a much, much closer tie with the royal family. Nothing can go wrong. Is that clear?'

'Crystal.'

'So, you'll do it?'

No. Both Emilia's head and heart spoke in unison. Emilia might be twenty-six now, all grown up with her own business and a family of friends she'd assembled herself, but where her father was concerned she was still a hurt, lonely child. And when it came to Simone she was a hurt, angry child. She kept an emotional and a physical distance from them for a reason; she didn't like who she had been when she lived with them, the way she had acted, her desperate bids for attention, each one more extreme than the one before, how out of control she had been. Better to stay far away. It was self-preservation and it had worked over the last few years.

But the event promised to be lucrative and generate a lot of publicity. This wasn't just about her; there were four of them with a lot invested in the future of the agency. She couldn't make a decision like this on her own.

'I need to talk to my partners. The notice is short and there is a lot to do; I'll have to leave for Armaria straight away and that means more work for everyone here. Look, I'll let you know in the morning. Send me numbers and a rough outline of what you need tonight and if they agree then I'll send through a quote first thing.'

'There's no need for a quote. I'll pay whatever you charge.' Simone got to her feet in one elegant movement. 'My assistant will email through the guest list and let you know your contact at the palace. Remember, I expect you to be professional, Emilia. Do not embarrass your father or yourself. No, don't get up. I can see myself out. I'll see you in three weeks. I'm expecting perfection. Do not let me down.'

CHAPTER TWO

'WELL, OF COURSE we'll say no.' Amber's green eyes burned with indignation as she paced up and down the small sitting and dining room housed in a conservatory at the back of the house. The whole of the ground floor was given over to office space apart from the galley kitchen and this light, if slightly cramped, area. Upstairs, the first floor and attic floor each housed two bedrooms and a bathroom; Alexandra and Emilia had one floor, Amber and Harriet the other.

Emilia wasn't sure what lucky star had been shining down on her the Christmas Eve she had decided to stay late at work rather than face her lonely rented room and ready meal for one. As she had finally left the modern South Bank building where she worked she had met first Harriet, then Alexandra and Amber, all, like her, in their early twenties and all with nowhere to go that Christmas. An impromptu drink had lengthened into a meal and, several years later, they were business partners, housemates and sisters, a bond even Harriet's recent engagement to their former boss, Deangelo Santos, couldn't break. Although Harriet officially now lived in Deangelo's penthouse apartment while she and her fiancé looked for the perfect home, she still had her own room at the Chelsea townhouse and often stayed over when Deangelo was out of town. And not even a billionaire fiancé could tempt her to stop working. The Happy Ever After Agency was born of their hopes and dreams. It was far more than a job. Making it work was their top priority and, although they all knew that Deangelo would gladly bankroll them, their independence was too important to allow them to accept a penny.

'Simone will pay whatever I quote, money no object. And think of the publicity, Amber.'

Alex nodded. 'The Archduke of Armaria is notoriously private. A ball hosted by him, the first in the royal castle in twenty years, will be headlines in all the gossip magazines, headlines which will give us the kind of boost we need to really get ourselves ahead.'

'We're doing okay and we can get ahead another way. Amber's right. You can't be an employee at your own father's birthday.' Harriet squeezed her hand. 'You should be there, dancing the night away, not worrying about missing musicians and whether there's enough canapés.'

'We all know the only way I'll be there is if I can invoice for the privilege. Family gatherings are not my style and it's easier for them to play happy, perfect families without me lurking in the background like the Ghost of Family Past. Look, if we consider this objectively then you know I would be mad to turn it down. It's a great job.' Part of her even believed what she was saying, another part, the bewildered little girl she tried hard to forget, just wanted to be at her dad's birthday party.

And the sensible part of her agreed with her friends. She would be much better off turning the event down.

But no way was she giving Simone the satisfaction.

'Do you want any of us there as backup?' Alexandra asked in her usual calm, cool way and Emilia seized onto the practical question gratefully.

'No, thanks. There is plenty to do here; in fact I have another two birthday parties for the pampered Princelings and Princesses of Chelsea, a Golden Wedding and an engagement party in the next three weeks, plus a restaurant launch and a charity coffee morning. Amber, I know you have a lot of your own work on; will you be able to manage?'

'With your notes and if you're on the end of the phone, of course,' Amber said stoutly.

Emilia smiled at her gratefully. 'We always planned to be doing huge charity balls and corporate launches; it's time we moved on from children's games, even if Pass the Parcel has a real diamond bracelet inside. How nice if we got to employ someone to take care of the small events and I could concentrate on the big league. Look, Simone thinks she's putting me down with this whole scheme, but she's actually doing us a huge favour so let's treat this like any other job. Who knows anything about Armaria?'

'Isn't it the smallest country in Europe?' Amber asked, but Harriet shook her head.

'Third, I think, or fourth. It's a principality, but the ruling Prince is actually an Archduke for various historical reasons I can't remember. Armaria is fiercely independent and proud, very patriotic, very beautiful.

It's in the sweet spot between France, Switzerland and Italy so gorgeous coastline, mountains and forests. Castles to die for; you couldn't ask for a more picturesque location, Emilia.'

'And how do you know so much about Armaria?' Alex arched elegant eyebrows at her friend.

'Deangelo considered investing there. The Archduke wants industry beyond tourism and farming without going down the tax haven route; it wasn't right for him then but he's been keeping an eye on the place to see how things change. The Archduke's father died when he was just a little boy and his mother was regent for many years and she concentrated on stability not growth, which means the economy has stagnated. It's still an absolute monarchy; there's some agitating for more democracy, but the last referendum was pretty decisive in favour of the status quo.'

Harriet clearly hadn't finished but she was interrupted by a squawk from Amber, who waved her phone in the air. 'According to Your Royal Gossip the pressure is on the Archduke to marry. The next closest heir is an older, unmarried second cousin who runs the local hospital and has no interest in changing that. Rumour is that Prince Laurent d'Armaria is looking outside the usual pool of local aristocrats and European royalty for fresh blood and fresh money…'

'Your stepsister is single, isn't she?' Harriet asked and Emilia nodded.

'As far as I know. Simone was hoping for a duke or one of the Windsors but obviously that didn't happen. I wonder if that's what she meant by closer ties? What's he like, the Archduke?'

'Handsome in a cold, blond way. Said to be proud, standoffish.' Amber held her phone out to Emilia but she waved it away. She'd see him for herself soon enough.

'Okay, I think we've decided that we're going for it, right? In that case I declare this meeting officially over. Let's celebrate our new contract the usual way.'

'Pyjamas, cheese on toast and mugs of hot chocolate?' Harriet punched the air. 'Bags me choose the film; Deangelo is on a nature documentary phase and it's interesting but I am gasping for a good old-fashioned romcom.'

They all smiled in agreement, but Emilia knew her friends' smiles all masked concern and that they would be watching her carefully all evening long to make sure she was okay. But as she watched Harriet start to slice the sourdough bread she'd brought over from Borough Market, and Amber grate the cheese while Alexandra began to heat the milk, Emilia also knew that she'd survive. She had before, and this time, thanks to the Agency and the girls who ran it, she wasn't on her own.

Emilia was doubly glad of the optimism and support of her friends when, two days later, she found herself suspended over the famous Armarian royal castle. The helicopter engine was so loud she could barely form a sentence, even in her head, but if she could she was sure that sentence would be *Help*. Human beings were not meant to travel in tiny metal cages held up in the air only by rotating rods.

The helicopter hovered over the castle for a brief moment, giving Emilia a bird's-eye view of the ancient building, all delicate spires and battlements, looking more like a child's dream of a castle than a real-life building, home to the royal family of Armaria, seat of the small country's Parliament and famous tourist attraction. Thanks to Harriet's detailed briefings and Simone's even more detailed notes, she knew that the Archdukes of Armaria had lived right here, in this very spot, for generations beyond memory, the original keep long since enfolded into the growing castle, the whole remodelled in the eighteenth century by an Archduke whose tastes had run to the gothic. The sun shone overhead and to one side the sea sparkled a deep blue, to the other the mountains rose up to meet the sky, the very furthest still topped with white. Even through her fear Emilia noted that she had never seen anything more idyllic in her entire life.

She sucked in a deep breath as the helicopter began to descend. She was here; there was no changing her mind now. And she didn't know what was more terrifying: putting together an event for hundreds of people, an event that would be reported on by every gossip magazine and blog in the western world, in just three weeks—or facing her father and his family.

With a final sickening lurch the helicopter juddered to a stop and Emilia gingerly undid her seat belt and alighted, head bent as far down as she could get it even though the blades were far above her. Glad she had elected to wear sensible flats and trousers to travel, she pulled her light linen jacket down and smoothed her hair back, checking it was still in its smooth ponytail. She was here to work and she needed to make the right impression straight off. This she could do. She'd been working since she was sixteen years old and that was the way she liked it. She'd soon learned that the busier she was, the less time she had to think. Or to feel.

A tall, angular woman was waiting at the far end of the helipad and, after seeing that her bags were being collected by a young, uniformed man, Emilia made her way over to her. 'Hi,' she said, holding out her hand in greeting. 'I'm Emilia, the event planner.' It was only as she spoke that she realised she had omitted her surname. Clayton was common enough a name but it might be easier not to be associated with the guest of honour or asked any difficult questions. Emilia only it would be then, unless anyone asked outright.

Her hand was ignored in favour of a condescending nod. 'Come with me. I'll show you to your office. You do not have much time so I hope you are ready to start straight away.'

'That's okay. I once organised a takeover announcement and launch of a whole new brand in just forty-eight hours. I thrive on pressure.' Uncomfortably aware she was beginning to sound over eager and might break out into the crazy metaphors of a reality show contestant any second, Emilia hurriedly changed the subject. 'It's very beautiful here; what an amazing setting. I usually like to start off by walking around a venue, getting to know it properly. Will there be any issue here if I do the same? I'm aware that the building has several functions and that the royal family actually live here and the castle is home to Parliament as well.'

'Your security clearance has been arranged.' As the older lady spoke they arrived at a small side door, guarded by a perspiring man in an antiquated-looking uniform, all braid and gilt. 'This is the door you will use to enter and exit the palace at all times. You need to show your pass here and then sign in once inside. No pass, no admittance, no exception.'

'Understood.' Emilia smiled at the guard, who stared woodenly back before she followed her guide into the long entrance hallway. It took a few moments for her details to be registered, her passport scrutinised and the all-important pass to be issued and she was then led down the corridor, rooms pointed out as they went.

'That's the main aides' office, the housekeeper's room and the *garde de campe*'s suite. You'll find the kitchens along there, turn right and down the stairs; the staff dining room is next to it. Breakfast is available between six and eight, lunch between noon and two and dinner from eight. If you require anything in the meantime, ask a page and she or he will get it for you. You do not help yourself. Most people are fluent in English; the official language is French, but day-to-day we speak an Armarian dialect which is a mixture of Italian and French.'

'I have passable Italian and my mother was French so I should be fine,' Emilia reassured her and the confidence elicited a begrudging smile. This lady was a difficult audience, but she'd had worse.

'Your pass gives you access to everywhere you should

need to go. If it's locked then it's a private area, accessible only to the royal family and their immediate staff. You are not to trespass. This side of the castle is the administrative and housekeeping wing and so the royal family are very unlikely to be seen back here, nor should you encounter any Members of Parliament; their offices and debating chambers are on the other side of the castle. If you should see the Archduke or his mother you curtsey and do not speak until spoken to. If you need to check anything with them, you ask me and I will arrange it.'

'Great. And you are?'

The thin lips pursed even tighter. 'Contessa Sophy D'Arbe. The Archduchess's secretary.'

'Got it.' Emilia looked around her with interest. Although the windows were narrow and glazed with ancient-looking glass, the curved ceilings high and the stone underfoot uneven, grey and very old, the corridors were still impersonal and corporate, with nondescript watercolours on the walls and the painted, closed doors were numbered like in any work space.

'Your office is on the floor below; it's small and a little dark, but it was the only space we had available. It should have everything you need, including lists of all the palace suppliers. Your bedroom is in the attic. The key to your room and directions to all areas of the castle are on your desk and your belongings have already been taken to your room.' The Contessa came to a stop by a narrow staircase and nodded to it. 'Your security pass will unlock your office door. Down those stairs, turn right, room twelve. If you need any refreshments, ask a page. I'll arrange a meeting with you tomorrow to

see how you've got on. Oh, and welcome to Armaria.'
And with that the Contessa nodded one more time before sweeping away without a backward glance.

Emilia stood at the top of the stairs, torn between
an urge to laugh and an urge to turn around and scam-
per back to the safety of her Chelsea home as fast as
she could. 'The Contessa and Simone seem destined to
become BFFs,' she muttered. 'I must introduce them.'
Right. She took a deep breath. Time to find and check
out the adequate office. Time to locate a page and order
some much-needed coffee. Time to write out her first of
what would be many to-do lists. And then time to famil-
iarise herself with the castle and the grounds. She had
all this wonderful, old, picturesque space to play with.
The more she had to do, the less time she had to worry
about actually seeing her father. It was time to get busy.

'Ah, Your Highness...'

'His Royal Highness will know the answer...'

Eyes forward, head up, Laurent silently repeated as
he swept down the grand corridor, determinedly not
looking left, right or up onto the gallery, where at least
three people were trying to grab his attention. He slid
his gaze slightly to the right to ensure his Armarian
Spaniel, Pomme, was following him, then snapped them
straight ahead, allowing one hand to briefly rest on the
dog's head as he marched on.

It came to something when a man couldn't find any
peace in his own castle. Laurent just wanted a corner to sit and read through the proposal his Chancellor
had pressed upon him earlier that day, but every corner

seemed to be full of cleaners or decorators or florists. There wasn't an inch of the palace that wasn't being buffed, polished, repainted or reupholstered and the air was thick with paint, dust and turpentine. Even his own suite of rooms wasn't immune, although he had made it very clear to anyone who would listen that they at least were strictly off-limits to cameras, guests and onlookers. Even a prince needed a room of his own—or, in his case, five rooms including a study and a bathroom, his bedroom, dressing room and en suite bathroom, neatly housed in one of the four turrets which rounded off every wing of the castle. Although he would never admit it, Laurent was still secretly glad that he had his own turret room. It seemed like the least a boy growing up in a castle could expect, a small consolation against the lack of privacy and tourists around every corner. Against the role he had no choice but to occupy.

'Just the man! Your Highness…'

But Laurent had long since learned the key to getting from A to B undisturbed. He simply strode fast, head high, eyes not focusing on a single face, not catching anyone's gaze. And because it was considered bad manners—if not downright treasonous—to accost the Archduke without an explicit invitation, this tactic usually worked. But it was hard to walk purposefully when one had to keep dodging ladders, buckets and toolboxes and every now and then Laurent would accidentally catch someone's eye and that would be considered the explicit permission that person needed to unburden themselves to their sovereign, as was their right and his duty. But when all they wanted was his view on paint colours or a ticket to this damn ball and he had a proposal to read, his patience was wearing thin fast. It was with a huge sense of relief that he finally reached the tiny side door to which only he owned a key and stepped out into the sunny courtyard beyond, the precious proposal a little more bent and dog-eared and still unread. He closed the door firmly behind him as Pomme made a dash for the nearest potted plant.

Laurent tightened his grip on the report. This was his chance: his chance to make Armaria truly independent and stable. Industry, jobs, investment… The Chancellor had gathered all the evidence, ready for Laurent to place it directly in Mike Clayton's hands. He just needed to pick when to present it. Before the ball or after? Before he proposed to Mike Clayton's beloved daughter or after…?

He'd always known he'd have to marry strategically; every Archduke did. Their title and position bartered carefully away for influence or money or hopefully both. Why should he be different just because some modern foreign princes and princesses had been allowed to follow their hearts? In a country where the monarch was more than a figurehead, hearts simply couldn't rule over heads. He'd always known this.

And now the time had come. Proposing to Bella Clayton was the most sensible thing he could do. He'd be fulfilling his duty to the country and to the throne. She was well-bred, well-educated and brought with her the potential of a new beginning for Armaria. She was perfect.

Whistling for Pomme to join him, Laurent walked

across the shady courtyard, filled with tall plants in earthenware pots and brightly flowering climbing plants. An arched door led into a walled garden, half a flower-filled lawn, half a small tangled orchard of fruit trees. At the far end of the orchard, a small wrought iron arbour stood by the wall, a shady respite from the relentless noon sun, and Laurent's favourite hiding place. Checking his phone—only eight missed calls, fifteen messages and thirty-three emails since he'd last looked half an hour ago—he headed straight there while Pomme, ecstatic to be freed from palace etiquette, made for the nearest tree. Laurent absentmindedly scrolled through the emails, deleting or forwarding as many as he could, flagging the rest to deal with later.

Intent on his phone, he didn't notice a leg lying in his path, not until he tripped right over it, recalled to his surroundings by an indignant, 'Ouch! Watch where you're going!'

Regaining his balance, Laurent turned and looked down at a young, slim woman, lying under a tree, long legs sticking out in a most dangerous way. 'I shouldn't need to watch where I'm going,' he said in his most repressive manner. 'This garden is private.'

It was only as he spoke that he realised the young woman had spoken and he had replied in English.

Flushing to the roots of her honey-brown hair, the young woman immediately scrambled to her feet, notebook in one hand, pen in the other. 'I did wonder,' she confessed. 'The door was so well concealed, but when it opened…'

'You slipped inside and hoped no one would see

you?' It should have been locked. Only two gardeners had the key; one of them had slipped up.

'That's about the truth of it. They gave me an office, but it's so noisy in the palace I couldn't think so I rewarded myself for a solid afternoon's work with an explore of the gardens. I couldn't believe my luck when I found this place. Not that the rest of the gardens aren't exquisite,' she added hurriedly. 'But they are so formal. I like a bit of wildness in my nature. I'm Emilia—' she stuck the pen into a pocket and held out a hand '—the event organiser. I am so sorry. I promise not to trespass again.'

Laurent was slow to take her hand, struck as he was by two things. One was the frank expression in her clear hazel eyes, an expression untinged by awe. The other was her surprising admission that she preferred this small, shady garden to the famous royal gardens of Armaria. He did, of course, but as far as he knew he was in a minority of one. 'You don't like the Royal Gardens?'

She stepped back, hand dropping as she looked around at the orchard as if seriously considering his question. 'Oh, no, they are beautiful and they will make a wonderful backdrop for the ball. But they're very...' she paused '...very grand. And perfect. I worry about crushing a blade of grass, or casting a shadow on a carefully cultivated scene. I'm much more of a throw myself on the ground and sprawl kind of girl, as you found out. Sorry again.'

'In that case,' Laurent said, 'you must come here whenever you wish. I'll order you a key.'

'But this is obviously private; won't the Archduke mind?'

For a moment all Laurent could do was stand there with an expression he was sure was the most undignified one he'd worn since ascending to the Dukedom at the tender age of seven. 'Mind?'

'If it's usually locked then isn't it his? That's what I was told—that all locked areas are private, for the royal family only.'

And that was when he realised what was odd about this conversation. There was no awe in her expression, no hesitation in her manner because she had no idea who he was. Laurent could not remember the last time that had happened—if indeed it ever had. True, he'd been helping shift furniture in the throne room and hadn't changed out of his oldest jeans, the ones that made his mother sigh on the rare occasion she saw him in them. His hair wasn't neatly combed but falling into his face, and his short-sleeved shirt was covered with dust. No one expected to see an Archduke look like one of the many labourers working away to make the palace perfect for the ball of a potential billionaire fairy godfather. For one moment he was tempted to pretend that he was one of them, to enjoy this pomp and ceremony-free moment a little longer.

He pushed the enticing thought aside. Surely she'd wonder how a palace workman could give her permission to be in a private place and, besides, such games were beneath him.

He held out his hand with the straight-backed formality that had been drilled into him since before he could

walk. 'I didn't introduce myself. I'm…' But the words
were thick in his throat. Oh, he had a few, a very few,
handpicked friends, men he could trust, who he could
be some semblance of normal with for a few precious
hours a week, but even with them there was an unspoken acknowledgement of his rank. When had he last had
a conversation this free and easy? He liked the frank
way she chattered on, despite her embarrassment at
having been caught trespassing. That would disappear
in an instant once he revealed his identity. 'I'm…' But
before he could complete the introduction Pomme came
bounding over, his interest in the pretty stranger clear.

'Hello, beautiful, who are you?' Emilia bent over
and found the exact spot behind Pomme's ears where
he loved to be scratched. Laurent grinned as he watched
his dog writhe with no self-consciousness whatsoever.
'What glorious colouring. Almost calico.'

'Pomme is an Armarian Spaniel. Originally bred to
be hunting dogs, but he's a pampered pet, aren't you,
Pomme?'

'He's absolutely gorgeous. Does he belong to you?'

'Yes. As you must have realised by now, he's Pomme
and I'm Ren…' The diminutive came easily to his
tongue. And it wasn't a lie; a very few people short-
ened Laurent to Ren. But never in public.

'Hi, Ren.' She straightened, one hand still buried in
the dog's thick ruff. 'It was nice meeting you but I'd
better go before we both get into trouble. I get the feeling the Archduke wouldn't be too happy if he caught
me here.'

'I'm sure he wouldn't mind.'

'Maybe not. But I'd still better go. It was lovely meeting you. And thank you for not arresting me!' And with one last pat for Pomme, a smile that didn't quite reach her eyes and a swish of her ponytail she turned and walked away. Laurent stood in the shadows and watched her walk out into the sunlight, the solitude he'd been craving suddenly not feeling as desirable as it usually did. 'Emilia,' he said softly, tasting her name, before heading over to the arbour to finally read the report that would help him save his country.

CHAPTER THREE

THE MOMENT OF stillness before an event took shape was always Emilia's favourite time. She loved the second an event became a success, of course, watching her hard work come to fruition. And she adored the exhilaration that always greeted a finished event. The knowledge that once again all her hard work, long hours, last-minute decisions and substitutions and occasional panics were worth it. But stepping into an empty space for the first time, visualising it filled with people, mentally dressing and decorating and transforming it, was always the best bit of the job. She'd created wonderlands out of bland conference rooms, fairy tale backdrops from ordinary gardens and come up with more innovative conferences than any one person should have to organise in one lifetime and they all started here: gazing out at a blank canvas, pure and mistake-free.

Of course her blank canvases weren't usually eighteenth century ballrooms, large enough to hold several hundred people, with doors leading to ante rooms, dining rooms and private nooks. They didn't usually have a wall of French windows leading out onto exquisite balustraded terraces. She would have to be a poor event planner indeed not to create the perfect ball with this backdrop, even with two very different but potentially demanding clients and just three weeks to work her magic.

On the one hand was her father's sixtieth birthday. Simone had emailed Emilia several lists of demands, from a wish for her father's favourite music and food to be included to a command for a themed ball. At the same time it was clear that, although the Midsummer Ball hadn't been held for over two decades, the night itself was an important one in the Armarian calendar and there were many traditions that had to be incorporated into the event, from country dances to a candlelit procession and special flower wreaths for unmarried women.

Tablet in one hand, tape measure in the other, Emilia started to examine the room, taking pictures of possible breakout and bar areas, and pacing out where the stage might be. The minstrels' gallery would be perfect for a small band but not for a full orchestra and other music acts needed for the dancing section of the ball.

The royal family had evidently taken the upcoming event as an excuse to freshen up the castle. Every corridor echoed to the whines of drills or the banging of hammers and the smell of paint and turps was omnipresent. Stepladders, ladders and stools were propped up in every corner and dust sheets shrouded paintings and statues. It was all a reminder of just what a big deal this ball was. A career-defining ball.

But, more than that, it was an opportunity to give something personal to her dad, something only she could give. He might not recognise her hand in the evening and she probably wouldn't even speak to him or acknowledge that she'd been involved in any way, but making his birthday special might be a way to…what? To make amends for her role in their estrangement.

At first she had blamed only him—well, her father and Simone. But with maturity had come a painful understanding that her own behaviour had by no means been beyond reproach. Hurting from her parents' divorce, grieving for her beloved *maman*, torn away from her home, she had retaliated with the only weapons she'd had—her tongue and her rebellious spirit. And what weapons they had been.

If only things had been different…

Closing her eyes, Emilia took a step and then another, whirling around as if she were in the middle of the ball. In another universe she wouldn't be an employee; she'd be the daughter of the guest of honour. She'd dance with him on his birthday, she'd dance with the Archduke; their names would be linked but she would laugh the rumours off because she would be more interested in working in her father's business than in marrying a public figure. At this ball she could smile and laugh with no regrets and her father would have no reproach in his eyes. There was no Simone, no Bella…

Abruptly Emilia stopped and opened her eyes. Daydreams were just that. Dreams. Inconsequential, useless. She needed to push them aside and concentrate on the ball. It was all she had.

The whole castle hummed with activity and optimism and Laurent found he was humming along with it. Usually his role demanded a certain distance and formality but it was all hands on deck to ensure that the castle would look its very best under the spotlight of the world's media. For the last few years many of the staterooms had been a little neglected as they were only open to tourists on one day a week, a multitude of cracks and faded plasterwork hidden by closed curtains and strategic lighting. Any formal receptions were held in the wing of the castle which hosted the country's parliament and, as a result, it was immaculate. It was nice to see the older rooms come back to life, just the way they had been when his father was still alive and Laurent was allowed to be just a little boy, not the Archduke, bowed by duty and expectation.

Pomme by his side, Laurent half jogged towards the ballroom. It wasn't often he got to do really practical things, despite a youth spent in the Army cadets and two years before university spent training as an officer. He might be able to create a bivouac out of three branches and some leaves, light a fire using flint, forage for and cook his own dinner and use every gadget on his army knife correctly, but he didn't get many opportunities. When he was in the castle his food was cooked and served to him, his baths run, his clothes laundered, put away and laid out. People's jobs depended on his inertia. It didn't make said inertia any easier to bear. But right now there were more jobs than people to do them and not only was he back in the disreputable jeans usually worn strictly in private, but there was a ladder and a tin of paint with his name on. Turned out this ball was a good idea after all.

Reaching the ballroom, Laurent skidded to a halt, Pomme one step behind. The room was already occupied by a slight brown-haired girl, twirling around at the far end, arms outstretched as if she were waltzing. Emilia. His chest tightened as he watched her turn, an almost overwhelming desire to walk over and take her hand, be part of her dance, enveloping him. Her eyes were closed, her expression unsmiling but serene, as if she were many miles away, in a different time and place. And then her arms dropped, she stilled and her eyes opened, her face dark with a melancholy and emptiness that Laurent recognised. A look he occasionally saw in the mirror but had never seen on another person's face. It made him profoundly uncomfortable, as if he were trespassing somewhere he had no right to be, and he stepped back, intending to make a noise as he re-entered the room and give Emilia warning of his proximity. But, somewhat inevitably, Pomme had different ideas. Recognising the person who gave such excellent ear rubs, he bounded past Laurent and, with a snuffly woof, collided with Emilia's legs and thrust his head under her hand, tail wagging at a speed of at least a hundred beats an hour.

'Pomme!' Laurent called, half amused, half exasperated by his dog's manners—and a little bit jealous. How nice to be so confident of your welcome by such a pretty girl—and so justified in that confidence, he thought, watching Emilia bend her knees in order to get closer to the squirming, happy dog. 'I do apologise. He has had training but he forgets himself when he sees a friend.'

Emilia looked up at that and an expression of such

utter joy passed over her face that Laurent nearly took a step back. She had a thin, rather solemn face, dominated by huge hazel eyes, but when she smiled it transformed from prettiness to a very real beauty, her eyes lit by gold flecks, her full mouth set off by identical dimples punctuating her cheeks. 'Am I his friend?'

'He seems to think so.'

'My first Armarian friend. And what a handsome one.'

'He knows it too,' Laurent said drily. 'I try to limit compliments to one a day, otherwise he gets a swelled head.'

She laughed at that and he was conscious of pride at her reaction. He sensed she didn't laugh often. 'You have more self-control than me. If I had a dog like this I would spend my whole time telling him how gorgeous he is and just what a good boy.'

'You don't have a dog? I assumed you did; you have the magic touch.'

'No—' she straightened and the light left her eyes as if it had never been '—I had one when I was very little but when my parents split up…' She didn't finish the sentence.

There was a world of unhappiness in the unsaid words. 'Everyone should have a dog.' Laurent was hit with inspiration. 'In fact Pomme is the proud father of a new litter. You could have one of his puppies as a souvenir of your time here.'

'You fathered a litter? What a clever boy.' Emilia addressed Pomme in caressing tones. 'But I couldn't possibly. I mean, his puppies are bound to be expensive. And I live in London. But thank you. That's a lovely thought.'

'Well, if you change your mind…' Laurent didn't know why it was so important to him, but he vowed to make sure that when Emilia left she took a puppy with her. A girl who obviously loved dogs like she did should have one. Sometimes it felt as if he could only really be himself with Pomme and he couldn't help guessing that she was similar; again he felt that odd sense of intimacy, as if he already knew Emilia, as if they were alike.

He shook the thought away. A smile and a quick conversation and he was making up a connection that couldn't exist, projecting his own feelings onto a strange girl because of a luminous smile and the sadness in her eyes.

'Don't tempt me; it wouldn't take much to change my mind, but it wouldn't be fair. A dog like this wants countryside and freedom, not city parks and bylaws. Besides, I share my home with two other girls and I have no idea what they'd say if I came home with a puppy. But it was a very kind suggestion.'

'Don't make your mind up completely until you've seen them. In fact, what are you doing now?'

'Measuring and planning. I'm thinking that with such disparate ages and types of people attending the ball it might be fun for several different bands to play concurrently and other entertainment to be on offer as well. Like a grand fete or a fair, a kind of festival vibe, you know? Make the gardens an extension of the ballroom, especially for the more traditional elements which feel like they belong outside. Apparently there are several marquees we can use and plenty of outside staging. At least the weather is pretty much guaranteed to be warm and dry, a definite bonus. In London we always need rainy day contingency, even—especially—in the height of summer.'

'Sounds good.' It really did—and refreshingly different from the balls of the past, grand formal occasions accompanied by the swelling tones of the orchestra, of waltzes and foxtrots, the gardens a mere backdrop and place for assignations. But this was a new start, a fresh dawn for a new Armaria, and Laurent couldn't help but be entranced by Emilia's vision—and by the animation in her voice, her face, in her whole body as she described it.

'I hope so. I have to run my ideas past the Contessa, and past Simone tomorrow. Unfortunately, they don't seem to actually speak so everything has to be conveyed through me. Luckily, there's a big enough budget and enough space to accommodate everyone's ideas, but I haven't broken it to the castle staff that Simone would like a themed ball—complete with costumes. I'm not sure how the Archduke and Duchess will feel about that.'

'Nor am I.' Laurent spoke with perfect truth. He suspected his mother would hate the idea but accept it philosophically if it helped them achieve their objectives. He, on the other hand, would do anything not to add to the little furrows creasing Emilia's forehead as she spoke. 'But the ball is in honour of Mike Clayton so I'm sure they will be happy to accommodate his wishes.'

'I hope you're right. I managed to talk her out of

fairy tales and medieval knights but I need to offer her something in return. I was wondering…' She paused.

'Yes?'

'Well, I know Shakespeare is English but he's kind of universal and lots of his plays are set around here. I was wondering about *A Midsummer Night's Dream* as a theme? Then people can wear pretty much what they like—go traditional in Greek chitons or Tudor clothing or anything else really. It fits in really well with the traditional Armarian wreaths and we can supply masquerade cloaks and masks for anyone who doesn't want to dress up. I thought we could hire actors to perform the play, just wandering the grounds.'

'Sounds like a great idea; I must get a donkey's head ordered immediately.'

'You'll be attending the ball then?'

'Yes…' Laurent remembered with a sinking feeling that he hadn't actually told Emilia who he was. 'I hope you'll save a dance for me.'

'Oh, I won't be dancing. There's always too much to do behind the scenes. My costume will involve trainers, black clothing so I can pretend to be part of the scenery and an earpiece. Not very glamorous at all. Less Titania, more a rustic. So what are you and Pomme up to now?'

Laurent nodded at the ladder. 'I'm painting. Pomme is waiting for me to finish so he can have a walk. He's not really any use at practical tasks.'

'It's amazing how hard everyone is working to get the castle ready. I mean, with candles and moonlight it would look incredible, but with all this buffing up it's really going to shine. I guess Mike Clayton really is important to Armaria.'

Laurent stilled. Was his wooing of the tech tycoon so obvious? 'What have you heard?' he asked, trying to keep his tone light as if the conversation was inconsequential.

'Not much, just that Clay Industries is looking for a new European headquarters and Armaria wants to encourage industry. You don't need an MBA to put two and two together and guess that this ball is a way of wooing them. Plus Amber said—' She stopped abruptly, her rather sallow cheeks turning pink.

'Amber?'

'My business colleague. She mentioned that there's a lot of chatter about the Archduke's marriage. Poor guy. Can't be much fun having the world's media watching your every move and speculating every time you speak to someone with working ovaries. Anyway, Amber said some of the gossip magazines are suggesting a closer tie than a business one between the palace and the Claytons.' She stopped, the pink now deep red. 'But I don't want to gossip; it's none of my business,' she finished, an odd, slightly bitter note in her voice.

'It's all right. You won't get arrested for gossiping about the Archduke's marriage. If it were a prosecutable offence half of Armaria would be in jail right now.'

'How horrid for him. I'm glad I don't have to deal with all that, aren't you? Even this glorious castle wouldn't make up for the lack of privacy and freedom. I've never fancied being royal or in the public spotlight. Not since I first saw *Roman Holiday*.'

'Since you went to Rome?' Laurent was slightly reeling from how accurately Emilia had summed up his situation. Most people told him how lucky he was, seemed to envy him the accident of birth that had placed him here. They didn't feel sorry for him or, if they did, they hid it well. It was bizarrely refreshing to hear such a different perspective. He needed more of that. Fewer courtiers and advisers, more straight talking.

'No, I've never been to Rome, although one day I would love to, not that that's relevant. No, I meant *Roman Holiday*. The film. You must have seen it. Audrey Hepburn? Gregory Peck?'

'An old film?' His mouth quirked in amusement, his smile widening as he watched Emilia bristle.

'A classic,' she corrected him.

'So no high-speed chases?'

'You need to watch more classics; there's plenty of high-speed chases in them. *North by Northwest*, *To Catch a Thief*, anything with Cary Grant.'

'But not in *Roman Holiday*.'

'No, but there is a scooter. I can't believe you don't watch classic films; you're missing out.'

Laurent leaned against the wall and folded his arms, Pomme coming to sit by his side. 'Let me guess. It's set in Rome and—who is it, Audrey Hepburn?—she's on holiday and meets an Italian millionaire played by Cary Grant and they don't like each other and then they fall in love. On a scooter.'

Emilia crossed her own arms in response and fixed Ren with what he assumed was her most withering glare. It was actually pretty adorable and his chest tightened again. Standing here, faux arguing, just hanging out with an intelligent, beautiful woman as if he were no more than the handyman she thought him was the most fun he'd had since, well, since he could remember.

'You couldn't be more wrong,' she said loftily. 'It's Gregory Peck for a start and he's American, not Italian, and a journalist looking for a big story.'

'My favourite kind,' Ren murmured. He couldn't quite keep the dryness out of his voice and Emilia glanced at him uncertainly.

'She's a princess in Rome for some big summit and she sneaks out of the palace for a bit of freedom.'

'That's more like it. I like the sound of her.'

'She's utterly charming. Very fragile but regal as well, with these huge sad eyes.' Laurent couldn't help but feel as if Emilia was describing herself. 'Anyway, Gregory Peck recognises her and thinks he's going to get an exclusive so pretends he has no idea who she is and takes her on this whirlwind tour of Rome while his friend takes loads of photos of her. She cuts her hair and they see all the sights and then they fall in love...'

'Is there a happy ending?' For one moment he felt wistful yet hopeful, as if this wasn't the plot of a film but a true story which promised hope for his own pre-destined path.

'No, I mean, it's more bittersweet. She goes back and he turns up at the press junket and she recognises him and thinks her secret escape will be front page news, but he just looks at her—in this absolutely amazing heart-in-his-eyes way—and she looks at him in the same way, only discreetly, so the rest of the journalists don't guess, and he manages to give her the photos so she knows she's safe. And when she does her speech it's all aimed at him, like a love letter wrapped up in the formal part. That's the film that made me not want to be a princess. It was far more fun to ride with Gregory Peck and drink Prosecco in Rome than deal with dignitaries and probably marry some boring prince.'

'Quite right too. Who would want to marry a prince?' She glanced at him and he made his expression as guileless as possible. 'So that's the end? She goes back to do her duty?'

'I used to imagine a sequel,' Emilia confessed. 'Her kingdom had been turned into a republic and she was free to marry whoever she wanted. She meets Gregory Peck again as she's trying to start a new life and this time they can be together. Not that I'm usually a hopeless romantic. Just in this case.'

'Even princesses in exile are expected to marry into other royal houses. I wouldn't count on your princess getting the normal life she wanted, even after a revolution.'

'But not today, surely. I mean princes marry actresses and princesses marry personal trainers. The rules have changed.'

'Maybe,' he allowed. 'But an heir to the throne or a ruler cannot always follow their heart. Sometimes they have to do what's right for the whole country. Even in a place like this. Especially in a place like this.'

And, just like that, they were back to where they'd started. 'So you think it's true? The Archduke is going to marry Bella Clayton?'

'I think the Archduke will recognise what economic and business sense it makes to create close ties with a man who can bring such wealth and prosperity into a country which desperately needs something new.'

'That seems harsh on both of them. But maybe we don't know everything. Maybe they're head-over-heels in love.'

'Maybe.' It was definitely time to change the subject. 'Do you have time for a quick break? Let me introduce you to the puppies. Even if you don't want to adopt one, you should still meet them.'

'How can I resist a puppy break? Let me just measure out the stage first. Here, take this end of the tape measure and keep walking back until I tell you to stop. Ready? Okay, keep going…further, further. Right there. Great!'

Walking backwards, Laurent had no idea that anyone else had entered the room until he stopped and heard a voice behind him, his heart sinking as he heard the cultured tones of his mother's private secretary.

'Ah, there you are, Emilia. Her Royal Highness was hoping for an update. Would you be able to spare five minutes right now?'

Laurent wanted to keep his back turned, to allow himself another day, another few hours of being Ren the handyman, of being able to spend a few more moments teasing Emilia about old films and listening to her speak with complete candour. But he knew his time had run out and he had barely half turned before the Contessa had sucked in a breath and fallen into a curtsey. 'Your Highness. I didn't expect to see you here.'

Emilia looked across at him, shock and disbelief darkening her eyes. 'Your Highness?' The question was so faint the Contessa didn't pick up on it.

'Of course, if you are busy with the Archduke then I am sure the Dowager Archduchess will not mind a slight delay. I'll tell her to expect you in, say, half an hour?'

'No, it's fine. I think we're done here, aren't we, Your Highness?' And Emilia gave him the briefest of curtseys and left with the Contessa before Laurent had a chance to say a word. But what could he have said? His brief trip into normality was at an end. It was probably for the best.

But he'd enjoyed being treated like a normal human being, found the way Emilia had teased him more than just refreshing; it was like peeping into an alternative world, one where he was free to make his own friendships, his own path. To meet a girl and pursue the attraction.

Laurent had no idea what would happen after the ball, if he would find himself an engaged man or not— but he did know one thing. He liked the way Emilia made him feel and he wasn't ready to stop feeling. Not just yet. If there was any way to salvage this new friendship then he had to give it a try. He'd been raised to do his duty by his country and he had every intention of doing so. But he still had three weeks before things potentially changed for ever. What harm was there in spending some of that time with Emilia? He quashed the dutiful voice pointing out his desire to see Emilia again had nothing to do with friendship and far too much to do with how much he was attracted to her. He spent his life dealing with inconvenient truths. He was allowed the odd illusion.

'What do you think, Pomme?' he asked his dog, who cocked an ear attentively at the sound of his master's voice. 'Have I messed up altogether? You'd like to see Emilia again, wouldn't you?'

Pomme whined and Laurent gave him a rueful grin. 'You're right; it won't be easy and it's probably a bad idea, but for once I say let's not think about all the reasons why not. Deal?'

Pomme sat down, his tail wagging enthusiastically. It was all the answer Laurent was going to get, but it was enough. He wasn't giving up on this new acquaintance, not yet. And he knew exactly the way to tempt her.

CHAPTER FOUR

EMILIA JUMPED AS her phone trilled, startling her out of a daydream. Flustered, she fumbled to answer the call and, as she did so, noticed the name doodled on her notepad.

Ren...

God, she was a complete and utter fool.

'Hello?' She did her best to sound like the competent person she usually was, grabbing a pen and furiously scribbling out the doodled name, cheeks flushing hot as she did so. What on earth was she doing, randomly inserting the names of young men she barely knew into the middle of her to-do list? Acting as if she were some love-struck teenager doodling on her pencil case? She was neither love-struck nor a teenager. She was a professional, and she needed to behave like one.

'Emilia? Hi, it's me, Harriet. Just checking in. Is everything okay? You sound a little flustered.'

'Flustered? No, not at all. Just deep in thought. There's a lot to do.'

'How's it going? Met anyone yet?'

Emilia looked around, suddenly suspicious. What

had Harriet heard? And from who? 'What do you mean, have I met anyone? Just because you're all loved-up doesn't mean everyone has to spend all their time thinking about romance.'

There was a startled pause at the end of the phone. 'Em! You know I didn't mean that. Have I turned into one of those people, the "everyone should get engaged" type, because you know I don't believe that…'

Damn it, now she had upset Harriet. 'No, no, of course you haven't. Ignore me. I was being silly.'

'You're sure?' Emilia couldn't blame Harriet for sounding hurt. The four friends had bonded through loneliness and they all found it hard to let people in, especially potential romantic partners. Harriet, like Emilia, had barely dated before she'd got engaged to Deangelo.

'Of course I'm sure.'

'I just meant have you spoken to anyone yet. Alex said you were buried alone in a basement office and sleeping in the attic. You should move to a hotel, Em. I'm more than happy to add it to Simone's gigantic bill. In fact, we'll get you a suite, champagne every night and fresh flowers and chocolates.'

'It's almost worth it just to imagine her face, but I'm fine here. Honestly, the office is perfectly adequate. Natural light would be nice, but it has everything I need, and the bedroom is clean and comfortable and has gorgeous views across to the mountains. It does me very well.'

'If you're sure…' Harriet still sounded doubtful and Emilia hurried to reassure her.

'Honestly, being here puts me at the centre of all the action and that's really important. You know I grew up bilingual, thanks to my mother? I barely use my French nowadays, but it's returned pretty quickly and I know enough Italian to manage to communicate well enough in dialect which, although everyone speaks English, they really appreciate. I've been helping out where I can; the whole palace is being overhauled, and it's paying off. Much easier to get people to cooperate with me if I've done them a favour first.'

'And what have you found out? Any gossip on whether the Archduke is going to propose?'

Emilia closed her eyes and saw Ren—Laurent—leaning against the wall, arms folded, blue eyes alight with laughter, disreputable old jeans moulded to strong legs like a second skin. He hadn't acted like an Archduke, nor a man considering marriage, two days ago.

But he was both.

'No, but everyone seems to think Dad's interest in moving the business here is a really good thing and they do seem to be taking it for granted that there will be an engagement within the year and Bella seems the most likely candidate. Apparently the Archduke has been to Dad's estate twice and Dad has visited Armaria, but the ball will be the first time Simone and Bella come here. I haven't told anyone what my relationship with them is. It's easier to keep work and complicated family life separate. Besides, everyone thinks Dad has just the one daughter,' she finished, trying to sound businesslike, but Harriet wasn't fooled.

'You need to spend some time with your father, Em. It's his birthday. You have every right to be there.'

'I don't think that's entirely true.' Emilia blinked suddenly hot, heavy eyes. All she wanted, all she'd ever wanted, was her dad to put her first. But he never had. And the more she'd tried to get his attention, the more he'd turned away, pushing her to more and more extreme behaviour. 'After all, I threw my drink at him on his fiftieth and told him I wished he'd died instead of Maman. And then I walked out of the fancy restaurant, leaving him covered in lemonade. Not my finest hour—you can see why he wouldn't want me around on this occasion.'

'You were sixteen and hurting.'

'He didn't come after me though, did he? Not that night—not ever.' She swallowed, pushing the hurt back down where it belonged. 'He might be a genius but he has no emotional intelligence whatsoever. I guess that's why it was so easy for him to just walk out on Maman and me when he met Simone. If Maman hadn't died I doubt I would have seen him more than twice a year growing up, if that. He was always cancelling my custody weekends because he had to work or he and Simone had plans. Sent expensive presents instead, as if a new laptop made up for him not being there. The truth is neither Simone nor he ever bargained on me actually living with them and when I left it made their lives easier.'

'And yet here you are, on the spot for his birthday and Simone put you there. This is your opportunity, Em, your chance to talk to your father, to tell him how you feel. Okay, I better go. This invoicing won't do itself, more's the pity. Call if you need anything, even if it's just a chat. Especially if it's just a chat.'

'Will do, thanks, Harriet.'

Finishing the call, Emilia wished she was the kind of person who could manage a casual 'love you' at the end of a sentence. But the words stuck in her throat. They made a person so vulnerable. She couldn't remember the last time she'd told someone that she loved them—or that someone had said those words to her.

Pushing the notepad away with a sigh, Emilia allowed herself to slump forward, head in her hands. It was all very well for Harriet to say this was her chance to talk to her father, but what would she say? She could apologise for her anger and behaviour as a teenager, but what if he didn't reciprocate? Still didn't see how he had let her down? After all, he hadn't tried very hard to reconnect with her over the last decade. What if she made herself vulnerable and at the end of it she still was on her own? All the hard work she had done to keep herself safe would be undone.

But watching Harriet deal with her father's dementia made Emilia yearn to at least try and put things right while she still had a chance. To be the bigger person, not the out of control teen pulling everyone into her maelstrom of misery. After all, whatever Simone's reasons for employing her, she had given Emilia the opportunity to show her dad how much she loved him. And, little as she had in common with her stepsister, to give Bella her due, she had always tried, inviting Emilia to lunches she was too busy to make, sending her gifts on her birthday.

But the thought of Bella brought her back round to Laurent again and Emilia groaned, grabbing her notebook and vowing to not think about anything but work again for the next two hours.

A rap at her door roused her from her thoughts and she called out for whoever it was to come in, surprised to see one of the pages carrying a silver tray with a brown envelope on it. The page, a boy in his late teens, wore the old-fashioned waistcoat and pin-striped trousers the role demanded with dignified pride.

'This is for you, *mademoiselle*,' he said in careful English, proffering the tray.

'*Merci.*' She smiled her thanks as she took the envelope, a little puzzled. The palace might have traditions and customs that seemed a thousand years old but behind the scenes it enjoyed the most up-to-date technology; the pages carried smartphones or tablets whilst Emilia had had no problem connecting to the palace's IT network. Who would be writing to her? Or—her heart speeded up as she felt something hard within the small envelope—sending her an object?

She began to open the envelope as the page left, tipping out a large wrought iron key. A tag was tied around the middle:

You are always welcome.

Putting the key onto the desk carefully as if it might explode, she reread the message, her heart thumping. It must be from Ren—Laurent. But why was he sending her an invitation to his private garden?

Sending her invitations, misleading her about his identity. What was going on? Emilia opened her top drawer and dropped the key and the message inside, closing it with a decisive bang. The answers to those questions didn't matter. She was here to do a job, not to speculate about the motivations of the Archduke. So he had sent her a key? She didn't need to use it. Her situation here was complicated enough. From now on she was steering clear of anything and anyone not related to the ball.

For the next twenty-four hours Emilia stuck to her resolution not to return to the walled garden, although she also didn't allow herself to speculate why she had retrieved the key from the drawer and stuck it into her bag, reading the note every now and then. Instead she threw herself into an orgy of spreadsheets, Gantt charts and costings, cajoling or bullying her most trusted suppliers to agree to her impossible timeline. Whether it was Simone's lavish budget or the prospect of supplying the Royal House of Armaria she didn't know, but most capitulated far more easily than she had anticipated. In fact, they gave in so easily it took half the fun out of her job. Her mood only lifted when the palace head chef said an instant *non* to the menu she'd put together and they then embarked on a two-hour battle in which they both emerged convinced they'd been victorious. But throughout the feverish hours she was all too aware of the heavy key weighing down her bag.

By the following evening her head was aching after too much coffee and not enough air and Emilia found herself sent outside for a walk by the stately house-keeper with strict instructions not to return until her colour had gone from corpse to cream. She put up lit-tle fight, the need for fresh air almost overwhelming.

It was a gorgeous evening. Armaria was blessed with long hot summers, crisp snow-filled winters and springs and autumns out of a child's book of seasons and the early June evening was warm enough for Emilia to be out with no coat or jumper, the light not quite as bright as during the day, but still sunny enough to make sunglasses a must. She pulled the bobble out of her hair, allowing it to swing free past her shoulders, and took a deep breath, letting the fresh flower-scented air fill her lungs.

The castle gardens deserved all the accolades heaped on them. An eighteenth-century designer had created a visual masterpiece of terraces, fountains and colourful flowerbeds, the whole divided by trees and hedges, wid-ening into more informal lawns and woodlands further from the castle. A maze at the foot of the terraces was known as the most fiendishly difficult in Europe, and the gardens were full of hidden nooks and secret cor-ners. But as she wandered through the beautiful rose garden Emilia couldn't help but think about the walled garden, about how each plant seemed to be there natu-rally, not because it fitted some overarching vision, how the orchard trees wound and bent around each other, not pruned to unnatural symmetry. The garden was obvi-ously tended, but it wasn't manicured.

And she had a key…

Of course she had told herself that going there would only lead to trouble. She had liked Ren. She might have only met him twice but she'd found him easy to talk to in a way that was unusual for her. In fact she'd been downright chatty. And although her life was a quiet one, she was still a warm-blooded woman. It was impossible not to notice that he was very attractive with his sudden, elusive smile and killer cheekbones. If Ren had sent her the key then, she would have been very tempted to visit the walled garden in the hope of meeting him there and seeing where their acquaintance took them. Tempted. Not that meeting strange young men was something Emilia habitually did. No dating apps for her, no accepting offers of coffee or dinner. Maybe she was a coward, but she knew all too well what could happen when you allowed your happiness to be held by someone else. That love had a toxic side, and not feeling at all was so much less painful than giving your heart only to see it disdainfully discarded. So no, she probably wouldn't have gone to meet Ren. But it was nice to think that maybe she would have summoned up the courage,

But *Laurent* had sent the key and she didn't know him at all. She would never have speculated about Bella and Clay Industries so freely if she'd realised who he was. And he hadn't denied that he was considering proposing to Bella, which made him doubly out of bounds and doubly dangerous—he had no idea who she was and her relationship with the man he so wanted to impress. So visiting the garden would be pure insanity and Emilia had only lived a sensible, planned existence since she had left home. This was neither the time nor the place to change that.

But as she neared the old wall set at the back of the

castle, near the kitchen gardens which groaned under the weight of beds and beds of vegetables and herbs, Emilia was aware of a sense of an unusual and sweet anticipation and, before she knew what she was doing, she had unlocked the small door and slipped into the secret garden.

Disappointment dropped through her as she realised she was the only person there. 'Don't be silly,' she told herself, speaking aloud so as to give the words more weight. 'It's better this way; you can enjoy the garden with no awkward encounters.' Determined to do just that, Emilia explored every corner from the old orchard, buds turning to leaves, the promise of fruit heavy in the air, to the rambling roses which climbed the high walls and the beds filled with fragrant herbs and flowers. She discovered an old arbour housing an obviously much-used seat, the cushion dented with use, a blanket slung over the neck of the bench, and an archway leading into a shady courtyard filled with potted plants. No castle windows overlooked the courtyard; it was completely private, a small wooden door set into the castle the only clue it belonged to the castle at all and wasn't some magical garden in an enchanted land.

Despite the courtyard's privacy she felt uncomfortable being so close to the castle, the key heavy in her pocket, and after a quick peek she slipped back through the archway and into the walled garden, returning to her favourite tree, its branches providing a shady respite from the evening sun which still burnt with Mediterranean intensity.

Leaning against the trunk, she closed her eyes, aware

the ache in her temple still hadn't quite disappeared, and breathed in the sweet evening air. It wasn't the work or the time pressure causing her sleepless nights and stress. It was knowing that she and her father would be occupying the same space for several days and that avoiding him for the whole time was unrealistic.

What if this ball was a sign that it was time to move on? To try and make amends. She wasn't foolish enough to imagine an ending where her father enfolded her in his arms and promised to make the last twenty years up to her, but she could walk away with her head held high, knowing she had done all she could. Maybe then she could finally move on. Find it within herself to be brave and search out the kind of happiness Harriet had embraced.

Her one attempt at a romantic relationship had backfired so horribly she'd steered well clear of any semblance of one ever since. But that had been a long time ago and she was older and wiser now. She had fought for and found her self-worth. Was she willing to let her father destroy it again? Especially now…

Her attraction to Laurent might be misjudged and mistimed but it showed she wasn't made of ice after all. If she could let her guard down once then maybe she could again. Only next time she'd investigate any potential interest to make sure he was who he said he was and not the ruler of a small Mediterranean country.

'Is everything okay?'

She jumped at the sound of a low masculine voice, opening her eyes to see Laurent leaning against the tree next to hers, his eyes crinkled in concern.

'Oh, hi.' She was conscious of a bubble of happiness expanding her chest at the sight of him. 'I'm fine, but thank you.'

'Are you sure? Is there anything I can help with?'

The offer, from a man she barely knew, touched Emilia deeper than she wanted to admit. Was she really that starved for kindness? 'No, honestly. I only came here to return the key.' She slipped the heavy iron key out of her pocket and held it out to him. 'Here.'

Laurent made no move to take it. 'It's yours whether you use it or not.'

Emilia replaced the key in her pocket, half relieved he hadn't taken it, but not wanting to dwell on why. 'Why didn't you tell me who you are?'

His mouth tightened. 'That was badly done of me.'

'I said things I wouldn't have said if I'd known. I'm sorry. I overstepped…'

'Don't apologise. I put you in that situation. The truth is I liked the way you spoke to me; I liked the things you said. I liked the connection we forged.'

'Connection?' She could hardly breathe as she said the word and his eyes darkened.

'It seemed as if we already knew each other. Or maybe it was just me.'

Honesty propelled her forward until she was standing next to him, close enough to touch. 'I felt it too. But it wasn't real; it couldn't be real. You're not who I thought you were. You have a life I can't imagine, commitments I can't comprehend. A duty I respect and all that goes with that.' She didn't—couldn't—say Bella's name but it hung there all the same and in that instant she realised she was just as culpable because wasn't she too hiding who she was? If Laurent realised she was Mike Clayton's daughter then what—would he want to court her instead?

Maybe it was a big leap from connection to courting but, even if it was, Emilia knew she would never want to be wanted because of what she was instead of who she was. And maybe Laurent felt the same way. With that thought came a flash of understanding about why he might have withheld his identity from her, and with understanding came sympathy. She couldn't look at him as she spoke. 'But even if I do admit I felt a connection, the whole situation is too complicated.'

'Even in here? Where I am just Ren and you are Emilia and there are no titles and there is no duty or expectation? Can't we be friends here?'

'Well…' She was more tempted to agree than she would have thought possible. She was Emilia Clayton, who always played by the rules and buried herself in work rather than think about all the ways she wasn't living. But this garden felt like a place where those rules didn't exist and where Emilia could throw off those shackles and just be. 'I have to go,' she said instead. 'I'll miss staff dinner if I'm much longer.'

'In that case, why not stay here and have dinner with me?'

'Here?' She looked around as if food might spring magically up from the ground and a smile softened his rather harsh expression.

'Here. I'll be ten minutes. Promise you won't leave?'

'I…' If she walked fast she'd make it to the staff dining room before the end of dinner. She could slip into her usual spot at the end of the table and, as usual, eat a hurried meal, not really talking to anyone, her position too temporary and too undefined for her to easily fit in with the hierarchical castle staff. How tempting to agree to stay in this walled garden with a man who looked at her as if he knew her and liked what he saw, and pretend that the world outside the walls didn't exist. 'Okay, on one condition.'

'Name it.'

'Pomme joins us. I don't want anyone saying I ate dinner with the Archduke unchaperoned.'

His smile was as sweet as it was sudden. 'I'm sure that can be arranged. But inside these walls there is no Archduke, just Emilia and Ren. Deal?'

She couldn't help answering his smile with one of her own. 'Deal.' Staying was probably, definitely, a bad idea but she couldn't walk away even if she wanted to. Emilia wasn't one for crushes or sudden fancies; she wasn't really one for romance at all, for putting her body or mind or heart in the hands of another, trusting someone else with her happiness. She knew all too well how dangerous that was. But there was a flutter of sweet tension down in her belly when she looked at Laurent, a thrilling in her veins at the burr of his voice. He was still a stranger but at some level something in her recognised something in him. The unwanted, unasked for attraction should terrify her—and usually she would run from it—but here in this garden it felt natural. Safe. Even if she knew that safety was merely an illusion.

* * *

'Laurent?'

Laurent turned as his mother called his name, masking his impatience at the delay. It was seven-thirty and that meant Emilia would be in the walled garden waiting for him. The castle kitchens would have sent up a basket of food and it would be placed by the small door that led into the palace courtyard. If any of the staff wondered why the Archduke had taken it into his head to dine outside and alone every night for the past week, they kept it to themselves.

The evenings were an oasis during increasingly busy days. The Prime Minister was making his impatience felt and, although there was little he could do, he made sure Laurent knew just how little faith he had in the proposed deal and Laurent's ability to pull it off. The Chancellor's worry about the next year's finances were infecting all of Parliament and Laurent knew that if Clay Industries decided against investing then he would have to capitulate on some of the Prime Minister's demands. The ball and its outcome was increasingly important.

But during the summer evenings, stretched out on a picnic blanket, none of these concerns felt so urgent. Emilia was an entertaining and intelligent companion whose stories of her life in events often kept him amused for hours. Every evening he felt more at ease with her; every evening felt more and more like coming home.

Only real life kept intruding. Simone Clayton had suggested he and Bella wore matching costumes, a clear signal of intent from the Claytons and one he couldn't ignore. And a signal Emilia was aware of; she was organising the costumes after all. That was why, despite the intimacy of the situation, they never touched, never strayed into personal territory. The more time Laurent spent with Emilia, the more he liked her. The more he saw of her, the more he admired her. And he was definitely attracted to her. But he respected her too much to cross a line that once crossed would spoil the first real friendship he had experienced for far too long. A line a man contemplating marriage to another had no right to cross.

A line he wanted to cross more every night.

'Hello, Maman.' He kissed his mother's cheek as she approached him, smiling down at her. 'You're looking well.'

'So are you, *mon fils*. Is everything okay? I've hardly seen you all week.'

'I've been busy, with the ball, Parliament, arranging a tour for Mike Clayton. These things all take time.'

'Just a few days until they arrive and less than a week until the ball. Are you ready, Laurent?'

The truth was, three weeks ago he had been ready. Three weeks ago he had seen his path clear in front of him and known that following it was the right thing to do. But now he couldn't help but be enticed by other paths, winding, hidden paths with twisty corners and beguiling destinations. He set his jaw. 'Don't worry, Maman, I'm ready.'

His mood was sombre as he collected the basket and carried it through to the walled garden, an eager Pomme at his heels. Emilia was in her usual place, curled up under her favourite tree, her tablet in hand, forehead furrowed as she tapped away. She smiled as Pomme bounded over, one hand automatically caressing the dog's ears as she looked up at Laurent. 'How much would you hate traditional Greek costume?'

'A lot,' he responded as he placed the picnic basket on the ground, pulling out the blanket and throwing it over to Emilia, who caught it with one hand.

'Tudor dress?'

'No, thank you.'

'Regency?'

'For *A Midsummer Night's Dream*?'

'Breeches are timeless and it has to be better than a tunic. We're running out of time to get costumes made so you really need to pick one. Bella isn't keen on Tudor either but she is happy with either of the other two.'

'You pick.'

She looked up, startled. 'Me?'

'Yes, your event, you know what will work.' He knew he sounded autocratic, every bit the spoiled young aristocrat some thought him, and Emilia's expression was troubled.

'If you're sure. No complaining—if I put you in a pink frockcoat and a white wig you'll accept it?'

'If you put me in a pink frockcoat I'll have you arrested for treason.'

'Go with Regency,' she said, getting to her feet and shaking out the picnic rug. 'It's a classic for a reason and you and Bella can be Theseus and Hippolyta just as much as if you were in tunics. The flower wreath will still work with a regency hairstyle.' She bent down to pick up her tablet and began tapping away again and Laurent watched her.

He knew every bit of her now, the way she moved, the way her eyes turned from green to gold to brown to match her moods, the way the light caught her hair, bringing out honey highlights, the shadows that darkened her expression when she lapsed into thought, the dimples that peeped out when she was amused. He knew how she never stopped, her tablet always by her side as she made notes, answered emails and researched ideas even as she ate. How she rose early and worked late, how she already knew every inch of the castle and had ideas to showcase every one of those inches.

But he knew nothing about her background or her family. Had no idea if she had ever been in love. Her secrets were locked up tight and he had no right to go prying. Not while he was planning to go to his ball with another woman on his arm. Not while he was still planning to propose to another woman.

Not while his country's prosperity could depend on that proposal.

Maybe these evening picnics were a bad idea. He saw them as his salvation but he had been content with his path before Emilia had turned up.

But in just a few days Bella Clayton would be his guest and, regardless of what that meant, he would have to give her the courtesy of his time and attention. Their picnics had an end date. The thought pulled at him. This friendship couldn't just fizzle out. They should do something special first.

'We should do something different tomorrow evening,' he said and Emilia put her tablet down and re-garded him in some surprise.

'Like what?'

'We could leave the castle while we can, before the ball guests arrive and your time becomes even more hec-tic. Let's hit the city. Where is your favourite place in San Tomare? The Italian quarter? The docks? The old town?'

Emilia's gaze shifted. 'I…well, I haven't had much of a chance to explore Armaria, not even the city. I've been so busy here, I haven't actually left the castle.'

'Not at all? You're not working twenty-four hours a day, surely?'

'No, but I am working all waking hours. Three weeks is not very long to put on a ball, especially one where most of the guests need travel and accommodation sort-ing as well.'

'Then tomorrow I will show you my city.'

Every instinct screamed at him that this was a bad idea. These illicit picnics were one thing; a night out, beyond the safety of the castle walls, was quite another. But Laurent needed one night before his life changed for ever, a night when he wasn't Laurent; he was Ren showing the city he loved to a pretty girl.

'You want to show me the city?'

'People pay good money for guided tours, and I am offering you one for free. It's a one-time offer though…'

'Then how can I resist? Thank you.' She smiled then, that sudden full smile which transformed her thin, sol-emn face into something else entirely, into an enchant-ing beauty of curves and dimples, of hints of fire and a sweetness which took his breath clean away. 'That's very kind of you.'

'Not at all.' He managed to somehow keep speaking although he wanted to stop time and drink her in. 'You're the kind one to take pity on me and grant me the pleasure of your company.'

She laughed at that, the usually hidden dimples deepening. Her laugh was husky, a little uncertain, as if she didn't unleash it often. 'I'll do my best to live up to that. Shall we meet here? Same time as usual?'

'No,' he said quickly. The last thing he wanted was for the soldiers who guarded all the entrances in and out of the palace to see them together, linking Emilia's name to his, exposing her to any resulting gossip. 'I'll pick you up at the crossroads, about quarter of a mile from the castle, if you go right when you leave the gates. Wear trousers, jeans if you have them, and a jacket,' he added and she stared at him, eyes wide with surprise. 'Sensible shoes are probably a good idea too.'

'Intriguing.' With that she opened the picnic basket and passed Laurent a perfectly chilled bottle of beer, taking one for herself as she did so. She raised hers to his. 'To new adventures.'

'To new adventures,' he echoed. But he knew that tomorrow wasn't about the new. It was about saying goodbye. To the old Laurent, to his old life and to the brief, sweet friendship that had so unexpectedly come his way.

CHAPTER FIVE

EMILIA SWIVELLED IN front of the narrow mirror. If she contorted and squinted she could just about see two-thirds of herself and that would have to do. Not, she reminded herself, that it mattered what she looked like. Going out with Laurent was a monumentally stupid thing to do. She'd allowed all those friendly evenings in the orchard to lull her into a false sense of security, but just because they'd fallen into an easy companionship didn't mean she could or should go out with him on the kind of evening that could be construed as a date.

Number one, he was an Archduke and she was an event planner from London who still shared a house with her friends. Her place was in the basement and the attic, not the ballroom. Number Two, he hadn't denied the rumours that he was going to marry another girl. Not just any girl: her own stepsister. A little fact she was keeping from him.

Their friendship might seem easy but it was based on evasion and half-truths and she was just as much to blame. And now it was going to be very difficult, if not impossible, to tell Laurent that she was the daughter of the man he was attempting to woo and the stepsister of his potential bride. Difficult and awkward.

Apart from anything else there was the small matter of the reconciliation she needed to attempt with her father. If Bella really was considering agreeing to be Laurent's Archduchess then nobody would be impressed if Emilia was seen swanning around with her stepsister's soon-to-be intended. They would assume that Emilia had done it on purpose, another attempt to grab the limelight and ruin her dad's birthday. No one would believe her friendship with Laurent was pure coincidence. Or innocent.

She wasn't too sure about the innocent part herself, even though they were both working very hard to keep it that way.

So the sensible thing to do would be to stop the evening picnics and stay home tonight with a box set and a box of chocolates. And Emilia could always be counted on to be sensible.

Couldn't she?

She looked down at her carefully chosen outfit. To be fair, nobody had actually said anything about a date. Tonight was a city tour—and she had been instructed to dress sensibly, which was not usually the precursor to anything romantic. So, sure enough, here she was, in a pair of jeans, trainers and a pretty flower-covered short-sleeved shirt, hair coiled up in her favourite messy bun, just enough make-up to look as if she wasn't wearing any. She was the epitome of 'just threw this on and yet somehow I look casually chic', a look that required forethought and ingenuity.

Forethought that would be wasted on dinner in the castle's staff dining room.

And, after all, she hadn't had an opportunity to explore the world-famous city of San Tomare yet and once her family arrived in just a couple of days it was unlikely she would find the time to eat, let alone explore.

Besides, there was nothing romantic between Laurent and her. Okay, to the untrained eye a week of picnic dinners in a walled garden might look like romance, but their hands had never so much as brushed together, they never held each other's gaze too long, and they hadn't spent their time together unburdening their souls. Emilia might not be that experienced in relationships but surely they couldn't—shouldn't feel so easy at the beginning, as if they had always known the other person? Shouldn't she be tongue-tied and overwhelmed, not so at ease she felt as if she might say anything and be understood? And all right, her heart might thump a little harder when she saw him, her palms tingle and her throat dry up. She might sometimes allow her gaze to dwell on his wide shoulders and long, muscled legs and allow herself to daydream about the shape of his mouth, but Laurent was absurdly handsome and she was young and single. It would be weirder not to be attracted to him. It didn't mean he was attracted to her. He liked her because she wasn't deferential, because she treated him like just a normal human being, not a deity.

So what was she so afraid of?

She spent her whole life fearing rejection, worrying she wasn't good enough, that she didn't deserve happiness. She hid away, avoiding all opportunities, reasoning that it was far better to be safe than sorry. What had happened to that teenage firebrand who said what she thought and didn't care who got caught up in her wake? It had scared her, the anger, the way it had consumed her, the havoc she had wrought, the things she had said. And in the end hadn't she been the one to suffer? The one who ended up a teenage dropout, with no formal education, no family she could rely on, making her own way in the world.

She'd woken up the day after her father's fiftieth and taken a good, hard look at the last four years—and she'd been ashamed of what she'd seen. So ashamed that she had promised herself she would change, that from now on she would be calm and hardworking and always in control. And she'd achieved that, but at what price? She hadn't just dampened her spirit down; she'd extinguished it completely. Was this how she wanted to live the rest of her life? Maybe she should just make a leap of faith and let tonight just be. No planning or worrying or thinking about the worst thing that could happen...

Right. She was going to do this. *Carpe diem* and all that. Grabbing her light jacket and shoulder bag, she marched out of her small but functional attic bedroom and down the several flights of winding back stairs until she came to the small side door through which she accessed and exited the castle. She showed her pass so she could be signed out, took a deep breath and stepped outside. She was doing this. She was really doing this.

It took longer to walk down the imposing driveway than it did to amble along the flower-filled roadside verge until she reached the crossroads where she had arranged to meet Laurent. Like everything else she had seen so far in Armaria, the crossroads had an old-world charm exemplified in the wooden road sign, which looked like something out of a fairy tale, with its white paint and curling script. Feeling a little foolish, Emilia propped herself next to the sign and waited, unsure of the right posture to pull off *I only just got here* nonchalance.

The evening was still lovely and warm, verging on hot. Slipping off her jacket, Emilia inhaled the sweet, fragrant air which bore little relation to the heavy, fume-filled air she breathed every day on the streets of London. Rural idylls certainly had their place. Closing her eyes, she tilted her head, letting the evening sun bathe her face, enjoying the prospect of just being for once. Apart from the stolen hour she spent each evening in the walled garden, Emilia had barely stopped since Simone had dropped in so unexpectedly. In fact she had barely stopped since they'd opened the agency, or indeed since she had turned sixteen and realised that the only person she could rely on was herself. Working hard was in her DNA but right now she was prepared to allow herself a few moments to slow down and smell the—well, whatever the flowers were—and take in every sensation, like the buzzing of a bee, for instance. A buzzing that seemed to be getting louder and louder...

Emilia's eyes snapped open as the buzz sharpened to a roar. Either that was one huge bee or... She stepped back as a sleek motorcycle swooped down upon her, stopping with a stylish turn. The rider, dressed in black to match the bike, she noted, swung one lean, muscled leg round in order to dismount, pulling the helmet off his head as he did so.

Laurent.

'Hi, you're here!'

Emilia was absurdly flattered by the frank pleasure in his smile. 'I almost thought better of it,' she confessed. 'But I wasn't sure what the penalty was for standing up an Archduke. I didn't want the guards to be put to the trouble of dragging me here.'

His smile ratcheted up a notch and Emilia's breath caught in her throat. 'I was hoping you'd come willingly.'

'On that?' She eyed the motorbike sceptically.

'It's quite safe.'

'Hmm.' But she couldn't help the thrill that ran through her at the thought of riding pillion, her arms around his waist, legs pressed to his. Emilia swallowed, convinced her thoughts must be showing on her face. The problem with not dating for several years was that it left a girl with no defences; she was as new to this kind of banter as a fifteen-year-old with a crush.

'Here.' Ren went over to the motorbike and returned with a second helmet, which he handed to Emilia, who clutched it, her arms barely managing to contain it. It was heavier than she had expected. 'Ever worn one of these before?'

'No. And I'm not sure I'm going to do so right now either.'

'I promise I'll be really careful. And you never know, it might be fun.'

'It's a very big bike,' Emilia said doubtfully. 'I'd be

more comfortable if it was one of those little pastel ones like in *Roman Holiday.*'

Ren merely raised an eyebrow. Of course he could raise just one eyebrow. And probably naturally; he didn't seem the type to practice in front of a mirror. She'd practised but never quite got the hang of it, much to her disgust. A sardonic raised eyebrow was much more useful than her dimples. They merely made her look cute, unthreatening.

She contented herself with matching his expression, only with both eyebrows raised as high as she could manage. 'What?'

'We're back to old films again?'

'Have you watched it yet?'

'Not yet.' His smile was rueful. 'It seems a little too close to home.' Her pulse sped at his words, at the hint that Laurent wasn't as reconciled to his path as he seemed.

'In that case I should be the one driving the motorbike and taking you on the tour.'

'Maybe.' Laurent looked directly at her, expression unreadable. 'Do you think she regretted it? The Princess? Did her escape make her life more bearable or did she spend the rest of her days knowing she'd tasted freedom and longing for it?'

Emilia took a deep breath, trying to work out the right thing to say. 'It may have only been one night, but she lived every moment of it. I guess that's all we can ask, isn't it? An opportunity to really live, even if we know it's not for ever.' And as she said the words Emilia knew that she hadn't been living every moment, not even half. She had shut herself away just as much as Audrey Hepburn's Princess Ann. Only she wasn't hemmed in by custom and duty, but by fear. Fear of finding love and losing it, fear of mistaking something darker for love. It was so easy to believe that she wasn't worthy of love, after all; hadn't she been shown that over and over?

But Harriet and Amber and Alex loved her and they were the best people she knew. And Laurent was standing close to her, his eyes focused on her, looking at her as if she had the answers he was searching for.

'Is that what you think? That we should grab every opportunity while we can?'

When had he got so close? Emilia blinked as her body registered his proximity, heating up as she glanced up at him and saw the smile deep in his navy eyes. A smile and a glint of heat that sent her temperature ratcheting up yet another notch. Her stomach tumbled, a mixture of desire and fear.

But at the same time she didn't want to step back.

What was he doing? A ride into the city was one thing, a guided tour harmless enough, even dinner was innocent. But if he kissed Emilia then that would be quite, quite different. It would be dishonourable and an Archduke should always act with honour. So it was best to step away and try not to notice how full and inviting her mouth was, how soft. Best not to notice the dimples at the corner of said mouth and how they gave her usually grave features a lightness and sweetness. Definitely best not to comment on the length of her dark eyelashes, a deep brown touching on black, only with a hint of gold, a hint echoed in the flecks in her hazel eyes which right now were more green than brown.

Better not to notice how her breath hitched as their eyes locked and need shimmered in the hot evening air, how her jacket hugged her, nipping her in at her narrow waist whilst emphasising the curve of her hips and her breasts. No, definitely best not to think about her breasts.

But it was hard to think of anything else. The air was sweet with night blooming flowers and the subtle scent of her light perfume. Like a Mediterranean garden, a little citrus, a little floral, a little sea salt. She smelt like Armaria and right now was infinitely more desirable.

But he wasn't free. Not entirely. Because desire was one thing but duty another, and duty always came first. And so, reluctantly, he stepped away, nodding at the helmet she still cradled in her arms. 'Are you going to wear that or hug it?'

Her eyes flashed golden green. 'Wear it.'

It took a couple of moments for Emilia to figure out how to fasten the helmet but Laurent didn't quite trust himself to help her, ungentlemanly as leaving her to struggle might seem. The problem was that he didn't want to be gentlemanly or princely or Archduke-ish. What he wanted to do was pull that damn helmet off her head and kiss her until he forgot who and where he was. Until he was lost in her. He'd kissed more than a few women in his life and had never got lost in any of them, but none of them had been as potentially dangerous as Emilia.

He stepped back again. 'Are you managing?'

'Quite well, thank you.' Her voice was muffled by the helmet but her glare quite visible through the visor. 'Very comfortable. This isn't hot and uncomfortable at all.'

'Better uncomfortable and safe.'

Her eyes narrowed. 'You said you would be really careful.'

He couldn't help his mouth curving into a playful grin. 'I also said it would be fun.'

She froze for a second and he could see the indecision in every inch of her, until she tilted her chin. 'I'm ready.'

She might be ready but Laurent soon realised he wasn't ready at all. Not for the clasp of her hands around his waist, or her thighs wrapped around his, her breasts pressing against his back. It was torture, the kind that would entice a man to spill every secret and beg for more. Exquisite as it was, it drove him nearly out of his mind, his whole being surrounded by her.

It had been too long since he had been so close to a woman. Dating Laurent came with a whole set of rules and attention that put off all but the most determined women. Add in the likelihood that the couple would be followed by paparazzi wherever they went and her life and previous relationships scrutinised in depth and it wasn't that surprising that women often decided that maybe they weren't keen on being with him after all. After a few uncomfortable and too public attempts at relationships with fellow students in his early twenties, Laurent had all but given up, save for a brief, secret fling with an actress who valued her privacy as highly as he did and had no interest in marriage or a throne, and a longer, more public relationship with a minor member of the exiled Greek royal family which had faded away, probably due to his preoccupation with matters of state. But that was a couple of years ago and since then he had been on his own.

It wasn't much to look back on at the age of twenty-eight, with probable marriage looming ahead. Maybe he should have been more reckless with his own heart, if not with other people's. But it was nearly too late for regrets.

Nearly...

Laurent took a corner with a flourish and Emilia's arms tightened as the movement shifted her even closer. Usually he loved the freedom of the bike as he navigated the winding clifftop roads which connected the castle to San Tomare, green hills on one side leading to the mountains which separated his small country from the rest of the continent, the sea down below. He loved the roar of the wind, the kick of the bike, the knowledge that for these moments at least he was the master of his own destiny.

But this evening he wasn't just aware of the elements and speed, or ultra-aware of the feel of Emilia, of how close she was, but of how her safety was in his hands. The trust she was placing in him. He wrenched his thoughts away from the warmth of her body, grimly focusing on the road ahead instead.

For once he was grateful when the city outskirts forced him to slow down, and he cruised along until he finally pulled up outside a gated villa overlooking the sea in a cultural and tourist hotspot on the outskirts of the city. The popular suburb had so many second homes and holiday lets that no one speculated about the owner of the seemingly innocuous white-washed villa set back from the road. Slowing, he turned in, the sensor recognising him and the gates slowly swinging open, and he felt Emilia tense behind him as he rode the bike through the gates and they closed softly behind them. He pulled to a stop on the driveway which ran up the side of the villa and dismounted, holding a still gloved hand out to Emilia. She took it but only lightly, dropping it as soon as she was safely on her own two feet, already fumbling at the helmet, shaking her head as she removed it so her light brown hair tumbled free of the loose bun it had been confined in.

'Where is this?'

'The Villa par la Mer.'

'Which is?'

'My villa. I come here sometimes, when I need to escape. But today it's just a parking spot. San Tomare is the safest capital city in the world—safest and smallest—but I still prefer to keep my bike off the streets. Besides, this is the scenic way into town; if we walk through the gardens and onto the cliffs we then finish our journey by boat. Or we could walk through the streets or get a taxi. Up to you.'

'The sea way sounds lovely,' she said at last and smiled, a slow smile which gradually lit up her narrow face, her dimples flashing into view and giving her rather austere beauty a puckish charm.

'Okay.' It was hard to tear his gaze away from her, but he managed it, hoping he was looking cooler and more relaxed than he felt. 'This way.'

He didn't tell her that she was the first outsider he had brought here. That this villa was his sanctuary, a place he rode to on the rare occasions he could leave the palace. A place he invited no one to, not even his mother. But he knew Emilia would love it as much as he did. And, for reasons he refused to dwell on, he wanted to share this part of his soul with her.

The gardens weren't extensive, not as manicured or designed as the famous and formal castle grounds, nor as wild and free as the walled garden. Herb and vegetable beds ran down one side; the whole was shaded by lemon and olive trees, shrubs and flowers grew in large pots. The long garden was terraced as it led to the clifftop, walled off on both sides, the innocuous whitewashed bricks hiding the sensors and cameras which were the price Laurent paid for his occasional freedom. He pretended not to know that the villa on one side was owned by the castle and soldiers occupied it day and night and that the villa on the other was lived in by a now retired bodyguard and his formidable wife. The illusion of escape, of privacy, was better than no escape at all.

'Did you design the garden yourself?' Emilia asked as she followed him along the gravel path, pausing to touch one of the ripening lemons hanging enticingly at head height.

'No, my grandmother did,' he said. 'She was Austrian, descended from royalty on both sides and rich with it. The perfect Archduchess for a small impoverished country. But she was never comfortable in the spotlight. She told me once her dream was to live in a small village and be a housewife, maybe run a shop. Instead she spent her days entertaining diplomats and opening buildings.'

'How sad.'

'She didn't see it that way. She knew it was her heritage, her duty to marry well; she'd been raised to it. But she adored nature and the outdoors—the walled garden was her sanctuary in the castle, this villa her escape from it. She left both to me.' He smiled, remembering how his grandmother, always so regal and proper, came to life in her garden, wearing old slacks, her hair falling out of its chignon, her elegant hands covered in dirt. 'She was always happiest when she was out here, weeding or planting or pruning.'

Emilia turned slowly, her keen gaze taking in every detail. 'My mother was a keen gardener. Keen but not as talented as your grandmother. To be honest, I don't think she had much luck at all but it didn't stop her trying. She was French and so she blamed the English weather, said it was too damp and unreliable!'

'Was?'

'She died when I was twelve.' Emilia swallowed, looking for a moment like the grief-stricken child she must have been.

'I'm sorry,' Laurent said. 'I know what it's like to lose a parent when you're too young to make sense of it.'

'Of course you do. You were even younger when your father died.' Her voice was soft with an understanding few could really comprehend.

'Seven,' he confirmed. 'I think that's why I was so close to my grandmother. She, of course, had lost her son, and I think she found some comfort in me. But also my mother had to step up, to become regent, and everyone told me I was the Archduke now, that I had to be brave and grown-up. It was only here, with my grandmother, that I got to be a little boy and just run around and play.'

Emilia smiled at him then, with an infinite tenderness that warmed his heart and his soul. 'Thank you for bringing me here.'

'How about you?' They resumed walking, a slow amble down the path, Emilia stopping frequently to examine a plant or a statue or to smell a flower. 'Are you and your father close? It couldn't have been easy for either of you.'

She didn't answer for a long while, blinking slowly, the shimmer in her eyes a tell-tale answer to his question. 'We were close once. It's easy to forget that, because we aren't now. I sometimes wonder if I made up my memories of him from books, because I remember a happy home and a father who carried me on his shoulders and a mother who was always singing and a dog I adored...'

'And your mother's death changed all that?'

'No, it changed long before. My father moved out when I was six. He'd met someone else. She had a daughter, a year older than me, and it seemed like, felt like he had a whole new family and just didn't want the old one any more. My mum stopped singing and gardening; she was so bitter and angry. And Dad, well, I suppose he didn't want to face up to what he'd done so he stayed away from her, and that meant staying away from me. Of course, I thought it was my fault. That he'd left me because I had done something wrong. Part of me still thinks that...'

'That's nonsense,' he said quickly and she shrugged.

'I know. I told myself that then, I tell myself that now, but it just didn't seem possible for my dad, the man I absolutely adored, to just not be in my life for no reason. And the only reason I could think of was that I had said or done something to push him away. Or that Maman had. Anyway, Dad kept the London flat we'd lived in and bought a huge new house out in Surrey as well for his new family. Meanwhile, my mother and I moved to a poky area on the outskirts of London. He was—is—well-off, but Maman was determined to be independent, so we had a little flat with no garden and she got a job teaching French. The worst part was when she gave my dog to a friend who didn't work. She said it was fairer for him, that he couldn't be alone all day, and she was probably right but I missed him more than my dad—does that sound silly?' The wistfulness in her smile tore at his heart and all Laurent wanted to do was try and fix all her hurts.

'Not at all.'

'It was hard at first. I was sulky and resentful and she was so angry all the time, but after a while the new became normal and we settled in. She liked her job and made new friends and I got used to the fact that Dad would cancel our weekends together and on the few occasions I did see him we never got time alone; instead he expected me to make a happy family with his new wife and daughter. His wife never seemed keen on having me around and I was really resentful of her daughter, because she got to live with my father, have inside jokes with him, see him every day. I wasn't very nice to her, I'm ashamed to say. But then Maman got sick and she just didn't get better. Next thing I knew, I was living with the man who walked out on me and the people he'd left me for. I was so angry and so grief-stricken.'

'I'm sure they understood.'

She shook her head. 'I felt like my presence was an inconvenience. They just didn't know what to do with me, I suppose. I didn't want to go to my stepsister's fancy school; I wanted to stay where I was, even though it was a really long journey to get there. I didn't want to be part of their family or adapt to their ways. It felt like betraying Maman. The truth is…' she paused, taking in a long breath, her face unreadable '…the truth is, I suppose, if I'm honest, that I behaved very badly, rebelled every way I could. Made unsuitable friends, stayed out late and didn't tell them where I was, missed school. I even shoplifted a couple of times, even though the one thing I had plenty of was money. I wore clothes they hated and dyed my hair any colour I could think of. The irony is Maman would have been appalled. She was so chic and French, she would have wept when I cut my own hair. I just wanted them all to feel as hurt and guilty and lonely as I did, but the more I rebelled, the more alone I was. The next few years were hell. So I left home at sixteen, after doing my best to tear us all apart. But all I did was isolate myself; they were closer than ever.'

'You were a child who needed unconditional love and safety.' It was hard to rein in his anger. What kind of family allowed a newly motherless girl to struggle on alone? At least Laurent had always known his mother loved him, even if she was so busy all the time, and he'd had his grandmother. Turned out he'd been lucky.

Emilia sighed and it was the loneliest sound he'd ever heard; his heart ached to hear it. 'Now I barely see him. I lost both parents. That's what hurts so much. It took a long time to come to terms with that.'

'And have you come to terms with it?'

'In some ways. It helps that I made my own family.'

Surprised, he glanced at her bare left hand and she laughed. 'Not a conventional one. I don't think convention and I work too well. No, I made three very dear friends and we set up our own business. I know, no matter where they are, what they do and who they're with that they have my back and I have theirs. They understand, you see.'

'Understand what?'

'What it's like to have no one.'

The words were uttered so simply, with no self-pity or despair, just a matter-of-fact statement but one that chilled Laurent through. Without thinking, without giving himself time to second guess, Laurent put his arms around Emilia and held her close. He had no thought beyond offering comfort, although he couldn't help but be aware of the floral scent of her hair, of the softness of her breasts and the way she fitted against him, but he made no attempt to tighten his hold, to do anything but give her the warmth and support of another human being. To show her that she wasn't alone. And to realise that, for the first time in a long time, he wasn't alone either.

CHAPTER SIX

EMILIA EXTRICATED HERSELF from Laurent's embrace, unable to look at him. What on earth was she thinking? Why had she said all that? She had never opened up this much before, not even to Alex, Harriet and Amber. They knew part of the story, of course, but not the whole sordid tale.

Not only had she ended up confiding in him, but she had allowed him to comfort her as well, to hold her as if she were in need of looking after, of rescue. And Emilia knew better than to trust any of her happiness to others.

Only right now, standing on a shady terrace, the scent of lemons permeating the air, the sound of the sea crashing against the cliff creating an oddly musical backdrop, the evening sun shining down, the memory of his touch buzzing through every vein, it was almost easy to forget that she didn't believe in fairy tales—or in handsome princes. Easy to forget when a pair of blue eyes regarded her with such intensity, eyes belonging to a man with shoulders broad enough to lean against and the kind of mouth a girl could fantasise about, if she was the kind to fantasise, that was.

The silence stretched until she could almost feel it, tension strumming the air. She wanted to say something—anything to break it, but found she couldn't, held in his gaze. He was making a decision, she knew that. But what that was she had no idea. To kiss her? Like he almost had back at the crossroads? Emilia shivered, imagining how it would feel, that hard yet elegant mouth on hers, his tall body holding her close, maybe backing her against one of the lemon trees, the bark rough against her skin. Her whole body goosebumped at the thought and she swayed slightly, closing the distance between them with the movement of her body.

'Ready to continue? We're nearly at the clifftop,' Laurent said at last, his voice hoarse and a heat in his eyes that burned straight through her, lighting a trail that ran right down her body, liquid fire in every vein. Was this desire? Lust? She'd never allowed herself to feel like this before. Not with furtive kisses in the park in her teens, or her desperately needy kisses with her one and only proper boyfriend. Emilia knew better now; she didn't trust, not with her heart or her body.

Or she didn't usually. But right now her body was ignoring her bruised heart, her pulse racing with need, stirring up every nerve with its relentless thrum. She wanted and she needed. Had from the moment she'd been disturbed in the walled garden, had in every second since, every evening they sat together deliberately not touching until the air between them hummed with desire. She didn't believe in love at first sight and wasn't fool enough to believe this, whatever it was, *was* love. But that didn't make it less powerful, and stronger women than she had fallen under its thrall. She swayed again and felt Laurent's gaze follow every tiny movement, the roll of her hips and the curve of her breast and, with deep feminine satisfaction, she watched him swallow, her eyes following the working of his throat, taking in the dark blond stubble covering his jaw, the vee of hard chest exposed by his shirt, at once vulnerable and strong.

She spent her life working hard, as if that made up for never really feeling, never really needing. She didn't so much as live her life as make sure she was always far too busy to think. She didn't want to start thinking now. Think about why her next words might be a huge mistake. 'We *could* walk on. Or we could stay here. For a little while longer.'

His eyes narrowed as he seemed to take in every word and examine it. 'We could stay; it's a pretty spot,' he agreed. 'I could go back to the villa and get some wine if you wanted to stop here for an aperitif?'

'That sounds nice.' But she didn't need Dutch courage—nor could she allow any time to elapse, not even the five minutes it would take to collect wine and glasses, otherwise she knew she would change her mind. No. She needed to act while she was still under this spell. It was Emilia's turn to swallow, with nerves, with anticipation, as she stepped towards him. 'Maybe later.'

He didn't reply, his mouth curving appreciatively although she thought she noted a hint of doubt cloud his expression, even as he visibly inhaled. She was affecting him. She was responsible for his preternatural stillness, for the way he watched her every move, half like a hunter, half like prey.

No, she amended as she looked straight at him and saw the way he seemed to be holding himself in check, the hunger in his eyes thrilling her even as part of her wanted to turn and run. She wasn't kidding anyone. He was all hunter.

But she wasn't anyone's prey.

She stepped again and then she was right next to him, almost within touching distance. She hadn't fully appreciated quite how tall Laurent was, how strong, despite his deceptive slenderness; every muscle was clearly defined. She was slim to the point of thinness and always felt angular, all corners, taller than her friends, yet looking up at Laurent she felt petite, delicate. Her jeans and shirt seemed girlish, feminine, *she* felt girlish in a way she had never felt before. If she'd been from a previous era she would be waving a fan right now in a deliberately provocative way.

As she stood there, mind for once at the urge of her body, Emilia remembered what Harriet had said about the moment she had thrown caution to the wind and kissed Deangelo for the very first time. *I was so tired of always being afraid. I wanted to really feel alive, just once.* Emilia bit her lip, the slight pain recalling her back to herself. She knew exactly how Harriet had felt. Knew exactly what it was like to live closed off and afraid and lonely. The last few months, she had begun to feel part of a family again, but Harriet's engagement showed how fragile those ties really were. Oh, their friendship would last, she had no doubt about that, as hopefully would the business, but Harriet's life had expanded, even as hers contracted even further until work was all she had.

One kiss. What harm would one kiss on a sunlit evening in a garden filled with the scent of lemons do? If she just dared. After all, no one would ever know…

She moved a little closer, her whole body now humming with need and want, delicious shivers running down her spine, aware of every nerve and how it sang with excitement. Reaching out, she touched Laurent's arm, warm and solid under her fingertips. He stood still, but a quiver ran through him as his eyes darkened even further to the almost grey of a storm-tossed sky. Emilia looked directly at him, allowing her desire to show in her eyes, for once hiding nothing, swaying further towards him, lips parted, and with a noise that was half a growl, half a smothered curse he tilted her chin, looking down at her for a long second before his mouth found hers.

Emilia had been expecting a slow warm-up kiss, maybe something gentle and tentative, a getting-to-know-you kiss, but why should a kiss be any different from their acquaintance so far? Hadn't they jumped from *Sorry for trespassing* to dinners for two without passing Go or collecting two hundred pounds? From the moment his mouth claimed hers the kiss spiked straight to incendiary, his lips provoking sensations and feelings she hadn't even known existed. Her hand still lay on his arm but otherwise their bodies didn't touch and, much as Emilia wanted Laurent's hands on her just as much as she wanted to claim every inch of his tall, lean body, touch every sinew and muscle for herself, she also knew if she did she would be undone.

No, better to lose herself in the kiss, to let his mouth take hers, at once hard and yet tantalisingly soft. Let herself get lost in his taste, in the ripples of lust shuddering through her body, in a rhythm that felt so right she could dance to it.

They could have been standing there for thirty seconds or thirty minutes or even, lost as she was, for thirty hours, but when he lifted his head and broke the kiss, it hadn't been long enough. One kiss? Who had she been kidding? Pandora had opened the box and she wanted more.

'Emilia…' Laurent's smile was a little rueful, a lot satisfied and a tinge wolfish, a combination that reached inside her and tugged hard down deep. 'I didn't bring you here to take advantage. I hope you know that.'

'Actually—' she tried for blasé and a little provocative '—I think I was the one who took advantage of you.'

'Is that so?' His smile was all wolf now and she wanted nothing more than to submit, but she lifted her chin and matched his smile with her own.

'Don't worry,' she said kindly. 'I like that you're not intimidated by strong women.'

His eyes flared with heat and a challenge she longed to answer, but his tone was cool and amused. 'That's good to know. What do you say, are you ready for that boat ride now?'

'Absolutely—lead the way.'

Emilia followed Laurent down the path, her head still

dizzy with lust, her mouth full of the taste of him and yet in some ways it was as if the kiss had never happened. Laurent made no effort to hold her hand or slip an arm around her as they made their way through the garden, but there was a tension between them, a crackle in the air, electricity any time their hands or arms accidentally touched, that showed neither were as impervious as they might pretend. Neither spoke until they reached the clifftop. A low wall was all that stood between the end of the garden and dramatic cliffs, with the sea tumbling against the rocks below.

'Do we abseil?' Emilia stared down at the churning white water. 'Is that why you told me to wear comfortable shoes?'

He smiled at that and her heart flipped. Princes shouldn't have such devastating smiles. It was most unfair.

'Not quite. Look this way.'

The tunnel was so cunningly hidden Emilia would never have noticed it on her own, the entrance concealed in a tangle of olive trees. A narrow steep slope led to a door, locked by an electronic keypad. Laurent led her down it, then punched in a long series of numbers and the door swung open. It was more like entering some vault than a path down to the sea.

'What is this?' The passage was tiled, the wall plastered and painted white. Lights were hidden in the ceiling illuminating the windy way down through the cliff. 'A smuggler's lair?'

'Once upon a time, yes. There was a time long ago

when all of coastal Armaria were smugglers and pirates, but now it's just a simple shortcut to the beach.'

'Is it safe?' She wasn't scared of heights or claustrophobic but the thought of walking through a tunnel dug out of a cliff, surrounded on all sides by tons of rock, made her heart beat faster and her palms dampen with nerves.

'Completely. My grandmother used it for sea bathing well into her late seventies. But we can always turn around if you're nervous.'

'No, I'm fine.' She wasn't going to be outdone by a septuagenarian grandmother. 'Just a little surprised, that's all.'

'I'm full of surprises.'

Emilia peered into the tunnel. Ever since she had first met Laurent her life had turned upside down. She'd found herself daydreaming at work. Flirting with a strange man. Confiding in a strange man. Getting on a motorbike with a strange man. Kissing a strange man. Now she was preparing to follow said strange man into a tunnel, trusting the destination was as he promised, trusting she'd be safe. But if she hadn't been here, what would she be doing? She knew exactly what—she'd be sitting at her desk, updating her project plan and budget, answering her emails, checking the plans the temporary event planners she'd hired to cover her work back in Chelsea had submitted for her approval. Burrowing into work, putting all her hopes and dreams into work, just as she had every day since she'd walked out of her father's birthday party, all her validation confirmed with every word of thanks, of praise. It had been enough. It had been all she had.

But something had changed in the last few hours. She had changed. And there was no going back.

'Okay then.' She reached out and took his hand, the strength in every sinew flowing into her. 'Let's go.'

Laurent was an honourable man. He had to be. He'd promised on his father's deathbed to behave with honour and put Armaria first. But he hadn't been thinking about honour or Armaria when he kissed Emilia. He hadn't been thinking at all. He had been all instinct and need and desire.

Technically he was still free to kiss anyone he wanted. He had said nothing to Bella Clayton that was even flirtatious, let alone a proclamation, made no promises and asked for none in return. She had no hold on him and he none on her. But he still needed her father's company to invest in Armaria and he knew there was plenty of speculation linking their names; by agreeing to joint costumes at the ball he was making a statement of some kind of intent, subtle as that statement might be. Joint costumes and gossip didn't tie him to Bella Clayton. But while he was still considering proposing, honour should have stopped him kissing anyone else.

True, he knew that if he proposed and Bella accepted, then she wouldn't be doing so in any expectation of love. No, she would be marrying him for position, as men and women had married for centuries. But she would have a right to expect her husband's respect, his fidelity, his honour. A right to know that if his heart wasn't hers it didn't belong anywhere else either.

He had always known that he owed his future Archduchess loyalty even if he wasn't lucky enough to offer her love and that was why in his few past relationships he had always been careful not to let his feelings grow beyond fond. To let his body and mind do the thinking, not his emotions.

He wasn't kidding himself that one kiss and a bit of flirting was enough to make Emilia fall in love with him. But neither could he kid himself that he wasn't falling for her. Hard. He was a rational, sensible man; he didn't believe in love at first sight. But the moment he had seen Emilia something in him had cracked. The way she had been lying under the tree, utterly absorbed in her work. The way she had responded to the garden he loved. The loneliness in her wary eyes. Her trust in him. The way she'd kissed him, fearlessly and sweetly. A kiss that should never be repeated. A kiss he would never forget.

For her he was probably a tryst at best and that was exactly as it should be. For him she was a glimpse of what his life could be like if he wasn't Prince Laurent d'Armaria, Archduke, absolute ruler and all that stood between his beloved country and bankruptcy.

So he allowed Emilia to take his hand and he vowed that he would treat her—and himself—to an evening neither would ever forget. And then he would let her walk away without a single reproach and he would get on with repairing his country.

Because that was what an Archduke should do.

The tunnel brought them out right at the foot of the cliff, onto a narrow ledge lashed by sea spray. There Laurent kept a small boat moored on a tiny jetty, sturdy and open, not robust enough to do anything but hug the rugged coastline, but still a taste of freedom found nowhere else in his narrow life except for those brief moments on his beloved bike.

'Your carriage, my lady,' he said as he pointed out the boat and her eyes narrowed.

'First a motorbike and now an open boat. Are you sure you're not trying to kill me?'

'The boat is completely safe.' He paused. 'You can swim, can't you?'

'I won't need to be able to swim if the boat is as safe as you say,' she pointed out and then relented. 'Yes. For a while I was in club training. As you can imagine, my mother hated it, all those five a.m. starts. I gave up after, well, when I went to live with my dad, but I'm still a strong swimmer.'

'Good. Sometimes I take the boat to deserted coves and swim. Maybe you could come with me one day.'

'That sounds lovely.' Emilia didn't point out that the chances of either of them having time to go swimming during the rest of her stay were slim at best and Laurent was relieved. Tonight he wanted to be like Ren, the man he had pretended to be when he'd first met Emilia, free of all ties and responsibilities, enjoying the company of a beautiful woman.

He helped Emilia into the boat and expertly steered it away from the rocks and along the shoreline, taking it further out as the cliffs gave way to harbours and beaches, the curve of San Tomare's famous promenade clearly visible with its waving palm trees and butter-yellow sand and elegant pastel-painted buildings, the mountains behind framing the picture-perfect whole.

Emilia said nothing during the boat ride but her eyes were wide as she took the scene in, her solemn mouth curved into a smile, showcasing her dimples. Fierce pride enveloped Laurent as he followed her gaze. San Tomare was the most cosmopolitan part of Armaria, but it was just one part of the country he loved; the mountains, the vineyards and olive groves, the alpine plains and the lowland rural grasslands, where the country's farmers still tilled and sowed as they had for hundreds of years, were just as important, just as impressive. But there was something special about the small capital city; no wonder tourists flocked here.

The city, the mountains, the plains, they were all in his keeping and he would do everything he could and all he should to ensure they prospered. But tonight… His eyes softened as his gaze moved to study Emilia, her straight hair whipped into a tangle by the sea breeze, her sallow cheeks pink with happiness, her eyes alight. He had never seen anyone or anything as beautiful as she was this evening, windblown in her jeans and jacket. He memorised every atom, knowing this memory would sustain him through the years to come.

Spotting the harbour, he steered the boat towards the long jetty he usually favoured, bringing the boat smoothly alongside with practised ease. Securing the boat onto one of the iron rings set into the jetty, he held his hand out to help Emilia from the boat. Her hand was cool and smooth in his, and yet he was aware of every millimetre of skin that touched his and he knew the feel of her hand in his would be imprinted on him for ever. How could a few hours change a man so profoundly? Maybe the Princess in *Roman Holiday* had a point— better a day of freedom than none at all.

'This is even more beautiful than the photos,' Emilia said, looking around as they started down the jetty, her eyes wide in appreciation, and Laurent was filled with a bittersweet happiness that he could show off the city he loved so passionately.

'A poet once said that San Tomare had all the history of Rome, the culture of Paris, the beauty of Vienna and the fierce pride of Tirana distilled into a few square miles of perfection.'

'I wouldn't want to contradict a poet,' Emilia said, her face glowing as they reached the end of the jetty, and Laurent couldn't help but remember Byron's immortal words: *She walks in beauty, like the night...*

'Come on then; let's see if you still agree after you've looked around.'

Laurent knew every inch of his city. Like all municipalities, San Tomare wasn't perfect. Some areas were far too expensive for locals, dominated by holiday lets and second homes, others needed investment, the inhabitants too often locked into a circle of poverty served by substandard infrastructure. If Clay Industries could be persuaded to invest here then all that could change, the opportunities for the youths and adults in the narrow streets transformed.

But this evening he would forget all his responsibilities and concentrate on all that the tourists flocked to San Tomare to enjoy, from the cobbled Italian quarter with its world-famous Roman amphitheatre to the celebrated beachfront promenade and the small but vibrant theatre district where Armaria's world-class ballet and opera companies were based.

At this time of the year the sun didn't set until late and they could wander through the soft pink evening light, Laurent pointing out the famous if slightly creepy puppet shops, stopping at a stand-up bar for bitter coffee followed by an eye-watering shot of the locally produced citrus liqueur sweetened with honey, and tiny plates of olives and cheese and tomato topped bread before they headed to the amphitheatre. Sometimes in summer the theatre companies staged plays or operas in the ancient space but tonight just a few tourists wandered around the circular stage, sitting on the stone seats or taking selfies against the dramatic backdrop. Laurent's heart swelled as he watched a young couple smiling into the camera, his arm protectively around her shoulders, the other angling the phone down as his girlfriend or wife snuggled in. What must it be like to be so carefree, to be able to choose where to bestow your heart?

But in the end did any of them have any choice at all?

'Come on,' Emilia said, tugging on his arm. 'Smile!'

To his surprise and slight alarm, Laurent saw her phone was in her hand, the camera switched on and toggled towards them. He always refused all requests for selfies and photos, wanting some little control over his life, to keep his inner self private. No wonder all his official photos and portraits were so stiff, like one of the puppets they had passed earlier, even the paparazzi shots showing a mannequin not a man. Was there a photo of him relaxed and smiling anywhere? Not that he was aware of.

His instinct was to pull away, but part of him wanted a memory of this evening's escape to be preserved on a cloud somewhere, for Emilia to come across it at some future date and remember the kiss they'd shared. So, instead of making his excuses, he smiled, leaned in so he could smell the sweet scent of her hair, so she fitted perfectly against him, and allowed her to take the picture.

'There you go,' she said, showing him the photo. 'Look at that backdrop.'

Laurent took the phone and stared down at the small screen and the two smiling faces. He barely recognised himself in the relaxed, laughing man, eyes glowing with happiness. 'Who is it that said that a photo captures a piece of someone's soul?'

'You've given me some of your soul then?' Emilia took her phone back and, although her tone was light, teasing, her eyes were full of questions.

'Yes,' Laurent said. 'And I gave it willingly.'

He'd told himself he wouldn't kiss her again, but how could he not when the sun was dropping below the horizon and the sky was purple and gold, when her face was full of hope and a tentative joy, when he knew it wasn't just part of his soul he had handed over this evening? She was still so close it was just a moment's work to turn to face her, to slip his arm around her slim waist and allow himself to savour the feeling of her skin under his touch, to imprint this moment firmly on his memories, to stare into the deep depths of her eyes and see her soul in turn and know he had been granted a rare and precious gift. One he would hold for just a few hours but remember for the rest of his life.

CHAPTER SEVEN

EMILIA COULDN'T BELIEVE this was her life. The whole evening was like a fairy tale. A dream. A soft-focus montage in a film.

It was like living someone else's life. Nights like this just did not happen to Emilia. She wasn't the kind of girl who got whisked off on a black steed—automatic horsepower rather than equine, but still—and kissed in a lemon grove and then again at the top of an amphitheatre as the sun set in a picture-perfect kaleidoscope sky. She had never before wandered hand in hand with a tall, handsome man through cobbled streets, stopping to kiss in doorways, before ending up in a tiny harbourside restaurant where flowers trailed from hanging baskets and violins played in the square beyond.

And yet here she was, champagne in hand, a plate of fresh seafood in front of her, a candle separating her from said tall, handsome man who was looking at her as if she—mousy, reserved Emilia—was the most enticing, brilliant thing he had ever seen. If this was romance then she had been wrong to scoff at it for all these years. She just needed to remember that it couldn't be real. People didn't actually fall in love at first sight or in one evening, or even in one week. They fell in lust maybe, desire certainly, but the bubbles frothing through her veins, the sweet tension low down in her belly, the sheer physical awareness of every part of her body and how it fitted with Laurent's, that couldn't be love. It couldn't be that easy, that simple.

A week simply wasn't long enough to get to know someone properly. She was all too aware that you could spend months, years with a person and they could still reveal a part of them you had never guessed was possible, show an indifference worse than any deliberate cruelty. But she did know that Laurent was a good listener and somehow she could open up to him like no one else. That he knew all the most picturesque spots in the city. That he kissed like an angel—or maybe a devil.

Even if she was the kind of girl to change her life for a man, it simply wasn't possible. Laurent had obligations and ties she simply couldn't comprehend, whether Bella was part of his future or not. No, better to take this evening as exactly what it was, a perfect evening. A gift from a universe which had finally seen Emilia's aching heart and loneliness and decided to show her another way. A better way. She could take this confidence and knowledge back to England and try to expand her limited life.

'What would you like to do next?' Ren asked as the plates were cleared and the waitress poured the last of the champagne into their glasses. 'We could go dancing— ballroom, disco, country—there's a nightclub for any type you fancy. Or we could go to a late-night concert.

Or we could just sit here and enjoy the view.' His gaze was fastened to her face as he said the last few words, not out at the moonlit sea, and Emilia's cheeks heated at the compliment—and at the desire clear in his eyes.

'They all sound appealing,' she said, picking up her glass and taking a too-large gulp of the tart champagne.

'Or,' Laurent said, his navy gaze intent on hers, 'we could head back to the villa. For a nightcap. See where the night takes us.'

'A nightcap?' Of course he'd suggested a nightcap. Wasn't that where evenings like this led? Walks and kisses and violins and champagne all led to nightcaps and then where? Her hand trembled as she held her glass, her smile less confident than she would like. But, for all her tell-tale nerves, she was tempted by the invitation, both spoken and in Laurent's eyes, the way his body leaned towards hers. She was sick and tired of re-grets, of fear of rejection. And her body hummed with his proximity. Why deny herself?

This whole job was about moving on. Moving on professionally by getting the kind of publicity which would push the agency into another league, making enough money to give them security for the next few, crucial months. It was her apology to her father and his family and a farewell gesture to a childhood full of anger. Why not move on emotionally as well, start to think of creating a life full of memories she wanted to carry rather than memories that held her back? Move on physically, banish the shadows that haunted her and stopped her getting close to anyone.

She wanted to, every atom ached to. But actually taking the step would be a whole other leap and she just didn't know if she was strong enough.

'Or a coffee. If you prefer.'

'That sounds tempting.' It was Laurent who tempted her, not the nightcap. But she couldn't let things go any further, not while there was so much left unsaid. Walks and kisses were one thing. A nightcap or coffee and where they might lead quite another. Laurent had no idea who she was, no idea she was related to the man he was putting so much work into attracting. No idea that the family she had told him about was the one he was considering marrying into. And even if she didn't tell him herself, he would find out soon enough. Her father, Simone and Bella were going to arrive in just a couple of days and she couldn't guarantee that her anonymity would be maintained. Better Laurent heard the news from her.

But what if the confidences she had so thoughtlessly shared made him confront her father and her dad didn't invest as a result? San Tomare was utterly charming, but Laurent had pointed out where it needed investment, jobs beyond tourism, farming and fishing, a reason for the university graduates to stay home rather than take their skills to France or Switzerland. Her father's company could be the first step in helping Laurent make the changes he needed. She would still be the selfish brat her father thought her if she got in the way of that.

And there was Bella. There was no love between the stepsisters, they weren't friends, spent no time together. But it wasn't Bella's fault. She had tried, back when they were children, and still made the occasional effort now. And she'd been in regular contact over the last two weeks, discussing costumes and dresses and asking for Emilia's opinion. Could Emilia really contemplate sleeping with the man her stepsister might marry? It seemed so sordid. In retrospect, all those cosy innocent picnics in the walled garden weren't half as innocent as they'd seemed. She was certain her family would not see them that way.

Twirling her glass, Emilia knew it was time to dissolve the spell and re-enter reality; she needed to find a way to tell him who she was. 'Can we walk?' she asked. 'By the sea?'

'Of course,' he said easily and if he was disappointed she had turned down the offer of a nightcap, he hid it. But then Laurent had plenty of practice at hiding his feelings. She just didn't want him to hide them with her.

It was a short stroll to the beach. The picturesque curve was lit up by the moon and the hundreds of fairy lights entwined around the palm trees fringing the road. Emilia inhaled the sea air and tasted salt on her lips. They passed a family as they headed to the shore, the parents holding hands while a small boy raced ahead and an older one walked by their side, exchanging greetings with a smile.

'Why has no one recognised you?' she asked, a question that had been hovering on the tip of her tongue all evening. 'You're on the bank notes, there's portraits of you everywhere and yet nobody has as much as done a double take.'

'You didn't recognise me when we first met,' he pointed out and she tilted her chin haughtily.

'I was new to the country and had yet to see a portrait or bank note. Besides, you looked most reprehensible. Who expects to see an Archduke in a dirty T-shirt and ripped jeans?'

'Exactly. Who expects to see an Archduke in casual clothes, taking a stroll with a girl in public? I learned a long time ago that the only way to have a private life is to do it publicly. The bike, the boat, the villa—no one expects me to own them and so they just don't see me. But if I was in my dress uniform with bodyguards then they'd know it was me. I like to hide in plain sight.'

'Very clever.'

'Very necessary. I don't get much time away from the castle, from Parliament and my duties, but just one bike ride, one night in the villa, one walk around the streets in a month reminds me of why I do what I do.'

'Did you ever question it? Ever think, *Sod it, I don't want to be an archduke and join the army and do a business degree. I want to ride my bike through Europe or be an artist. I want to marry whoever I want. Be whoever I want?* Did you ever rebel?'

Laurent was silent for so long Emilia feared she had overstepped. When he spoke at last his voice was quiet, pensive. 'The night my father died he called me to him. He told me that people would think that being an Archduke was fun, that having the power we still have in Armaria gave us freedom. He told me that those people were wrong. That my inheritance was a great privilege and a great responsibility. That Armaria was my destiny and I needed to treat the country and my role with respect and honour. I have always tried to live up to his words, even when they seemed like an unbearable burden. Even when, yes, I wanted to take my bike and roar off into the distance, although not to be an artist. I'd soon have starved. But how could I when my father laid this charge on me? Gave Armaria into my keeping? I always knew my destiny and tried to embrace it, not resent it.'

Emilia had promised herself no more touching but she couldn't resist reaching out and taking his hand. His fingers closed around hers, reassuringly strong. 'What would you be? If you weren't an Archduke?'

'No one has ever asked me that before.' They walked a little longer while he thought. 'I always liked buildings. Maybe an architect, although the lack of drawing ability might be a problem. Or an engineer of some kind. How about you? Always wanted to organise events?'

Emilia was guiltily aware that she was supposed to be confessing who she really was but the evening was so warm, the sound of the sea lapping on the shore so beguiling, the conversation so easy, she put off the moment for a while longer. 'I fell into it really. When I left home I obviously needed a job and got one at a hotel, just as a chambermaid; I wasn't really qualified for anything. But the manager was really kind—and French. He liked it that I was half-French. So he trained me as a receptionist and then after another year I started to work in events at the hotel. A couple of years after that I went to work in conferences for a big corporate company and that's where I met Harriet, Amber and Alex. The rest is history. But it suits me. It's all-encompassing; when I plan an event I don't have the time or energy to think about anything else. And it's always a huge adrenaline ride. I'm at the centre of this whirlwind, you know? Everyone needs me and I control it all. It's terrifying and wonderful all at once.'

'Alex? One of your friends is male?'

She couldn't help smiling at the studied casualness in his voice. 'Short for Alexandra.'

'So who else is in your life? Any hopeful potential boyfriends sitting at home and checking their phones, wondering why you haven't texted this evening?'

She swallowed, looking down at their clasped hands. 'No.'

'Then English men are even more cold-blooded than their reputation,' he said.

'That's very kind of you.' She could barely speak, thanks to the lump in her throat.

'I'm not being kind; I'm being serious. What are they thinking?'

'I work all the time. I don't have time to date. And I haven't really wanted to.'

He stopped and she was forced to stop too. She still couldn't look at him. 'Ever? My every public move is followed by the world's media and I still managed to have several semi-meaningful relationships.'

'Did you love any of them?' she managed to ask, her throat still thick with fear and memory.

'No. I always knew that my marriage wasn't about me, it was about my country. Becoming an Archduchess—it's like you described running an event, standing in the middle of a whirlwind, trying to maintain control. It's not for everyone. Love seemed like a luxury. What if I fell for someone who didn't want to live such a life or couldn't cope with it? I didn't realise at the time, but I always kept something of myself back in those few relationships. And maybe that was a good thing. The girls I dated when I was younger found the public pressure far too much. If I'd loved them then imagine how hard that would be, knowing my country was the reason we couldn't be.'

'I fell in love once. At least, I thought it was love.' Was that her voice, so scratchy and raw? And what was she saying? No one knew this story. Not even her friends.

'But it wasn't?'

Emilia tried to loosen her hand from his grip but Laurent held on; instead she resumed walking and he kept pace beside her. 'No. It was infatuation on my side.'

'And on his?'

She'd asked herself that question a million times. 'Power, I think. It's an old story. Young, friendless girl meets older sophisticated guy and falls head over heels. Guy makes her feel like the most special thing in the world one minute and the most useless person alive the next. Girl never knows which guy she'll get, the romantic, loving one or the cold, critical one and she spends her life trying to please and appease him, desperate for his approval.'

'Oh, Emilia...'

She shook her head, not able to cope with sympathy. 'My attraction was my vulnerability. I see that now. I was like a puppy dog, just desperate for attention, for love. Willing to put up with anything for the pretence of it.'

'Did he hit you?' His voice was so cold it made her shiver.

'No. It never got that far. He moved on, thank goodness, bored of me and how pathetic I was. Found someone else desperate for his attention. But he made sure I knew he'd just been using me first. Made sure I knew just how easy I was, how useless. The words cut so deep because they were true. I tried to change my whole self to please him but, whatever I did, it was never enough. I just couldn't trust my own judgement after that. First my dad and then him. I put all my self-worth into their love and approval and when they withheld it I felt like nothing… It just seemed safer to be alone.'

'I don't want you to be alone.' His grip tightened on hers. 'You deserve so much more, Emilia.'

It was all too much. The confidences shared, the kisses, the whole evening. Emilia had worked so hard to keep her heart, herself, safe and she could feel her armour cracking and peeling off, her defences loosening. But there were things Laurent still didn't know and, whatever happened, only heartbreak awaited her. He was not free to love her and, even if he was, she wasn't exactly an Archduchess type, a former teenage tearaway with only one sordid relationship to her name.

All she knew was that she needed to feel something, do something. Breaking away from Laurent, she kicked off her trainers and waded into the warm sea waist-deep, her jeans instantly heavy and clinging.

'Emilia? What are you doing? Are you all right? Emilia!' Laurent called her name again but she kept going until the water reached her chest, soaking through to her bra, the sensation reminding her that she was still here. A survivor. She could survive this too, whatever this was. She turned at the sound of someone wading through water, only to step back as Laurent reached her.

'What are you doing? You're still dressed,' she said foolishly and he looked at her incredulously before his mouth found hers in a kiss so deep and so full Emilia had no defences left, even if she had wanted them. She allowed him to pull her close to his cold, wet body, pressing even closer as if she could climb inside him, returning his kiss with a fierceness she didn't know she possessed, her arms sliding around his neck to pull him harder against her, mouth open to him, wanting all he was giving and more. Her breasts were crushed against his chest, her legs against his, and still she moved closer. She was dimly aware of a flash of light, of noise on the beach, but none of it mattered, only this kiss, this man, this moment.

When Laurent pulled away she couldn't help but mutter a moan of protest, her mind and body and lips aching for more contact. 'You're soaking,' he said ruefully and she laughed.

'Says you.'

He looked down at his dripping body almost in surprise. 'It's a good thing I have clothes back at the villa. Come on…'

Hand in hand, they waded out of the sea and weaved quickly through the promenading crowds enjoying the summer evening, slipping down side streets, Laurent pausing only to back her against a wall for another, fierce kiss.

* * *

Walking fast, they could have been back at the villa in less than fifteen minutes, but every few yards one or the other would stop to pull the other back into a desperate hot embrace. Laurent knew he should be cold in spite of the warm Mediterranean night, his clothes soaked through with sea water, but the spark between them didn't allow anything but heat. He'd never felt anything like it, this want. He couldn't fight it, not any longer. It was a sign that his life had to change. There was no way he could propose to anyone while feeling like this for another woman. And now his life had exploded into Technicolor he couldn't walk willingly into a monochrome future. He'd find a way to take care of Armaria and live the life he realised he craved. There must be a solution…

The villa gates swung open as he neared them, the door unlocked, not thanks to the sensor on his keys, wet through in his pocket, but his unseen bodyguards, and he cursed them as he shut the door firmly against the cameras and sightlines that invaded so many of his moments. But not this one. This was his alone. There were cameras in the house but not in his private suite, and he led Emilia up the stairs to the corner room with sea views and the large bed that dominated the high-ceilinged room.

'You better get out of those clothes,' he said, walking past her to the bathroom and grabbing a large towel. 'Here.'

Emilia leaned against the door and removed one boot and then the other, sliding her feet out of her socks with an almost balletic grace before shrugging her jacket off and unbuttoning her jeans. She made no move to take the towel he held out as she shimmied out of the tight, wet denim, pulling her shirt off in one fluid movement so she stood before him clad only in her still wet pink bra and pants.

'Your turn,' she said, her voice shaking despite the confident words, and Laurent knew he was undone.

He kicked off his wet shoes and socks, peeling off sodden trousers and shirt, dropping the towel as he did so. Emilia was staring at him, eyes wide, her sweet mouth slightly open, the heave of her breasts in the flimsy silk her only sign of life. Laurent was beyond thought as he drew her close, his touch both gentle and possessive. He was drowning in her, in her scent and her long smooth limbs and her touch. He skimmed his hands over her back, round to the dip of her waist, the swell of her hip, then back to the softness of her breast and heard her gasp as he did so.

'Laurent…'

She wanted *him*, not the Archduke, not the ancient name, not the castle. She wanted him and that thought was more intoxicating than any moment in his rigid dutiful life had ever been.

Their gazes snagged and held. 'Do you want me?' she whispered.

'More than I have ever wanted anything in my life.'

'That's all I need to know.' And, not taking her gaze away from his, she unhooked her bra and let it fall to the floor. 'And I think we've done enough talking for one night, don't you?'

Her words and gaze were bold but the wariness hadn't

quite left her eyes—wariness and apprehension, maybe fear, as if she thought he might reject her. Reject her? It was laughable. She stood there, topless, her hair falling around her shoulders, emphasising the swell of her breasts. Laurent drank her in, unable to move. She was very slim, long-limbed, strong—a survivor, and he knew that her trust in him was a gift and not one she gave often or easily. 'You're so beautiful.'

'Tonight I feel beautiful. You make me feel beautiful,' she whispered and with that admission any thought, any vestige of hesitation was gone. All Laurent could do was take her into his arms once again, her skin smooth and warm against his, inflaming nerves he had thought dormant, turning his body into an explosion of touchpoints and sensation everywhere their bodies met. Chest, stomach, thighs, hands, mouths—he'd never been so overwhelmed before, never so lost in someone else's scent, their body, their whole being. As he scooped her up and carried her over to the bed Laurent vowed that this was just the beginning. That he would never hurt Emilia. They had met for a reason and he was never letting go. He'd find a way to make it work. He had to.

CHAPTER EIGHT

EMILIA STRETCHED IN the mid-morning light and glanced at the watch she always wore, a slim gold Swiss watch that had belonged to her mother. Gracious! She had overslept, and her desk wasn't a five-minute sprint down stairs and along corridors but several miles away…

And with that realisation the memory of the rest of last night came flooding back. The motorbike, the tour of the city, the meal, the way she had opened up as never before, the way she had trusted as never before. And the way she had felt as never before…

She wriggled, half in embarrassment, half in pleasure. Had she seduced Laurent or he her? Probably a little of both. She had never been so vocal, so demanding, so upfront about what—and who—she wanted before.

Closing her eyes, she relived the night, the touch and sensation, the gasps and exhortations to not stop, not yet, the low-voiced murmurs and laughter. She straightened, pulling the sheet up with her as she did so. How had this happened? How had she, Emilia Clayton, sensible and measured and always, always careful, fallen into bed with a man she hardly knew? A man who wasn't free to be there with her?

Maybe that was why. There was no future for them. She knew the ending before they started. How could she be hurt by him when he had never been hers? He was safe. Her heart should be safe.

But she had seen the way his eyes darkened when he told her she was beautiful. She had felt his soul when he kissed her. She would stake everything she had that he felt more for her than a fleeing attraction. But what he felt didn't matter. What she felt mattered less. Better to accept what was and move on. Let the night they had shared become a sweet memory. Their own *Roman Holiday*.

Sitting up, she looked around at the tidy, sparsely furnished room, all whitewashed walls and polished wood. There was no sign of either Laurent or his clothes, no sign that two of them had shared the bed, shared their bodies, were responsible for the rumpled sheets. Emilia rolled over and tried to block out the creeping negativity shivering through her despite her good intentions to approach her future with positivity, despite the look she had seen in Laurent's eyes, the way he had held her. Had she got it all horribly wrong? Misjudged everything? Trusted a man who was just after a night's fun before marriage put an end to his freedom? Had the connection she felt been nothing but a carefully planned seduction? Every instinct screamed no, but she had been so very wrong before. How could she trust her flawed instincts? Better to go on evidence, and the empty room spoke volumes.

She rolled back over, staring at the white-painted ceiling with its ornate plasterwork, and inhaled several deep calming breaths. Right, it wasn't as if she had slept with Laurent in the hope of a happy ever after. It was a one-night stand, no matter what his motivations. All she could do was control *her* thoughts and actions, no one else's. And right now her thoughts and actions needed to get her into the office, behind her desk and making sure every single detail for the ball was nailed down.

Mind made up, she slid out of the bed and padded to the bathroom, gathering up her clothes and bag as she went. Someone—Laurent—had picked them up from the floor where she had discarded them and hung them by the window so the sun had dried her damp jeans and top. He must have been up for some time. They were bone-dry.

The bathroom was as simple and elegant as the bedroom and the villa gardens. A quick shower and a face wash and Emilia felt ready to face the day, aided by a sweep of the deodorant and lipstick she always carried in her bag. Getting into yesterday's clothes wasn't too bad, although the jeans and jacket seemed too warm for what looked like another lovely hot day.

Returning to the bedroom, Emilia pulled her phone out of her bag, wanting to read her emails and anchor herself back in her world, but her battery had died in the night and her phone was unresponsive. Sighing, she returned it into her bag, knowing there was nothing else she could do to delay the inevitable and she was going to have to exit the bedroom and go in search of Laurent and a ride back to the palace. Wandering to the window, she looked out at the lemon trees in the garden and the sea beyond and was filled with a sudden intense urge to stay in this sheltered villa, in this moment. To be the girl who'd woken up in a rumpled bed, the sunlight slanting through the shutters, mouth swollen with kisses and a sweet ache deep inside for a while longer. But that girl was just an illusion. The real Emilia belonged at a desk with a phone in one hand and a to-do list in the other. It was time she remembered that.

As she turned, stomach quaking at the thought of searching the house for Laurent, of finding the right words to say to him after her abandoned frankness last night, the door opened and he appeared, holding a tray. Emilia smiled, trying to hide her foolish relief. Of course he hadn't just abandoned her, wasn't regretting the night before. That wasn't how most people operated. But, she noted with a sense of foreboding, although he looked delectably morning-after-the-night-before, hair rumpled, chin and cheeks covered in morning stubble, his smile looked a little forced and wasn't reflected in his eyes, more grey than blue in the morning light.

'Morning, sleepyhead,' he said. 'I brought coffee; we don't have any tea. I hope it's all right.' He put the tray down on a small table near the other window; it was flanked by two armchairs. Her mouth watered; the tray was heaped with coffee, fresh fruit and delicious-looking pastries.

'Perfect. I usually have coffee in the morning,' Emilia reassured him. She hovered, unsure whether to kiss him or not, but he made no move towards her and so she stayed where she was. 'Do you have a phone charger?

I really should check my emails. I had no idea it was so late.'

Laurent's smile dimmed. 'Yes, of course, but sit and have some coffee first.'

The sense of wrongness rolling around Emilia's stomach grew as she took the chair he indicated and accepted the cup of deliciously rich coffee he handed her, but shook her head as he offered her a pastry. 'I'm fine, thanks. Maybe some of that fruit first.' She paused, feeling foolish, but her instincts were screaming that something was wrong. He hadn't greeted her with a kiss or any kind of touch, his bearing formal and removed. 'Is there something wrong? It's okay,' she tried to joke. 'I'm not expecting a proposal. We both were carrying a lot of emotion last night.'

There was no answering smile. If anything, Laurent looked more serious than he had before. 'Do you remember when I told you last night that I always had to keep a little part of me aside? That the demands of being my girlfriend often outweighed the benefits and that's why I stopped dating?'

'Yes, I remember.' She put down her cup, the faint foreboding that had shadowed her from the moment she realised she was alone intensified. 'What's going on?'

He didn't answer at first, pouring himself a black coffee and selecting a pastry he didn't eat, putting it down on his plate, crumbling it absently between his fingers. 'Very soon the Claytons arrive.'

'Yes.' Was this the *It's not you, it's me and my need to save my country* speech? He needn't worry. With all the hormones bombarding her last night she hadn't had an opportunity to tell Laurent the truth about who she was. When he found out she'd been less than honest she wouldn't blame him for walking away rather than nobly renouncing her. Maybe that kind of break was for the best rather than the *Roman Holiday—If things were different* type Laurent was heading for.

'I thought I knew exactly what I had to do. And what I wanted to do. Because no one was pushing me or forcing me. Wooing Bella Clayton was my decision. I need an heir, an Archduchess, and she ticked all the right boxes. I never expected more than compatibility in marriage and so how could I be disappointed when compatibility was my future?'

'Laurent, you don't have to explain. I knew what the deal was, what I was getting into. It's all right.'

He carried on as if she hadn't spoken. 'But then last night happened. Truth was, it didn't occur to me to factor something like you in, why would I? My world was so structured, so planned, random meetings and new acquaintances just didn't happen. But there you were, under my favourite tree. In my soul… You changed everything. You changed me.'

This was not how Emilia had expected this conversation to go. 'Me?' she managed to say.

'Duty didn't seem too much of a burden when I didn't know anything different. But, although my mother knows what I was considering, although I am very sure Simone Clayton was also aware of my thoughts, I haven't committed myself to Bella, to anyone, not in any way. There, at least, I have nothing to reproach myself for. I promise you, Emilia. My heart was free for me to give where I chose.'

'I know all this,' she half whispered, both desperate and dreading finding out where this conversation was heading.

Putting his coffee cup down, Laurent straightened and looked directly at her, and with an effort Emilia met his gaze. 'Last night I made a decision. Duty is important, compatibility is essential. But love also has a place in marriage, even that of an Archduke. Bella is a very nice woman, but I don't love her and she doesn't love me. How can I ask her to share her life with me? How can I pursue a relationship with her when I have spent the last week falling in love with someone else?'

'I…' This was so not how she had expected this conversation to go. They were supposed to agree that last night had been lovely, that it shouldn't have happened, return to the castle, and that would be that. Sure, it would have been difficult to watch Laurent with Bella but she had known the score before they started. She would have buried herself in work; it was always the remedy.

Now everything had changed and Laurent had said it was because of her. He had talked about love. Emilia's blood heated at the thought even as her mind recoiled in panic. 'Last night…' She shook her head, unable to stop her cheeks heating, to look directly at him. 'Last night was incredible. I've never felt like that before. Never imagined I would ever feel so…' She stopped again, not wanting to reveal so much, not even to Laurent, to whom she had already shown so much. 'But this is the next day and we're back to reality, Laurent.'

'The amazing thing about reality is that we get to shape it, if we want.' Laurent was watching her closely, so sure, so confident that this was right, and how she wanted to believe him. But she hadn't come here to fall in love. She wasn't prepared.

'Laurent, I don't know what to say,' she said almost desperately. 'To be honest, I didn't think that this was how this morning would go. It's not that I haven't started to develop feelings for you but we come from different worlds, different countries. Last night was supposed to be a one-off as a start; we both knew that. And that made sense. Apart from anything else, neither of us have time to start shaping reality. I have an incredibly busy few days ahead, you have guests to entertain.'

'Duty comes first?'

'I guess we have that in common.' She tried for a smile, needing to get away, to think. 'Look, I need to get to work. Can we meet and talk about this later? In the garden this evening?' The garden was their safe place. Maybe she could make sense of his words, of her heart, there.

'It's not quite that simple.' Laurent took his phone out of his pocket and slid it across the table. 'As you'll see.'

Emilia picked it up after a quick glance at Laurent, her mouth dry. As she tilted it towards her a picture flashed up, a wet-through Laurent kissing a brown-haired girl very thoroughly. Kissing her... 'The flashes of light,' she remembered, her heart sinking.

'Thumb through,' Laurent commanded and Emilia

obeyed with shaking hands. Another shot of them kissing, one of them holding hands, heads tilted together, the desire on their faces so blatant Emilia gasped, feeling as exposed as if she had been naked.

Prince and Mystery Brunette! the headline read, followed by a breathless article detailing the Archduke's secret date and the mystery girl he hadn't been able to keep his eyes or hands off all night.

'Oh, my God.' Emilia set the phone back down, sickened. 'This is horrible. How can they publish these?'

'We were in public. I just didn't think. I thought we—I—hadn't been recognised. I often go out incognito, but I don't usually let my guard down to this extent.'

'I can't believe this is happening,' she whispered. Her father would see the photos, Bella would. Of course they would think she had sabotaged things on purpose. This ball was supposed to be her way of making amends and moving on, not building an even bigger wall between them.

'I'm sorry. I should have warned you this was a possibility. I thought we had covered our tracks, but I can never guarantee privacy. Do you regret last night?'

Emilia stared down at Laurent's phone, at the photo of her standing by the water's edge, her clothes wet through and clinging so that every part of her body was visible. She looked so vulnerable, every thought right there for anybody to see: hope, desire, need. How many people were looking at her right now? Sneering at her naked want, at her messy hair and see-through top. But then she looked up and saw a flicker of sadness in Laurent's otherwise perfect poker face. She wasn't alone here. Standing up, she walked over to Laurent's chair and lifted his head with her hands so he was looking directly at her.

'Neither of us know what's going to happen. We wouldn't if you weren't the Archduke, we wouldn't if those photos hadn't been taken. But one thing is certain. Last night was the best night of my life and if that's the one shot we get then that was a pretty good shot. You made me feel in a way I didn't know I could. You made me believe I was beautiful and desirable and I am so grateful—will always be grateful for that.' Emilia leaned down, her heart flipping as she inhaled his scent, sea and lemon and something uniquely masculine that was pure Laurent, pressing a gentle kiss on his mouth.

He didn't respond for a single surprised second, but then he deepened the kiss, pulling her down so she was on his lap, his arms around her, kissing her greedily, desperately, as if he was trying to fit a lifetime in the one kiss. Emilia matched him, hungry kiss for hungry kiss, her arms entwined around his neck, fingers in his hair, pulling him closer until the shrill ring of his phone made them both jump and pull apart.

'I should get that…' he said and Emilia slid off his lap, trying not to touch her swollen lips as she did so.

'Yes. And then we had better get back. I'll wait downstairs.' And she was at the door before she could change her mind. She stopped as she reached it, turning back to look at Laurent. His eyes were fixed on her and she paused for a moment, allowing her heart to shine through her eyes, before turning and hurrying downstairs, feeling as if she had said goodbye before they had got much past hello.

Laurent walked heavily down the steps of the villa. It was so different to last night, pulling Emilia up after him, breathless and thrumming with need and desire. Last night had been a beginning, this morning a kiss goodbye. They had barely got started.

It was easy, too easy, to blame the pictures. Nobody wanted to be photographed during their private moments, for the whole world to share what was meant to be intimate. But Emilia had begun to withdraw before then. She had withdrawn the second he had mentioned love.

He was a fool. He'd rushed into a huge declaration because of the photos, wanting her to know how he felt before she saw them. He'd forgotten how vulnerable she was, how damaged by her past. She needed wooing gently, not big gestures.

He could do that. It was almost a week until the ball. He had time. Of course first he needed to deal with the fallout of the pictures. The Claytons were due to arrive the day after tomorrow. He couldn't exactly apologise—that was the problem with unspoken understandings—nor did his carefully arranged programme for getting to know Bella Clayton better seem appropriate. But he could still entertain the family, showcase the best of Armaria and ensure that the Midsummer Ball was as magical as its reputation.

Clay Industries' investment didn't depend on an engagement, thank goodness. It had just seemed like a

neat way to tie the family to Armaria, but all the reasons
Mike Clayton had been interested in the first place were
still valid. The sun, wind and tides, the educated, multi-
lingual workforce, the rail, sea and air links… He just
needed to sell those benefits as never before and hope
Bella Clayton hadn't invested too much in the idea of
becoming an Archduchess, for both the sake of the investment and also her own happiness. She wasn't in love
with him, he knew that, but that didn't mean he wanted
her humiliated. Thank goodness he had said and done
nothing she or her family could reproach him with, and
he was even more thankful she seemed far more interested in meeting Pomme and riding Armaria's famous
bridle paths than spending time with him.

Emilia hadn't gone very far. She was curled up on
the chaise in the hallway, scrolling through her phone—
she must have found a charger somewhere. Her face
was very pale, her eyes glassy and brow furrowed. Her
tiredness didn't look like the result of a sleepless night, it
looked like plain old exhaustion and all Laurent wanted
to do was keep her here until her colour returned. In
fact…

'Why don't you stay here for a few days?' he said,
inspired. 'It's private, there's plenty of space. I could
have a car take you anywhere you needed to go.'

'That sounds lovely, but I need to be on site.' She held
out her phone towards him. 'Besides, there's something
I need you to see.'

Laurent stepped over and took the phone, eyes creasing in disgust as he realised he was looking at yet another gossip site, another photo of a soaking-wet Emilia,

her top almost transparent. 'Why are you looking at this? The best thing to do is ignore them; believe me, I know.'

'Read it,' she said.

After shooting her a troubled glance he quickly scanned the text.

Royally Yours *can exclusively reveal that the mystery brunette who indulged in a spot of late-night swimming with Europe's most eligible bachelor Laurent d'Armaria, Archduke and royal hottie, is none other than Emilia Clayton, who is in Armaria to organise the Midsummer Ball—which will also commemorate her father's sixtieth birthday.*

Emilia is the only biological daughter of tech king Mike Clayton, who has been rumoured to be looking at Armaria as a base for his newest factory.

Palace sources had hinted that Bella Clayton, Mike Clayton's socialite stepdaughter, was in line to be the new Archduchess. Was it all an elaborate bluff or has Emilia cut out her stepsister?

Either way, we can't wait to see what happens next.

Laurent read it again before looking over at Emilia, confused. 'I don't understand. How have they made such a mistake?'

'I was going to tell you last night…'

It took a moment for her words to sink in. 'It's true? The man who let you leave home when you were just a child? That's Mike Clayton?' Laurent just couldn't comprehend it, couldn't marry the serious but kind man he had met with the uncaring father Emilia had described, the close-knit family who had welcomed him into their home with the people who had excluded a hurt, grieving teen.

'Yes. At least…'

'Emilia, either it's true or it's not.' His chest tightened. How could he do business with such a man? But how could he not? He needed the Clayton millions—Armaria needed it.

'Everything I said was true,' she told him with quiet dignity, her chin high. 'My father had an affair, he left my mother and she was heartbroken. I didn't see much of him from the day he left until the death of my mother. He's not the only man to start a new family and see little of the old; it happens all the time. But that doesn't make it easier or right.'

'I know.'

'It's hard to explain, to put into words how angry I was, Laurent. Simone didn't want me but, to be fair to her, maybe she tried as much as she was able. She is so different to Maman, though. So calm and emotionless. I couldn't read her at all; I still can't. And Dad was so different when he was with her. It felt like a betrayal of all we had been, of Maman, of my whole life.'

'None of that excuses what they did.'

'No, it doesn't. And I don't excuse them, Laurent, but what I have realised as I've grown older is that there are always two sides to every story and their story would have some validity. I was very, very difficult. I already told you

I used to stay out, truant from school, shoplift. I was also rude to Simone, always, not that she ever showed that she noticed, rude to Bella when I spoke to her. And when I say rude—' she shook her head '—sullen was a good day.'

'Emilia, I don't care how badly behaved you were. They were your family.'

'No, they weren't. That was the problem. It is the problem. They were—are—a family, and Dad and I should have been a family but we weren't; he belonged with them. The more I wanted him to show me that he loved me no matter what, the worse I got, the more he stepped back—I told you he had no emotional intelligence.' She paused, looking down at her phone, her eyes clouded.

'Maybe part of me thought if I was bad enough I could scare Simone and Bella away and then it would be just Dad and me and I'd get some part of my life back. Part of me just wanted them to hurt like I did. And I just wanted them to see me, to really see me, to acknowledge how I felt, to tell me it was okay. I wanted more from them than they could give, I think. It was like we spoke different languages and they just couldn't understand what I was begging for. I wish my father hadn't had an affair, I wish he had tried harder to see me after he left. I wish he'd shown me he wanted me and loved me. But in the end I was the one who walked out and I'm the one who stayed away. It was the only way I could protect myself. But when I look back I feel sorrow for how sad and lonely I was, but also shame for some of the things I said and did, and guilt for how much I tried to destroy his happiness. That's why, when Simone asked me to do the ball, I agreed. It was a chance to say I was sorry. A chance to show him who I am now, what I do. Maybe it still won't be enough, but I couldn't go on hiding away. I had to try.'

'But why didn't you tell me who you were?'

She tried for a smile. 'So many reasons. I couldn't work out if asking me to do the ball was Simone's way of keeping me in my place or an olive branch. I didn't know if Dad would know I was involved, if I wanted him to know. All the publicity says that Dad has one daughter—and they don't mean me. It's so humiliating. Plus there were the rumours about Bella and you… It just seemed safer to stay anonymous. But I was going to tell you last night, until circumstances overcame us.'

'Right.' It wasn't often Laurent was at a loss but right now he didn't know what to say or to think. Emilia had been the most real thing to happen to him, but it looked like he didn't know her at all. He hadn't even known her name. Plus the already awkward situation with the Claytons had just taken on a whole new dimension. How was he going to explain to them why a member of their family had been plastered all over the tabloids, why their family was now in the gossip columns? He wouldn't blame them for taking their investment and walking straight out.

'There's a car outside to take you back to the castle. I'm afraid there's a lot of press around so it's not safe to use the bike. You go—there's something I have to sort out here.'

'Okay.' Emilia got to her feet, making no move to touch him as she left, as if the passionate kiss they had shared had never happened. 'I'm so sorry. I know I've ruined everything again, but I'll try and put it right. Goodbye, Laurent.'

Laurent watched her go, wanting to call her back, to tell her he didn't care who she was and what she had done. But he couldn't find the words, his mind still taken up with wondering how to unravel the mess he had somehow created, the deal to save his country looking more and more unlikely. He had to put Armaria first. His own heart would have to wait.

CHAPTER NINE

'YOUR HIGHNESS.' SIMONE CLAYTON swept into an elegant low curtsey, her daughter following suit, and with a laugh Laurent hoped didn't sound too forced he bade them rise.

'You are my honoured guests,' he told them as he led them from the helipad to the front of the castle with its imposing entrance. 'No formalities necessary. How was your journey? Let's get you settled; I believe your suite is ready. I hope Miss Clayton doesn't mind sharing a suite with her parents? You have your own bedroom and bathroom, of course. But we have so many people coming to the Midsummer Ball the castle is actually almost full.'

'Of course that will be fine,' Bella Clayton assured him, her smile seeming genuine if her gaze a little curious. She didn't seem at all put-out, to Laurent's relief. Her mother was cool, but then she usually was, and he recalled Emilia's words; she didn't show much emotion at all. Bella laughed. 'As long as the stable is expecting me and I get a chance to see the famous Armarian Spaniels then I am completely happy.'

'A suitable mare has been selected for you and the daughter of one of my aides has offered to show you some of the best rides around here. As for dogs, my own dog Pomme has recently fathered a litter. I'm looking forward to introducing you to the puppies and to the proud father, of course.'

'That sounds awesome; thank you so much.' Bella paused and touched his arm, her expression serious. 'I just want you to know I got my own costume. There's been so much silly stuff on all those gossip sites, and it just seemed best. I didn't want to fuel any more crazy talk by matching with you. I hope that doesn't put you out?'

'No, not at all. Very sensible.'

'Good.' She looked relieved. 'Where is Emilia? I thought she'd be here? I wanted to chat about my new costume; she's good at things like that. The ones she found for us were great, so I wanted her input on this one.'

'I believe she's in her office; it's where she seems to be all the time. There's a lot to do.' Laurent was very aware of Mike and Simone Clayton's heavy stares at the mention of Emilia's name. A difficult conversation needed to be had—and soon. 'My mother is very much looking forward to meeting you,' he said, falling in next to Simone and escorting her up the grand stone steps at the front of the castle. 'She's arranged some excursions around the country—the joy of being so small is that everywhere can be reached in a day. I do hope you enjoy them.' If Simone Clayton realised what a huge honour having the dowager Archduchess as a tour guide was she didn't betray it by so much as the flicker of an eyelid. Laurent could see how her *froideur* must have been difficult for a hurting, lonely child to cope with.

He was still unsure how he felt about Emilia's revelations. Of course he had kept his identity from her at the beginning—who knew how long he might have continued to lie if the Contessa hadn't unwittingly outed him? He could hardly occupy the moral high ground. And he understood the awkwardness of the situation, why she would want to avoid speculation if people had realised who she was. But not to tell him? To sleep with him whilst keeping something so important concealed?

But, as she had said, she had meant to tell him that night, but instead it had swept them both away. It was unfair for him to blame her for that. Things had escalated so very quickly...escalated and then stopped and he hadn't seen her since. She hadn't appeared in the garden over the last couple of evenings and he hadn't wanted to fuel speculation by visiting her in her office.

But although he had hoped she would come to talk to him, even if it was for the last time, he hadn't been surprised when she didn't appear. He'd had the feeling she was saying goodbye before the revelation about her identity.

So here he was with her family and yet without her. It seemed wrong, but for the Claytons it had been this way for a decade. Emilia obviously believed she was as much to blame for the family estrangement as her father and his wife, and in some ways that seemed the worst thing of all. How could she think that a child had equal responsibility, no matter how badly behaved she had been? Laurent knew many people who had lost their way mid-teens, only to grow into fine adults. They had had firm, loving families to help steer them though. Emilia herself had grown into a responsible, hardworking, intelligent young woman, but that lack of stability had left deep scars.

That was all Emilia needed. Stability and unconditional love. And, much as Laurent longed to rush to her and promise her his heart, he held back. He had to fix the relationship with Clay Industries for his country's sake. Armaria came first; he knew it, Emilia knew it. And if that was the case then was he the right person to fix Emilia's bruised heart after all? Or should he step away and free her for someone who had no other ties? Who would always put her first. Would that be the right thing to do? It would be catastrophic if he got it wrong, let her down. Dishonourable.

For the first time in his life his head said one thing, his heart another. Maybe if he just saw her then things would fall into place.

They reached the top of the steps and the guards who stood on either side of the main doors, grand in their ornate uniforms, saluted smartly as Laurent ushered the Claytons into the castle hallway. The main doors led straight into a huge hallway, part of the original medieval keep, with thick stone walls covered with tapestries and huge wrought iron chandeliers suspended from the high ceilings. Corridors led off on three directions and wooden staircases on either side led to the gallery.

'This is the original part of the castle. It was modified and extended through the centuries and three hundred years ago turned into the structure we see today—but all those original parts are incorporated within the castle. This is the main ceremonial wing; the residential wing is to the left, the business wing to your right, and that includes the parliamentary chambers, and the domestic and administrative wing is at the back.' He frowned. 'I'm not sure if wing is the correct term when the building is a square?'

'Are the turrets original?' Bella asked and Laurent smiled.

'Sadly not. Most of the bits that look really medieval are eighteenth-century follies. Apart from this hall, which dates back to the twelfth century in parts.' So much history and he could trace his line right back to that twelfth century duke. Some Archdukes had managed peace, others had fought wars they might or might not have been responsible for. Some had built, others had plundered. His grandfather had tried to take a country ravaged by two World Wars in twenty years and give it stability, a goal his father had inherited. Their hopes rested on Laurent's shoulders now.

'Would you like to go to your rooms now or would you like some refreshments?' he asked. Both women elected to head to their suite to freshen up, but Mike Clayton asked for refreshments and Laurent led him to the library, ordering a coffee tray to be brought to them there.

'You are, of course, welcome on any of the excursions we have arranged for Mrs Clayton,' he said once the drinks had been brought in and the coffee poured. 'I have arranged some field trips for you as well; I hope that's acceptable. One to the sites that I thought might appeal to you if you did decide to locate your factory here and a visit to the university, and a tour of some of our transport facilities.' He paused, searching for the right words to say next. 'I owe you an apology. It can't have been pleasant seeing your daughter in the gossip columns. For me it's a way of life; I ignore them. But for the uninitiated it can be brutal. The speculation about your family must have been difficult.'

Mike Clayton added milk to his coffee before replying, his shrewd gaze fixed on Laurent as he did so. 'It hasn't been easy. We're not used to that sort of publicity. I thought it was Bella you were interested in. I wasn't aware you even knew Emilia. To be honest, I wasn't expecting to see her here. We're not close.'

'I believe your wife asked her to help plan the ball,' Laurent said and Mike Clayton nodded.

'So Simone said. It seemed a little risky to me; Emilia can be a little volatile. She takes after her mother. But apparently she's good at what she does. It will be nice to see her. It's been a while. Look, don't worry about those pictures. Emilia always had a knack of getting into trouble, of demanding attention. I'm just surprised this hasn't happened before.'

Laurent stared at the older man in disbelief. 'The Emilia I have come to know is steady and hardworking,' he said. 'And the only reason she was in that situation is because of me. I took her out without bodyguards and I'm the one the paparazzi are interested in. Believe me, your daughter has been nothing but professional since the day she got here.'

Not wanting the conversation to escalate, Laurent

switched back to discussing the itinerary for the next few days until the coffee was finished and the two men moved onto the local brandy. Mike Clayton picked up his glass and swirled the amber liquid thoughtfully. 'I suppose you think I'm a terrible father?'

Laurent paused, torn between good manners, the knowledge that he needed to keep this man on side and his wish to tell Emilia's father exactly what he thought of him. 'Emilia said she wasn't an easy child,' he admitted. 'And from things she's mentioned it sounds like she wasn't. But she was very young. I lost my father when I was young, sir, so I don't know a lot about relationships between fathers and their children. But I hope mine would have stood by me no matter what.' He kept his voice polite but his expression was hard and fixed on the older man, who nodded as he absorbed the words.

'Her mother was a very emotional woman. She hated how much I worked, wanted a marriage of ups and downs, full of big dramatic gestures, whether that was breaking every glass in the house or some spontaneous romantic adventure. And for a while it was exciting, but then it was just exhausting. Simone was so calm; meeting her was like coming home after a storm. She was interested in my work, supportive… I could have handled the divorce better, but Marie made it hard, which was understandable but helped no one, let alone Emilia. I offered Marie the Kensington flat, but she refused and moved out to north London, blaming me for the upheaval. She didn't want me to see Emilia. She would cancel weekends or holidays, rearrange when we had plans…and when Emilia was with us it was clear she didn't want to be. Simone said we shouldn't give in, that it should be business as usual, but I wonder now if that was the right tack.' He downed the brandy. 'It's too late now.'

'Emilia said you didn't want to see her back then,' Laurent said slowly, unsure of how much of Emilia's confidences he could reveal. Mike Clayton nodded.

'To be fair to Marie, she believed her own dramas. I'm sure she thought it was true. She didn't even tell me she was ill; the first I knew of it was when the hospital called and we hadn't seen Emilia for months. I know,' he said, looking up at Laurent, 'that I have little excuse here. I'm just telling you how it was. The business was taking off so quickly I worked eighteen-hour days, seven days a week. And Emilia didn't want to be with us anyway. I assuaged my conscience by sending her things rather than trying to force her to see me. Then Marie was gone and Emilia blamed me for everything. The next four years were almost unbearable; she waged a constant war. When she left, we could breathe for the first time in years.'

'So you just let her go?' Laurent couldn't keep the blame from his voice.

'I arranged a job for her with an old friend of mine, a job that came with a room. I made sure she got the training she needed to move up, even though she'd not even taken her school exams. I paid off that unpleasant young man she took up with when she was eighteen, and I have put money aside for her every month. She could buy a house if she wanted to, invest it in that business of hers, but she doesn't want to know. She doesn't reply to my texts, never comes to the house. I know why, but I have no idea how we can start anew or if she would even consider it.'

'Does she know any of this?'

'I don't know,' Mike Clayton said heavily. 'I doubt it and now it's too late. But she looked happy with you. Once I'd got over the shock, it was nice to see her happy.'

Guilt stabbed at Laurent. She had looked happy in those pictures—he'd been so horrified on her behalf, at the invasion of her privacy, he hadn't taken the time to see beyond the headlines. And he'd made no attempt to see her since. He was no better than the man sitting before him. She deserved better than both of them.

'She was happy,' he said slowly before looking directly at the older man. 'Look, it's none of my business but I think you should talk to your daughter. Tell her what you told me. She needs to hear it and she'll only believe it if it comes from you. You owe her that.'

His bluntness might have just lost him a deal, but Laurent needed more than honour and duty. He needed integrity. And he needed to find Emilia.

The evening was drawing in, but Emilia barely noticed the pink streaks highlighting the sky; instead her gaze returned again and again to the archway that led into the courtyard. Of course Laurent might be too busy with his guests to come here tonight, or assume that she wouldn't be there herself after the two evenings she had missed. Or maybe he simply didn't want to see her, thanks to her lies.

Coming here was foolish; she knew that. But she

needed to tell him goodbye before all the guests arrived and gossiped about them, before she had to keep a careful distance in public so as not to fuel that gossip. Goodbye and thank you. Tell him what his friendship had meant.

Closing her eyes, Emilia inhaled the now familiar scent of flowers and herbs. She had never been as drawn to a place as she had this garden. It had felt like home. But her home was back in Chelsea with her friends. A place where she could work and not think, where she was safe. Chest aching, she walked around the garden a couple of times listening to the evening birdsong until she heard footsteps in the courtyard and halted, her heart hammering in her chest. She pulled the key out of her pocket and held it with trembling hands until Laurent came through the archway. He stopped when he saw her, an incredulous smile curving his beautiful mouth, and she held up a hand to stop him coming closer.

'Hey,' she said.

'Hey.'

He looked tired, shadows purpling his blue eyes, his cheeks hollow, and her heart turned over at the sight. She wanted to hold him, to support him, but all she could do was stand there. 'How are my family?'

'Okay, I think. Bella adores the horse I picked out and she is in love with all the puppies. I suspect she'll be begging for one to take home. Remember I promised you a puppy too; you need to go and visit them.'

'Maybe later. Bella was raving about how sweet they are. I saw her yesterday. She's changed costume. She is now full-on Titania in white and silver robes.'

'Probably for the best,' he said and she nodded agreement, guilt coursing through her. Bella hadn't reproached her in any way, but her sister seemed instantly at home in Armaria. In less than a day she had made friends and knew her way around the castle. She would have made a good Archduchess. If Emilia hadn't got in the way.

Her guilt recalled her reason for being here. 'I wanted to return this to you.' She held out her hand, loosening her clasp so that the key to the garden was clearly displayed. Laurent closed his eyes briefly and her heart ached at the hurt on his face.

'It's yours,' he said roughly. 'I had it cut for you. Use it, don't use it, leave it at the bottom of a drawer, do whatever you want, but it's yours.'

'Laurent…'

'Don't worry, Emilia, I get it. I understand. And I don't blame you. My world is intense. It's not for everyone. Those not born into it are wise to run away while they still can because, believe me, if we were to see each other again, those photos would have been just the start. You're doing the right thing.' She stepped back at the bitterness in his voice. 'You deserve better,' he added more gently.

'No, you deserve better,' she told him, clutching the key so tightly it cut into her hand.

'I wish things were different, Emilia. I wish I was Ren, that my life was uncomplicated and free, that I could take you out and no one would notice us. That I could woo you and we could fall in love slowly and sweetly. But that's not who I am. I come with all this…' He made an expansive gesture, taking in the castle. 'I come with press intrusion and all-night policy sessions and pomp and ceremony. And it's exhausting. Whoever marries me marries all this as well. It's not easy. But I'd be there, supporting them every step of the way. Supporting you. If you would stay here a little longer. Let us get to know each other properly. See if this is real or not.'

She squeezed the key harder until her hand whitened around it, welcoming the discomfort. His offer was so tempting and who knew? Maybe back at the villa she might have agreed. But she'd had a lot of time to think since then. A lot of time when he hadn't called and she'd remembered how much relying on someone else for your happiness could backfire. A lot of time to remember how much worse it was to love and lose than just keeping yourself away from anyone who could hurt you.

'What about my dad? About Clay Industries?'

'I don't know. He's agreed to the itinerary I prepared. It's a start. But I think he loves you, Emilia, in his own way.'

'Don't,' she whispered, holding up her hand again, needing him to stop. 'I can't hope, Laurent, because it will tear me apart to lose him again. Maybe I'm a coward because I can't take a chance on him or on you. One day you'll realise that I'm no one special and I won't be able to take it. So this has to end now. While I can walk away with my head high and memories to light up the darkest days. Please understand.'

'You are special,' he said roughly. 'Why can't you see that? Why can't you believe in yourself the way I believe in you?'

'Everyone leaves me, Laurent.' She was willing herself not to cry, willing the tears to stay in her throat and her chest and the heat of her eyes. 'Please don't ask me to try.' She knew she was probably passing up the greatest chance of happiness she would ever be offered, but she didn't know how to grab it. Didn't know how to risk it all.

'I'll tell you what's real. How about the ball you have put together with love and care and attention especially for a father you love despite everything? What about the friends you talk about all the time? The business you're building up? You can love and be loved, Emilia; I see it in everything you do. Won't you let me try to show you?'

His words were intoxicating but she couldn't let them go to her head. 'Your friendship has changed me, Laurent. I know I must look pathetic to you, but it has. The evening I spent with you was the most romantic evening of my life, the night we spent together...' She paused, cheeks hot with memory. 'That night... I never thought it could be like that, that I could *feel* like that. I've spent my life trying to mean something, to be someone, working harder and harder looking for approval, to be needed, and in one night I finally felt whole. Like I mattered. And it was the most wonderful gift I could ever have had. I will never forget it and never forget you.'

'But you won't stay?' The disbelief in his voice almost undid her but she had to stay firm.

'You need a proper Archduchess, someone brave and strong.'

'I need you,' he said but she shook her head.

'I can't, Laurent.'

He looked as if he were about to say something; instead he paced up and down the path for a moment before coming to a halt in front of her. 'You deserve so much more than you'll allow yourself. And it's out there for you, Emilia. Please don't be afraid to try. Don't be afraid to reach for what you want.'

Emilia stared at him, tears clouding her vision. 'I…'

'Promise me,' he said, taking her hand. 'Promise me you won't hold back. I can't guarantee you that everything will work out. I can't promise you a happy ever after and that everyone you want will stay with you. But I can promise you that life is so much more worthwhile if you live it. I realise that now. I know it, thanks to you. It might be safer to live life with no ups and downs but if you do, Emilia, you will never get to enjoy the view. I'd like to think that one day you'll allow yourself to enjoy the view, even if I'm not standing next to you. And promise me that you'll remember that I tried. That I love you. That I saw you.'

She could hear no more. Emilia's mouth trembled as she extracted her hand from his. Standing on her tiptoes she pressed one brief kiss onto his cheek. 'I'll try,' she promised. And with that she turned and was gone. It wasn't until the gate closed behind her that she realised the key was still in her hand.

CHAPTER TEN

LUCKILY FOR EMILIA the work piled up so high that even she began to feel overwhelmed, six hours' sleep dwindling to five and then four, and yet her to-do lists got longer and the amount of unread emails lengthened. But she was glad. Her workload meant she didn't have time to wonder if she'd made a huge mistake—and it gave her a legitimate reason to steer clear of her family.

All she had ever wanted was someone to really see her, to want her. Yet, instead of embracing it—and him—she was walking away without a fight. Was she walking away because she felt that Laurent was genuinely better off without her, that she was the wrong person to be an Archduchess, or was it because she was scared? Probably both, but whatever the answer she felt constantly empty, a gnawing pain in her chest and stomach.

Was she being incredibly brave or actually a coward, giving up far too easily, keeping their relationship as one perfect night, a dream that would never be sullied by reality?

Emilia huffed out a sigh, rubbing her temples as she

did so. She didn't have time to keep turning the situation around and around. Not every guest wanted to dress up and follow a theme so she had ended up buying several hundred cloaks and masks for guests to use and discard after the midnight midsummer celebrations and needed somewhere to display them near the entrance. She had also needed to rethink some of the decorations and reorder the order of the music, her father's favourite band being more rock than classical, a strictly after midnight affair. Not that she minded being busy. Better too much to do and no time to think than actual time to sit, brood and mourn.

Thank goodness the ball was tomorrow and she would be home by the end of the week. Home to lick her wounds, regather her thoughts and whatever other clichés would help her get through this mourning period.

She opened up her email, wincing at the sheer number to have invaded her inbox in the last couple of hours, when her door swung open with a bang.

'I don't know, this isn't as bad as you claimed. Sure, there's no natural light, and the stone does rather scream ex-dungeon, but you've got a potted plant so it's all looking good to me.'

'Alex?' Was she dreaming? But no, there was her friend and business partner, as tall and effortlessly elegant as ever in a wafty maxi-dress which would make Emilia feel as if she were wearing a sack but on Alex looked like the cutting edge of fashion. Her hair was swept up into a chignon, her make-up perfect. Of course it was; Alex always looked perfect. 'What are you doing here?'

Alexandra didn't answer; instead she placed a tablet on the desk in front of Emilia. The screen wavered for a moment and then came to life to show two smiling faces; her heart swelled as she saw Harriet and Amber.

'Hi, Em,' Amber said.

Harriet chimed in with, 'Emilia! How are you?' at the same time.

'Radio silence, Em, not cool at all.' Amber shook her head reproachfully.

'I haven't been silent. I have emailed you approximately one hundred times a day.'

'You haven't spoken to any of us since those photos were published.' Harriet's brow creased with concern. 'We need to know you're okay.'

'Come on,' Emilia tried to joke. 'Which of us hasn't been photographed in a compromising position with an Archduke and had the pictures sent around the world?' But her joke fell flat.

'Are you two together? Does Simone know? I'd love to see her face when you sweep into the ball on his arm and she has to curtsey to you!' Amber's green eyes gleamed. 'I want an enlarged photo to hang on my wall.'

'It'll have to be Photoshopped as it won't happen. There's no together, Amber. Sorry to puncture your romantic dreams.' Emilia hadn't meant to sound so curt and she tried to force a smile. 'Look, I didn't realise Laurent was who he is when we met. I thought he was a handyman or a gardener or something.'

'He lied to you?'

'Way to go, Em!'

Her friends' contrasting reactions made Alex and Emilia exchange smiles.

'Do we need to kick his ass?' Alex asked. 'Archduke or not, no one gets away with messing my friends around.'

'No ass-kicking required. We parted by mutual consent.' That wasn't exactly true, but if she admitted that he'd asked her to try and she'd walked away her friends would be horrified. 'He has a country to put first, and you have to admit I'm not Archduchess material.'

'You could be anything you wanted to be,' Amber said loyally.

'No, lust and liking isn't enough, not for someone like Laurent. People like him marry for security, money, power. And who's to say that those marriages aren't successful? At least you both know exactly where you stand and what you want.' Say it enough and she might believe it. Forget the hurt in his eyes when he'd realised she wasn't going to even try.

'And how do you feel about this?' Harriet asked.

Emilia grimaced. 'My feelings don't matter, Harry. I'm not here for romance. I'm here to do a job, and that's what matters.'

'You like him though, don't you?' Alex asked, her dark-eyed gaze unreadable.

'Yes,' Emilia admitted. 'I do.'

'Do you love him?' Amber asked.

'I barely know him, Amber!'

'That's not what those photos looked like.' Amber's grin was gleeful. 'I'd say you know him rather well indeed.'

'I like him, I fancy him, I respect him. Are you satisfied? But love? I don't know what love is, I've never been in love, not the real thing. I think it might have been possible, in another world, another situation, one day. But I'll never know; it's just a might-have-been. Something short and sweet.'

'I think the lady protests too much,' Amber yelled as Harriet dug her in the ribs. 'Ouch! Harriet!'

Harriet ignored her. 'You didn't answer, Em. How do you feel? This whole situation is messed up. Your dad is there, along with your stepmother and Bella and now there's this whole situation with Laurent. That's a lot for anyone. So don't tell me you're fine. Tell me how you feel.'

Emilia made a point of sighing loudly but no one responded. Alex folded her arms and leaned against the office wall as if she had all the time in the world and Amber and Harriet stayed so still they seemed more like a screenshot than living, breathing women.

'I don't know, okay?' Emilia said finally. 'I don't know how I feel about any of it and I think it's better that way, better not to think or feel, because that way I can get up every day and arrange a party for the father who replaced me with a new family, and pretend not to hear people talking about me while I do my job and be brave and say goodbye to a man who might be my only chance at happiness. The man I think I might have loved tells me he thinks he might be falling in love with me and yet I let him go because I'm too scared to trust in him. And he's a good man, an amazing man, and he respects my feelings and that should make me happy, but actually I want someone to fight for *me*. I want Laurent to fight for me, even though I told him goodbye. I want someone to think I'm worth everything. I'm so tired of being replaceable…' She stopped with a gasp, aware that her voice had got louder and louder, that her eyes were hot with tears, her throat ached. She couldn't give in now. She couldn't feel, not properly, because if she did she wouldn't be able to carry on.

'Oh, Em,' Harriet said softly.

'I'm…'

'You're not fine,' Alex said firmly. 'And that's okay, Emilia. We don't need to be fine all the time and it's not weakness to let our friends take care of us.'

Emilia didn't point out that Alex never let anyone take care of her, that she kept herself hidden away behind her cool façade. She knew why the other two had no family, why their friendship was so important to them. Harriet had lost her mother at a young age too, something the two girls had bonded over, and she had spent her teens and early twenties caring for her father until his dementia advanced to a stage where she couldn't manage any more. Harriet had been the loneliest person Emilia had ever met—except when she looked in the mirror—but since her engagement she had transformed into a lighter, brighter version of herself. Amber had walked away from a family who had wanted her to live in a way they approved of, shaking off their rigid constrictions for freedom and a life she chose for herself. It was a brave choice and Emilia could only applaud her friend for her unfailing optimism and belief that happiness awaited her. But Alex? None of them knew why she had been alone the Christmas Eve they'd first met and every Christmas after that, why she'd shared her inheritance with them, giving them both a home and business premises, who her family was and why she was estranged. They didn't know and they never asked. There was a wall around Alex even they couldn't push through.

'I don't need taking care of,' she said instead. 'I appreciate you coming here, Alex, but it's unnecessary. I just need to keep working.'

'I'm here to do the PR,' Alex said coolly. 'The guest list, the castle, the entertainment all is very tabloid friendly—even without the Archduke's much photographed amorous encounter. I offered our services to the castle press office and they agreed to let me come over and handle it as you're here anyway. I get the impression they usually find it much easier to control the story; this ball and the speculation around it is out of their league.'

'But while she's there,' Harriet said, 'she can make sure Amber and I are in the loop so we can manage any other issues from here, and that means you, Emilia, my dear, are free to go to your father's ball.'

Panic seized her chest. 'No. Impossible. I don't have a dress.'

'I brought one with me for you,' Alex said.

'It needs to be a costume…'

Alex didn't bother replying but her look said it all. Of course she'd bought a costume—and shoes and evening bag and jewellery and anything else Emilia might need.

'And I have a whole timetable to oversee—there are eight different bands in three locations, a formal sit-down dinner, a buffet, chocolate fountains, cheese buffet, cana-pés and an ice cream truck. There are acrobats and ballet dancers and a magician, a children's choir and a troupe of Shakespearian actors. There's a candlelit procession, country dancing and a midsummer celebration at midnight. Champagne bar, gin bar, craft ale bar and a speakeasy in a marquee outside, complete with cabaret. To say nothing of approximately five hundred guests arriving today and tomorrow.'

'Five hundred guests whose accommodation has been organised, transport from the train station or airport sorted, and coaches to and from the castle booked, each one with a steward to look after any mishap?'

'Well, yes, but…'

'And the castle housekeepers and stewards all have copies of this timetable?' Amber said, waving the carefully updated and very lengthy event plan that had been Emilia's bible over the last few weeks.

'Yes, but…'

'We can manage from here. And you've got your watch.' Emilia had a very expensive smartwatch that looked like an evening watch but received messages and allowed her to send them, which she often used when carrying her phone around was impractical. 'We can contact you if we need you.'

'And I'm right here,' Alex reminded her.

'But I'm not invited.' And that was the crux of the matter. She wouldn't push into an event she wasn't part of, into the family that didn't need her. Watch a man she knew so intimately dance with other women and smile as if her heart wasn't breaking. As if she hadn't walked away from a chance of real happiness.

'You're the guest of honour's daughter,' Alex said.

'And you could dance with Laurent,' Amber said softly, but Emilia shook her head.

'No. I shouldn't. I bet Gregory Peck didn't follow Princess Ann around like a constant reminder of what might have been.' Three blank faces greeted this pronouncement and Emilia vowed to make them all sit down and watch *Roman Holiday* once she was back.

'Em, don't turn this opportunity down. Don't look back with regrets,' Harriet said. 'I know it's not easy, just be there to wish your dad Happy Birthday.' Her smile was wistful and Emilia knew that her friend was thinking of her own father, now living permanently in a past where Harriet didn't exist.

'Okay.' Much as she hated to admit it, her friends were right. She didn't want to watch her father's birthday from the sidelines, not again. And the costume element gave her the advantage of a disguise. She could take the opportunity to wish her father a happy birthday—and then make sure she disappeared before Laurent knew she was there. 'I'll put the dress on and I'll go for a bit, if you promise five-minute updates and to let me know immediately if anything isn't perfect so I can fix it. I will not have Simone finding fault with a single thing.'

'Deal.' Alex smiled as if she had no doubt that this was where they would end up. 'Let Amber and Harriet take care of all those last-minute details I can see you fretting over and I'll show you the dress I brought. It should fit, but better to find out if it needs altering now rather than tomorrow. And then you can show me this beautiful castle and the city and let me know everything I am going to need to run this event and any potential PR stories, positive and negative. I'd rather have all the responses drafted out in advance. This event is really going to put the agency on the map. I need to make sure we get the recognition we need.'

It was the calm before the storm. After all the painting and re-plastering and buffing, all the threading of fairy lights and erecting of marquees and stages. After weeks of frantic preparation the castle was ready, humming with anticipation. Laurent strolled through the beautifully decorated ballroom, admiring the flowers which brought the midsummer theme inside, the beautiful table decorations and all the love and care bestowed on the event. Emilia's hand was everywhere.

She'd be at the ball tonight; he'd made sure of it, contacting her friends and asking them to stage an intervention. She deserved to enjoy all her hard work. The big question he had yet to answer was whether he would respect her decision to say goodbye or fight for the woman he knew he loved.

He wanted to swoop in with an answer for every objection and show her he was there for her no matter what. But he also knew how scarred she was, how frightened. She needed to be shown respect, to know that he understood her and listened to her. Somehow he had to find the line between respecting her and giving her the reassurance he knew she wanted. It was a fine line and he had to tread more carefully than he ever had before. He still wasn't sure what to do. He just knew he couldn't let her leave without trying one last time.

The alcoves had been disguised with gossamer curtains ready for dancers to sit and cool down or couples to slip away from the crowd and Laurent sat down inside one, enjoying the momentary peace. He had spent the last few days being the most gracious host he could, selling Armaria as subtly but clearly as possible. He could do no more. The only misstep had been the moment he'd showed Mike Clayton exactly what he thought of the way he'd treated Emilia and he wouldn't change that moment even if he could. Not even for the guaranteed investment.

Lost in thought, he didn't realise anyone else was in the room until he heard voices. A familiar voice that haunted his dreams.

'Dad? What are you doing here? You should be getting ready. Happy Birthday, by the way.'

'Thank you,' Mike Clayton replied. Laurent looked around for a way out of the alcove without being seen but there was none. He froze. If he left now would he interrupt the conversation, maybe kill it before it got going? But eavesdropping was dishonourable.

He sat back. Maybe it was dishonourable to stay, but he'd learned this week that sometimes honour wasn't the most important thing. Emilia needed to have a conversation with her dad; nothing should get in the way, especially not him. He grabbed his phone and tried to distract himself with emails, but the curtain was thin and their voices clear.

'It all looks amazing, Emilia; you've worked very hard.'

'Well...' he could hear the smile in her voice '...Simone pays well. Besides, I owed you about a decade worth of birthday presents and I did make a fool of myself at your fiftieth.' There was a long pause and when she spoke again she was barely audible. 'I should never have said what I said. Or thrown that drink.'

Thrown a drink? Well, she said she'd been a teenage tearaway and, knowing her history, Laurent didn't altogether blame her.

'We never meant to make you feel like we didn't want you, Emilia. I hope you know that.'

'Part of me does. I'm sorry about the photos too, Dad; they were embarrassing for all of us. I hope Bella wasn't too disappointed. Or you. I know you hoped that she and Laurent...'

'That she and Laurent?'

'That she became an Archduchess.'

There was a startled pause before Mike Clayton laughed. 'I'm not denying that Simone probably fancied being the mother-in-law of an Archduke but you know Bella; she was far more excited about seeing the puppies than she was about seeing Laurent again. No, when she settles down it will be in a large country house full of animals and kids and the kind of chaos that makes Simone shudder. She's made to be a farmer's wife, Bella, not an Archduchess. What about you? The two of you seemed...' he paused awkwardly '...close.'

'Oh, Dad, can you see me as an Archduchess?'

'Once no, but we all grow up, Emilia. And you've

grown up into a fine young woman. Your mother would be very proud. That agency of yours is well thought of, you're good at what you do, people admire you. I don't see why not. If that's what you want.'

'You think Maman would be proud?'

'How could she not be? I am, Emilia. What you have achieved here is amazing.'

'You are?' Through the curtains Laurent saw the outlines of two people embracing and his heart nearly burst at the realisation that Emilia was finally getting the affection she craved from her dad. He glared at his phone as he concentrated on his messages with every bit of willpower he had, managing to give the pair the privacy they deserved until the sound of his name distracted him.

'He seems like a nice young man, your Laurent.'

'He's not mine.' Yes, he vowed, he was. 'Have you had a good visit?'

'It's an interesting country all right.'

'Interesting enough to build your factory here? Oh, Dad, please consider it. I know you want renewable energy and the conditions are perfect; Armaria is already much further along than most countries. The links are perfect, sea, air, rail, road and river, the education system is good. And Laurent is an amazing Archduke. He really cares, Dad, wants Armaria to be the best it can be, for the people here to have every opportunity. He'd work with you to make sure you had everything you needed, I know he would. You couldn't do better.'

'You're quite the ambassador.'

'I've been here for just three weeks and it feels like

home. I can't help but care about what happens here, even after I leave.'

'Well, just between us, I am very close to making a decision. I was very impressed with that Laurent of yours. He isn't afraid to stand up for what he thinks is right and I respect that. I'd better go—we have a formal dinner before the ball and Simone will want me to start getting ready. Save your dad a dance tonight.'

'I will.'

'And Emilia? I'm glad you're here. Let's do better. Both of us.'

Laurent stayed still until he was sure both Claytons had left, his mind whirling. Not only had Mike Clayton practically assured Emilia that he was going to build his factory here in Armaria, but he had told Emilia he was proud of her. The words he knew she'd needed to hear.

Not only that but it seemed as if Laurent's intervention had been the right thing to do. Here it was, proof that seizing the moment was as important as planning. Emilia would be at the ball tonight. He had one last chance to convince her to trust in him and their relationship, one last chance to show her she was worthy of love. He could plan—or he could look for the right moment and seize it.

He'd been too cautious earlier, talking about getting to know each other better, thinking she needed slow and gentle wooing, allowing her self-doubt to push him away, aware as he was of all the problems being with him could entail. And those problems existed, but surely together they were strong enough to cope. Maybe he needed to go all in, show her just what she meant to him.

Mike Clayton was right—she had been a brilliant ambassador for Armaria, and she would make a brilliant Archduchess if she just believed in herself. In him. He'd known her the moment he'd laid eyes on her, fallen a little harder every stolen evening they'd spent together. He could live without her, but he didn't want to. Now he just had to convince her that he loved her, and find out if she loved him enough to try.

CHAPTER ELEVEN

'I LOOK RIDICULOUS.' Emilia stared at herself in the mirror and just about managed not to laugh. 'How on earth did you get this dress here, Alex? There's no way it would fit in a suitcase.'

'You look perfect,' Alex assured her. 'Very in keeping with the theme.'

'It's not very practical, not when I might have to come and help out at any moment.' She smoothed down the fabric of the dress. It was ridiculous but she couldn't help but admit that it was actually very pretty too. If she was five it might be the perfect dress... It was strapless and tight fitting around her bust and waist, before flaring out into a very full skirt. It ended mid-calf level at the front, curving to a small train at the back. The creamy buttery yellow looked warm against her sallow skin, the whole embroidered with shots of silver thread so the dress sparkled as it caught the light. A pair of silver shoes fitted perfectly, the heels surprisingly comfortable, her only jewellery a pair of sparkling statement earrings. Her hair was piled up into a chic knot, a mask, also silver, covering just her eyes.

'There is no need for you to come and help. Everything is under control. The masks and cloaks are being handed out as guests arrive to those that need them, all the food is ready, the musicians are here, the entertainers are warming up and the formal dinner is nearly over.' Alex shot her a hard stare as she spoke. She'd tried to persuade Emilia to go along to the dinner, but Emilia hadn't been able to face the idea of the other guests watching her and Laurent. Besides, for all Alex was willing to help, there were a hundred and one last-minute things that only Emilia could check.

But she had been fine not going because she had had the first real conversation with her father in two decades. A conversation in which he had told her he was proud of her. A conversation in which she had persuaded him that Armaria was the right place for him.

It had been easy to do. She hadn't realised until that moment how much she loved the country. Partly because of its charm and partly because it meant so much to Laurent.

Laurent. Her stomach tumbled. Had she done the right thing? How could she think so when knowing her stay was nearly over and she might not see him again felt like the end of the world?

'I think we're ready,' Emilia said, the nervous knot in her stomach partly the adrenaline that any large event always produced, especially one put together on such short notice, and partly nerves at the evening ahead. 'But call…'

'Call you if I need you. I know. I got it the first ten times.' But Alex smiled as she spoke. 'So what's your plan?'

Emilia inhaled to calm her churning nerves. 'I'm going to find my dad and say Happy Birthday and give him my present, have the promised dance. Not pour a drink over him, so already we're doing a lot better.'

'And Laurent?'

'I...'

'Look, Emilia. I understand, I do. Of course you want him to fight for you; that's completely understandable. But sometimes we have to fight for ourselves. If all that's standing between you and him is your fear then the only person who can really overcome it is you. It's your battle. He can't win this one for you.'

'I...' She stared at herself in the mirror, almost unrecognisable in the beautiful dress, her skin olive from the Armarian sun, her hair naturally highlighted, her eyes bright. 'You make it sound so easy.'

'Oh, Em. It's not easy. That protective shell has kept you safe. Telling Laurent how you feel about him, letting him convince you to believe in him, is going to take a huge amount of courage. But I know you have that courage,' Alex walked around Emilia, pulling the dress into shape.

'Do I? Sometimes I think I do, but then it all seems too much.'

'We've been friends for—what?—three years? In all that time you have never put yourself out there, Em. You've kept your heart hidden. Look,' she added quickly, 'I know—pot, kettle and all that. But I'm not the one about to go to a ball where the man I love will be and hide from him all evening because that's safer than being honest with myself, safer than being vulnerable—you are. Do you really want to come home with me, knowing you didn't even try to talk to him? To tell him what you told us? To tell him you love him.'

All Emilia could do was stand and gape. Alex's words were so close to her own thoughts it was uncanny—and painful to hear them spoken out loud.

'I don't know what to do, Alex.' She could barely get the words out, her voice small, the admission of failure difficult to say and acknowledge.

'You love Laurent?'

'I do. I love him.' Saying the words so plainly shocked her; the lightness in her heart as she said them was even more of a shock. She turned her bewildered gaze onto her friend. 'I do,' she repeated. 'How is that possible? After so short a time? Maybe I'm mistaking lust for love? Because I certainly feel that too…'

'I know,' Alex said. 'I saw the pictures.'

'But it's more. I love how he cares for this whole country, every person in it. How I can talk to him and he seems to understand when I barely understand myself. And I love the way he makes me feel, like I'm precious and special…'

'Don't tell me,' Alex said. 'You need to tell him.'

'But what if he changes his mind, or I mess up…?'

'No, no more excuses. Tell him. What's the worst that will happen?'

Emilia's stomach lurched. 'He'll laugh. Or he'll freeze me out. Or he'll tell me it's not me, it's him. Or he'll feel the same way but decide that he needs to marry someone more suitable.'

'Or none of the above. There's no guarantees, Em.

It's safer not to try; I agree with you there. But then you'll have to live your whole life wondering what-if. Are you ready to do that?'

She'd thought she was. She'd written the book and bought the T-shirt. But when it came down to the line, all her very valid reasons seemed a lot less valid. 'No,' Emilia said slowly. 'I'm not.'

'If the worst comes to the worst, we're here for you, we're your family, we'll pick you up and heal you. But going through life too scared to put yourself out there isn't living, it's existing, and you deserve more. We all do.'

Emilia turned to her friend, so grateful for her wisdom. All this time she had worried about not being enough, about losing the people she cared about while the women who loved her were supporting her, selflessly making her dreams come true. 'Thank you, Alex. For everything. You, Harriet and Amber are the best family in the world. I am so lucky to have you. I don't know what will happen when I get in there, if things will still be okay with my dad or if I will know what to say to Laurent but, whatever happens, knowing that in two days' time I'll be home with you three makes anything possible.'

Neither Alex or Emilia were the tactile type. Amber was the hugger in their house, Harriet more so since her engagement, but Emilia stepped forward and held her friend close and after one rigid second Alex returned the embrace. Emilia inhaled, drawing courage and strength from the other girl. Alex was right. Emilia had spent her whole life battling with what-ifs. Tonight she was going to lay her ghosts to rest. Tonight she was going to start the rest of her life. She was going to stop being afraid and live.

The dinner passed with excruciating slowness, Laurent placed between Simone and Bella. He still couldn't read Emilia's stepmother although at times he thought he detected a humour so dry he wasn't sure it was there at all. Bella just wanted to talk puppies and that was a subject he was happy to indulge her in. She was a nice girl, but he realised that she would be bored by the duties an Archduchess needed to take on; like his grandmother, she longed for a simpler life.

But Emilia would handle those duties with aplomb. She was used to being firm and diplomatic, to juggling myriad responsibilities, to long meetings and quick meet and greets. She had everything he needed in an Archduchess.

But even if she hadn't he would want to marry her anyway.

Finally dinner ended and thankfully Laurent escorted the Claytons into the ballroom where the remaining four hundred or so guests waited to greet Mike Clayton and wish him a happy birthday. The room looked magical, like the *Midsummer Night's Dream* Emilia had promised, flowers and fairy lights bedecking every beam and pillar, the guests dressed in a gorgeous display of costumes and gowns.

Laurent took to the stage to welcome everyone officially, to present Mike Clayton with the case of Armarian brandy which was the castle's birthday gift and to remind everyone to be back in the ballroom at midnight for the official birthday cake, and then declared the ball open. Excited chatter broke out as all the guests headed out into the gardens to sample the delights Emilia had planned, or stayed in the ballroom to dance. Although many of the guests had simply added cloaks to cover normal party attire, plenty of others had gone all-out, some in Tudor costumes, others Greek tunics or fairy dress, and some in barely-there strips of glitter or the frock coats and breeches Emilia had threatened him with.

If this had been a traditional ball then Laurent would have been expected to lead the dancing, starting with Simone as wife of the guest of honour, followed by his own mother and then Bella, but the three separate dance areas swept away the usual etiquette and Laurent thankfully slipped away to explore. He had elected to dress simply in his dress uniform. If anyone asked he would claim to be Theseus, the general. All he needed was his Hippolyta. But he snagged a cloak and mask from the table to give himself some privacy, covering his uniform with the cloak and hiding his features with the half-mask.

The disguise was liberating. When he returned to the ballroom it was with complete and rare anonymity; he was free to wander through the ballroom and stand by the French windows, open onto the terrace beyond, without acting either the host or the Prince. In fact, he could go anywhere and nobody would be any the wiser. Now he just needed to find Emilia. He knew she was here somewhere.

Deciding to start in the gardens, he began to turn, only to come to a stop as a girl entered the room.

She wore a soft yellow dress shot through with silver, the same silver covering half her face, soft brown hair piled high on her head. Hazel eyes searched the room and his pulse began to thrum as they rested on him. He was cloaked and masked, anonymous, but her soft smile recognised and beckoned him. Wordlessly he crossed the room to stand before her.

He bowed with a flourish and she responded with a low gracious curtsey.

'You came?' he said.

'I decided I'm tired of hiding away in the kitchen.' Her gaze swept the room and she sighed in relief. 'It's all going well?'

'Whoever organised it did a brilliant job,' he assured her and was rewarded with another smile.

'It's easy when there is a backdrop like this.'

'How did you recognise me?' he asked.

'I'd know you anywhere.'

At her soft words his pulse sped even more, his blood roaring as it rushed around his body, primal possession seizing him. She knew him and he knew her. She was his as he was hers and nothing could change that. It was wrong to even try.

'I heard you earlier today,' he said quickly, needing her to know before they went any further. 'I heard you with your father, I heard what you said. Thank you. But I didn't need to hear it to know that you are exactly what Armaria needs, because you are what I need.'

'Laurent…'

'I know we haven't known each other long. I know my life is unusual. I know being photographed and speculated about is uncomfortable, but that's not all my life is about. It's about this amazing country and its amazing people. It's about taking chances. There's fun and laughter and love in there, even though I sometimes let duty overwhelm me. I want to share that love and laughter with you. I think I rushed in too quickly before. I don't think you should stay. I think I need to see your life and you need to see mine, that we should date. I think we should get to know each other. I think we should go to the cinema and out for dinner, take long walks and spend slow afternoons just talking, weekends away, maybe a trip to Rome. I'd like to take a Roman holiday with you, scooter and Prosecco and all. I would like to get to know you properly, Emilia. I would like to have the opportunity to woo you.'

'To woo me?' There it was, the dimple at the corner of her mouth, peeping out. He reached out and touched it, relishing the feel of her skin under his.

'To woo you,' he confirmed. 'You see, I already know you're the one for me. I knew it the minute I first saw you, only it took me a while to make sense of what my heart was telling me. But I can see that it might seem a little crazy to you, that you may need some time.'

'Walk with me,' Emilia said. 'I want to see what's outside.'

It wasn't a yes, but nor was it a no and, as Laurent took the hand she was holding out to him, he felt more full of hope than he had for a long, long time.

She couldn't believe that she was here, walking through the magical light-filled wonderland she had created, listening to the music and the chatter. Actors performed Shakespeare in the rose garden and in the distance, through the trees, acrobats performed a gravity-defying set. To her right, on an outdoor stage, two dancers performed a *pas de deux* of such breathtaking beauty all she could do was stand and stare until the last lift. In the marquee ahead of them partygoers danced to the rock her father adored, in the ballroom behind her couples were sweeping around the floor in a traditional waltz. People walked by, holding a whole variety of drinks or foods, their costumes bright and ornate.

And as she walked and stood and marvelled there was Laurent, solid and real, his hand in hers. The cloak hid his uniform, the mask half his face, but she'd know that mouth anywhere, the blue eyes, the way he held his body. The way he looked at her as if he saw her soul.

Happiness rippled through her, so rare and fragile but real. It had been so long since she had felt this way and it was down to the man next to her. The way he made her feel, the way he felt about her. 'You talked to Dad about me?'

She felt him tense and squeezed his hand reassuringly.

'A little, the first day they arrived.'

'I don't know what you said but he said you didn't mince your words. You didn't need to do that for me, Laurent—what about the factory?'

'The factory is important, you know that. But integrity is important too. What kind of man would I be to sell out love for profit?'

Love. Emilia took a deep breath. It was time she dared

to show her feelings, time to dare to be vulnerable. 'You told me once that duty dictated who you are and what you did. But it doesn't. You just know what's right. It's part of you, innate. But me? Fear has dictated everything for me. Fear of not being enough, fear of being left.'

'That's understandable. Your experiences would make anyone feel that way.'

'I told you I couldn't be with you and I meant it. I thought that the memories of one night would be the most I would ever get. That a lifetime with someone is too scary to dream of, too out of reach. Better to flame briefly and brightly and die than burn out.'

His clasp tightened and he turned to face her, tilting her chin so she met his fearless gaze. Emilia's stomach tightened as she saw the heat in the depths of his eyes, a heat her whole body yearned to match. 'You told me to go and, like a fool, I listened. But I've changed my mind. I'm not going anywhere. A flame doesn't have to burn out; it can be constant. You light up my life, Emilia Clayton. I want to learn to read your every thought and fleeting look. I want shared jokes and known danger areas. I want to see you first thing in the morning and last thing at night. And I'll be dammed if I spend the rest of my life thinking *What-if?* because I *know*. I shouldn't know because I'm a rational man and I don't believe in love at first sight, but I *know* we'll be happy. If I was writing that film of yours then your Princess and Cary Grant...'

'Gregory Peck.'

He squeezed her hand. 'Your Princess and Gregory Peck get on that scooter and they ride off into the sunset together. I want to ride into every sunset with you. I am not going to leave you.'

'I wanted you to,' she confessed. 'Because that was easier than actually trying and it not working out. Of really getting to know you and care for you and then you leaving. That scared me—scares me—most of all. You can't promise that won't happen—no one can.'

'Are you saying you don't want to try?'

'No. At least, a bit of me is still yelling loudly that this is too much of a risk, that it's better to walk away now. But I am sick of being afraid, tired of letting what happened in the past define me. I don't want to look back at a life half lived, half loved. I want to look back at a life where I gave it my all.'

'And is there space in that life for me?'

Emilia took a deep breath. 'It seems so absurd after so short a time, but I can't imagine my life without you in it. I don't want to imagine my life without you in it. So if you want to be there, then yes, there's space.' She trembled as she said the words, at how vulnerable she was making herself, knowing that now they were said there was no unsaying them, now she was allowing herself to really feel there was no way of guarding her heart. 'There's space to learn each other's worlds. For films and walks on the beach, for dinners and brunches. For all the in-betweens.'

'I want to be there. I know it won't be easy. You live in England, I here, we both have lives and duties. But I promised to woo you, Emilia, and that's exactly what I intend to do.'

'I like a man who keeps his promises,' she whispered

as his mouth found hers. The ball, her fears, her responsibilities all disappeared under his embrace. She pulled back, cupping his face in hers. 'I don't need wooing, Laurent. I'm in. I'm yours if you're sure.'

'I'm sure,' he vowed. 'I know where the end point is. I know that in six months, or a year, one day I'll know the time is right, that you'll be ready and I'll ask you to be my Archduchess and you'll make the most splendid Archduchess Armaria has ever known. But, more importantly, I'll ask you to be my wife. Not just because you're suitable, but because I love you and I can't imagine a life that doesn't have you in it.'

'Keep remembering those words,' Emilia said, eyes burning with unshed tears—but, for the first time she could remember they were tears of happiness. 'They'll be perfect for the proposal.'

'Come on.' Laurent started to walk and Emilia allowed him to pull her along.

'Where are we going?'

'I want to dance with my beautiful duchess-to-be. In front of everyone.'

They'd reached the ballroom. Emilia could see her dad twirling Simone around. He looked so happy, Simone smiling up at him. She might not like the way they'd found each other but she couldn't deny they suited each other. In the opposite corner Bella was dancing with Laurent's second cousin, her face lit up. Laurent halted and then slowly, deliberately removed his gown and mask before taking Emilia's mask off her. She shivered as his fingers brushed her cheek.

'No more hiding,' he told her. 'From now on we're a team—and we face all our fears together.'

Emilia could barely speak. She was no longer alone. This glorious, strong man needed her—and she needed him. 'Together,' she repeated. 'I'll do my best to make sure we both live happily ever after.'

'In that case—' he bowed '—will you do me the honour?' Laurent held out his hand and she took it.

'Always,' she promised.

His eyes flared and as he swept her into the dance his mouth found hers. Emilia kissed him back with all the intensity and passion and love she had, not caring who was watching. No more being afraid. No more watching from the sidelines. With Laurent by her side she could face and be anything. With Laurent she was finally free.

She broke the kiss and cupped his face in her hands. 'I love you,' she said. 'Not because you're an Archduke and a prince, not because you're the best person I have ever met, not because you make me feel invincible. I love you because you have the biggest heart, because you make me laugh, because you knew me the moment we met and I knew you too. I love you because the thought of spending my life with you makes me impatient to get started. I love you because you're you.'

Laurent smiled down, infinitely tender, infinitely dear. 'I love you, Emilia Clayton,' he said. And as the music swelled and he twirled her back into the waltz Emilia knew she would never be alone again.

* * * * *

THEIR INHERITED TRIPLETS

CATHY GILLEN THACKER

Chapter One

"What are *you* doing here?" Lulu McCabe rose to her feet and gaped at the big, strapping cowboy with the wheat-blond hair and the mesmerizing gold-flecked eyes. Even with a good ten feet and a huge table between them, just the sight of him made her catch her breath.

Sam Kirkland strolled into the conference room at their Laramie, Texas, lawyers' office in his usual commanding way. He offered her a sexy half smile that warmed her from the inside out. "I could ask the same of you, darlin'."

With a scowl, Lulu watched as he came around the table to stand beside her.

Clad in jeans, a tan shirt and boots, his Resistol held politely against the center of his broad chest, he was the epitome of the highly successful, self-made rancher. The way he carried himself only added to his inherent masculine appeal.

Ignoring the shiver of awareness pooling inside her, Lulu looked him square in the eye. "So, you don't know what this is about, either?" she guessed finally.

"Nope." He gave her a leisurely once-over, then narrowed his eyes at her, as always appearing to blame her for every calamity that came their way. "I figured you engineered it."

Anger surged through her, nearly as strong as the attraction she'd worked very hard to deny.

Lulu drew a breath and inhaled the brisk, masculine fragrance of his cologne and the soapy-fresh scent of his hair and skin. Determined to show him just how completely she had gotten over him, she stepped closer, intentionally invading his space. "Why would I want to do that?"

He held her eyes deliberately. Gave her that slow smile, the one that always turned her legs to jelly. "Honestly, darlin'," he taunted in a low tone, "I don't know why you want to do *lots* of things."

Really? He was going to go back to their last argument, claiming she was not making any sense? Again? Slapping both her hands on her hips, she fumed, "Listen, cowboy, you know exactly why I want to join the Laramie County Cattleman's Association!"

His gaze drifted over her before she could make her proposal again. "And you know exactly why, as organization president, I'm not about to let you."

She had a good idea. And it had a lot to do with what had secretly happened between them a little over a decade ago. With exaggerated sweetness, she guessed, "Because you're not just a horse's behind, but a stubborn, sexist mule, too?"

Finally, his temper flared, as surely as her own. He blew out a frustrated breath, then lowered his face to hers. "It's not enough to just own a ranch in Laramie County, Lulu," he reiterated.

Both hands knotted at her sides, she glared up at him, aware her heart was pounding, and lower still, there was a building heat. "Well, it should be!" she argued right back.

"You have to raise cattle. Not honeybees."

"Okay, you two, calm down." Family law attorney Liz Cartwright Anderson breezed into the conference room, her husband and law partner right behind her.

"Or someone might think something besides a show of heat is going on with you," Travis Anderson quipped.

"The only thing we share is an immense dislike of each other," Lulu grumbled. *Well, that, and an unwillingness to forgive.* Because if they had been able to do that... things might be different now. But they hadn't... So...

Liz sent a questioning look at Sam. He lifted an amiable hand. "What she says," he quipped.

An awkward silence fell.

"We could meet with you separately," Travis offered finally. "Since Sam is my client, and Lulu is Liz's."

Lulu shook her head. They wouldn't have been called in together unless the matter involved them both. "Let's just get it over with," she groused.

"Okay, then." Liz smiled. "Travis and I called you both here together because we have some very important things to discuss," she began, as a somber-looking man with buzz-cut silver hair walked in to join them. He was dressed in a suit and tie, carrying a briefcase and appeared to be in his late fifties.

Travis made the formal introductions. "This is Hiram Higgins. He's an estate attorney from Houston. He's enlisted our help in making what we hope will be a smooth transition."

"*Transition?* For what?" Lulu blurted, glancing over at Sam. For once, the big, sexy cowboy looked as clueless as she was. Unsure whether to take comfort in that or not, she opened her mouth to speak again.

Liz lifted a hand. "It will all become clear in a moment. Why don't we all sit down?" she suggested kindly.

Everyone took the chair closest to them, which put Sam and Lulu on one side of the table and Liz and Travis opposite them.

Hiram took a chair at the head of the table and opened up his briefcase. "There's no easy way to say this," he said, "so I am going to plunge right in. I'm handling the estate of Peter and Theresa Thompson. They were killed in an auto accident in Houston two months ago."

Lulu sucked in a breath. She hadn't seen her sophomore year roommate, Theresa, and her husband, Peter—one of Sam's old college friends—since the two had eloped years before, but shock and sorrow tumbled through her. Sam seemed equally taken aback by the tragic loss. He reached over and put his hand on top of hers.

Normally, Lulu would have resisted his touch. But right now, she found she needed the warm, strong feel of his fingers draped over hers.

She actually needed more than that.

Given the grief roiling around inside her, a hug wouldn't have been out of bounds...

Had the person beside her been anyone but the man who had stomped her heart all to pieces, of course.

Unobtrusively, Lulu withdrew her hand from his.

Hiram continued, "Peter and Theresa left three sons, two-year-old triplets."

Lulu struggled to take this all in. Regretting the fact they'd all lost touch with each other, she asked hoarsely, "Where are the children now?"

"In Houston."

"With family?" Sam ascertained.

Hiram grunted in the affirmative. "And friends. Temporarily. We're keeping them together, of course. Which is where the two of you come in." He paused to give both Lulu and Sam a long, steady look.

"Peter and Theresa came to see me shortly after their children were born. They wanted to make out wills, but sadly, were never able to agree on who should take care of their children in the event something happened to them. So, they did what a lot of people do when it comes to thorny guardianship issues. They agreed to discuss it some more…and put off finalizing anything with my office."

He cleared his throat. "In the meantime, they went on one of those do-it-yourself legal websites and made out practice wills. They never had those notarized, so they aren't official and may or may not hold up in probate court. But thanks to the copies they left behind, we do have their wishes on record, which is what we are using to guide us now."

"And those wishes are…?" Sam prodded.

After a long silence, Hiram finally said, "Sam, you were Peter's third choice for legal guardian. And Lulu, you were Theresa's fourth choice."

Third! And fourth! "Who was first?" Lulu asked, curious.

Hiram looked down at his notes. "Theresa chose the great-aunt who raised her. Mabel had the boys for about two weeks, before she fell and broke her hip."

Sam and Lulu exchanged concerned looks.

"From there, they went to Peter's first choice—his best friend, Bob, who is also a father of three, all under age five."

Sam nodded, listening.

"The kids all got along great, even if it was something of a madhouse. Unfortunately, Bob's wife is pregnant and had to go on bed rest for the duration of her pregnancy."

Lulu sighed in dismay.

"So, the triplets then went to Theresa's second choice—a cousin of hers who is a flight attendant." Hiram frowned. "Olivia had them for a week and a half before deciding there was no way she was cut out for this."

He looked up. Adding in concern, "From there, they went to Peter's second cousin. Aaron's engaged and wants a lot of kids, but his fiancée is not on board with the idea of a ready-made family. So that trial run also didn't work out."

"And now...?" Lulu asked, her heart going out to the children for all they had been through.

"They are with Theresa's business colleague and her husband. Unfortunately, although they adore the boys and vice versa, they both travel a lot for work, so permanent guardianship is not a viable option there, either. Which brings us to Sam, the last person on Peter's list."

"Or...actually, me," Lulu interjected with her usual gung ho enthusiasm for all things family. She was more than ready to take on the challenge. "If you just want to cut to the chase."

Sam didn't know why he was surprised Lulu was jumping headlong into a situation neither of them was cut out for. She'd always been romantic and impulsive. Never more so, it seemed, than when she was around him.

The trouble was, he felt passionate and impractical around her, too.

Part of it was her looks. She really was drop-dead gorgeous, with that thick mane of sun-kissed, honey-brown hair, those long-lashed turquoise blue eyes, elegant cheekbones and cute, determined chin. And she had impeccable fashion sense, too. Her five-foot-eight-inch frame was currently decked out in a short-sleeved black polo, bearing the Honeybee Ranch logo above one luscious breast, a snug-fitting dark denim skirt that made the most of her trim hips and long, lissome legs, and a pair of Roper boots that were as sturdy as they were feminine. She had movie-star sunglasses on top of her head, a leather-banded watch on her left wrist and four handmade bracelets, probably made by her four nieces, pushed high on the other.

But it was the skeptical twist of her soft, kissable lips as she leaned toward him and shot him a disdainful look that captivated him the most.

"Let's be real here," she said, inundating him with the scent of her signature fragrance, an alluring combination of flowers and citrus, along with a heady dose of that saucy attitude he recalled so well. "There's no way you're going to take on two-year-old triplets for more than a week or so without changing your mind, too, the way everyone else who's had them already has."

The fact she had such a low opinion of him stung. Unable to keep the growl out of his voice, he challenged, "What makes you think that?"

"Because." Lulu shrugged, her eyes taking on a turbulent sheen. "You're a man…and you're busy running a big cattle ranch…and you're single…"

All of which, last time he'd heard, were facts in his favor. "And you're a woman. And you're busy running a honeybee ranch and now a food truck, too. And you're single."

Lulu's mouth dropped into an O of surprise. She squared her shoulders and tried again. "The point is, *cowboy*—" she angled her thumb at her chest "—I'm cut out for this."

He let his glance sift over her from head to toe before returning, with even more deliberation, to her eyes. "Really?" he countered softly. As always, when they were together, the world narrowed to just the two of them. "'Cause I am, too."

Indignant color flooded her cheeks. "Sam, come on, be reasonable!" She gave him a look he was hard-pressed to reject. "I've wanted a family forever."

He cocked his head to one side, once again forcing himself to do what was best, instead of letting his emotions get the better of him. "Mmm-hmm. Well, so do I, darlin'."

She stared at him. He stared back. Years of pent-up feelings entered the mix and combined with the ever-encompassing grief and sense of loss. Both feelings she seemed to be struggling with, too. Then, breaking the silent standoff, she pushed her chair back from the table and pivoted to face him. As always, when overwrought, she let her temper take charge. "You're just volunteering to do this in order to be difficult."

Actually, he was trying to honor their late friends' wishes, and keep them all from being hurt any more than they already had been. "You couldn't be more wrong, Lulu."

"Is that right? Then please, enlighten me."

With a grave look, hoping to get through to her once and for all, he said, "I'm taking this on because Peter was once a very good friend of mine, and he trusted me to care for his sons, if the worst ever happened. Since it has…" Sam's voice caught. Pushing his sorrow aside, he went on huskily, "I will."

Hiram interjected, "Y'all understand. The request isn't binding. You both are free to say no."

Lulu turned back to the children's lawyer. "And if we *were* to do so?" she asked in concern.

Hiram said, "Then we'd notify social services in Houston and have the agency start looking for suitable adoptive parents."

Not surprisingly, Sam noted, Lulu looked as upset by the thought of leaving the kids at the mercy of the system as he was. Once again, without warning, the two of them were on the exact same page.

"And in the meantime?" he asked gruffly.

Hiram explained, "They'll be put in foster care."

"Together?" Lulu queried.

Hiram's face took on a pained expression. "I would hope so. But honestly, there's no guarantee a placement like that could be found, at least right away."

Lulu sighed, appearing heartbroken. "Which would likely devastate the children."

Hiram nodded.

She swung back toward Sam, and concluded sadly, "So, it's either going to be you, or it's going to be me, taking these three kids on and raising them." She gave him a long, assessing look. "And you have to know, deep down, which one of us is better suited for parenting toddlers."

He did.

Although he doubted they agreed.

"Which is why, given the options that are left," Sam said, pushing aside his own welling grief, and ignoring the pleading in her soft turquoise blue eyes, "I think I'm the right one to assume responsibility."

"Okay, then," Hiram declared, looking happy everything had been resolved so very quickly. He reached into the folder in front of him and brought out a file of paperwork. "I'll make arrangements to have the boys brought to Laramie County as soon as possible. All you'll need to do is sign here—"

"Whoa! Wait! *That's it?*" Lulu sputtered. "You're not even going to ask me if I'm interested in being the triplets' legal guardian?"

Hiram paused, papers still in hand. "Are you?"

"Yes! Very!" Hands clasped tightly, she leaned toward the estate lawyer urgently. "I would love to do this for Peter and Theresa's boys!"

"Until it starts to get hard and reality sinks in," Sam muttered, thinking of their torrid past, and knowing there was no way he would visit such a reversal of fortune on those boys. "Then we both know where you will be, don't we, darlin'?" he returned bitterly. "Out the door. Without so much as a look back."

Lulu glared at him. "I'm not a quitter, Sam," she told him fiercely.

Wasn't she? It seemed like that was exactly what she had done ten years ago, albeit in a roundabout way. He regarded her skeptically. "But you are still very emotional. And impetuous." Two character traits that were intensified by their mutual sense of loss.

Lulu winced. "And you're overbearing and hopelessly set in your ways, so—"

Travis let out a referee-style whistle, signaling everyone needed to stop before anyone else said anything regrettable, no matter how upset they were. He turned to his wife, giving her the floor.

"Obviously," Liz interjected gently but firmly, "this has been a tremendous shock, and we're all feeling a little emotional and overwrought right now."

"Which is why, on second thought," Hiram concurred, putting the papers back in his briefcase before leveling a look at Sam, "I'm going to ask you to take a little more time to think about this." After a beat, Hiram continued, "If, after due consideration, you still feel inclined to accept temporary guardianship, you can call me and let me know, and I'll arrange to have the boys and their belongings driven here. The guardianship papers can be signed when you take custody of them."

"What about me?" Lulu said, clearly hurt and disappointed.

Hiram stood. "As I said, you're next in line if things don't go well with Sam and the boys. But for right now," the lawyer said firmly, "he is the one being tapped to take care of the triplets."

The meeting broke up.

Sam and Lulu walked outside.

As they reached their respective vehicles, she studied him with wary reserve. "How are you going to do this?"

It irked him to realize she did not think he could. He squinted down at her. "One step at a time."

"I'm serious, Sam!"

He shrugged. "Obviously," he drawled, "I'll need help."

Lulu opened her mouth to respond just as her cell phone went off. She plucked it out of her purse and stared disbelievingly at the text message.

Concerned, Sam stepped closer. "What is it?" he asked.

Her brow furrowed. In a dumbfounded tone, she admitted, "The sheriff's department has been called to my ranch!"

Chapter Two

An hour and a half later, Lulu stood at the entrance of the apiary on her ranch, staring at the empty field. Bare spots where the boxes and pallets had been. A few wooden lids scattered here and there. The occasional honeybee buzzing around, wondering where in the world the hives had gone.

"Are you okay?" Sam asked, standing next to her, looking more solid and imperturbable than ever.

Was she?

Resisting the urge to throw herself into his arms and ask for the comfort only he could give, Lulu turned away from his quiet regard. Her heart aching, she watched the patrol car leave her ranch. The only time she had ever felt this devastated was when Sam had walked away from her years ago in Tennessee. But she had survived heartbreak then, she told herself steadfastly. And she would survive it now.

"Lulu?" he prompted again.

She pivoted back toward him and lifted her chin, hating that he had to see her at her most vulnerable. "Of course I'm all right," she muttered. Although the devastation might have been easier to bear had he not gallantly insisted on accompanying her to the scene of the crime. And then, once amid the devastation, done his best to assist her and the sheriff's deputy who'd been sent to investigate. Because that had made her want to lean on him, the way she once had. And she knew she could never do that again.

Oblivious to the morose direction of her thoughts, Sam put a staying hand on her shoulder. Moved so she had no choice but to look into his face. Solemnly, he reminded her, "It's been a hell of a day, darlin'. First, we found out about the death of our close friends. Learned their boys had been orphaned. And found out we had both been tapped as potential guardians. Now, you just had all three hundred of your bee boxes, as well as your entire stockpile of honey, stolen."

Which left her with exactly nothing, she realized miserably. Seven years of hard work, building up her hives, gone. The only thing she had left of her business, aside from her small 150-acre ranch property, was her Honeybee Ranch food truck, and without her signature honey, the food she served out of that wasn't going to be the same, either.

His gaze drifting over her with unexpected gentleness, Sam told her, "I called the other officers of the Laramie County Cattleman's Association while you were talking to the deputy, and put out the word. Everyone's offered to do whatever they can to help."

Lulu was grateful for the assistance. Even if she wasn't entirely sure it would do much good now, after the theft. With a grimace, she stepped back. Despite her efforts to the contrary, she was unable to control the emotions riding roughshod inside her.

Bitter tears misting her eyes, she blurted out, "If only you had made that offer prior to today, cowboy, I might not be in such a mess."

Recognition lit his gold-flecked eyes. "Wait..." He touched her arm and surveyed her. "Is *that* why you were so determined to join the Laramie County Cattleman's Association? Because you were *afraid* something like this could happen?"

Shoulders stiff, she shrank from his touch. "What did you think?" she scoffed. "That it was for your charming company?"

Stepping closer, he cupped her shoulders between his large palms, preventing her escape. "Why didn't you just tell me this?"

As if it had been that easy, given his resistance to cutting her even the slightest bit of slack, after what had happened between them.

His tranquil manner grating on her nerves as much as his chivalrous attitude, Lulu broke free from his hold and spun away. Her pulse skittering, she headed toward the barn. "I would have, had I felt you would be the least bit sympathetic or helpful." She tossed the words over her shoulder, then turned her glance forward again. "But you weren't...so..." An ache rose in her throat.

Sam caught up with her, matching her stride for indignant stride. "Come on, Lulu," he said. "It's not as if you've ever been afraid to fight any battle with me."

Lulu stopped dead in her tracks. He was right. She wasn't afraid to go toe-to-toe with him. Never had been. With effort, she forced herself to be honest. Wearily, she said, "In the end, I didn't come to you with my fears because even though I knew it was happening in other parts of the state, big-time, I wasn't really sure something like this could ever happen here in Laramie County." She sighed. "Or maybe I just didn't want to believe that it would. Especially since I'm the only beekeeper who runs—or did run, anyway—a big commercial operation."

"And the other beekeepers?" Sam didn't take his eyes off her.

Lulu felt the heat of his gaze like a caress. "Are simply hobbyists, with one or two hives, so it really wouldn't be worthwhile for anyone to go in and try to locate and then steal their boxes."

She went into the barn, came out with a wooden pallet and carried it over to the apiary. She wanted any remaining bees in the area to have a place to go.

Sam kept pace with her, inundating her with his brisk, masculine scent. He watched her set down the pallet in the middle of the barren field. "Why would they want to do that, anyway? I mean, given the risk of getting caught?"

She returned to the barn for a brand-new wooden bee box bearing the Honeybee Ranch brand and a metal water pan. Already thinking about getting a new queen for the hive. "Because adding hives to orchards can increase the yield up to four hundred percent." At his look of amazement, she added, "I've had offers to rent out my bees to almond orchards in California, watermelon fields in south Texas and cranberry bogs in Wisconsin."

His large frame blocking out the late-afternoon June sunshine, Sam stood back and gave her room to work. "And you said no?"

Acutely aware of his fiercely masculine presence, she carried both items over to the pallet inside the apiary. Set the lidded box down, filled a water pan from the outdoor faucet and left it nearby. "Every time."

His brow furrowed. She could see he didn't understand.

Sighing, she explained, "I could earn money that way, but it'd be hard on my bees, and it would bring with it risk of mites and disease and infection to the hives. Which would not be worth it in my opinion, since I already have a very good market for my honey. Or had."

Briefly, guilt and remorse etched the handsome features of his face. "I'm so sorry, darlin'."

Again. Too little, too late.

Arms folded, she moved even farther away.

Gruffly, he promised, "We'll find your bees, Lulu."

She dug in her heels. Now was not the time for idle comfort, just as earlier had not been the time for idle promises. "And if we don't?" The tears she'd been holding back flooded her eyes. "Then what?" She blotted the moisture with her fingertips. "I'm going to have to start my honey business *all over*, Sam."

He shook his head, stubbornly nixing even the possibility of that outcome. "Someone had to have seen something unusual, even if they didn't put it together at the time. With the sheriff's department and the cattleman's association both working on finding answers ASAP, we should know something soon."

Would they? Lulu wished she could be as certain of that as Sam. Heck, she wished she had even a tenth of his confidence.

"In the meantime," he continued in an agreeable tone that warmed her through and through, "I'd like to help you in whatever way I can."

Lulu studied him. "Do you mean that?" she asked thickly, turning her attention to the other big challenge currently facing her. The one with even more potential to break her heart. "Because if you do," she said slowly,

"I've got a proposition for you." She paused, bracing for battle. "I'd like to be the children's nanny."

Sam had known that Lulu would not accept him as the triplets' guardian when she was next on the list. And hence she would continue to fight the decision, in one way or another.

But he hadn't expected her to offer this.

"*You*...want to be the triplets' nanny?" he repeated in disbelief, staring down into her pretty face.

Lulu tossed her head, her dark hair flowing over her shoulders in soft, touchable waves. And as she stepped closer, tempting him with the scent of her perfume, it took every ounce of self-control he had not to haul her into his arms and simply breathe her in.

"Well, I'm right in my assumption, aren't I?" she demanded. "You are planning on hiring one to help you with the three little boys."

"Yes." He intended to call a five-star service as soon as he got home and have them send someone out. Hopefully, by tomorrow evening. "I was."

"Well, I'm telling you there is no need for that," she went on sweetly, "when you have *me*, volunteering for the position."

Actually, there were a lot of reasons, Sam thought. Starting with the fact he had never really gotten over Lulu. Or the way their relationship had ended. Or the fact that, even now, he found himself wanting to take her to bed and make love to her over and over again.

Was she feeling the same damning pull of attraction? And if so, where would that lead them? "Why do you want to do this?" he asked.

She shrugged, suddenly holding back as much as he

was. She spread her hands wide. "Well, at the moment, it's not like I have anything else to do."

Uh-huh. "And if I believe that, you have some prime swampland to sell me."

"Okay." She flushed guiltily and her tongue snaked out to wet her lower lip. "You're right." A small sigh. "I do have an ulterior motive."

Now they were talking.

"I want to be there for the children in case things don't work out with the four of you."

"Except...they're going to work out, darlin'," he promised, just as persuasively.

At his assertion, an inscrutable veil slipped over her eyes. Her slender body stiffened and he took in the gentle rise and fall of her breasts.

"You seem sure of that," she said finally.

Sam nodded. Trying to keep his own latent anger and disappointment at bay, he replied, "When *I* make a commitment, Lulu, I keep it." Their eyes locked, held. Memories came flooding back.

Reminded of their falling-out all those years ago, and the reason for it, the color in her cheeks grew even rosier.

"Even if they do work out just fine with you...as their *single* daddy...you're going to need loving backup for them. And what better person for that role than their next, and *only remaining*, named legal guardian?"

She had a point. What she was suggesting did sort of make sense. At least when it came to doing what was best for the three little ones.

"You'd have to come to my ranch," he warned.

"Obviously."

"And be available to help whenever, wherever, however I need you."

He expected her to resist. Instead, she did not so much

as flinch. She rocked forward on the toes of her cowgirl boots, patient and ready. "I can make plenty of sacrifices, when necessary."

There had been a time, he thought irritably, when that wasn't the case.

"In fact, if you'll let me take charge of them, you won't even have to pay me or be anything more than an admirable father figure in their lives. I'm perfectly willing to handle everything on my own."

She was deliberately calling the shots and shutting him out. He frowned, warning her, "I intend to be a lot more hands-on than that, darlin'. And if you take this on, I will pay you the going rate."

"Okay. Well, then, if you want, I'll do the days while you're out working. When you get home at night, you could take over completely in the evening."

As much as he wanted that to be the case, he knew that might be a little much for him. Especially in the beginning, until the kids got settled in and developed a routine.

As if sensing that, she continued, "Or you could have me stay and help you until they're all in bed for the night. And then I could still head home to my place. After all..." Lulu sighed, pausing to look him in the eye, letting him know that nothing essential would ever change between the two of them, even if two-year-old triplets were involved, "...like oil and water, you and I will never really mix." She pivoted and headed for the barn. "Not for long, anyway."

We could, Sam thought, with a ferocity that surprised him, *if you would ever give us even half a chance.*

But Lulu wouldn't, he realized, watching her long legs eat up the ground. Not back then, when they had loved each other, and clearly not now, given the lingering animosity between them.

He caught up with her, overwhelmed yet again with the desire to sweep her into his arms and kiss her until she melted against him. Pushing the impulse aside, he retorted gruffly, "We need to think about what is right for the kids, Lulu." *Not what either of us wish could happen in some fantasy world.*

She shut one barn door, then the other. Over her shoulder, she sent him a contemplative look and said, "I am thinking, Sam." She brushed past him and headed for the porch of her small and tidy cottage-style home.

She settled on one of the cozy wicker chairs on the front porch. With a gesture, she invited him to make himself comfortable, too. "In fact, I haven't stopped mulling over what to do since the moment I heard about the triplets being orphaned. Which is why I know in my heart that the boys need to be here in Laramie County, where they will be well cared for and loved. Not just by you or me but by the whole community."

Sam wasn't surprised Lulu was feeling protective. She had always been sweetly maternal. An emotion that as of late had been bestowed upon her bees.

She had also switched gears pretty quickly. From cantankerous ex slash opponent, to heartbroken business owner, to ferociously determined nanny-to-be. He couldn't help but wonder if they were moving too fast, if they shouldn't ask for an extra few days to think about what they wanted to do, before they gave Hiram their answer.

Able to see how Lulu might take such a suggestion, however, he said only, "You're really willing to go all out to lend a hand, even after what happened here at the Honeybee Ranch today?" A theft that had left her devastated?

She gave him a look that said, *Especially after this.* "First of all, Sam," she reflected sadly, "we owe it to our friends to do everything we can to protect and nurture their three little boys."

Renewed grief wafted over him, too. "I agree," he said gruffly.

"Second, it'll keep me busy until I see *if* my hives will ever be recovered." As she seemed to fear they wouldn't be. "Third, to make this work, you're going to need help. Lots of it."

He leaned against a post on the porch and studied her. Aware the impulsive, reckless, romantic side of her was simultaneously the most thrilling and the most irritating. Which made him wonder just how long she would last, in what was likely to be a very challenging—and potentially heartbreaking—situation.

He sauntered toward her. "I don't half do anything, Lulu." A fact he'd made perfectly clear ten years before.

Her lower lip slid out in a delicious pout. She rose with elegant grace to face off with him. "Unlike me, I suppose?"

He let his gaze drift over her, taking in her luscious curves and lithe frame, her elegant arms and long sexy legs. "I wasn't talking about our previous big mistake."

She sent her glance heavenward. Sighed, with what seemed like enormous regret. "It was that, all right."

He jammed his hands on his waist and lowered his face to hers, wishing she had realized that a whole lot sooner. Like at the beginning of their spring break, instead of the end. "It was your idea in the first place."

She glared back at him. "Yeah, well, you went along with me, cowboy. At least initially."

Until she'd begun to panic. And suffer regret. Then, well, it had been clear their relationship was all over.

Emotion rose as their stare-down continued.

Realizing she had almost goaded him into losing his

cool, Sam shoved a hand through his hair and stepped away. Deciding it might be best to be more direct, he said honestly, "This is what worries me, darlin'. The fact we can hardly be around each other without quarreling."

Lulu nodded. Sober now. "It would worry me, too, if we didn't have something much more important to worry about. The health and welfare and happiness of Theresa and Peter's three boys."

She released a soft, empathetic sigh and compassion gleamed in her eyes. "You heard what Hiram said. They're at the end of the line of the named guardians. If we don't want them to end up separated and in foster care, you and I are going to *have* to find a way to make it all work." She paused to draw a deep, enervating breath that lifted the curves of her breasts against her polo shirt. "I don't think, under the circumstances, that this is too much to ask of us. Do you? Especially since Peter and Theresa named both of us in their wills?"

"All right," Sam said, deciding he could be as selfless as she was being and more. "I'll agree to this arrangement for one month." *Which should be enough time for you to realize how unworkable a situation this is going to be for the two of us, and then decide to simply take on the role of close family friend.* "At the end of that time," he said sternly, "we reassess. And if we need to find a professional nanny, we will."

"Agreed. Although I have to warn you, I'm not going to change my mind."

That, Sam thought, remained to be seen. From what he'd observed, one two-year-old could be a lot. Three… at one time…who were also in mourning…? But in the short-term, there were other important things they needed to worry about, too. Her personal safety being paramount.

"Where are you going to be this evening?" he asked,

guessing she hadn't yet told her family what had happened. Otherwise her cell phone would have been ringing off the hook and the place would have been inundated with McCabes.

But they would know, as soon as the ranchers in the family got the alert from the cattleman's association. "Are you going to stay with your parents?"

She blinked, confused. "Why would I want to do that?"

"In case the rustlers come back."

She pooh-poohed the notion, fearless as always. "They already took everything of value."

She had a point. They hadn't touched her house. And they certainly could have looted it, too, if they had wanted to do so. Still… He gazed down at her. "I think until we know more about who did this and why, you'll be safer elsewhere, Lulu."

"And I think I'll be just fine right here." She took hold of his biceps and steered him toward the porch steps, clearly done with this topic.

But he was not satisfied. Not in the least. Because the need to protect her was back, stronger than ever. "Lulu…"

She peered up at him from beneath a fringe of dark lashes. "You just worry about contacting Hiram and getting the triplets here as soon as possible. I'll handle the rest." She went into the house and shut the door behind her.

Chapter Three

"Sam's *still* out there?" Lulu's mother, Rachel, asked during the impromptu family phone call an hour later.

Grimacing, Lulu peeked out the window of her living room, catching a glimpse of the ornery cowboy through the dusky light. Cell phone still pressed to her ear, she confirmed, "He's sitting in his pickup truck, talking on the phone and doing something on what appears to be a laptop." Looking as devastatingly handsome and sexy as ever with his hat tossed off and his sleeves rolled up, another button of his shirt undone. Not that she was noticing the effect the summer heat might be having on him...

"Good for him," growled her father. He had heard all about the theft from other members of the cattleman's association before she'd even managed to call home to tell them. "Since Sam obviously doesn't think you should be left alone right now, either."

But Sam had once, Lulu thought. When the two of

them had been at odds, he'd had no problem issuing an ultimatum. When he'd become deeply disappointed in her and walked away.

"Now, Frank," her mother warned, "Lulu can make her own decisions."

On the other end of the connection, her father harrumphed.

Lulu didn't want what she saw as her problems bringing conflict to her family. "It's not that I don't appreciate the offers made by you and my brothers," she said soothingly. All five of whom wanted to help out by either temporarily taking her into their home or standing guard over her and her property. "It's just that I need some alone time right now."

She needed time to think, to figure out how she and Sam were going to manage the triplets. Without continually bringing up any of their former angst.

With uncanny intuition, her mother asked, "Is there anything else going on?"

Glad she had opted not to FaceTime or speak with her parents in person, at least not until after Sam had formally become the triplets' guardian and she their nanny, Lulu tensed. "Like what?" She feigned innocence. Knowing her folks, they were going to have a lot of opinions about her decision to become a parent this way, too.

"I'm not sure." Her mother paused.

Lulu's heartbeat accelerated as she saw Sam get out of his pickup truck and stride through the twilight. He still had his cell phone and a laptop in his big hands. "Listen, Mom, Dad, I've gotta go. Talk to you soon." She hung up before they had a chance to reply.

The doorbell rang.

Her body thrumming with a mixture of impatience and anticipation, she switched on the porch light and opened the door. She stood, blocking him, and gave him a deadpan look. "Yes?"

His legs were braced apart, broad shoulders squared. Looking as confident and determined as ever, he turned his ruggedly handsome face to hers. "I wanted to tell you what the cattlemen have unearthed thus far," he said in the low, masculine voice she knew so well.

Lulu blinked in surprise and glanced at her watch. "It's only been a few hours."

A stubble of evening beard, a shade darker than his wheat-blond hair, lined his jaw. A matter-of-fact smile turned up the corners of his sensual lips. But it was the compelling intensity of his eyes that unraveled her every time. No matter how fiercely she determined that he would not get to her. Not again. "When it comes to rustlers, it's important to strike before the trail gets cold," he explained.

She couldn't argue that.

Their eyes met for one brief, telling moment, that— however fleeting—had them on the exact same page.

Gratitude oozing through her and figuring they might as well sit down for this, she ushered him in. He followed her past the cozy seating area and over to the kitchen island, where she'd been working on her own laptop, notifying fellow beekeepers of what had transpired.

Sam set his belongings down but remained standing. "First," he said, "I want to tell you that I phoned Hiram and told him you and I were going to be jointly caring for the boys, at least in the interim. Me as their permanent legal guardian, you as their nanny. He was on board with the idea of the two of us joining forces during the kids' transition, so the triplets are being brought to my ranch tomorrow afternoon around 3:30 p.m."

Wow, Sam worked fast. On multiple fronts. But then

he always had. His ability to really get things done was one of the things she admired most about him.

He paused to check an incoming text on his phone, then turned his attention back to her. "Apparently, they are going to have everything they need with them for the short-term, and the rest of their belongings will be delivered by movers the following day."

She nodded, trying not to think about how attracted to him she still was.

His gaze roving her head to toe, he continued, "So, if you would like to be at Hidden Creek with me to greet them…"

There were times when he made her feel very comfortable, and then there were others, like now, when he made her feel very off-kilter. Lulu moved around to the other side of the island. "I would." She busied herself, putting a few dishes away.

He smiled. "Great. And second of all…" He settled his six-foot-three-inch frame on the bar stool, opened up his laptop and, eyes locked on hers, continued, "I know that you gave some of this information to the sheriff's department regarding the theft, but I want to make sure I didn't miss anything, if that's okay."

Ribbons of sensation ghosting down her spine, Lulu dipped her head in assent. He nodded back at her, then typed in a few words. "The burglary happened sometime this morning."

His manner was so businesslike, Lulu began to realize she could lean on Sam, at least in this situation, if only she allowed herself to do so.

Determined to keep him at arm's length, she fought the waves of sexual magnetism that always existed between them. "Sometime between eight o'clock, when I left for town to set up my lunch service for my food truck," she confirmed. "And when the sheriff's department notified me at around five o'clock, to let me know there had been a break-in."

Which left a huge nine-hour window.

His big hands paused over the keys. "A customer reported it?"

Aware she was suddenly feeling shaky again, Lulu moved around the island in search of a place to sit down. "Lucille Lockhart came out to buy some honey. She hadn't read my social media page advertising the location of my food truck today, so she didn't know I wasn't here." But the thieves likely had.

Sam made a low, thoughtful sound. "And everything was gone when Mrs. Lockhart arrived?"

She settled in the high-backed stool next to him and swiveled to face him. The sincerity in his gaze was almost as unnerving as his unexpected, unrelenting kindness. "The entire apiary was emptied, and so were the storehouse shelves. Panic-stricken, Mrs. Lockhart tried to call me, and when she couldn't reach me, she notified the sheriff. We don't know much more than that right now."

"Actually, we do." He swiveled toward her, too, and braced one elbow on the counter next to his laptop. His other hand rested on his rock-hard thigh. Nodding tersely once again, he added, "I put out the word when we got here. I've heard back from almost all our members."

She caught her breath at the worry in his eyes.

"Apparently two trucks were spotted on the farm-to-market road that goes by here around one o'clock this afternoon. They seemed to be traveling together and were headed north. One was a white refrigeration truck, the other a flatbed loaded with two off-road forklifts." His lips compressed, and his gruff tone registered his disappointment. "We didn't get an actual license number, but someone noticed the plates were from Wisconsin."

Hope mingling with dread, Lulu laid her hand across her heart. "They're sure it was a refrigeration truck?"

"It had the cooling unit on top of the cab."

Relief filtered through her. She didn't know whether to shout hallelujah or sob with relief. In truth, she felt like doing both. "Oh, thank heavens," she whispered finally.

"That's important?" Sam guessed.

Lulu swallowed around the ache in her throat. "Very. The bees wouldn't survive in their boxes if they were transported a long way in this kind of heat." She ran her hand over the side seam of her denim skirt. Sam's glance followed her reflexive move. Realizing the fabric had ridden up, Lulu did her best to surreptitiously tug it down. Yet, maddeningly, the hem remained several inches above her bare knees.

Knees he had once caressed with devastating sensuality.

Pushing aside her rush of self-consciousness, she added, "Moving bees is hard on them as it is."

Sam lifted his glance and locked eyes with her yet again. He regarded her with the respect of a fellow rancher. "Makes sense they'd do better if they were kept cool." He rubbed his jaw. "That kind of truck will also make the thieves easier to find."

Glad he had taken it upon himself to help her, even when she had preferred he leave her to handle everything on her own, Lulu drew a breath. It would be so easy to lean on him again. Too easy, maybe, given how acrimoniously they had once parted. "So what now?" she asked quietly.

Sam sobered, the corners of his lips slanting down. "I've already notified the sheriff's department with all the information I was able to compile, and they in turn have put out an APB and will be checking with truck stops and weighing stations for any vehicles fitting the description."

Feeling her first concrete ray of hope, Lulu asked, "You really think we might find them?"

He nodded. "Trucks like that can't stick to country roads without drawing a lot of attention. On the highway, they'll be a lot easier to find. Hopefully, we'll know something soon."

He shut the lid on his laptop and stood.

Feeling surprisingly reluctant to see him go, Lulu rose, too. "Sam…" She touched his arm, delaying him. He turned to gaze down at her and her heart rate kicked up another notch.

"I really… I don't know how to thank you," she continued sincerely. "A few hours ago, I had very little hope I'd ever see my beehives again. Now, well." She struggled to put her gratitude into words. As she gazed up at him, she pushed through the wealth of conflicting emotions suddenly racing through her and tried again. "I never would have expected you to…help."

Something dark and turbulent flashed in his eyes. "Well, you should have," he said, as if fighting his own inner demons.

The next thing Lulu knew, she was all the way in his arms. His head was lowering, his lips capturing hers. His kiss was everything she remembered, everything she had ever dreamed of receiving, everything the wildly impulsive and romantic part of her still wanted.

From him…

Because the truth was, no one had ever affected her like Sam did. No one had ever made her want, wish, need… And as his lips ravished hers, she moaned at the sweet, enervating heat. The touch of his tongue against her sent her even further over the edge. Wreathing her arms about his neck, she shifted closer. Nestling the softness of her breasts against the solid, unyielding warmth of his broad chest. His hand swept lower, bringing her even nearer. And, just like that, the walls she'd erected around her began to crumble and her heart expanded, tenfold.

One kiss melded into another. And then another…and another. Until he had her surrendering to the firm, insistent pressure of his mouth as never before. She clung to him, soaking up everything about him. His strength, his scent. His warmth and tenderness. Years of pent-up emotion poured out of her as she rose on tiptoe and pressed her body even closer against the hardness of his.

And still he kissed her. Slowly and thoroughly. Softly and sweetly. With building need. Until a low, helpless moan escaped her throat. And she recalled everything that had once brought them together…and had ultimately torn them apart…

Sam hadn't meant to kiss her. Hadn't thought he would even come close. But when Lulu had looked up at him with such sweet surprise in her expression, well, it triggered something in him. Something primitive and hot and wild.

It had made him want to claim her again.

As his woman.

As his…

He cut off the thought before it could fully form. Knowing there was no way either of them could go back to that tumultuous period of time, even if the hot, intense connection that had always been between them was definitely still there. And she knew it, too, as he felt her begin to tense the way she always did when she began to have second thoughts.

With a sigh, he drew back. Sure of what he was going to see.

She gazed up at him, eyes awash with the kind of turbulent emotion that had always signaled trouble for them. Lower lip trembling, she flattened her hands over his chest and pushed him away. "We can't do this again."

And once again, the need to possess her got the better of his common sense.

"Why not?" he demanded gruffly.

"Because we already proved it will never work between us," she whispered, the shimmering hurt back in her pretty eyes, "and I really don't want to go there again."

To Lulu's relief, after a moment's consideration, Sam seemed to concede it wouldn't be wise to complicate their situation any further.

And when he greeted her at the door of his sprawling ranch house the following afternoon, his manner was appropriately circumspect.

Which left her free to forget about the heady aftermath of their passionate embrace and concentrate on the changes made to the Hidden Creek cattle ranch since she had last been there.

The thousand-acre spread was as tidy and filled with good-looking cattle as ever, the barns, stables, bunkhouse and other buildings meticulously well kept. He had updated the main house with dark gray paint on the brick, white trim and black shutters. She admired the beautifully landscaped front lawn and the circular drive directing guests to the covered porch and inviting front door. A quartet of dormer windows adorned the steeply pitched roof.

Most arresting of all, though, was the ruggedly handsome rancher who ushered her inside. The corners of his sensual lips lifted in an appraising smile. He came close enough she could smell the soap and sun and man scent of his skin. "A little early, aren't you?"

Hcr heart panged in her chest. "I wanted to make sure I was here when they arrived, but if you'd like me to wait in my SUV…" Aware she was fast becoming a bundle of nerves, she gestured at the Lexus in the driveway.

"Don't be ridiculous." He ushered her inside.

Aware the atmosphere between them was quickly becoming highly charged and way too intimate, Lulu turned her attention elsewhere. There'd been a lot of changes since she'd been here last, she noted as she followed him. The ecru walls and dark wide-plank wood floors were the same, but the fancy upholstered pieces and heavy custom draperies favored by his late mother had been exchanged for large leather couches, mahogany furniture and modern plantation shutters. A lot of the knickknacks and elegant paintings were gone, replaced by a handsomely redone white brick fireplace and mantel, a complete wall of built-in bookshelves and a state-of-the-art entertainment center.

His gaze dropped to the hamper in her hand "Planning a picnic?" he drawled.

Lulu's hands curled around the wicker handle. "I'm open to whatever the kids need, although I don't really know what to expect when they do arrive." Which was one of the reasons she was so uncharacteristically on edge.

Evidently that was something they had in common. Sam sighed. "Me, either." He led the way down the hall to the back of the ranch house, where changes also abounded. The kitchen's flowered wallpaper and frilly curtains were gone, replaced by stainless steel appliances and concrete countertops and sleek white walls washed in sunlight. The breakfast room table and eight captain chairs were the same, although all had been refinished with a glowing golden-oak stain. The family room had become a work space, with file cabinets, a U-shaped computer desk, scanner/copier phone and printer.

He squinted at her. "Meet your approval?"

With effort, she met his probing gaze. She set the hamper on the island—also new—in the center of the large square kitchen. "It's very nice. You've outdone yourself," she said.

He shrugged, all affable male again. "Can't take all the credit. My sister Lainey is an interior designer now, so she helped. Tara, the computer expert, set up all my business systems for me. Liza, the chef, taught me how to cook. Betsy, the innkeeper, showed me how to properly stock a pantry and freezer."

Like the McCabes, the Kirklands always had each other's backs. "Your sisters are scattered all over now, aren't they?"

"Yep." He lounged against the counter, arms folded. "I'm the only one left in Texas."

Trying not to notice how well he filled out his ranching clothes, she asked, "You miss them?"

His gaze skimmed her appreciatively. "They visit."

Not an answer. But then, he had never been one to own up to anything that hurt. He just moved on.

As he was about to do now...

He inclined his head. "So what's in there?" he asked.

"I wasn't sure what you had on hand or what they were sending with the kids, so I brought some toddler favorites like applesauce and kid-friendly mac and cheese for their dinner, just in case."

Another nod. "Thanks," he said, as a big, sleepy-looking Saint Bernard came around the corner. The brown patches of fur over the pet's eyes and back and chest contrasted with the fluffy white coat everywhere else. An extremely feminine flowered pink collar encircled her neck.

Lulu watched the big dog pad gracefully over to stand beside Sam. She sat down next to him, pressing her body up against his sinewy leg and hip. Tail wagging, she gazed up at Sam adoringly. Waited, until he petted her head, then let out a long, luxuriant sigh that Lulu understood all too well.

Pushing aside the memory of Sam's gentle, soothing touch, she asked, "Who is this?"

"Beauty. As in *Beauty and the Beast*."

Unable to resist, Lulu guessed, "And you're the Beast?"

Although he tried, he couldn't quite contain a smile. "Very funny."

Lulu chuckled. "I thought so."

Although, the moniker fit. The 120-pound dog was absolutely gorgeous. And not really the type of canine she would have expected a rough-hewn rancher like Sam to choose.

"When did you get her?" Lulu smiled and made eye contact with Beauty, who appreciated her right back.

Tilting his head, Sam paused, calculating. "A little over four years ago."

"As a puppy?"

"She was about six months old at the time."

Lulu paused. "I didn't know you wanted a dog." He certainly hadn't mentioned it when they were together.

Back then, all he'd talked about were horses and cattle. And of course the importance of keeping one's commitments. Which he definitely did not think Lulu had done.

He smiled as his dog stood again and then stretched her front legs out in front of her, dipping her tummy close to the floor in a play bow. "She's not mine. She belongs to my sister Hailey."

Hence, the romantic pet name.

Lulu turned back to him, confused. "But…you're keeping her?" She watched Beauty rise again and turn back to Sam for one last pet on the head.

His big hand sank into the soft, luxuriant fur on the top of Beauty's head, massaging it lightly in a way that made Lulu's own nerve endings shudder and her mouth go dry.

"It was never the intention," Sam admitted, oblivious to the effect his tender ministrations were having on Lulu. "But Beauty was too big for Hailey's apartment, and she suddenly had to travel internationally for her job. Constantly boarding Beauty didn't seem fair. My sister asked me to help out temporarily, since I have plenty of room. I agreed."

Lulu observed the free-flowing affection between man and pet. "Looks like you made the right decision."

And possibly, Lulu thought as Beauty lumbered over to stand next to her, the right decision regarding the three kids, as well.

Because if Sam wouldn't turn out a dog who had come to live with him, she knew he would never abandon three little orphaned boys. And that meant if she was going to form a permanent, loving connection with Theresa and Peter's triplets, she would have to forget the difficulties of their past and find a way to forge an enduring, *platonic* connection with Sam, too.

The next twenty minutes passed with excruciating

slowness. Sam settled down to do something at his desk while Lulu paced, looking out one front window, then the next.

Finally, a large dark green van made its way up the lane. It stopped next to the ranch house. The doors opened. Hiram Higgins and three other adults stepped out. And even though there was no sign of the children they were going to care for just yet, Lulu's heartbeat quickened.

"Sam! They're here!" she exclaimed.

He rose and strode briskly through the hall to her side.

Together, they walked out the front door and down the porch steps. Hiram introduced his wife, Winnifred, a kind-faced woman with gray hair, and Sandra and Jim Kelleher, the thirtysomething couple who had been looking after the triplets.

Seeing that Lulu and Sam were chomping at the bit to meet the kids, the Kellehers proceeded to unfasten safety harnesses and bring the children out, one by one. All three were holding stuffed animals and clutching well-loved blue baby blankets. In deference to the shimmering June heat, they were wearing blue plaid shorts and coordinating T-shirts, sandals, plaid bucket hats and kiddie sunglasses. All appeared shy and maybe even a little dazed. As if they'd been napping and were still trying to wake up.

"This is Theo," Winnifred introduced the most serious-looking toddler.

Sandra brought forward the one with the trembling lower lip. "And Ethan."

"And Andrew," Jim said, shifting the weight of the only one starting to fidget.

"Hello, Theo, Ethan and Andrew," Lulu greeted them in turn.

They simply stared at her, then eventually turned away.

Her heart sank. She was a McCabe. She'd been around children all her life. Not once had one responded to her with such indifference.

But then, these children had been through hell. It was probably no surprise they'd become…numb.

Hiram retrieved his briefcase and inclined his head at Sam. "We probably should sign the papers first and then unload the belongings they brought with them today."

"Lulu," Sam said, "you want to take them all on in?"

"Sure." She led the way inside as Sam and Hiram adjourned to a corner of the front porch. Winnifred and the Kellehers took a seat in the living area, a child on each lap. Once they were all settled, Lulu sat down, too, and they got down to business.

"I brought a folder with me of everything I've been able to piece together about the children's previous routines, plus everything that did or did not work for us, in terms of their care," Sandra said.

Jim exhaled, then turned to look at Lulu. "I hope Sam has better luck with them. It's good you're going to be helping out, too."

Winnifred chimed in, "Hiram and I can both attest to that. They can be a handful."

Suddenly feeling a little unsure they were up to the task, Lulu nodded her understanding. Had she and Sam underestimated the task of helping the orphaned triplets?

Sam and Hiram walked in. After Sam set the papers on the entry table, Jim handed the still-fidgety Andrew to Lulu and all three men headed back outside. Short minutes later, a trio of car seats, travel beds, booster seats, suitcases, and a big box of toys were stacked in a corner of the living room.

"Probably best we be on our way," Hiram said.

Lulu expected the kids to wail in protest at the impending departure of yet another set of guardians. Instead, they took it stoically in stride. Too stoically, in fact, to be believed.

Chapter Four

"How long do you think they're going to sit there like that, before they decide to get comfy and stay awhile?" Sam quipped to Lulu a good half hour later. Although he was the one with legal responsibility for them, she was the one who seemed to inherently understand what was going on with them. That put them all in the awkward position of really needing her soothing maternal presence in a way Sam hadn't expected. And that he wasn't sure how to deal with, given his ever-present desire for her.

Oblivious to his chaotic thoughts, Lulu looked up from the toy fort she was building in the center of the living room floor and turned her glance in the direction Sam indicated.

The triplets were right where they'd initially settled. Cuddled together in the middle of his big leather sofa. All still wore their hats and sunglasses. Their blankets and stuffed animals were on their laps. Thumbs in their mouths. All previous attempts, and there had been three thus far, to gently separate them from their head-wear had failed.

"I don't know." With a shrug, Lulu continued pulling toys from the box. Unlike him, she was completely at ease, despite the fact that, like him, she'd been rebuffed at every attempt to get acquainted with the children, too. Her turquoise eyes sparkled with amusement and her soft lips curved into a sweet, contented smile. "Until they're ready to do something else?"

Sam edged closer and caught a whiff of her signature fragrance. With effort, he concentrated on the problem at hand. Helping the boys acclimate.

"With those sunglasses on, this place has to look dark to them, even though we opened up the blinds and turned the lights on." He wondered if they were scared.

Lulu dusted off her hands and stood. Looking incredibly fetching in a pretty floral sundress and casual canvas flats, she came close enough to go up on tiptoe and whisper in his ear, "Would you relax, cowboy?" Her hand curved over his biceps. "I think your anxiety is making them tense."

Was it his imagination or was it getting hot in here? "I'm not anxious."

Clearly, she didn't believe him.

She let go of him for a moment and stepped back to study him from beneath a fringe of thick, dark lashes, then lightly clasped one of his forearms just above his wrist. "Let's just give them a moment to acclimate without us staring at them, okay?" She gave a little tug when he didn't budge. "Come on. You can help me set their booster seats up at the kitchen table. Maybe set out a snack or…" she glanced at her watch, noting that it was nearly five o'clock "…dinner."

Her soft skin feeling like a silky manacle around his

wrist, she guided him down the wide hallway to the kitchen. Sam pushed away the evocative memories her touch engendered. Exhaled. For once, he was all too willing to let her be in charge of what went on with the two of them. In fact, the knowledge that she had some idea of what to do was reassuring.

His sisters had done all the babysitting when they were growing up. Not him. And the truth was, he had no idea at all how to handle a situation like this.

Sam peeked back into the living room, far enough to be able to surreptitiously check on the three little boys and see they were just where they had been.

Then he moved back toward Lulu. Stood, back braced against the kitchen island, feet crossed at the ankle, arms folded. "You think they're hungry?"

She ran a hand through her sun-streaked honey brown hair, pushing the silky waves off her face. As she squared her shoulders, the luscious curves of her breasts pushed against the bodice of her dress. "I'm sure they are. Thirsty, too." She removed three small cartons of apple juice and a container of Goldfish crackers from the bag, then set them all on the counter.

"I also know they've had a very rough time, being shuffled from home to home for the last two months." She paused to look into Sam's eyes. "They've got to be very confused."

He let his gaze drift over her, surprised at how good it felt to have her here, in his home, with him. When all they'd done for years was try to stay as far apart from each other as possible. He was beginning to see what a mistake that was. Clearly, there was a lot of unfinished business between them. Aware they were definitely on the same page about one thing—making the triplets happy again—he murmured, "I want them to feel good about being here."

"I'm sure they will," she reassured him softly. "But we have to give them time, Sam."

Without warning, Beauty, who'd been sleeping on her cushion in the corner of the kitchen, lifted her head. Got to her feet. And ever so slowly moved toward the hall.

Wondering what the Saint Bernard had heard, Sam turned in that direction.

There it was.

The unmistakable sound of childlike chatter.

Lulu started in surprise. Pausing to give him a quick, excited glance, she tiptoed down the hallway toward the living room. Sam was right on her heels, moving just as soundlessly.

And there they were. All three boys. Finally sans bucket hats and sunglasses, sitting on the floor, in the middle of their toys.

"You were right," Sam murmured, standing close enough to feel the heat emanating from her slender body. "All we needed to do was give them a little room to maneuver."

Lulu nodded, although to his consternation she didn't look nearly as relieved as he felt to see them up and about.

Figuring it was his turn to comfort her, he reached over to give her forearm a companionable squeeze. "Maybe acclimating them won't be so difficult after all," he theorized.

Except as it turned out, Lulu noted in despair many times over the next eight hours, it absolutely was.

The three boys all refused their snack, and, except for a few sips of their apple juice, also made a mess of their dinner. Squishing the mac and cheese between their fingers and smearing it on their plates and the table in front of them. Banana slices, applesauce and chopped green beans shared a similar fate. In fact, once they'd finished, it looked as if there had been one heck of a food fight in Sam's kitchen.

Once down from the table, they began to run and climb and shout, while Beauty lay on the floor, watching over them with a sweet maternal grace. As if the Saint Bernard knew exactly what they were thinking and feeling.

Which was good, Lulu thought with increasing disquiet. Because neither she nor Sam had a clue. A fact that really hit home when she decided to take matters in hand and put the overtired little munchkins to bed.

Her old camp-counselor smile plastered on her face, Lulu approached the boys. "Guess what, fellas?" she said. "It's almost bedtime."

"That's right, bedtime," Sam echoed cheerfully.

"Nooooo!" all three boys yelled in unison, then went racing off in all directions.

Sam and Lulu leaped into action. He plucked Andrew off the top of the sofa, then intercepted Ethan, who was scurrying up the stairs to the second floor. Meanwhile, Lulu scooped Theo into her arms before he could reach the remotes on the third shelf of the entertainment center. "Who wants to take a bubble bath?" she asked, even more enthusiastically.

Theo wriggled like a tadpole in Lulu's arms. "No bath!" he shouted.

Ethan and Andrew echoed the sentiment as Sam lowered them onto the living room floor. Lulu followed suit with Theo.

The mania increased.

Sam looked over at her, clearly at wit's end. "We have to do something," he said firmly.

Lulu struggled to catch her breath while the boys began doing somersaults in the middle of the rug. "Agreed."

"Then...?"

She knew she was the one with all the childcare experience, from her high school and college days. But even some of the most difficult situations at summer camp had never been like this. No wonder none of the other guardians had been able to handle the triplets.

"Maybe we should pass on the baths and just put them in clean diapers and pajamas before starting the bedtime routine," she said.

He nodded, clearly ready to comply with anything she suggested. Which was unusual. He generally liked to be in charge.

"Got anything to bribe them with?" she asked.

His broad shoulders lifted in an amiable shrug. "Cookies?"

"Worth a try!"

He disappeared and came back with a transparent bakery container. "Who wants a chocolate chip cookie?" he said, holding it aloft.

The boys stopped.

Lulu could see they were about to refuse this, too.

Sam lowered the container so they could get a better look at the confections inside.

Three thumbs immediately went into mouths. They were thinking. Checking with each other silently. Considering.

Good. "All you have to do," Lulu coaxed, "is get ready for bed. Then you can have a cookie *and* a bedtime story. Maybe even a glass of milk, okay?"

The triplets stood still.

Being careful not to spook them, she got out the necessary items, and with Sam's help, swiftly got them all changed. When all were ready, Sam doled out the cookies as promised.

The three of them climbed up onto the center of the sofa and began to chomp away. While Sam watched over them, Lulu raced into the kitchen and brought back three sippy cups of milk.

One by one, they drank that, too.

Pleased she and Sam had been able to work together to bring peace to the household, Lulu smiled. Indicating Sam should take one end of the sofa, she slipped onto the other and began to read a story that—from the well-worn condition of it—appeared to be one of their favorites. It was about a dog who went into his little house to find shelter from the storm and was soon joined by every other animal nearby. By the time the storm passed, the doghouse was full. New friendships had been formed. And everyone was still safe and warm and happy.

As she hoped they would soon be here, at Hidden Creek.

"Would you like another story?" Lulu asked as the triplets blinked sleepily and their heads began to droop.

To her disappointment, there were no nods of agreement.

But no shouts of outright refusal, either. So taking that for a yes, Lulu grabbed another book and then another and another. By the time she hit the fifth story, all three toddlers were sound asleep.

Sam, who'd been hanging out simply listening, gestured toward the three carrying cases in the foyer. "Where do you think I should set up their travel beds?" he whispered.

That was easy, Lulu thought, already thinking about how hard it was going to be to say good-night this evening. But she and Sam had a deal, so…

She drew a deep, bolstering breath. "Close to you, in case they wake up."

He paused, blond brow furrowing. "I know our agreement," he said. "But…are you sure you can't stay? At least for tonight?"

The truth was, Lulu had been hoping like crazy that he'd ask. Partly because she didn't want to leave the boys, given the highly agitated state they'd been in. And also because she wasn't any more confident Sam could handle this on his own than he was.

"I'll have to run home and get a few things," she said, doing her best to hide her elation.

He nodded his assent and rose as she walked over to get her bag. Then, stepping closer, murmured in the same tender tone he had used before, "Think we should get them settled into their beds first?"

Her body tingling at his nearness, she shook her head. "I'd let them get a little deeper into sleep first."

"Okay."

Another silence fell.

He looked so momentarily unsure of himself, her heart went out to him. So she moved in to give him a quick, re-assuring hug. "I know we've had a rough start today, but it's all going to work out, Sam," she promised fiercely.

"I know," he whispered back. His arms went around her and he pulled her in close, one hand idly moving down her back, reflexively calming her, too. She sank into his warmth and his strength, wishing things were as simple as they once had been. When need…want…love… were the only things driving them. But they were different people now. She needed to remember that.

Forcing herself to do what was best for all of them, Lulu drew a breath and stepped back from the enticing circle of his arms. She flashed a confident smile she couldn't begin to feel—not when it came to the two of them, anyway.

"I'll be right back," she promised. And while she was gone, for the sake of everyone, she would do her best to get her own feelings in order.

Two hours later, Sam was feeling much better. Lulu had returned with an overnight bag, honey-grilled chicken sandwiches for their dinner and the makings for a pancake breakfast the next morning. He'd cleaned up the kitchen and breakfast room and set up the three toddler travel beds in the master bedroom upstairs in her absence.

Now, with their own hunger sated, all they had to do was figure out how to move the still-snoozing tykes from the sofa to the travel beds on the second floor.

"Want me to go first?" Lulu asked as they stood shoulder to shoulder, gazing down at their little charges.

Doing his best to contain all he was feeling, Sam nodded. "I'll follow your lead."

With an adeptness Sam well remembered, Lulu eased in to remove Theo first. He was sleeping half on Ethan and had one leg beneath Andrew. She slid her hands beneath him, careful as could be not to disturb the other two. Theo shifted and sighed as she lifted him into her arms and then situated him with his head on her shoulder, his body against her middle.

"Wish me luck," she mouthed and glided off toward the stairs.

When she'd made it all the way up without incident, Sam copied her movements and eased Ethan into his arms. The little boy stirred and sighed but did not wake as Sam headed up the stairs. Slowly, he went down the hall, then into the master bedroom where Lulu was still bent over one of the travel cribs, tucking Theo in. She helped him ease Ethan down, and together, they went back to get Andrew. He slept through the move to bed, too.

Ten minutes later, all was set.

They tiptoed into the upstairs hallway. Lulu looked at him in question.

"Take any guest room you want," he said.

She chose the one two doors down. Which was probably an effort to put a little more physical space between them, since the bedroom she passed over, with a queen-size bed and adjoining bath, was almost identical.

When she turned to glance up at him, she looked tired, vulnerable and very much in need of a hug. But a hug would lead to a kiss, and a kiss would lead to everything they didn't need right now.

An electric silence fell between them and his heart kicked against his ribs.

"You'll let me know if you need me?" she said finally.

I need you now, more than I ever thought I would. He returned her half smile, promising, just as kindly, "No question."

Aware there was nothing else to say, he went back down the stairs and retrieved her overnight bag for her. They said good-night quickly, and both turned in.

Sam had no idea if Lulu fell asleep right away or not. He lay there for a while, thinking about all the mistakes they had made, everything they'd lost. How good it had felt to kiss her again the night before.

Still thinking about that, he drifted off. And it was shortly after that when the crying started. First Ethan, then Theo and Andrew.

Heart pounding, Sam threw back the covers and raced over to the travel cribs at the foot of his bed. All three boys were sitting up, distraught, rubbing their eyes.

Lulu rushed in, clad in a pair of blue-and-white-striped linen pajama pants, her hair gloriously mussed. In that instant, giving Sam an insight into what kind of mother she would be, she tenderly scooped up one child.

He reached down and lifted the other two.

"Hush now, baby, it's all right," she cooed, over and over. As did he.

To no avail. The crying continued in concert, long into the night. Sam's only comfort was the fact that Lulu was right there with them, steadfastly weathering the storm.

Chapter Five

Lulu woke slowly, aware of three things. She was incredibly exhausted, curiously weighed down, at least in the region of her midriff, and was that Sam…in all his early-morning glory…sleeping next to her? With two toddlers in his arms?

She blinked. And blinked again.

Yes, it was Sam, clad in a pair of pajama pants and a V-necked T-shirt. With his hair adorably rumpled and a morning beard rimming his chiseled jaw, he looked incredibly masculine and sexy. He was also sound asleep, his breathing as deep and even as that of the two little boys curled up on his chest, their heads nestled between his neck and shoulders.

Better yet, she had a tyke in her arms, too, snuggled up close, his head tucked between her head and shoulder. And all five of them were cozied up in Sam's king-size bed.

Without warning, he stirred slightly. Drew a deep, bolstering breath and opened his eyes.

He turned to look at her, his lips curving up in that sleepy-sexy, good-morning way she recalled so well.

Contentment roared through her, making her feel all warm and cozy inside.

His glance roved her slowly. It seemed like he might be feeling some of that contentment, too. "Some night, huh?" he murmured huskily.

It had been. The boys had cried off and on for hours. Every time they thought they had one asleep, another woke him.

The only thing that had soothed any of them was being walked. And so they'd roamed the master bedroom, crooning softly, Lulu with one toddler in her arms, Sam with two in his.

Until finally, around four in the morning, the boys had drifted off, and wary of disturbing them yet again, Sam and Lulu had eased onto the center of his big bed, children still in their arms. They lay there gently, daring to relax fully and close their eyes. And then, finally, slept.

Admiration shone in Sam's eyes. "You were great with them last night," he said.

She knew the memory of the boys' first night would stick with her. "So were you…"

Theo snuggled close, yawned sleepily, squirmed again and then lifted his head. Andrew and Ethan swiftly followed suit. All looked expectantly in the direction of the open bedroom door. "Mommy?" Theo said.

"Daddy?" Andrew asked.

"Go home?" Ethan demanded.

The plaintive requests, along with the confusion and lack of comprehension in the boys' eyes, tugged on Lulu's heartstrings and filled her with sorrow. She mourned Peter and Theresa, too. She could only imagine how poignant the loss was for the boys. No wonder they were out of control. They didn't understand where their parents were. And at their young age, there was no way to explain.

Her vision blurred.

Sam cleared his throat. "Mommy and Daddy are in heaven," he said gently. "But you know who we do have?" He indicated the stuffed animals scattered around them. "Tiger and Elephant and Giraffe!"

Grinning, the boys picked up their stuffed animals and clutched them to their chests.

"And blankets, too!" Sam declared.

They grabbed those, as well.

Her heart aching with an emotion that was almost primal in its intensity, Lulu did her best to smile, too, and affect an air of normalcy. Her grieving would have to come later, privately. "How about we all go downstairs and I'll rustle up some breakfast?" she suggested.

Sam reached over and squeezed her shoulder. Although the boys' hurt and confusion had affected him, too, he had regained his composure swiftly. "Sounds like a plan to me..."

Sam had to hand it to Lulu. Even though he could see her heart was breaking for the boys, as was his, she pulled it together with feminine grace. Helped with the three diaper changes and, along with Beauty who'd been sleeping on the floor of his bedroom as per usual, escorted the boys downstairs.

While the triplets played with their toys in the living room, she went into the kitchen to start breakfast. He let Beauty outside and put on a pot of coffee. She was still dressed in blue-and-white-striped pajama pants and a white scoop-necked T-shirt that nicely outlined her slender body. Her dark hair was tousled, her cheeks pink with sleep, her turquoise eyes red-rimmed with fatigue.

He cupped a hand over her shoulder as she passed, temporarily stilling her. "Hey. If you want to go back to bed for a while..."

She pivoted another quarter turn, so she was looking up at him directly. Acting as if that were the most ridiculous suggestion she had ever heard, she wrinkled her nose at him. "Ah, no."

"Sure?" he pressed. Aware he was still holding onto her, dropped his hand. Filled with the surprising urge to protect her, too, he said, "You only got two or three hours of sleep."

Propping one hand on her hip, she looked him over, head to toe. "Which, as it turns out, was exactly what you and the boys got," she retorted. "Seriously." Her gaze gentled. "I'm fine. I want to be available to the kids whenever, however they need me."

Before he could respond, the doorbell rang.

"Expecting someone?" she asked.

"No." Sam went to get the door while Lulu remained in the kitchen.

A uniformed Laramie County sheriff's deputy was on his doorstep. And not just any deputy, but Lulu's brother, Dan.

He touched the brim of his hat in an official manner, the grim look in his eyes indicating that although they were longtime acquaintances, this was not a social call. "Sam," Dan said.

Sam nodded back, just as officiously. "Dan."

"My sister here?" Dan asked, looking anything but pleased.

Her brother had to figure that she was, Sam thought, since Lulu's SUV was parked in his driveway. "Yes."

"Can I speak with her?"

Sam wasn't sure how to answer that. Generally, Lulu didn't want her family interfering in her personal business. And this definitely looked personal.

Before he could say anything further, Lulu strode across the living room and into the foyer. She regarded her brother with a mixture of annoyance and concern. "What's going on?" she asked.

Her older brother gave her a look that was strictly family-drama. He compressed his lips, looking over her pajamas. "I could ask you the same thing," he groused.

It didn't help, Sam thought, that with her flushed face and guilty eyes, it appeared as though Lulu had tumbled straight out of bed. *Sam's* bed.

She folded her arms, stubborn as ever. "I asked first."

Dan squinted at her. "I've been trying to get a hold of you since last evening."

"I was busy."

"Yeah, well, that's no reason not to answer your phone," he chastised.

"Actually," Lulu shot back, "it kind of is."

The siblings stared each other down.

Sam cleared his throat. He was all for gallantly coming to Lulu's aid, even if they were no longer a couple. On the other hand, he had no wish to insert himself into another family's drama. Plus, the boys, who were still busily building a block tower, didn't need to witness any quarreling. He cleared his throat and looked back at Lulu, who was still blocking the doorway. "If you'd like, I can step in so you can step out and talk in private," Sam offered mildly.

"Nope." Lulu lounged against the door frame, one ankle crossed over the other. She stared at Dan, nonchalant. "Whatever you have to say to me, big brother, can be said in front of Sam. And how did you know I was here, anyway?"

Dan shrugged. "Simple deduction. Sam was at your place yesterday, helping out and watching over you. Neither of you have been answering your phones. I figured something was going on."

Taken aback, Lulu paused. "That's no reason to spy on me."

"I wasn't spying," Dan continued quietly. "I just wanted to make sure you're safe."

Sam couldn't blame him for that.

And neither, as much as she wanted to, could Lulu. "Well," she said finally, "as you can see, I am."

"Uh-huh. It still doesn't explain why you're here now," Dan said.

"I would think that would be obvious." She pointed to Theo, Andrew and Ethan who were all still playing happily with their toys.

Dan turned to Sam. "So the word in town is true? You've just become legal guardian to three little ones?"

"Yes."

He turned back to his sister. "What do you have to do with this?"

She tensed. "I'm here, helping out."

Dan lifted a curious brow.

"By…um…nannying," she concluded reluctantly.

Her brother eyed her pajamas, which were quite chaste compared to some of the things Sam had once seen Lulu in. And would like to see again.

"Do Mom and Dad know you're now *working* for Sam?"

It felt more like working *with*, but whatever, Sam thought. It was clear they were going to have to renegotiate their deal, anyway.

Meanwhile, Lulu wasn't about to quibble over semantics. "What do you think?"

Dan squinted. "That you were probably afraid to tell them about any of this, never mind your sleeping over, for fear of what they'd say."

Lulu turned to Sam, clearly feeling that was out of line, even if Dan was family. "Would you deck him for me?"

"No." Although he wouldn't mind taking her in his arms again.

Her eyes lit up like firecrackers on the Fourth of July. "Why not?" she demanded, looking both confused and incensed. "You've never had trouble defending my honor before!"

True, Sam thought, but this was different. They weren't a couple now, although for parts of the previous night and this morning it almost felt as if they *could* be again. And because, as the primary caregiving adults in three vulnerable little boys' lives, they had to be adult about all this. She especially had to not care about what others thought, as long as the two of them knew what they were doing was right. "Because there are better ways to resolve conflict," he said wearily.

Lulu flushed again, for an entirely different reason this time, it seemed. Temper dissipating, she turned back to her brother, contrite. "Okay, sorry for overreacting."

He lifted a hand, understanding. "It's okay, sis. I know you have a lot going on."

Lulu regarded her brother intently. "Why did you want to talk to me, anyway?"

Dan relaxed as peace returned. "I wanted to tell you there was some news about your hives. The driver of the tractor trailer hauling the off-road forklifts was apprehended last night in Missouri."

Lulu bit her lip. "And the bees?"

"We don't know where they are yet. The two vehicles apparently split up. The guy who loaded the beehives into the refrigeration truck said he thought it was a legal transport."

Her shoulders slumped in disappointment. "What about all the honey that was stolen?"

"The jars are in crates, on the same truck as the beehives. He thought those were authorized to be removed, too."

Appearing distraught, Lulu moved closer to Sam. It was all he could do not to put his arm around her and hug her close. Figuring that was the last thing she would want him to do in front of her protective older brother, he remained where he was.

"Did the officers believe him?" she asked in a low, quavering voice.

Dan's brow furrowed. "Not sure, but the guy is cooperating, so there's a chance we might recover your bees yet."

"Thank heavens." Looking like she needed a moment to compose herself, Lulu went back into the ranch house without another word.

Dan declined to stay for breakfast. Intuiting Lulu's brother had a few more things he wanted to say, man-to-man, Sam walked him to his squad car.

"You and Lulu an item again?" Dan asked casually.

Sam shook his head. "No." *But after last night, I wish we were*, Sam thought. And how crazy was that?

The lawman slanted him a warning glance. "You know in addition to her usual impulsiveness, Lulu has baby fever…"

"She's also the next and last guardian on the list for the kids. She wants to be involved in this."

"You break her heart again," Dan warned, "friend of the family or not, you're going to be dealing with all five of her brothers. You get that?"

Sam nodded.

For a moment, neither of them spoke.

"So how is it going with the kids?" Dan asked.

Sam gave him the recap of the first eighteen hours.

Dan blinked, then offered empathetically, "I'm off at eleven. If you'd like, Kelly and I could round up our kids and come over this afternoon to lend a hand."

His wife was not only a preschool teacher, but mother to triplets, too. Sam spread his hands, for once open to any assistance offered. "Actually," he said sincerely, "if Kelly would like to visit, whatever tips she can give us would be great."

For the first time since he had arrived, Dan smiled. "I know she'd be glad to help," he said. "As would I."

Kelly, Dan and their triplets arrived shortly after noon, with a picnic lunch and a large box of toys their children had outgrown. Two-year-olds Theo, Andrew and Ethan were immediately taken with four-year-olds Michelle, Michael and Matthew.

Who had *lots* of questions.

"Are these your babies, Aunt Lulu?" Matthew asked.

"No." Looking gorgeous in a pair of coral shorts and a sleeveless white linen blouse, her hair swept up in a clip on the back of her head, Lulu knelt and lined up toy cars and trucks on the floor next to a play garage. Briefly, regret flashed in her long-lashed eyes. "I'm helping to take care of them," she explained, "but they're staying with Sam."

"So you're their daddy," Michael concluded with furrowed brow.

"Guardian," Sam corrected gently. *Although I'm beginning to think I'd like to be more than just that...*

Oblivious to the overemotional nature of his thoughts, Michelle sized up her aunt Lulu, then Sam. "Are you having a romance? 'Cause if you are," she added helpfully, "then you could get *married*."

Sam watched Lulu tense, the way she always did when the subject of her and marriage came up.

Kelly blushed. "Sorry." The lively preschool teacher lifted a hand. "She's been obsessed with love and weddings and marriage since..."

"Forever," Dan chuckled.

Michelle beamed. "Our mommy married Dan so he could be our daddy. They could show you how to fall in love. Then you could become a mommy like you want, Aunt Lulu," she finished sincerely.

So it was true, Sam thought. Dan hadn't been wrong in his analysis. And Lulu hadn't been exaggerating when she'd said she had wanted this forever. She did have baby fever. Enough to skew her judgment? Cause her to behave as recklessly as she had before they'd broken up? Only to regret her overly impulsive actions later? He sure as hell hoped not. Their first breakup had been excruciating enough. And now Theo, Andrew and Ethan were involved.

Seemingly aware of the delicate nature of the circumstances, Kelly took charge. "I think Sam and Aunt Lulu can figure out their own situation, honey."

"Let's show the boys the rest of the stuff we brought for them to play with," Dan said, digging into the big box of toys.

The kids immediately became enthralled, as everything old became new again.

Which was good, because it was only a few minutes later that the small moving van from Houston arrived.

"Where do y'all want this?" the workers asked. The crew boss opened up the back to reveal about twenty cardboard moving boxes, various toddler riding toys, a trio of toddler beds, a bureau, an oversize rocker-glider and a matching footstool.

Sam looked at Lulu, once again very glad she was there. "What do you think?" He had no idea where to put all this stuff.

"If it were me, I'd put the boxes containing Peter and Theresa's belongings in a storage area like…"

"The attic?"

"Yes. And then clear the large bedroom next to yours and set up a nursery for all three boys in there. Maybe figure out where to put the playroom stuff later."

Sam considered the suggestion. "Downstairs, off the kitchen, where my home office is now?"

"That would certainly be practical. You could toddler-proof the space and keep an eye on them while you prepare their meals. Maybe move your home office upstairs to one of the spare guest rooms you aren't really using. Where it'll be quieter."

Sam nodded gratefully. "Sounds good." He offered to pay the movers a little extra to lend a hand with the reorganization efforts. Two hours later, with Dan and Kelly still downstairs supervising both sets of triplets, he and Lulu remained upstairs, unpacking the nursery linens.

"You really don't have to help me with this," Lulu said. "Now that the beds are assembled and put in place, I can get it all set up from here. So, if you want to hook up the stuff in your new office space—" which was at the far end of the hall "—or go downstairs and work on the new playroom area…"

Why was she suddenly in such a hurry to get rid of him, now that the movers had left? Sam could only come up with one reason.

"Afraid what Kelly and Dan will think if you're alone with me for too long?"

"No." Her cheeks lit with embarrassment, she swooped down to pull pillows, mattress pads and sheets out of boxes.

Aware that everything but the possibility of making love to her again had temporarily left his brain, he lifted his brow. "Uh-huh." He watched her deposit the appropriate stack of linens on the end of each toddler bed with more than necessary care. "Then why didn't you tell anyone in your family that you were going to be the boys' nanny, at least temporarily?"

"Maybe I didn't have time."

He let their glances collide, then linger. "And maybe things haven't really changed since we were together before."

Looking adorably flustered, she whirled away from him and went back to the bed against the far wall. "I know what you thought back then. And apparently now, too," she said, her emotions suddenly as fired up as his. "But I was never ashamed to be with you."

"But you were reluctant to tell them just how serious we were about each other. Isn't that right, darlin'?" He paused to let his words sink in.

Her upright posture emphasized the soft swell of her breasts. His body hardened in response. "You may have been twenty-one," she mused, "but I had just turned nineteen…"

"Which was old enough to go to Tennessee with me for spring break."

"Yes, but my parents didn't know that." She bent to

put on the first mattress pad and gestured for him to do the same. "All they knew, or know even to this day, was that I was going to go with Theresa to visit Graceland and Dollywood and Gatlinburg, and then enjoy the music scene in Nashville…"

He tore his eyes from her sensational legs and the sweet curve of her hips, recalling, "They had no idea that you were going to be maid of honor and I was going to be best man at Peter and Theresa's elopement."

Cheeks turning pink, Lulu moved around to the other side of the bed to snap the elastic hem into place. "They wouldn't have approved."

He imagined they would have approved even less if they'd known she was deliberately keeping them in the dark. He finished putting the mattress cover on the second bed, then stood. "Are they going to approve of you nannying here?"

Lulu drew a deep breath. "If you want the truth…"

He did.

She put on the top sheet, then the quilt. "Probably not."

Finished, they both headed for the remaining toddler bed. Her head bent—to avoid his gaze, he imagined—she worked swiftly and methodically. He would have helped had she not edged him out with her hips.

Folding his arms, he moved around so he could see her expression. "You know you can't keep being here a secret from them, don't you?" Laramie County was a close-knit community, where families watched out for other families. Which meant that word would spread quickly.

Finished, Lulu punched the pillow into place. "I wasn't planning to."

"What's going to happen if they do express their displeasure?" he said, goading her. "Will just the *thought* of disappointing them make you run away again?"

She marched toward him, unafraid. "I never ran away." She poked a finger in his chest. "*You* were the one who threw down the gauntlet, *forcing* us to call it all off."

He went toe-to-toe with her and lowered his face until they were nose to nose. "For good reason, Lulu. I wasn't going to hide how I felt!"

"But you did," Lulu whispered, tears gleaming in her eyes. "We both did," she admitted in a choked voice, filled with the kind of heartache he, too, had experienced. "For a long time after that…"

Suddenly, Sam knew, he wasn't the only one who had been carrying a torch for the last ten years.

The next thing he knew, she was all the way in his arms. Her face turned up to his, and in that instant, all the pain of the last decade melted away. Their lips fused. A helpless sound escaped her throat and she pressed herself against him, yielding to him in a way she never had before.

And damn it if he wasn't giving his all to her, too. He gathered her even closer, let the kiss deepen, all the while savoring the sweet womanly taste of her, her fiery temperament, her warmth and her tenderness. Whether or not they'd be able to work it all out in the long haul was still questionable, but there'd never been anyone else for him. Never would be, he knew…

Lulu hadn't meant to let her feelings slip out. It wasn't surprising they had. She'd never been able to be around Sam and keep her guard up for long. He had a way of seeing past her defenses, of giving what was needed, even when she didn't exactly ask for it.

And what she needed right now, she thought as she

sank even deeper into his tantalizing embrace, was his strength and his tenderness, his kindness and perceptiveness. She needed to know if there was still something really special between them, or if their all-consuming feelings for each other had faded.

True, they hadn't made things work when they'd had a chance. And there was no way they could go back and undo any of those mistakes, much as she might wish.

They could, however, find a way to forge a new path, one that gave them both what they needed and wanted, she thought as his tongue swept her mouth and mated ever so evocatively with hers. What she wanted right now, she realized, pressing even closer, was a second chance.

For him. For her. Maybe even for the three kids that were legally in his charge and emotionally in hers.

Who knew what would have happened if not for the sounds of a delicately clearing throat? The sight of her sister-in-law in the doorway?

"Sorry to interrupt," Kelly said, her cheeks flushing. "But the kids are all getting hungry. Would you all be up for taking them into town for pizza?"

Chapter Six

"You really think this is going to work?" Sam asked Lulu at seven thirty that evening. He lounged against the bathroom wall, smelling like soap and man and brisk cologne. He also needed a shave. Although, truth be told, the rim of evening shadow on his jaw made him look rakishly sexy.

Trying not to think about how much she wanted to kiss him again, never mind how intimate and somehow right this all felt, Lulu squirted bubble bath soap into the big soaking tub in the master bathroom. As she turned on the warm water, she reflected how much better the triplets' second day at the ranch had gone, compared to the first. It gave her hope the boys might settle in after all. That with a little time and a lot of love and effort, she and Sam *could* handle this.

And if they could handle the boys' adjustment, what else might they be able to handle? she wondered. A real, enduring friendship? An affair? One thing was clear: the hot kiss they'd shared earlier was still resonating within her. And maybe him, too, if the veiled looks he'd been giving her were any indication.

With effort, she forced herself back to the matter at hand. "You heard what Kelly said at dinner. A familiar routine is crucial in helping kids to feel safe and happy."

He cocked a brow, his gaze drifting over her lazily. In the same casual tone, he returned, "And the second thing is making kids *want* to do what they need to do."

"Right." Lulu smiled. Hence, the stop at the discount superstore on the way out of town to let Ethan, Andrew and Theo all pick out new bath toys. The boys had ridden back to the ranch with their treasures clutched in their little arms. And now that Sam had removed the packaging for them, it was time to play.

He walked back into the bedroom, where the triplets were enthusiastically climbing up onto the storage bench at the foot of his bed, and from there, onto the mattress. "Who wants to put their toys in the bubbles?" he asked.

"Me do!" Andrew said, hopping over to the edge and leaping unexpectedly into Sam's arms.

"Me first!" Theo dropped down and scooted over to the edge of the bed, putting his feet over the side of the mattress and onto the wooden bench, then down onto the floor.

Ethan held out his arms joyously and waited to be scooped up. "Me, too!"

"Okay, fellas," Sam said, once they'd all been ushered into the bathroom. "Let's see which new toys like the bath the most."

Andrew dropped his rubber whale and dolphins in. The creatures shimmied but remained upright. Theo added his waterwheel, sieve and cup. Ethan added his three boats. Sam nodded approvingly at them. "Looking good," he said.

"Play?" Theo asked. He already had one leg up.

"Sure," Lulu said matter-of-factly, "but you have to take your dirty clothes off first, before you get in."

Immediately, all three boys began to undress. Lulu and Sam helped. A minute later, they were all in the tub, playing merrily. And were so entranced by their toys, they endured quick shampoos and rinses, too.

Eventually, they had to get out.

They did not want to do that.

Lulu said, "We have cookies and milk and bedtime stories for three little boys, as soon as they get their jammies on."

They had to think about it. But eventually caved. And by eight thirty, the five of them were on Sam's sofa again, enjoying what was to become their new bedtime routine. She and Sam alternated the reading of the stories, while the boys snuggled close, and cozy contentment flowed through them all.

Once again, the boys fell asleep sprawled together like a pile of puppies on the center of the sofa. Sam looked over at her. The tender regard he bestowed on the boys seemed to include her, too.

A shiver of awareness went through her.

"Move them now, or wait?" he inquired huskily.

It was a toss-up either way. Lulu studied their cherubic faces, then said, "Let's give them a few minutes." Aware her heartbeat had accelerated for no reason she could figure, she gathered up the basket of the boys' laundry that she'd left at the foot of the staircase. "Okay if I use your machine?"

Sam eased away from the sleeping trio, while Beauty dozed nearby, watching over the triplets. "Sure. I'll help."

They went into the laundry room together. Began sorting. Light colors in one pile, darks in another. They added their clothes, too.

He stepped back while she put in the first load, added detergent, switched on the machine. In the small space, it was impossible not to notice the silky smooth skin of her legs beneath the hem of her shorts. He lifted his gaze, taking in the curve of her hips, her slender waist and full breasts, before returning to her face. "It was a much better day," he remarked, aware he hadn't felt this relaxed and happy in a long time.

She smiled back at him. "It was."

As she started to move past him, he captured her in his arms. "On all scores," he rasped, then lowered his head and kissed her tenderly.

She caught her breath, even as she softened against him. Splaying her hands across his hard chest, she submitted to another kiss and then surprised him with a passionate one of her own. "Are we really doing this?" Lulu whispered. "Flirting with romance again?"

They'd be doing more than just flirting if he had his way. Knowing, though, if they were to have any chance at success, they'd have to slow down a bit, Sam gave her waist a playful squeeze. "We really are," he said.

Knowing they could have a rough night ahead, they both turned in shortly after that. Ten hours later, Sam woke slowly, feeling an incredible sense of well-being, a weight on his chest and each shoulder, and the soft press of a female body draped against his right flank. The fragrant scent of citrus and flowers teasing his nostrils, he turned his head slightly as he opened his eyes. Caught a glimpse of Lulu's lustrous hair as the top of her head pressed against his cheek. She shifted slightly, sighing drowsily. Snuggled deeper into the crook of his shoulder. She had a little boy in her arms, too.

In a rush of memory, it all came flooding back to him.

They'd had another night of the kids waking after a few hours with night terrors, crying incessantly, refusing to be soothed. He and Lulu had paced the floor in tandem, toddlers in their arms. Until finally, exhausted, they all climbed into his big bed, and still holding on to each other, slipped one by one into an exhausted sleep.

Made easier by one thing, the fact they were all in this together.

Lulu sighed again and opened her eyes all the way. She appeared to struggle to orient herself, just as he had, then relaxed as the events of the night came flooding back. She turned to gaze into his eyes. "Morning," she mouthed, as if leery of waking the little guy draped across her chest.

"Morning to you," he mouthed back with a grin. There was at least one perk to another stressful, sleepless night. He had forgotten what it had been like to wake up with her beside him. Not that he'd enjoyed it too many times before Tennessee. But the week they'd spent together prior to their breakup, that had been something special.

And now, thanks to the arrival of the triplets, he and Lulu were back to spending lots of time together again.

Without warning, three little heads popped up, one by one. The boys studied Lulu and Sam. Grinned at each other and scrambled upright. "Hungry," Ethan announced.

"Want 'cakes," Andrew said.

Meaning pancakes, Sam thought, recalling how more had been squished between little fingers and smeared across plates than eaten the previous day.

"No. Eggs," Theo declared.

"No, cereal!" Ethan disagreed.

"How about all three?" Lulu said.

Sam grinned. "Given how hungry I am, sounds good to me."

They worked together, cooking and supervising. Of course it was a lot easier, now that they'd moved the boys' toys to the adjacent family room.

"Well, that went better," Sam said half an hour later.

"It did, didn't it?" Lulu replied, pleased.

She looked gorgeous, lounging around his kitchen. He tore his gaze from the flattering fit of her pajamas and moved it to her tousled, honey-brown hair and pink cheeks. "So well," he added expansively, "that if you'd like time off to go to the McCabe family potluck at your brother Jack's house this afternoon, I think it would be okay."

Lulu's brow rose. "You know about that?"

Sam sipped his second mug of coffee. "Dan mentioned it last night at dinner, when he and I went up to the counter to collect our pizzas. He said we would all be welcome, of course, but that if the kids and I were to go with you, there might be..." He paused, unsure how to word it.

"Flack from my parents?" Lulu guessed. She reached for a bottle of spray cleaner and began wiping down the counters for the second time.

Sam concentrated on the smooth, purposeful movements of her hands. His mouth suddenly dry, he shrugged. "Anyway, I know that they both think I'm a fine enough person, apart from you."

Lulu dropped the used paper towel into the trash. Straightened. "They haven't exactly been your cheerleader, when it comes to me, anyway. Not since we broke up years ago," she concluded.

That was putting it lightly, Sam thought. Maybe it was time they talked about this. "I think they blame me—

and the animosity of our breakup—for the fact you've never married anyone else and have yet to get the family of your own that you want." He knew the same could probably be said of him.

"And they're probably right." Lulu raked the edge of her teeth across the soft curve of her lower lip. "You are the reason I've never been serious about anyone else."

She hadn't meant to blurt that out. But now that she had…maybe, given the fact they were trying to get their relationship back on an amiable track…it was time the two of them were more forthright with each other than they had been. She closed the distance between them and slid her hands into his.

"No one has ever compared, in terms of the way you made me feel back then," she confessed. Aware the past tense wasn't entirely accurate, given the whirl her emotions were in.

"Same here," he said gruffly, the expression on his face maddeningly inscrutable.

"But that doesn't mean marriage isn't in both our futures. Someday," she continued hopefully. Even though the only person she could imagine tying the knot with was Sam.

An awkward silence fell.

Lulu reluctantly disengaged their palms and stepped away.

"Back to the potluck at Jack's today," Sam said finally.

She walked over to look out the window. Although rain was predicted for that evening, it was bright and sunny now. "I want you and the boys to go with me."

"Sure?" His gaze roved over her.

Lulu turned back to face him, certain about this much.

"If I'm going to be your nanny, my family needs to get used to seeing us together."

The rest of the morning was spent supervising the kids, finishing the laundry they'd started the evening before and showering. They also dealt with their personal responsibilities.

Sam talked to his foreman about the work being done on his ranch.

Lulu called a couple of her beekeeping friends, explaining that in addition to the theft, she was now busy helping out a friend who was weathering a family crisis. She arranged for them to install a new queen and help her tend her remaining hive for the next two weeks.

And of course, they all had to get dressed for the potluck.

By the time they had everyone ready to go, it was nearly one in the afternoon, and the kids, who were sleep deprived, were getting cranky and yawning. Beauty, looking ready for peace and quiet, climbed onto her cushion in the corner of the kitchen.

Sam's hand lightly touched Lulu's waist as they moved through the doorway, then just as easily fell away.

Yet the moment of casual gallantry stayed with her a lot longer than it should have.

Doing her best to disguise the shiver of awareness sifting through her, she guided the boys into the back seat of Sam's extended cab pickup. He went around to the other side and leaned in to help fasten the safety harnesses. "Think they'll sleep on the way into town?" he asked.

Lulu climbed into the pickup, too, then handed the boys the bucket hats and sunglasses they wore in the car. "I hope they can power nap." She smiled as they put them on, then glanced over at Sam, looking across the row of three car seats. "Or will at least behave long enough for me to dash into the market and pick up the loaves of bread I was requested to bring."

Five minutes later, Sam said, "Luck is with us."

Lulu followed his glance.

All three boys had nodded off. Blankets and stuffed animals clutched to their chests. Lulu sighed, the affection she felt for them nearly overwhelming her. "They look so sweet right now," she whispered, stunned by the ferocity of her feelings. She turned back to Sam and, unable to stop herself, asked, "Is it weird for me to be so attached to them already?"

He shook his head. "They need us." His sensual lips took on a pensive curve as his hands tightened on the steering wheel. "And I'm beginning to think we need them, too."

His husky observation sent a thrill down her spine. She shifted in her seat to better view his ruggedly handsome profile. "How so?"

"To rekindle our friendship, for one thing."

He was so matter-of-fact, so certain. Her heart skittering in her chest, Lulu drew in a whiff of his tantalizing aftershave. "Do you think this is all part of some big predestined plan for our lives?" That everything they'd experienced up to now had led them to this day?

A muscle ticked in his jaw. He seemed so serious now, in the way that said he wanted the two of them to get closer. The hell of it was, she wanted that, too. "How else to explain it?" he asked.

How else indeed, Lulu wondered, if not fate?

When they stopped at a traffic light at the edge of town, he turned to her. His gaze swept over her, lingering briefly on her lips, before returning to her eyes. "Neither of us had seen Peter or Theresa for years, yet they both put us on the potential guardian list. Everyone else ahead of us failed. And the triplets end up here in Laramie County with us."

What was that, if not some sort of sign? Lulu did her best to keep from overreacting. "According to the will, they were just supposed to be with you, though," she pointed out softly.

He looked deep into her eyes, his gratitude apparent. "But, darlin', you knew without even seeing them that they were going to need both of us. And you stepped in, initially over my reservations. And now—" he reached over to briefly squeeze her hand "—barely three days later, we're together twenty-four-seven and feeling like our own little family unit."

For now, Lulu thought worriedly.

What if they got to the point where he didn't need her at night? Or left the boys with her, by herself, all day? As they had originally planned?

As much as the hopeless romantic in her wanted to wish otherwise, she had to remember that she was still involved only because he was allowing it. She had no legal standing here. So, if they were to start not getting along again…or decide there was no rekindled romance for them in the cards…their situation could change in a heartbeat.

The light turned green and Sam drove on.

"Um…speaking of destiny…" Lulu drew in a shaky breath.

Sam quirked a brow, listening.

"As heartbreaking…and yet simultaneously incredible…as this has all been for us," she began, knitting her hands together in her lap, "I still feel it's an awfully fragile situation."

Sam turned into the supermarket parking lot. He parked in a space and left the motor running. The boys slept on. One hand resting on the steering wheel, he turned and took in the anguished expression on her face. "Something on your mind?" he asked.

Lulu nodded, her heart in her throat. She didn't want to do this but she knew it had to be said. Sooner, rather than later.

Still holding Sam's eyes, she vowed softly, "I just want you to know that whatever happens…" *between you and me and the rest of it* "…I'm never going to emotionally abandon those boys."

Not exactly a ringing endorsement of their future, Sam thought, stunned by the sudden doubt she was harboring about this situation working out as they hoped.

He was about to ask what had caused her to be so on edge. But before he could speak, she slipped out of the truck, eased the passenger door shut and headed for the supermarket entrance.

As Sam had feared, the lack of forward motion had an effect.

By the time she returned a few minutes later with four bakery-fresh loaves of bread and a basket of fresh Texas peaches in hand, the boys were all awake and kicking their legs rambunctiously. Lulu seemed just as impatient. "On to Jack's!" she said.

Although Sam knew all the McCabes and their loved ones, he had never spent a lot of time in their company. The year he and Lulu had been dating, she had preferred to keep their relationship separate from her family obligations.

And while part of him had felt a little excluded back then, the rest of him had been happy to have Lulu all to himself. So it felt a little different now to be walking in with her and the boys when the rest of her family, sans her parents, was already there in Jack's big shady backyard.

Together, they made the rounds, saying hello to everyone. Her brother Matt was there with the love of his life, Sara Anderson, and her nine-month-old son, Charley. Matt looked happier than Sam had ever imagined he could be again when he'd first returned from war.

Cullen and his newly pregnant wife, Bridgett, introduced their adopted eighteen-month-old son, Robby, to the boys, who were immediately taken with him.

Jack's three daughters, Chloe, Nicole and Lindsay, ages three, four and six, also came over to say hi.

Lulu's brother Chase and his wife, Mitzy, introduced their ten-month-old quadruplet sons.

And of course the triplets were already acquainted with Dan and Kelly's four-year-olds—Matthew, Michael and Michelle.

In no time, the fifteen kids were scattered on the blankets spread across the lawn, playing with the toys that had been set out. Jack had the grill going, and all the other adults were gathered around, talking in small groups.

And Lulu, it seemed, couldn't wait to get away from him, Sam noted, as she touched his arm, her manner pleasant but oddly aloof. Like he was just another random guest in attendance at the barbecue. Not her old friend, not her potential love interest and certainly not her date for the occasion.

"Can I get you anything?" she asked, an officious smile pasted on her face. "A cold drink, maybe?"

He thought of the afternoon ahead. The fact he was suddenly and unexpectedly being pushed out of Lulu's life, just as he had been before.

Aware they had an audience, he smiled back at her in the exact same way. "Sounds great. Thanks."

* * *

Lulu made her escape, just as her parents' Escalade pulled up in front of Jack's home. She didn't know what to expect from them when they finally talked. She just knew she was dreading it.

"So what do you ladies have planned for Father's Day?" Kelly was asking when Lulu walked into Jack's kitchen to see what she could do to help.

"Don't know yet." Bridgett sighed.

"Me, either, although the kids and I still have a few days to figure it out," Kelly said.

"Should one of us ask Jack's girls what they'd like to do for him?" Lulu's mother, Rachel, asked as she came in, carrying a large platter of veggies and ranch dip.

Bess Monroe, Jack's friend—and constant platonic companion—smiled shyly and said, "I could probably do that if y'all would like." Although technically not family to anyone here besides her twin, Bridgett, Bess was around enough to be unofficially considered so.

Lulu smiled. "I think that would be great."

Rachel set the platter down, then turned back to Lulu, wasting no time at all in doing what Lulu had feared she might. "Sweetheart," she said softly, "could we have a word?"

"Sure." Lulu followed her mother into Jack's formal living room at the front of the big Victorian. Her dad was waiting there.

"What's this we hear about you becoming a *nanny* for the three kids Sam is guardian to?" Frank asked, his brow furrowed in concern.

Briefly, Lulu explained the situation while her parents listened.

"I understand he's probably got his hands full, but do

you really think you should be this involved?" Rachel asked kindly.

Yes, Lulu thought. "I'm next on the list of potential guardians, Mom."

To Lulu's relief, her parents weren't as disappointed in her as she had feared they might be.

"*Next* being the operative word," her father pointed out gently.

"We just don't want to see you get too attached, sweetheart," Rachel said, "since the boys really are Sam's charges."

Frowning worriedly, her dad added, "And the two of you have a history of not getting along…"

That they did, Lulu admitted reluctantly to herself. But all that had changed. The last three days were proof of that. She and Sam had been not only getting along splendidly, but working like a well-rehearsed team. "That was because we were broken up," Lulu explained practically.

Her mother did a double take. "Are you saying you're *not* broken up any more?"

Lulu flushed, not sure how to respond.

Rachel lifted both hands, pleading, "Oh, Lulu." She came forward swiftly to embrace her. "Please don't do anything reckless that you'll regret later!"

"I don't intend to, Mom," Lulu said, returning her mother's hug.

"Good," her dad said in relief. He embraced her, too. Stepped back. "Because the last thing we want to see is you heartbroken the way you were before."

Lulu shoved aside the memories of that awful time. "I'm not going to be." She looked both her parents in the eye.

Her mom paused. "How can you be sure of that?"

Easy, Lulu thought. "Because Sam and I are not the

naive kids we were ten years ago. We've grown and matured," she insisted, doing her best to reassure her parents. "There is no way we're making the same mistakes."

Different ones, maybe.

But even those they should be equipped to handle, she promised herself resolutely.

Rachel exhaled. "So you *are* back together?" she pressed.

Knowing a few stolen kisses did not constitute a reconciliation, Lulu shook her head. "No, Mom, we're not." The hell of it was, she just wished they were. And she wasn't sure how any of them, her parents or herself, should feel about that.

Chapter Seven

"Are you avoiding me?" Sam asked an hour later, when he finally caught up with Lulu in the walk-in pantry off the kitchen.

Actually, yes, I am.

Determined not to give her parents anything to discuss later, she looked behind him, saw no one in their line of sight and slid him a glance. If only he weren't six feet three inches of masculine perfection, didn't know her inside and out and didn't kiss like a dream, this would be a whole lot easier.

Lulu continued counting out paper plates and putting them in the wicker basket at her hip. Wishing he didn't look so big and strong and immovable standing next to her, she asked, "Why would you think that?"

"Oh, I don't know." His lazy quip brought heat to her cheeks. "Maybe the fact that you've managed to stay as far away from me as possible since your parents got here this afternoon."

Aware he was watching her, gauging her reactions as carefully as she was measuring his, Lulu lifted her chin. "It's just…there's a lot to do," she fibbed, "if we're going to get this meal on before the rain starts…" Hoping to distract him, she asked, "By the way, who's watching the boys?"

"Your mom and dad."

Lulu winced. Of all the people to tell he was going in search of her.

"Why? Is there something wrong with that?" Sam asked. Clad in a blue short-sleeved button-down, jeans and boots, he looked sexy and totally at ease. "They offered, and they've obviously got plenty of experience handling little ones."

"I know."

"Then?" he asked. His gaze roved her knee-length white shorts and sleeveless Mediterranean-blue blouse before returning to her face.

"It's just…the boys can be a lot."

They both stopped as the sound of…was that rain…?

"Oh no!" Lulu exclaimed, pushing past Sam, seeing through the kitchen windows that a sudden downpour had indeed begun. "Everyone's still outside!"

They took off at a run.

Theo was in the sandbox, trying to protect his creation from the torrential downpour to no avail. He was screaming in distress, along with two of Jack's daughters who also did not want to see their castles destroyed. Neither were listening to Lulu's mom, who was trying to coax them inside.

Andrew was standing on the top of the play-fort slide, along with three-year-old Chloe, enjoying the downpour and also refusing to get down for Bess Monroe—who might have been able to handle one child but definitely could not pick up two simultaneously.

Ethan, wide-eyed with a mixture of surprise and dismay, had taken cover beneath an umbrella table and was also refusing to be coaxed out by Lulu's dad.

Plus, the food on the long picnic tables needed to be rescued. Luckily, it was covered with plastic wrap, but still…

"You get Ethan, I'll get the other two," Sam said.

Every adult jumped in to help.

A frantic five minutes later, their meal had been salvaged, and everyone was inside. And while Jack's Victorian was pretty spacious, the fourteen adults and fifteen children had the first floor bursting at the seams. So, as soon as the meal was over, cleanup done, the great exodus began.

Not surprisingly, the triplets were having so much fun playing with the other kids, they did not want to leave.

"Five more minutes," Lulu said firmly.

"And then we're going back to the ranch to see Beauty," Sam added.

The mention of the beloved pet had all three boys hesitating but not for long.

"No! Stay!" Andrew shouted cantankerously.

"Play! More!" Theo added while Ethan pretended to ignore it all and kept right on driving his toy trucks around in circles.

Sam and Lulu exchanged the kind of looks parents had exchanged forever. A fact that, unfortunately, did not go unnoticed by Lulu's mother.

"One way or another…" Sam murmured.

Lulu nodded. "I agree." The kids had to have boundaries. And when they were overtired, their belligerence only got worse. So even if it meant they were unhappy, they were still going to have to leave when the time was up.

Sam moved off to talk to Dan, to see if there had been any update on Lulu's bees. There had not.

Meanwhile, Kelly noted sympathetically, "The boys really seem to enjoy playing with other children. Did they go to preschool previously? Do you know?"

"From what Sam and I have been able to glean from their records," Lulu said, "Theresa went back to work part-time when the triplets were a year old. They went to school five mornings a week, from nine to one, for about six months, then bumped it up to six hours a day. They usually got picked up right after nap time."

"You could enroll them at the preschool where I teach. Especially if you think that would help them acclimate."

Lulu hesitated.

Kelly continued, "Cece has the two-year-old class, and she's great with them."

Reluctantly, Lulu admitted, "Well, Sam is the one who has the say on that, but I don't know that he'll want to leave them. Especially since they've been moved around so much already in the last two months."

Kelly smiled. "I understand. If you change your mind, let me know because I can really expedite the process for you all."

"Thanks, Kelly."

Sam approached. "Ready to give it another try?"

Feeling as much a mommy as he appeared to be a daddy, Lulu nodded.

They tried reason, cajoling and firmly ordering. No approach worked when it came to getting their way-too-overtired children to cooperate. In the end, they had no choice but to carry all three boys out to Sam's pickup in the still pouring rain. Jack loaned them some beach towels to throw over their heads to keep the boys from getting wet, but Sam and Lulu both got rained on nevertheless.

Sam seemed impervious to the chill. Lulu was not

so lucky. Shivering, she draped one of the damp towels across her shoulders and chest, like a shawl, the other over her bare legs as they drove away.

By the time they reached the first stoplight in the downtown area of Laramie, the boys had stopped their protesting and were already yawning. They were sound asleep at the town limits.

Lulu told Sam what Kelly had said about enrolling them in preschool.

"Hmm."

"What does hmm mean?"

He slanted her a self-effacing smile. "It means, like you, I'm on the fence. I think it would be good for their social development, but I worry that more change might make things worse."

Lulu blew out a breath. Not really all that surprised to find them feeling the exact same thing. "Being a parent is hard."

He reached over and squeezed her knee through the towel. "We'll get used to it," he promised.

We'll...

He had said *we'll*.

They really were in this together, Lulu thought.

It was still raining pretty hard fifteen minutes later when they arrived back at the ranch. Sam parked as close as he could to the covered front porch, and they carried the boys in one at a time, with Sam easing the sleeping children from their car seats and Lulu holding a towel over them to keep them dry. They put them all on the sofa, placed their stuffed animals in their arms and covered them with their baby blankets.

Beauty strolled in to say hi. After she'd been let out for a quick potty break, she sank down next to the boys and curled up with her back to the sofa to nap while guarding her little charges.

Arms folded, Sam stood back to look at them. Tenderness sweeping through him, he leaned down to whisper in Lulu's ear, "Boy, they are really out."

"I know," she whispered back fondly.

And it was way too late for them to be taking a long nap. He glanced at his watch. "It's five o'clock."

She wrinkled her nose in concern, a sentiment he shared.

Hand beneath her elbow, he steered her a distance away. "Think we should wake them up? Or let them snooze a little while longer?"

She sent another affectionate look at the boys. As she swung back to him, he couldn't help but admire the sheen of her honey-brown hair. "I don't know." Lulu bit down on her lower lip, and heat pooled through him as she came intimately close. "What do you think?"

As if he were the expert here.

Still, it felt good to be sharing responsibility with her. To be able to lean on each other, whenever, however, they needed. Had they been able to do that before, they probably never would have broken up.

"Maybe a little while longer?" Sam supposed, inhaling her intoxicating perfume. "Until six?"

Their gazes met and she drew a breath. "Then we can let them play a bit before dinner, give them baths and go through the normal bedtime routine?"

"Sounds good," he said, his gaze dropping to her mouth, then lower, to the damp clothing clinging to her supple curves.

"What isn't good," Lulu said, holding her shirt out away from her breasts before allowing it to fall into place again, "is how I feel."

His body hardening at the sight of her nipples show-ing through her drenched shirt, he looked down at his own clothes. "We did get a little wet, didn't we, darlin'?"

Lulu grimaced. "I need to change. Unfortunately, I'm out of clean clothes, and I'm reluctant to leave you alone with the boys to make the run back to the Honeybee Ranch."

Not wanting her to go, either, Sam shrugged. "You can borrow one of my shirts." The way she had when they'd spent their spring break in Tennessee. When their attraction to each other was white-hot. Life was so much simpler back then.

Her brow pleated. She didn't appear to be affected with the same memories. "You wouldn't mind?"

"Nah. Besides..." he let his glance sift over the damp, mussed strands of her sun-kissed honey-brown hair "... there's no point in going home to get more clothes when you can throw your laundry in my machines, get it washed and dried in an hour and a half or so. Probably be easier than running back and forth."

"Okay. Thanks." She squared her shoulders and took another deep breath. "You want to get me a shirt, then?"

Sam studied the color that had swept into her fair cheeks. He shrugged. "Just go to my closet and take any one you want. They're all on hangers."

Her flush deepened. "I think I'd feel better about it if you went with me."

Grinning, he gestured broadly. And tried not to think about how much he wanted to make love to her again. "If the lady insists..."

She led the way, with Sam behind her, admiring her every languid, graceful step. When they reached the bed-room doorway, she hesitated. He walked ahead to throw open the closet door, then stepped back. "Take your pick."

Bypassing the nicer ones at the front, she selected a worn blue chambray at the very back. Holding it in front of her, she pivoted back to face him. "This one okay?"

He nodded. "Perfect," he said huskily.

She read his mind, as their eyes met. "Oh, Sam…" she said, her hushed voice sliding like silk over his skin. The shirt she was holding fell to the floor. She stepped into his arms, rose on tiptoe and pressed her lips against his. Her kiss was everything he wanted. Tender. Searching. Sweetly tempting. A rush of molten desire swept through him. This was what he needed. *She* was what he needed. And damn it, he thought as her soft, pliant body surrendered all the more, if she didn't realize it, too.

Kissing Sam again was going to be a risk, Lulu knew. And she had avoided risks like the plague since the two of them had broken up. But the last few days had ignited a fire in her unlike anything she had ever felt, then or now. For good reason, it seemed. Sam was right to think this was all part of some larger destiny that brought them back into each other's lives, just in time to be able to help the boys and resurrect a replacement for the complete family they'd lost.

They were meant to be.

And what better way to prove it than through renewed lovemaking?

Giving in to the passion simmering between them, she dared him to take full advantage of fate and be as impulsive as she was. When he kissed her back with equal fervor, elation flowed through her. Caught up in the moment, she poured everything she had into their embrace. Her knees weakened, her whole body shivered. She hadn't ever felt this much like a woman, or wanted Sam with such unbridled passion. But she wanted him now, wanted him to fill up the aching loneliness deep inside her. She wanted him to help her live her life fully again.

And still he kissed her, hard and wet and deep. Masterfully taking charge, until she shifted restlessly against him, wanting more. His hands slid beneath her blouse to unfasten her bra and caress her erect nipples. His lips parted hers, his tongue sweeping into her mouth, until her entire body was on fire. She moaned at the delicious pressure, the taste and feel of him. Yanked her blouse over her head, let her bra fall to the floor.

His eyes darkened. "So beautiful," he said, his thumbs gently tracing the curves of her breasts, caressing her sensitive nipples. "More so…" he bent to lay a trail of kisses over her throat, collarbone, the tips of her breasts "…than I remember…"

Lord, he was gorgeous, too. All over. She tugged off his shirt, ran her hands over his chest. Explored the satiny warmth of his lean waist, muscled torso and broad shoulders. It had been so long since they'd made love. Too long, she mused as she ran her fingers through the crisp hair arrowing down into the waistband of his jeans.

Quivering with excitement, she slid her hands beneath. Cupped the hot, velvety hardness. He dropped his head, kissing her again, bringing forth another wellspring of desire. Their tongues tangled as surely as their hearts, and he groaned, resting his forehead on hers. "Lulu…" he whispered, the last of his gallantry fading fast.

She knew how easy it would be to fall in love with him all over again. Knew it and welcomed it. "I know what I'm doing, Sam," she whispered. She went to shut the bedroom door, then took him by the hand and led him toward the bed.

"Do you?" Eyes dark, he watched her continue to undress.

She knew what he was thinking; there had been so much hurt between them in the past. Too much. But that was over. It was a new day. One that held the promise of so much more.

There would not be regrets this time, she told herself fiercely. Even if they'd been brought together again by circumstances not of their own making, and were moving a little too fast.

"I know this feels reckless," she whispered. Her heart skittering in anticipation of the mind-blowing passion to come, she helped him disrobe, too. "But I want you. I've never stopped wanting you," she confessed with a ragged sigh.

Shouldn't that be enough?

Now that they were both adults with another full decade of life experience informing them?

With long-established ways to guard their hearts?

Suddenly, she wasn't the only one shuddering with pent-up need. "Well, in that case…" His sexy grin widened. All too ready to oblige, he dropped a string of kisses down her neck, across the slopes of her breasts to the crests, then he sank to his knees and his lips moved lower still. The white-hot intimacy had her arching in pleasure. Making her feel ravished and cherished all at once.

Closing her eyes, she fisted her hands in his hair and gave herself over to him. Fully. Completely. And she lost what little was left of her restraint as a soft moan and a shudder of overwhelming heat swept through her.

Hands on his shoulders, she urged him upward. Not about to be the only one to find release, she whispered against his shoulder, "My turn now."

Sam laughed quietly, as she'd hoped he would.

Determined to keep it light and sexy between them,

she was eager to tantalize his hot, hard body as he had hers. She lay down beside him, kissing and caressing him until everything fell away but the feel and touch and taste of him. Until there was no more holding back.

He found a condom. Together, they rolled it on. Suddenly, she was on her back. One hand was beneath her, lifting her, the other was between her thighs. She surged against him, softness to hardness. He stroked his thumb over her flesh, and she was flying, gone. And still he kissed her, again and again, until there wasn't any place she would rather be.

Needing him to find the same powerful release, Lulu wrapped her arms around him and brought him closer. He groaned, rough and low in his throat, and her muscles tautened as he found his way home in one long, slow, purposeful slide. Allowing her to adjust to the weight and size of him, he went deeper still.

Needing more, she wrapped her legs around his waist, opening up to him, and then there was nothing but the sensation of being taken, possessed. Treasured. And for the first time in an extremely long time, she felt connected to him in that very special man-woman way.

Sam had known it was a mistake to make love to Lulu on a whim. Because it was when Lulu did things on impulse that she was most likely to regret them later. But when she'd reached out to him, he hadn't been able to resist. Now, he was beginning to wish he had, as he watched Lulu silently come to the same conclusion that he had already reached. That once again, they'd let their emotions get the best of them, and had gone too far, too fast. "Us being together this way doesn't have to complicate things unnecessarily," he said, stroking a hand through her hair and soothing her as best he could. "We can still take things one day, one moment at a time, dar-lin'. Do whatever feels right."

Like make love.

And get closer yet.

"You're right." Lulu let out a long sigh. Pressed her hand against the center of his chest, insinuating distance between them. As their gazes locked, something came and went in her pretty eyes. "This doesn't have to mean anything more than any other fling would."

He held tight when she would have fled, aware once again she was taking his intentions all wrong. "That's not what I said," he told her gruffly.

"Isn't it?" she returned with a casual smile that did not reach her eyes. Before he could say anything else, she lifted a hand. "It's okay, Sam." With typical grace, she eased away from him. "We're both sophisticated enough to handle just having sex."

Which was obviously all it had been to her.

"And you're right," she finished with a weariness that seemed to come straight from her soul. "It really doesn't have to change anything." She rose and pulled on her panties and his shirt, then, scooping up her damp clothes, padded down the hall to the guest room where she'd been stowing her belongings.

He rose and dressed, too, in dry clothing. Emerging from his bedroom, he caught sight of her as she headed downstairs, small mesh bag of dirty clothes in hand.

Sam went back to gather up his own laundry, then found her in the utility room, sorting clothes, her head averted. He noted she had added an above-the-knee denim skirt and pretty sandals to her ensemble.

"Are we really just going to leave it like this?" he said, dumping his own clothing into a separate hamper.

Cheeks slightly pink, she kept her attention on her

task. "What's there to say?" They both reached for the detergent at the same time. Their shoulders and arms brushed before they could draw back.

Wishing he could make love to her again—without driving her further away than she was at this moment—he stepped back to give her the physical space she craved. He focused on the tumult in her eyes.

"Maybe you should tell me."

She looked at him for a long moment. "Well, it was probably important for us to satisfy our curiosity, given the situation."

She focused on her task, added soap, set the dials and closed the lid. Turned on the machine.

He stayed his ground. "Curiosity," he repeated. *So that's what they were calling it now.*

"We probably also needed to find out if the sparks we used to have still existed." She drew in a deep breath and finally pivoted to meet his gaze. Her chin lifted. "And now we know."

Now they did know. Though he had the intuition that they had arrived at completely different conclusions…

"Meaning what?"

She walked past him, down the hall, peered around the corner into the living room. The triplets were all still fast asleep. She returned to the kitchen, still not clarifying what she meant.

Knowing nothing would ever be solved by pretending there wasn't a problem, he edged closer. Needing to know where he stood with her. Guessed, "Meaning…it's not going to happen again?" Or it would?

She leaned against the kitchen island, her back to the still-pouring rain, and let out a slow breath. "I'm not sure."

He switched on the overhead lights, bringing light to the gloomy room. He moved so she had no choice but to look at him. "Hey," he said softly, not about to let her deny it. His gaze roved her. "I know it was good for you."

She blushed at his needling tone. "I know it was good for you, too." Seeing Beauty heading for the back door, she moved to open it. Stepped out under the overhang. "But as you noted earlier, our life is pretty complicated right now, with the kids and all," she said, keeping her voice low as the damp warmth surrounded them.

Sam gave his pet room to move down the steps, into the yard, then eased next to Lulu. "And making love just now makes it even more so. I get that. It doesn't mean we can pretend it didn't happen," he pointed out. Or that he even wanted to.

Regret pinched the corners of her mouth. "Sure about that?"

Because she sure seemed able to do so, Sam noted bitterly as Beauty came back up the deck steps and walked on into the house.

Lulu grabbed a dog towel off the hook and bent to dry off Beauty's thick coat. When she was done, she gave the Saint Bernard a fond pat on the head and watched as the dog padded soundlessly back to the living room, to stand guard once again over the kids.

Lulu hung up the towel, then, glancing over at the family room, zeroed in on the toys that had been left all over the place. She breezed past him and began picking them up. Although he didn't care whether the toys were neatly put away or not, he followed and began to help.

An even more conflicted silence fell. Which was a shame, Sam thought, since they didn't often have time to themselves. "You really don't want to talk about this any more?" he said, wishing like hell that she would.

Still bearing the glow of their lovemaking, she bit her

lip. Ambivalence flooded her expression. "I really don't," she returned, just as softly.

And suddenly, Sam knew what the real problem likely was.

"Then how about you tell me what happened at the picnic today, when you and your parents went off for a private chat?"

Chapter Eight

The last thing Lulu wanted to do was tell Sam her folks' doubts about her ability to make wise decisions in her life. On the other hand, he was involved, too, if only by circumstance.

She knelt beside the wooden toy box emblazoned with the triplets' names. He knelt on the other side. Wearing a washed-till-it-was-soft cotton shirt, much the same as the one she had borrowed and was still wearing, and faded jeans, he was every inch the indomitable Texan.

Trying not to notice how sated and relaxed he looked post-lovemaking, she forced a smile and an attitude of nonchalance. "My mom and dad cornered me."

Handsome jaw tautening, he regarded her. "And?" His voice dropped another husky notch, in a way that sent heat flashing through her.

She flushed under his scrutiny. As always, his ultra-masculine presence made her feel intensely aware of him. "Bottom line? They're concerned I'm getting too involved with you and the kids."

Something flickered in his gold-flecked eyes, then maddeningly disappeared as he watched her drop more toys into the storage container.

"Is that what you think?" he asked, his expression closed and uncommunicative.

No, I think I've had the brakes on for way too long. But maybe that was the old Lulu talking. The reckless, restless, impulsive Lulu who once fell in love with Sam and ran off with him and then panicked and made the biggest mistake of her life...

The Lulu who was ruled more by emotion and the fear of disappointing anyone than logical, practical thought.

The Lulu who just gave in to the buildup from the most emotional four days of her life and recklessly made love with Sam again.

And worse, she couldn't quite bring herself to regret it. Much as the practical side of her wished that she could.

Not that he looked as if he were lamenting it, either...

Even though, as he said, none of this had to change anything between them.

When to her, it already had...

Oblivious to the conflicted nature of her thoughts, Sam persisted, "What did you say to them?"

Feeling a little unsteady, she drew a deep breath, glad to have someone to confide in about this. "I told them they were wrong," she said softly, lifting her chin. "That the kids need us both."

"They do." Finished picking up, he lifted the box and carried it over to the corner where it usually sat. Taking her by the hand, he led her to the breakfast room table. The corners of his eyes crinkled. "Which is why I've been thinking, you shouldn't just be their nanny, Lulu.

Or a concerned friend helping out." He waited for her to take a seat and then settled opposite her.

He paused to look her in the eye, then said, even more resolutely, "You should be their legal guardian, too."

Legal guardian!

She caught her breath, feeling thrilled and stunned. Still, this was awfully sudden. Too sudden, maybe?

Swallowing, she lifted a halting hand. "Sam…"

He reached across the table to take her hands in his. "I'm serious, Lulu. Your parents were right. It isn't fair for you to be so involved if you're not a guardian. So why not be a co-guardian with me? It's obvious I can't do it alone."

Lulu sighed. "Neither could I."

Sam nodded his agreement, all matter-of-fact rancher now. "Even more important, you love the kids and they love you. They need a mom." Warmth spread throughout her body as his fingers tightened on hers. "I need a partner…"

Aware his grip felt as masculine and strong as the rest of him, she withdrew her hands from his. "Are you saying that because I just put the moves on you?"

A look of hurt flashed in his eyes, then disappeared. "Our lovemaking just now has nothing to do with this."

"Doesn't it?" she returned.

He kept his gaze locked with hers. "No." His expression sobered, becoming all the more sincere. "These are two separate issues."

For him, maybe. But for her?

Her desire for him seemed an integral part of her. Aware she could fall way too hard for him if she wasn't careful, she folded her arms.

"You say that now." She drew a deep breath, wishing he weren't so sexy and capable and kind. So tender and good with the kids. "But what happens if you and I start down that road again and then don't work out as a couple again?" she challenged, feeling self-conscious, as he ze-roed in on her nervousness. "How would you feel about sharing guardianship duties with me then?"

"If that happens, and I don't think it will, we'll do exactly what we're doing now and figure out how to continue to make things work—as friends," Sam said firmly. "But in-stinct tells me that we will work out, Lulu. And if you listen to yours, I imagine you'll be convinced of the same thing."

He was right about that. Only it wasn't her feminine instinct doing the talking. It was her heart that wanted to be with Sam and the kids…

"So what do you say, darlin'?" he proposed softly, gripping her hands again and looking deep into her eyes. "Will you be their co-guardian with me?"

Lulu might still be confused about what she wanted when it came to Sam, but there was no doubt at all about what her heart wanted in regard to the three little boys. Or what would be best for them. They needed both a mother figure and a father figure in their lives.

Joy bubbled up inside her. She'd imagined she would have to fight to make this happen. Instead, once again, she and Sam were on the exact same page.

She returned his searching gaze and said, ever so softly, "Yes, I'd love to be legally responsible for the triplets, too."

Their new deal would inadvertently solve another problem she had not been looking forward to contend-ing with. She pushed back her chair and rose, aware it was time for them to wake the children for dinner. "This way, you won't have to pay me for caring for them."

"I'll still owe you…"

"No," she cut him off, feeling vaguely insulted by his insistence, although she wasn't sure why, "you won't."

Their stare-down continued.

"This isn't about the money, Lulu," he warned.

"I know it isn't," she agreed. "For you." But for her…the thought of him being her boss…giving her a paycheck… Well, that might have been their *initial* agreement, the only way she'd gotten herself in the door to help. Yet from the first moment the children arrived at Hidden Creek Ranch, she hadn't felt like his employee so much as she'd felt like his comrade in arms.

"But I still prefer it this way," she reiterated, "with us equally responsible. And absolutely zero money changing hands."

"I owe you…"

"And you've paid me," she stated, just as vehemently, "in room and board."

His eyes glinted, the way they always did when he let her have what she wanted. He exhaled, his gaze drifting over her with lazy male appreciation before finally returning to her face. "I'm not going to win on this. Am I, darlin'?"

"No, cowboy," Lulu shot back sassily. Knowing the only way they would ever truly be able to come together was as equals. She whirled on her heel and marched off. "You are not!"

As for the rest…

She sighed.

Sam was right. They could figure it all out later. In the meantime, the first thing they needed to do was take care of the legal formalities.

"I think that's wonderful," Hiram said when Lulu and Sam called his office the following morning, just after breakfast.

Sam looked over at Lulu, who was smiling from ear to ear. He felt relieved and happy about their new agreement, too. As far as it went, anyway. They still had a lot to work out about their own relationship, but he could be patient on that front. In the meantime, as far as the caretaking went, he and Lulu were in this together. And as they'd already more than proved, he thought, returning her excited grin, they made a very good team.

As unaware as Lulu of the romantic nature of Sam's thoughts, Hiram concluded, "I'll send the appropriate papers to Liz and Travis. You can go to their law office to sign them."

"Thank you, we will," Lulu replied.

They all signed off.

And just in time, too, Sam thought. Behind them, a cacophony of toddler voices sounded.

"Horsey!" Theo yelled.

"Me ride!" Andrew insisted.

"No! Doggy," Ethan disagreed. Not sure what was going on, since the boys had escaped to the living room while they were on the phone, Sam and Lulu headed off in their direction. They found Beauty standing parallel to the big leather sofa. Ethan was standing just in front of her and petting her face gently while Theo and Andrew tried to simultaneously climb on her back and ride her like a horse.

"Oh dear!" Lulu rushed to rescue the remarkably patient Saint Bernard.

Sam plucked both little cowboys off her back and deposited them on the far end of the sofa, out of harm's way. "Fellas, Beauty is not a horse," he scolded. "So you *cannot* climb on her back." He gave his dog a consoling pat on the head, then lifted Ethan out of the way, too. With a beleaguered sigh and the way now clear, Beauty lumbered down the hall, over to her cushion in the corner of the kitchen, and sank into the bed.

All three boys began jumping on the sofa, as hard and high as they could. "Want friends," Theo shouted loudly.

"Play now!" Andrew agreed.

"Go car," Ethan explained.

Lulu went to her phone. "I'll see if I can arrange a playdate," she called over her shoulder.

She came back five minutes later. The triplets had given up jumping but were now attempting to climb onto and slide down the bannister. Every time Sam plucked one off, another climbed on.

"Everyone is at preschool," Lulu informed him, lifting her brow at the boys. Like magic, they all stopped climbing on the stair railing. Only to resume jumping and shouting from the sofa. Lulu shouted to be heard above the bedlam. "Kelly said the triplets could be visitors in her three-year-old class today, which in the summer runs from nine to one o'clock."

Knowing the only thing that ever entertained the boys for long was other children, Sam replied, "Sounds good."

The boys were even more delighted.

While they drove to town, Lulu called their attorney and arranged to visit their office to sign the guardianship papers Hiram had sent.

"You sure you don't want to think about this?" Liz and Travis asked them, after they'd dropped the kids off.

To Sam's relief, Lulu shook her head, looking prettier and more determined than ever. "No. Sam and I agree they need both of us."

They walked out of the office building into the late-morning sunlight. For a moment, they just looked at each other. He studied the rosy color in her cheeks and the shimmer of excitement in her eyes. He was happy she was finally getting the children she had wanted, too. They were all lucky to have each other.

Her gaze swept over his form, making him glad he had taken the time to iron his shirt instead of just shave and shower and put on the first set of clean clothes he pulled from his closet.

Instead of going to the passenger side of his pickup, she remained in the sunlight. "You know," Lulu mused, "this is the first time we've been without chaperones in almost five days. I almost don't know what to do with myself."

He had to fight not to reach out and touch the silky strands of her honey-brown hair. "I know."

An awkward silence fell. He observed the pulse throbbing in her throat.

She raked her teeth across the lush softness of her lower lip. "I don't want to go too far, though, in case the triplets suddenly decide they don't want to be at preschool after all."

"No kidding," Sam said, wishing it were appropriate to take her in his arms and kiss her.

She cocked her head to one side, as if thinking the same thing. He was about to reach for her, figuring they could at least hug each other in congratulations, when Lulu's phone rang.

"Oh no," Lulu said, plucking it from her purse.

"Don't tell me it's the school already," Sam said. Which in one sense would not be surprising, since the drop-off had been almost *too* easy to be believed, with the kids going right in without batting an eye.

"No." She exhaled, looking distressed. "It's not them. It's Dan."

To Lulu's relief, Sam was happy to accompany her to the sheriff's station.

Her brother ushered them into a conference room and,

as usual, got straight to the point as soon as she and Sam sat down. "We found your bees."

Lulu had figured as much, when he'd said he had *news*. "Where are they?"

"A commercial melon farm in Wisconsin. The owner thought it was a legitimate lease. When he saw your brand listed as stolen on the state agricultural website, he notified authorities there immediately. They, in turn, contacted us."

"Thank goodness for that," Lulu said as Sam reached over and squeezed her hand. "How are my hives doing?"

Dan looked down at his notes. "Apparently, there was some loss, but the majority of the hives seem to be doing well. The question is what to do now. The farm owner still needs your bees for his crops, but he understands if you want them shipped back immediately."

Her heart racing, Lulu asked, "Do you have his contact information?"

Dan handed her a piece of paper.

Lulu called the melon farmer. They talked at length. Finally, she hung up. Her brother had gone off to attend to other law enforcement business. But Sam was still there, waiting. Patient and calm as ever.

"Everything okay?" he asked, his handsome face etched with concern.

Her emotions still in turmoil, Lulu nodded and led the way into the hall. She waved to the front desk and, aware it would soon be time to pick up the triplets, headed out into the summer sunshine. "The farm owner is going to pay the going rate, which will be negotiated through our lawyers, and keep the hives until late August."

Easing a hand beneath her elbow, Sam matched his steps to hers. "And then what?"

"I'll either ship them back home or sell them outright to a beekeeper where they are now."

Sam stopped in midstride. "You'd really do that?"

Not willingly. She also knew she had to be practical here, now that she was co-guardian to the triplets. "It might make the most sense."

"Those bees are your life's work," he reminded her, clearly disappointed.

Lulu tensed. She didn't like him judging or second-guessing her. Shifting her bag higher on her arm, she returned in a cool tone, "That's true. They were." She paused to look him straight in the eye. "But things are different now I'm going to be raising the triplets. Already, I've had to ask beekeeping friends to install a new queen for me, and tend my remaining hive on an emergency basis, because I just don't have time to get over to the ranch. That being the case, it might be better for me to pocket the cash from the sale and concentrate on the kids for now. Worry about resuming my beekeeping career later."

Sam stared at her. Feeling like he had gone back in time to their college years, when Lulu had flitted from one thing to another, changing her major almost as often as she changed hairstyles. A pattern that had continued for at least three years after the two of them had broken up.

In fact, to date, beekeeping was the one thing, the *only* thing, she seemed to have stuck with.

Her lips slid out in a seductive pout. "You don't approve?" she challenged.

He rubbed his jaw, considering. The last thing he wanted to do was make an emotional situation worse. "I know it's hard now, but I think if you give it all up you might regret it, darlin'."

Her eyes turned dark and heated. "Exactly why I'm putting off the decision for a couple of months, so I will have time to think about what I want to do."

With a scowl, she pivoted and continued on to the parking lot, walking briskly ahead of him. "I'm not going to lean on you financially, if that's what you're worried about. Whatever I decide to do, I'll have enough to pay my share of the kids' expenses. And of course all my own, too."

He caught up with her, sliding his hand beneath her elbow once again. "That's not what I'm worried about and you know it."

She whirled, coming close enough he could inhale her tantalizing floral scent and feel her body heat radiating off of her. "Then...?"

His gaze drifted over her pretty turquoise sundress and silver necklace. It was all he could do not to touch her.

Aware this was something they did need to discuss, even if it was unpleasant, he stuck his hands into the back pockets of his jeans instead. "I just wouldn't want you to change your mind about other things down the road, too."

"Like...?"

He shrugged. Was she really going to make him say it? Apparently, she was. "The kids."

Color swept into her high, sculpted cheeks. "Did you *really* just say that to me?"

"Look, I wasn't trying to insult you—"

"So you did accidentally?"

He tracked the silky spill of hair across her bare shoulders. Figuring if they were going to be co-guardians, they ought to be able to talk everything out together, he shrugged. Given what she'd just said about the business she'd spent the last seven years building…which was also the one thing, the only thing, he'd seen her feel maternal toward, up to now. "It's a legitimate worry."

Hurt sparked in her gaze. "No, it isn't, Sam," she disagreed quietly. "And if you really feel that way…"

What he really felt was the intense urge to haul her close and kiss her until the tension between them went away. The fact he'd been brought up a Texas gentleman kept him from doing so, but—

Her phone pinged to signal an incoming text.

She paused, brow furrowing, and read the screen. "It's Kelly," she said in concern. She looked up at Sam. "She said there may be trouble at the preschool. She wants us to come now to get the kids."

Fortunately, they were only a couple of minutes away. Sam climbed behind the wheel and Lulu settled in the passenger seat. He stretched his arm along the back of the seat and looked behind them as he backed his truck out of the space. He paused before he put it in gear. "She didn't say anything more?"

She shook her head. "Nope."

Sam drove through the lot and turned onto the street. Hands gripping the wheel, he asked, "You don't think they caused some sort of ruckus, do you?"

Lulu sighed, and put a hand over her eyes, looking like a harried mother. She pressed her soft lips together ruefully. "I wish I could say no, but you know how they are when they're overtired."

He did, indeed.

It seemed to take forever to make it to the school, a fact hampered by the number of cars lining up in the driveway and down the street. They bypassed the drop-off and parked. Still not speaking to each other, they headed inside.

There were no sounds of crying or wild behavior as they moved through the hall.

When they cleared the doorway to Kelly's classroom, the boys were huddled together anxiously, watching the portal. Other kids were being escorted out by their moms and dads.

"Hey, guys." Lulu knelt down to say hello. Sam hunkered down beside her. "How's it going?"

"Want *Mommy*," Theo said fiercely.

Andrew folded his arms militantly. "Want *Daddy*."

"Go *home*," Ethan said, his lower lip trembling.

Too late, Sam realized it might have been a mistake to bring them to a setting that so closely mirrored the place where they'd been when they'd received the news that something terrible had happened and their parents weren't coming back.

Sam started to engulf them in a reassuring hug. "We're going to take you home, fellas," he said.

"No!" Theo shouted, pushing him away. "Want Mommy!"

"Want Daddy," Andrew agreed, wriggling free.

"Me scared," Ethan collapsed to the floor in a limp heap and sobbed outright.

The hysteria spread. Within seconds, other preschoolers were welling up. Some sobbing. Others loudly demanding their own parents take them home. And so it went, well after the classroom was cleared.

The triplets, it seemed, weren't going anywhere. Not willingly, it seemed.

Kelly disappeared, then came back a few minutes later. "I called the head of grief counseling over at the hospital. She's on her way over now."

"Thank heavens," Lulu whispered, moving closer to Sam as if for protection while the boys clustered together on the play rug on the floor, stubbornly waiting.

Kate Marten-McCabe breezed in.

The silver-haired therapist had a small cooler and a big bag of books and toys. "I've got some things for us to do," she announced with soothing candor. She glanced at the three adults remaining. "Could y'all could give us a little time to talk? Maybe wait for us on the playground, where we'll have Popsicles later?"

Sam and Lulu nodded.

They walked to a bench beneath a shady tree in silence. "Well, you were right," Sam admitted ruefully as they took a seat side by side.

Lulu slanted him a questioning glance.

He cleared his throat. "Maybe we're both going to have to step back from our jobs for a while." He paused to look deep into her eyes, intensifying the intimacy between them. He took her hand in his and squeezed it affectionately. "And I'm sorry I didn't realize that as quickly as you did."

Lulu knew it was a big step, and an important one, for Sam to say he was wrong when they differed. He had never done so in the past. Instead, had just expected her to come around to his way of thinking or accept he wasn't going to change his opinion and deal with it.

She looked down at their entwined fingers. Realizing she could have done more to intuit the reason behind his worry and reassure him on the spot that she would never ever abandon him or the kids, rather than simply go on the defensive.

"Apology accepted," she said quietly. She turned to face him, her bent knee nudging his thigh. "But as for your work, running Hidden Creek... Could you really step back for more than a week or two?"

The reservation was back in his eyes, along with a

lingering desire she felt, too. "My foreman and the other ranch hands can handle everything day-to-day until the boys are really settled."

"That could take a while."

He exhaled roughly. "I know." But seemed prepared to make the sacrifice nevertheless.

Silence fell between them.

"What do you think is going on in there?" he asked finally.

Lulu turned toward the school, saw no sign of anyone coming outside. "Kate's probably explaining to them that their parents aren't coming back."

His expression turned brooding. "You think they'll accept that?"

Recalling the raw grief the triplets had exhibited, their emotional expectation that their parents would magically appear to take them home, Lulu drew in another jagged breath. She looked down at her and Sam's entwined hands. Realized they really did need each other to see the boys through this rough patch. "At their age? I don't know."

Another silence fell.

This time they didn't talk.

Finally, Kelly came out of the school with two sets of triplets, hers and theirs. All six had Popsicles. As she neared, Sam and Lulu disengaged their hands and stood.

Kelly gave them a smile. "Kate would like to talk to you inside."

They found the grief counselor in the classroom, packing up. She gestured for them to have a seat. "I explained to the boys that their parents are in heaven, but they don't really comprehend what that is yet. They just know their parents won't be coming to pick them up today." She brought a notebook and pen out of her bag. "How have the kids been doing at home?" she asked kindly.

"Better every day," Sam said.

"Is there any hyperactivity?" Kate asked.

Reluctantly, Lulu admitted, "Pretty much all the time."

"Their sleeping?"

"Fitful at best," Lulu said.

They went on to explain about the night terrors and their inability to get them to lie down in their own beds.

"In fact," Lulu added, "the only way they will rest at all, for any length of time, is if we're holding them."

Kate did not look surprised. "How is their eating?"

"They like sweets," Sam replied, "but when it comes to anything else, they're pretty picky."

Lulu nodded. "They'll ask for something, like pancakes or scrambled eggs, but then they don't really eat much of it."

"Have they had any temper tantrums?"

Sam and Lulu nodded in tandem. "At least once a day."

"These are all signs of toddler grief. Healing is going to take time. But the good news is, we have programs at the hospital for all of you that will help."

Sam and Lulu exchanged relieved glances. Feeling more like a team than ever, Lulu asked, "What can we do in the meantime?"

"Reinstate as many familiar routines from their old life as you can, including preschool. Get them on a schedule and sleeping in their own beds. Help them remember their parents and the love they received in a way that is comforting and heartwarming rather than grief-provoking. And…" Kate handed them a storybook for orphaned children and a packet of information with her card attached "…bring them to the children's grief group at the hospital on Saturday morning. The two of you can attend the one for guardians and caretakers."

"Thank you." Sam and Lulu shook her hand, promising in unison, "We will."

Kate smiled. "Call me if you have any questions or concerns." She slipped out of the classroom.

Sam and Lulu turned to face each other. Aware what a sticky situation they had found themselves in, it was hard not to feel completely overwhelmed. Especially when the two of them were still privately mourning the loss of their friends, too. "Looks like we have our hands full, cowboy," she murmured in an attempt to lighten the mood and dispel some of the grief they were both feeling.

He returned her quavering smile. "And then some." His gaze stroked her features, every one, ending with her eyes. With his customary confidence, he promised, "Together, we'll make it all work out. But first things first. You've got to move in."

Chapter Nine

Lulu gaped at Sam. His thick blond hair rumpled, his gold-flecked eyes filled with worry, he looked a little ragged around the edges. Which, after the afternoon they'd had, was exactly how she felt. And they still had the rest of the day, and night, to get through.

"You want me to actually move in?" she repeated in astonishment, not sure she'd understood him correctly. "With you?"

"And the boys, obviously," Sam said. He appeared perfectly at ease with the idea of them residing together under one roof, full-time.

"Temporarily," Lulu ascertained.

He shook his head, correcting, "From here on out."

Lulu was still trying to wrap her mind around that when he moved closer. His gaze caressed her face. "You heard what Kate said." He tucked his hand in hers, gave it a tender squeeze. "If we want the boys to recover, we have to give them as much security as possible. Get back to familiar routines." He paused to let his words sink in. Once again, a thoughtful silence brought them together.

"And what was normal to them," he continued practically, "was living with a mom and a dad under one roof."

A tingle of awareness sweeping through her, Lulu hitched in a breath. "That's true," she managed around the sudden dryness of her throat. The thought of making love with him again dominated her mind. "But…" It would be impossible to ignore their attraction for long under such intimate circumstances. A fact she guessed he knew very well!

Dropping his grip on her, he stepped back. Cocked a brow. "What?" he prodded.

This was the kind of impulsive thing *she* would do. Not him. Doing her best to control her soaring emotions, she studied him from beneath her lashes. "Are you sure you really want to do this?" Thus far, their arrangement had been only temporary. Meant to last only until the boys adjusted and were sleeping peacefully through the night.

They'd yet to discuss what would happen after that.

"If we're going to raise them together, as full-time co-guardians, we need to be *permanently* under one roof." He lifted a hand. "We could do it at your place, of course, but it's so much smaller…"

They would be tripping all over each other.

"And the boys are already sort of used to staying at Hidden Creek. I don't think it would be smart to uproot them again, do you? Especially after what happened a little while ago." He jerked his head in the direction of the classroom floor.

Aware that Kelly and the two sets of triplets were waiting for them on the playground, Lulu began moving about the classroom, gathering up the boys' things. "No. Of course it wouldn't be wise to move them again," she said.

He held her carryall open while she slid their belongings inside. "Then…?"

The two of them hesitated just inside the door. Lulu hated to admit it, but she was worried about how it would look. "If I actually move in," she murmured, looking up at him, "people are going to probably assume, because of our romantic history, that you and I are a couple again."

Sam lounged, arms folded, with one brawny shoulder braced against the wall. His glance drifted over her intimately. "So?"

"So," Lulu said before she could stop herself, "that could put a crimp in your dating life." *Oh my god! Where did that thought come from?*

To her embarrassment, her flash of jealousy did not go unnoticed.

Male satisfaction tugging at the corners of his lips, he stepped closer, gently cupped her shoulders and told her exactly what she had hoped to hear. "I'm not going to have any dating life when I have three kids to take care of."

A thrill swept through her. She forced herself to calm down. Just because they'd had a brief fling did not mean he would ever fall in love with her again, or vice versa. And from what she'd seen in the time since they'd broken up, he'd suffered no shortage of attractive female dinner companions.

Shrugging, she stepped back, away from the enticing feel of his warm, calloused hands on her bare skin. "You might be surprised. A lot of women my age have baby fever." *A lot of women lust after you.* She pretended an insouciance she couldn't begin to feel. "Three adorable toddlers could make you a very hot prospect."

Just that suddenly, something came and went in the air between them. The slightest spark of hope of renewed passion and a rekindling of the love they had once shared.

"Is that why you made love with me?" he chided, in a tone that was half joking, half serious. "Because you have a well-known case of baby fever? And wanted in on the bounty of family I suddenly found myself blessed with?"

Wondering just what it was about him that made her unable to get over him, she said, "Of course not."

To her chagrin, he looked skeptical.

"As I said before, I made love with you because I was…" *nostalgic for what we once shared*, she wanted to say "…curious," she fibbed instead.

His eyes darkened with a mixture of masculine pride and intense interest. Oblivious to the leaping of her heart, he mused in a low, husky voice that made her want to kiss him passionately, "You wanted to see if it was as good as we both recalled."

"Yes," she replied in a strangled voice.

Seemingly in no hurry to leave until he had the answers he wanted, Sam tucked a hand behind her ear. "And was it?"

Lulu swallowed around the building tightness in her throat. "Physically, you know it was." She shoved her hands into the pockets of her sundress skirt. In an attempt to appear oh-so-casual, she leaned against the bulletin board decorated with pictures of family. Children, parents, grandparents, pets… The sum of which made her want him, and everything he offered, all the more.

"And emotionally?" His gaze dropped to her lips and he came closer still.

She planted a hand on the center of his chest before she gave in to the temptation to kiss him again. "Whoa there, cowboy." She stepped aside. "I'm not going there."

Sam shrugged. And straightened. "We're going to have to eventually, if we plan to adopt the kids."

Wow. The man just didn't stop. But then, she remembered that about him, too. When he wanted something, he worked single-mindedly until he achieved his goal.

Her eyes widened. "If *we* plan to *adopt*?" she echoed.

Talk about acting impulsively and going way too far way too fast! Had the two of them exchanged personality flaws or what?

Shrugging, he straightened to his full six feet three inches. "You didn't think I'd be content to be just guardians forever. Did you?"

Honestly, she'd been so busy trying to keep pace with the swift moving events she hadn't given it any thought. Although in the back of her mind, she had always thought, if she were lucky enough to be given the chance to raise the kids, she would certainly adopt.

None of that meant, however, that she and Sam should rush into anything again. No matter how selfless the reason.

She folded her arms. "First of all, Sam, at this point, the boys are so young they don't know the difference between us being their guardians versus their adoptive parents."

"But they will, probably before we know it. And if we want to give them the most stable family possible, we should probably be married, too."

Of course he would throw in a matter-of-fact proposal. Sam was a get-things-done kind of person. He never put off for tomorrow what could be done right now.

The thing was, to her surprise, she could see them eventually deciding to get married, too, if it meant giving the three little boys more security.

Still, she had to make sure she and Sam were on the

exact same wavelength when it came to their future. That she wasn't jumping to erroneous conclusions. "And we would eventually do this as a convenience," she said, trying not to think what his steady appraisal and deep voice did to her.

"Yes. And a way to ensure sexual exclusivity."

Leave it to him, she thought with a mixture of excitement and exasperation, to spell it out when she would rather have left it undecided.

"Because you're right, Lulu," he continued in a way that seemed designed to curtail her emotional vulnerability. And maybe his, too. "If we're just living together, acting as guardians and taking care of the kids without having made a formal public commitment to each other, people will speculate about the state of our relationship."

And that could hurt the kids at some point down the road, Lulu realized.

"So, if we find we have needs…" She kept her eyes locked with his, even as her heart raced like a wild thing in her chest.

He squared his shoulders. "Then we satisfy them with each other."

It was certainly a practical, adult approach to what could be a very thorny situation. There was also no doubt they'd both lost the naivete that had once made them believe in fairy-tale romance and happy endings.

Even so, thinking about adoption and eventual marriage was a risk. One she wasn't sure she was ready to take, even if he wanted to go ahead and get everything settled. "What makes you think a marriage of convenience would work?" she challenged. Were they even really discussing this? "When our previous romance crashed and burned?" *Big-time.*

"There would be less pressure on us, as a couple and

a family, if you and I went into it from a practical stand-point, as friends and co-parents."

And less pressure, at least in his view, meant it might work.

"And maybe, at some point, lovers, too." Doing her best to protect them both, she went back to his previous point.

A corner of his mouth quirked. "Yes." He looked as pleased as she was by the prospect of never having to imagine each other with anyone else. His gaze drifted over her lovingly. "I could see that happening," he rasped, taking her hand and rubbing his thumb along the inside of her wrist, starting a thousand tiny fires. "Especially after what happened yesterday."

Lulu flushed. Their lovemaking had been spectacular. No question. All she had to do was think about what it had felt like to be with him again, and renewed need pulsed inside her. Pushing aside the lingering thrill, she cautioned, "We need to slow down, Sam. Take it one day, one step at a time."

He glanced at her, as if his heart were on the line, too. "But you'll think about it?" he pressed.

Was he kidding? She wouldn't be able to do anything but!

An hour and a half later, all three boys shouted and giggled as they bounced wildly up and down on the center of Lulu's queen-size bed.

"Whoo whee!"

"Jump!"

"Me fun!"

Keeping watch to make sure the boys remained somewhat contained and didn't tumble off the mattress, Sam asked, "Can I help you?"

Lulu could tell he wanted her to go faster. It wasn't easy to pack when she was so completely distracted.

"Yes," she said, getting a handful of frilly bras and panties from her drawer and stashing them as unobtrusively as possible in the duffel she had looped over her arm. Noting Sam's glance tracking a silky burgundy thong hanging over the side, she hastily stuffed it out of sight. In an effort to direct his attention elsewhere, she inclined her head toward the boys. "Make sure they don't fall off and land on their heads."

"Okay, guys, settle down a little bit. We don't want anyone getting hurt."

The triplets responded by hopping around even higher.

Lulu sighed. What was it about guys and danger?

"I've got this," Sam said, scooping them up into his arms. "Time to sing the monkey song!"

The boys, who'd been hyperactive since their expression of grief earlier in the day, paused. All three tilted their head at Sam.

He sat down on the bed and gathered them onto his lap. "Everybody knows the monkey song," Sam said. He sang, "One little monkey jumping on the bed. He fell off and bumped his head. Momma called the doctor and the doctor said…" he wagged his finger in theatrical admonishment "…no more monkeys jumping on the bed!"

The boys began to grin. Clearly, they'd heard this children's song before.

He glanced over at her. "You could join in."

Still gathering shirts, shorts, pajamas and the occasional summer dress or skirt, Lulu winked at the guys in her life and, as requested, added her voice to Sam's baritone. "Two little monkeys…"

The boys chimed in, too, their words and tune garbled and mostly nonsensical but cute.

To Lulu and Sam's mutual relief, the switch in activity helped bring about much needed calm. They were up to ten monkeys by the time Lulu had what she needed for the rest of the week in two clothes baskets.

"Sure that's all?" Sam asked when she showed him what he would need to carry down to her Lexus for her while she shepherded the boys outside.

"Yep."

He quirked a brow.

She knew what he was thinking. If she was really moving in, she should be taking a lot more with her. For lots of reasons she preferred not to examine too closely, she needed to keep one foot out the door. Leaving the majority of her summer clothes at the Honeybee Ranch would accomplish that.

That evening, they closely followed their nighttime routine. Dinner, bath and then, at long last, story time. With Lulu and Sam sitting side by side on the sofa and all three boys sprawled across their laps, they read a few of the favorite tales. Then injected the book Kate Marten-McCabe had given them, about children whose parents had gone to heaven.

The boys listened, but did not seem to connect it to Peter and Theresa or themselves.

Sam and Lulu continued reading, alternating stories, until the boys fell asleep, then carried them one by one upstairs to their toddler beds.

With the boys asleep, Sam went to take Beauty out while Lulu stayed nearby, putting her things away. Shortly after Sam returned, the boys awakened. And once again, Sam and Lulu walked the floor with them, only to end up for the rest of the night snuggled with all five of them together in Sam's big bed, Beauty sleeping on the floor next to them.

The following morning, as per Kate's advice, they went into town and formally enrolled the boys in preschool, from nine to one o'clock every day.

"So what's next on the list Kate gave us?" Sam asked as they walked out of the preschool.

Relieved the drop-off had been so easy and feeling a lot like the co-parents they aspired to be, Lulu fell into step beside him. "We need to find a way to help the boys remember Peter and Theresa."

Sam matched his long strides to her shorter ones. "All their belongings are in the boxes in my attic."

Lulu pushed aside the dread she felt at having to tackle such an emotional chore. They had to do this for the kids. "Want to go have a look?"

He nodded.

Like the rest of Sam's home, the third floor of the ranch house was clean, well lit and spacious. They pulled the boxes to the rug on the center of the wood floor and wordlessly began going through them, finding clothes of Theresa's and Peter's. A huge cache of old photos. Theresa's perfume. Peter's aftershave. Photos of their Memphis elopement.

"Here's a few with us in the picture, too," Sam said thickly. He handed over a photo of the four of them. The guys were in suits and ties, the gals in pretty white spring dresses. The guys wore boutonnieres, the girls carried bouquets.

"We were so young," Lulu murmured.

"And happy and idealistic," Sam said, studying their smiling faces.

If only they could have stayed that way, Lulu thought wistfully. But they hadn't, so...

She handed the photo back to Sam. And took out another. This one of Peter and Theresa at the hospital with their three newborns. Their first Christmas, the boys' first and second birthdays. One from Easter that year, which had to have been taken just before Theresa and Peter's death. A folder of the children's artwork from school. Another with newspaper articles detailing the eight-car pileup on the Houston freeway during morning rush hour that had killed them and seriously injured a dozen others.

Suddenly, the loss was too much. The grief hit Lulu hard, and she began to cry.

"Hey," Sam said, folding her close. After reading the articles, his eyes were wet, too. "Hey…" He stroked a hand through her hair. "I've got you…"

Needing the comfort only he could give, she snuggled into the reassuring safety of his strong arms. "Oh, Sam," she sobbed. "This is all just so unfair!" Her chin quivering, tears still streaming down her face, she struggled to get her emotions under control. "How are we ever going to fill the void their parents' deaths have left?"

Sorrow etched the handsome contours of Sam's face. "The only way we can," he countered, cupping her face between his big hands. "By taking it one day, one moment at a time. And becoming a real family in every possible way."

Lulu thought of the boys' meltdown the previous day, their sad little faces, the heartrending sounds of their sobs when they awakened at night.

"But what if we fail them?" she asked, knowing she'd never been so scared and so overwhelmed. "The way we once failed each other?"

Chapter Ten

"We're not going to fail them, darlin'," Sam said.

The depth of her despair only made her look more vulnerable. He wiped away her tears, cuddling her even closer. Still caging her loosely in his arms, he gently kissed her temple. "We never fail when we're together. It's only when we split up that we make a mess of things."

For a brief second, she seemed to take his assertion at face value. Then worry clouded her eyes. "I wish I shared your confidence."

But she didn't. She didn't believe in herself. In him. Or in the two of them.

So he showed her the only way he could what an excellent team they made. Determined to convince her, he lowered his mouth to hers and delivered a deep and sensual kiss. As he hoped, she opened herself up to his embrace just as swiftly. Wreathing her arms about his neck, she let out an involuntary moan and curled against him. Returning the hot, riveting kiss again and again and again. Blood rushing hot and needy through his veins, he slid his hands beneath her shirt and her nipples pearled against the centers of his palms.

"Oh, Sam," Lulu whispered, as he trailed kisses along the shell of her ear, down the nape of her neck. The tears she'd shed still damp across her face.

She whimpered, another helpless little sound that sent his senses swimming even more. Aware he had never wanted a woman as much as he wanted her, he deepened the kiss. Her mouth was pliant beneath his, warm and sexy, her body soft, surrendering. And still they kissed, sweetly and languidly, hotly and passionately, slowly and tenderly. Until worries faded and pleasure reigned.

Not about to take advantage, though, Sam reluctantly drew back. "Now's the time," he teased, looking deep into her eyes. "Tell me to stop." He caressed the damp curves of her lip with his fingertip. "Or go."

Her turquoise eyes smoldered. "Go," she said, smiling and taking him by the hand and leading him down the stairs, away from everything that had been so upsetting, to her bedroom. She shut the door behind them. She plucked a brand-new box of condoms from the nightstand drawer.

"Definitely go." She shimmied out of her skirt. Drew her blouse off, too.

"Gotta say," he drawled, enjoying the view of her in a peach bra and panties set, knowing she had obviously planned ahead. "I like the way this is going." The fact she'd known, just as he had, that despite all the problems still facing them, they would make love again.

She toed off her sandals. "Good." She motioned toward his clothes. "Your turn, cowboy."

Appreciating the reckless, sexy side of her, he stripped down to his boxers.

Her delicate brow lifted. "Keep going."

He didn't need to glance down to know he was getting pretty far ahead of her. "Ah…sure?"

Mischief and her typical zest for life sparkled in her smile. Tilting her head to one side, she gave him a lusty once-over. "Mmm-hmm."

"What the lady wants." He obliged and saw her eyes go wide.

Rationally, Lulu knew they shouldn't be making love again, at least not so soon, when the last time he'd been so casual, and she'd felt so inexplicably conflicted, afterward. But for now, as she sauntered toward him, took him in her arms and kissed him again, all she could think about was how much every one of them had been through in such a brief span of time, how short life was. How unpredictable. The only thing she could count on, besides this very moment they were in, was how good she felt whenever she was with him. How grateful that they had found each other again.

With a low murmur of appreciation, Sam stopped kissing her long enough to ease off her bra and panties. Her hands rested on his shoulders while he helped her step out. Still kneeling, he savored the sight of her, then kissed her most sensitive spot. She quivered, clinging to him like a lifeline, aware that she was on the brink.

He left her just long enough to retrieve a condom and then roll it on. Then he settled her against the wall. She wrapped her legs around his waist and they were kissing again. Touching. Caressing. Finding and discovering every pleasure point.

She was wet and open. He was hot and hard. So hard.

And then there was no more waiting. He surged inside her and she welcomed him home. All was lost in blazing passion and overwhelming need. Pleasure spiraled. Soared. And then they floated blissfully down into a satisfaction unlike anything she had ever known.

Afterward, they clung together, still pressed up against the wall, their bodies still entwined and shuddering with release. Eventually, he let her down. Sam kissed her shoulder tenderly as her feet touched the floor, and she continued leaning up against him, snuggled into the warm, strong embrace of his arms. "Feeling better?" Sam asked.

Suddenly realizing that she and Sam and their three little boys might comprise the perfect family after all, Lulu murmured against his shoulder, "Always, when we make love."

"Same here." Sam gave her another angel-soft kiss, then drew back just far enough to see her face. "Anything else on your mind?"

"I was thinking about what you said, about us never failing when we're together."

He tucked a strand of hair behind her ear. "It's true."

Lulu thought about what else she had learned from growing up McCabe. Mindful of the time, she eased away from him and began to dress. "When you add the reality that the foundation of every happy family is the relationship of the couple at its heart." She drew a deep, bolstering breath, as she shimmied into her panties. "It makes sense that we need to be united in every way we can be."

Sam pulled on his boxers and stepped behind her to help her fasten her bra. Grinning, he said, "Including bed?"

Lulu sighed luxuriantly. "Definitely including bed. Though I'm still not sold on the two of us actually getting married in order to make that happen," she cautioned candidly while she pulled on her blouse.

Sam tensed, as if an old wound was reopened. "Because you don't want to be married to me?"

Lulu flushed self-consciously, warning herself she had nothing to feel guilty about as long as she was being completely honest with him. "Because I don't think that legal formality is even necessary these days," she clarified.

An indecipherable emotion came and went in Sam's eyes.

"But," she went on with heartfelt enthusiasm, "I am definitely on board with co-adopting the children with you." She paused to look him in the eye. "And I want to start that process as soon as possible."

To get things moving, Sam called their attorneys that same afternoon. Liz and Travis agreed to meet with Lulu and Sam the following day while the triplets were in preschool. Their two attorneys listened while Sam and Lulu outlined their plans, occasionally exchanging lawyerly looks and appearing concerned about the speed with which Lulu and Sam had reached their decision.

"Travis and I understand you want to protect the triplets," Liz said gently. "But there is a big difference between being co-guardians and adoptive parents, at least in terms of the court."

"Meaning?" Lulu asked nervously.

Sam reached over and squeezed her hand. A week ago, Lulu would have pulled away. However, today, feeling like they were members of the same family unit, she relaxed into his reassuring grip.

Both their attorneys noticed. Sobering all the more, Travis said, "To become a guardian, when you've been named by the parents in their will, is a fairly simple matter. You express a willingness to do so, papers are signed, and it's a done deal. Unless of course, there is some obvious reason why it shouldn't happen."

"But when you petition to adopt," Liz continued where her husband left off, "you have to complete a formal application and petition the court, undergo home studies and background checks."

"What are they looking for?" Sam asked.

Liz spread her hands. "Any signs of potential problems. Or instability."

"You mean mental instability?" he asked, perplexed.

"Or personal," Liz explained. "Like if someone's had multiple marriages or ones that only lasted a day, has been consistently fired from or quit their jobs, things like that…"

Lulu froze.

Travis jumped in. "Everything is looked at. Your finances, your family histories, your lifestyle. You have to provide character references and show proof of any marital history or divorce. It's a lot to undergo. Particularly when you already have your hands full just trying to acclimate the kids to their new circumstances."

Liz lifted a soothing hand. "It's not that we're expecting anything problematic to come up."

Unable to prevent herself from worrying, Lulu tried to figure out how to ask the question without revealing what she was really stressed about. "But what if it did? What if there were, I don't know, say, unpaid parking tickets? Or a noise violation?" *Or other evidence of reckless behavior.* "From years ago?"

Sam turned to look at Lulu. Poker-faced, but concerned.

"Then we'd address it," Liz said soothingly.

"But of course it would be better if we knew about any

potential issues before making any formal application or getting social services involved," Travis said.

"Agreed." Sam suddenly looked every bit as on edge as Lulu felt. Still, he sounded calm when he added, "Which is why we should probably go ahead and have your law firm do complete background checks on both of us. Just so we can see what does come up, and if there is anything, deal with it."

"I agree with Sam." Lulu did her best to mimic Sam's laid-back attitude.

Liz and Travis seemed a little surprised by their request, but readily agreed.

Trying not to look at Sam, for fear she would give away what it was they were both trying like hell to hide, Lulu asked, "How long will it take?"

Travis shrugged. "Depends on how far back you want our investigator to go."

"As far back as they can," Sam said. He was no longer looking at Lulu, either.

Travis made a note on the legal pad in front of him. "Probably seven to ten days."

"Relax." Liz smiled. She got up to walk them out. "Knowing the two of you and your squeaky-clean reputations, I'm sure it will be fine."

But would it? Given Lulu and Sam's rocky romantic past?

Sam looked over at her as they left their attorneys' office. "I think we need to talk."

"I agree."

They walked over to The Cowgirl Chef and picked up a couple of cold drinks—a mocha frappé for her and a black iced coffee for him—and then headed for the park in the center of town. As they moved across the grass toward one of the benches in the shade, Lulu sent him an anxious glance. "Do you think that what happened in Tennessee is likely to come up?"

Sam sat down beside her and draped his arm along the back of the bench. He kept his voice low as she settled beside him. "No idea if it will or not, darlin', since there was never any follow-through on our part and therefore nothing put on record. But it will probably be good to know for sure."

Lulu worked her straw back and forth between her fingertips. "What about my business? The theft I just had?" She took a long sip of her drink, then dropped her hand and ran her fingertip along the hem of her pretty cotton skirt. It had ridden up above her knee and showed several inches of bare, silky skin. "Will that make me look irresponsible for not having had a security system installed on the property?"

He moved his gaze upward, past the scoop-necked knit top cloaking her slender midriff and the swell of her breasts, to the flushed pink color in her face. She had put her honey-brown hair up in a neat knot on the back of her head before the meeting. She looked beautiful and kissable and frustrated as all get-out. He moved his hand from the back of the bench to cup her shoulder gently.

"It's Laramie County, Lulu. We don't usually need security systems here since pretty much everyone who resides here is honest and neighborly. The court will understand that."

She shifted toward him, her bare knee brushing up against his jean-clad thigh. "Yes, but will they understand I haven't decided whether or not I even want all my bees back?"

"The court will probably want to know what your plans are in that regard. If you decide not to work, at least for now in order to take better care of the kids, I'm sure the court would be okay with that. Especially since we can well afford to take care of them on my income alone."

Lulu met his eyes, then shifted forward again. "I know but I really don't want to look like a dilettante. And we both know, during college and for a couple years after, I was pretty flighty."

Sam liked the idea of her leaning on him, even if it was just for moral support. "And you worked through that and built a business to be proud of. I really don't see it as a problem."

Shame flushed her cheeks. "I really don't want anyone to find out about the choices we made on spring break."

"Hopefully, they won't."

Lulu crossed her arms beneath the soft curves of her breasts and took another sip of her coffee. "And if they do?"

He paused, taking in the anxious twist of her lips. Unlike her, he didn't regret what they had done, not then and not now, just how they had let it end. But he had been older at the time of what she had once referred to as Their Big Mistake.

He squeezed her shoulder. Knowing he would do whatever he had to do to protect her, he leaned down to whisper in her ear. "Then we'll deal with it, Lulu. The best way we know how."

"Well, there's one good thing about having the kids in preschool five half days a week," Lulu said the following morning. They'd returned to the ranch after drop-off, ready to tackle that day's To Do list. "It gives us time to do the things we couldn't do otherwise."

Sam followed her up to the second floor. "Which would normally be sleep," he joked.

"No kidding." Lulu walked into the boys' room, where the beds were still unmade. She reached for the covers on one bed. Sam, another. "I never thought I'd want just *one* solid night of shut-eye so badly."

Looking sexy as could be in a T-shirt and jeans, he arranged blankets and stuffed animals against the pillows. "That's what being a parent is all about, isn't it?" He straightened and waggled his eyebrows at her. "Losing sleep? For the best possible reason?"

To comfort them. And each other. Speaking of which… Lulu glided into Sam's arms. Hugged him fiercely. "I love those little guys."

Squeezing her back, he rasped, "So do I." They stayed that way another long moment. Sam stole a few kisses, as Lulu knew he would. Then gave her another long, affectionate hug. "Now, if we could just figure out how to get them sleeping through the night, in their own bed," he murmured against her hair.

Lulu thought for a moment. "Maybe it would help if we set up their bedroom more like it used to be. We have photos." She went to get some.

Sam studied the layout with her. "Definitely worth a try."

Together, they shifted the three toddler beds from the U shape they had been in, with the beds pushed up along the sides of the bedroom, into a neat dormitory-style row, with all the headboards against the same wall. They took the rocker glider out of the corner, as well as the box of toys, and put both out into the upstairs hall for later rearranging.

Hands on her hips, Lulu studied their handiwork, lamenting, "They won't be able to play in here at all."

Sam moved behind her. He wrapped his arms around her and rested his chin on the top of her head. "Well, maybe that was the idea," he said, bringing her softer form back against his hard body. He pressed a kiss into the top of her hair, the shell of her ear. "Theresa and Peter wanted their bedroom to be a dedicated sleeping space and nothing more."

"Maybe." Lulu leaned against Sam another long moment, then went over to stack their bedtime storybooks on top of the room's lone bureau containing their clothing. Among them was the one Kate Marten-McCabe had given them.

Sam frowned, and, as was happening more and more these days, seemed to read her mind. "I know the grief specialists said reading this to the kids would help," he ruminated, "but I get the feeling they think it's just another story, and one they don't really want to hear."

"I know what you mean." Lulu sighed. "I don't think they make the connection between their own grief and the loss the little boy and girl in the storybook experience."

Sorrow clouded Sam's eyes. "Me, either."

For a long moment, neither of them spoke.

"Maybe it will come in time," he offered finally.

"And maybe," Lulu said, knowing they needed more than hope, they needed action, "what we really need is a book about the boys and their journey."

Crinkling his brow, he walked over to look at the book she was holding. "You mean superimpose their pictures and names in this storybook?"

"Actually, I think we should go one better." Lulu gestured for Sam to follow her and walked into the guest room she was using, where she had stashed several of the boxes of old photos and mementos.

"Maybe we should put together a story about Peter and Theresa. How they fell in love. Had the triplets. And all lived together happily. And then there was an accident. Their parents went to heaven. The boys went to stay with a number of other people. Before they ended up with the two of us and Beauty."

Sam ran his palm across his jaw. "So they would understand."

Eager to get him fully on board with the idea, she clamped her hands on his biceps. "Maybe we could end it with them blowing kisses at their parents in heaven, and their parents looking down on them, happy they are okay. So they can see there is still, and will always be, some connection."

"That could work." Sam grinned down at her, his enthusiasm building.

"It *will* work," Lulu said. Happy she and Sam were becoming such a good team, she rose on tiptoe and kissed his cheek.

He squeezed her waist affectionately. "Then let's get to it!" he said.

Lulu downloaded self-publishing software that helped her write and format the custom story that evening, after the kids were asleep, while Sam sorted through the photos, selecting the ones she needed.

Together, they put the book together, and while it would never make bestseller status, it did explain with words and pictures how many people loved the triplets and how they had come to live at Hidden Creek Ranch.

They printed it out, took it into town the following day to have it laminated and bound at the copy shop, and read it to them that evening after their baths. Sam and Lulu sat together with the three boys sprawled across their laps, the homemade storybook held out in front of them.

"Again," Theo said enthusiastically when Lulu had finished.

Ethan pointed to the photos of Theresa and Peter. "Mommy," he said. "Daddy!"

Andrew leaned his head on Sam's shoulder. "Heaven," he murmured.

Beauty, who had been stretched out at their feet, sat up. As she looked from one triplet to another, she seemed to be offering comfort and condolence.

The only problem was, all three boys wanted to take the new book to bed with them. To the point where there was almost a free-for-all.

"Hang on, guys," Lulu said, rushing off. She returned with a photo of Peter and Theresa for each of them. "Would you like to sleep with these tonight?" she said.

Three little heads nodded.

"Okay, then, up you go." Sam picked up Ethan and Andrew. Lulu hefted Theo in her arms. They went up the stairs.

Although the new bedroom arrangement hadn't done much to relax the boys the night before, they weren't giving up. Lulu put on a CD of lullabies she had found in one of the moving boxes. As the soft orchestral music filled the room, the boys perked up, listening, then snuggled down on their pillows, photos, stuffed animals and blankets in their arms.

Sam sat, his back to the wall, between beds one and two, while Lulu planted herself between beds two and three.

The boys continued listening. Child by child, eyes shuttered closed.

Sam and Lulu turned on the monitor and eased from the room.

"We should do more of this," she whispered. "Helping them remember, like Kate suggested. I think it really might help."

Sam took her hand and led her down the hall. He bussed her cheek. "Maybe you and I should do some re-membering, too."

Chapter Eleven

"What are we going to be remembering?" Lulu asked, her heart fluttering in her chest. The look in his eyes was so incredibly romantic!

Sam walked into his bedroom, shut the door and turned on the monitor on the bedside table. Then, pivoting back to her, he lifted her up, so she was sitting on his bureau, arms wrapped around his neck, his strong, hard body ensconced in the open V of her legs. The insides of her thighs rubbed the outsides of his. "Our first date," he murmured.

She trembled as his palms molded her breasts through the knit of her shirt and the lace of her bra, his thumbs rubbing over the tender crests. His mouth hovered above hers and Lulu felt herself surge to life.

"Our first kiss," he whispered as their lips met in a melding of want and need.

Yearning spiraled through her and she ran her hands

through his hair, giving back, meeting him kiss for kiss. The feel of his mouth on hers imbuing her with the kind of love she had wanted all her life. The kind of love only he could give.

She kissed him passionately, adoring the way his tongue stroked hers, once and then again and again, all while he never stopped touching her. Caressing her breasts, the curve of her hips, cupping her buttocks in his palms, before moving around to trace the lines of her pelvic bones and the sensitive area between her thighs.

Aware it was her turn, Lulu reached between them to unclasp his belt. Dropping hot kisses along his neck, she slid her hand inside his jeans. Felt the velvety heat and hardness, even as his mouth moved on hers in a way that was shattering in its possessive sensuality. "The first time I touched you," Lulu whispered, when they finally came up for air.

He found his way beneath her panties. "And the first time I touched you."

Deciding it was time they both got naked, she lifted his shirt over his head and tossed it aside. Taking a moment to admire him, she let her glance sift over his bare chest. His skin was golden and satiny smooth, covered with curling tufts of golden-brown hair that spread across his pecs, before angling down toward his navel. Lower still, his hardness pressed against the front of his jeans. "The first time we were together all night, in Tennessee."

Sam grinned, recalling. He helped her off with her shirt, bra, skirt. "If I could do that entire trip over, I would."

Lulu lifted up enough so he could dispense with her panties. "So would I," she admitted huskily, as the rest of his clothing followed suit. He came back to her once again, and she wound her arms about his neck. "But I'd make sure we had a different ending this time." One rife with love and tenderness, instead of heartbreak and anger.

Sam smiled over at her in a way that made her feel beautiful inside and out. He tucked an errant strand of hair behind her ear. "We may not be able to go back in time and have a do-over," he said, kissing her thoroughly and claiming her as his. "But we can certainly put all our mistakes behind us and start fresh again."

Lulu luxuriated in the feel of his mouth on hers. "I'd like that, Sam," she whispered back, pulling him close once again. "I really would…"

Sam knew Lulu was still afraid their reconciliation would turn out to be short-lived. But *he* knew better. He'd lost her once; he wasn't going to make the same mistake again. He set about showing her that he was in this for the long haul as they resumed kissing again, long and deep, soft and slow, sweet and tender.

She ran her hands over his back, across his hips. He luxuriated in the soft, silky feel of her. Caressing, exploring, entering and withdrawing in slow, shallow strokes that soon had her arching against him, clamoring for more.

And still they kissed. Taking up the rhythm he started. Until their breath caught and their hearts thundered in unison, and there was no more playing and delaying. She held fast, claiming him as he claimed her. Giving and taking everything. Tumbling into the sweet, hot abyss.

Afterward, they snuggled together, the aftershocks every bit as potent as their lovemaking had been. "This was nice." She sighed, looking utterly fulfilled as they moved from bureau to bed.

Aware he felt the same, he lay on his back. With her draped over top of him, her head nestled against his chest, he stroked a hand languidly down her spine. "Ah. You mean Sam-and-Lulu time?" he teased. Knowing he never wanted to be without her again.

She bantered back, "Where we see to our own...very adult...needs."

Realizing she looked for comfort from him as much as he yearned to receive it from her, Sam nodded. A contemplative silence fell. Moments drew out. He could feel Lulu drifting away from him, the way she usually did when her guard went back up, but he was determined not to let their closeness fade. "What are you thinking, darlin'?" Sam rasped, still enjoying how beautiful and utterly ravished she looked.

Lulu drew the sheet up over her breasts and rolled onto her side, facing him. Her honey-brown hair spilling over her shoulders, she rested her arm on the mattress and propped her head up on her hand. She met his gaze equably and drew in a bolstering breath. "That maybe we should just stop fighting our attraction to each other and accept it."

Glad she'd told him what was eating away at her, he traced the curve of her lips with his fingertip. "I haven't been fighting mine."

"I know." Their glances met, held. Her turquoise eyes sparkled ruefully. "But up to now, cowboy, I have."

How well he knew that! He took her free hand and lifted it to his mouth. Gently kissing her knuckles, he felt comfortable enough to ask, "Any particular reason why?"

She wrinkled her nose at him and let out a beleaguered sigh. "I just don't want either of us to be disappointed if things don't work out in the end."

The fact that she was beginning to feel the kind of heartfelt emotion that had drawn them to each other in the first place, in addition to the sizzling physical attraction that had always existed between them, made Sam very happy. To his frustration, however, beneath her outward pragmatism and acceptance, Lulu still seemed somewhat ambivalent.

Up one moment. And fully on board with their increasing intimacy. Wary—and down—the next.

"You don't sound deliriously pleased with the situation," he deadpanned, trying to make light of the maelstrom of emotions running through him.

"No, it's not that at all," Lulu explained. "I've just been trying really hard to keep our situation from becoming overly complicated." She shifted slightly, and the sheet moved lower, giving him a seductive glimpse of her breasts.

He felt himself grow hard again.

She raked her teeth across her lower lip and shyly admitted, "And I don't want us to have expectations of each other that we can't possibly meet, the way we did before."

He could see why she didn't want them to be disappointed in each other. Again. But it bothered him that she always expected less of them than they were capable of giving.

Still, this was progress. It was the first time they'd made love that she had expressed acceptance instead of worry or regret, at least since they had come together to care for the triplets.

"So." She waggled her brows at him mischievously, looking happy and relaxed again. "As long as this is good...for the both of us..."

"We can make love however, whenever, wherever you want," Sam promised her gently, folding her close. And as her body began to respond to the urgency of his, he made love to her all over again.

Saturday morning, Lulu and Sam attended the grief group for parents of orphaned children. As was her custom with new attendees, psychologist Kate Marten-McCabe asked them to stay after for a few minutes. "So how are things going?" the silver-blond therapist asked.

"Better." Lulu explained what they had done thus far to help the children remember their parents.

"The storybook sounds wonderful." Kate smiled.

"We still can't get them to spend the night in their own beds though," Sam said.

"Although we did get them to actually go to sleep in their beds last night," Lulu added.

"It'll come," Kate promised, and then gave them a few more tips.

"Kate's right," Lulu's brother Jack said. Sam, Lulu and the triplets had stopped by his home for lunch and an afternoon playdate with his three little girls and Jack's old friend, rehab nurse Bess Monroe. "Progress does come. But it's often in infinitesimal degrees."

"Are you trying to encourage me or discourage me?" Lulu joked while making lunch with Bess. Her famous honey-grilled chicken salads for the adults, PB&J and apple slices for the kids.

Sam and Jack stood in the doorway of the kitchen and kept an eye on the six nicely playing kids. "I'm just saying the sleep thing is a hard thing to work out," Jack retorted, sadness creasing his face.

Concerned, Lulu went over to hug her brother. His surgical skills were legendary among the returning veterans that he and Bess both helped. However, he was not so great at dealing with the grief left by the death of his wife, Gayle.

Lulu stepped back to take him in. "Are you okay?"

"It's Father's Day," Bess put in.

Jack shot her a massively irritated look.

She raised both hands. "Well, it is. You get like this every year."

Lulu turned back to Jack. "Why would this make you sad? Your children love you! I'm sure they made you gifts at school."

"They do and did," Bess put in.

Pushing aside his usual stoicism, Jack said thickly, "It's just that Father's Day reminds me of Mother's Day. Which makes me think about Gayle. And all the holidays she's never going to celebrate with us."

Lulu understood, and she knew Sam did, too. Her eyes suddenly glistening, Bess slipped from the room. She disappeared down the hall and into the bathroom. Which was no surprise, Lulu noted, since Bess and Gayle had been very good friends.

Lulu wrapped Jack in another consoling hug. "I miss her, too," she admitted, tears welling.

Sam walked over to clap Jack on the shoulder. "We all do. She was a real force of nature."

A recuperative silence fell.

Seconds later, Bess emerged. Her nose was red and her eyes too bright, but she had a cheerful smile plastered on her face. Completely ignoring what had just happened, she asked, "What do you all think? Should we eat lunch inside or outside?"

The rest of the afternoon went pleasantly. Mostly because the kids played well and the adults avoided talk of anything the least bit sensitive or uncomfortable.

As they were getting the kids ready to leave, Jack took Lulu and Sam aside. "About the nighttime travails… My only advice is to comfort them when they wake and then always put them back in their own beds for the remainder of the night, even if it means you're stretched out on the floor next to them, so they get the idea that *their* beds are for sleeping, not yours. Unless it's very special circumstances, like they're running a fever or there's a big thunderstorm or something."

"And that works?" Lulu asked as Bess came to stand next to Jack.

Jack smiled. "It does."

The events of the day stayed with Lulu.

On the way back to Hidden Creek, Lulu said to Sam, as casually as possible, "Hey. What do you think about stopping by the Honeybee and letting me and the kids off for a few minutes, and then you going and getting lost for, oh, an hour or so?"

He slanted her a quick glance. Clad in his usual snug jeans, custom-fitted boots and solid-colored cotton shirt, he looked so ruggedly masculine and handsome it was enough to make her go weak in the knees. "You serious?"

She shrugged and checked out the kids in the rear-view mirror. They were all wearing their bucket hats and sunglasses, looking cute as could be, and were surprisingly wide-awake. "You must have some stuff to check on at your ranch."

"Tons."

Which was no surprise, Lulu thought. Since they'd taken custody of the triplets, Sam had been all kids, all the time.

He made the turn into the Honeybee Ranch and drove up to the house. He put the pickup in Park, then turned to look at her with a mixture of curiosity and affection. "You sure you can handle them by yourself?"

She was going to have to if she wanted to succeed with her secret plan. Lulu smiled. "Yep."

Sam reached over to cup her face in one hand. He rubbed his thumb across the curve of her cheekbone.

Said admiringly, "Your older brother sure did infuse you with confidence."

Tingling all over, Lulu smiled back at him. "And good ideas," she said mysteriously.

As Lulu expected, the boys were delighted to sit at her kitchen table and play with the kids' craft stuff that she kept for her preschool-age nieces and nephews when they visited. The triplets were covered with washable glue and glitter and colorful markers and still working on their "projects" when Sam came back an hour later.

"Surprise!" they shouted in unison. "Happy Day!"

They rushed at him, wet and sticky artwork in tow. "Here! For you! Sam!"

Looking surprised and touched, Sam hunkered down and wrapped them all in a hug. "You fellas did all this for me?"

For the second time that day, Lulu felt herself welling up. She edged closer to indulge in the group embrace. Knelt down. "Even though we're technically still guardians, they wanted you to know what a fabulous father figure you've become to them," she said hoarsely.

Sam wrapped an arm about her waist and drew her in close. He pressed a kiss to the top of her head. "Right back at you, darlin'."

One day, they would be Mommy and Daddy. But for now, Lulu thought, returning Sam's warm hug and cuddling the boys, this life they'd fashioned was more than enough.

Chapter Twelve

"Congratulations." Lulu toasted Sam three days later.

Aware how right it all felt, having her and the boys in his home, he clinked his coffee mug against hers. Who would have thought the five of them could become a family so fast? Or that mornings would become so blissful? "To you, too, darlin'."

"Can you believe it?" she whispered. Fresh from the shower and clad in yellow linen shorts, a striped tee and sneakers, she looked pretty and ready to take on their day. "The boys spent the whole night in their beds!"

His gaze drifted over her appreciatively. She'd put on makeup sparingly. Damp honey-brown hair twisted in a knot on the back of her head, she smelled of the citrus-and-flowers shampoo and soap she favored. Lower still, he could see her sleek and sexy legs.

Doing his best to tamp down his desire and focus on the conversation at hand, he lingered next to her. Enjoying their camaraderie, he leaned over to buss the top of her head and reminded her, "We did have to go back in and sit propped against the wall next to them, twice, to get them to fall back asleep."

"I know," she acknowledged. As she shifted toward him, the soft swell of her breasts rubbed against his arm. She stepped back to gaze up at him, and the absence of her touch had him feeling bereft. "But they stopped crying almost immediately and we didn't have to pick them up and walk the floor with them to calm them down. All we had to do was reassure them."

He nodded with a depth of parental satisfaction that surprised him and set his coffee mug aside. "It was a lot better than it ever has been."

She put her own mug down, then splayed her hands across his chest. "Jack's advice is really working."

He wrapped his arms around her waist and tugged her so they were touching in one long, tensile line. Burying his face in her hair, he thought of all they'd managed to accomplish in just under two weeks. Then murmured, "A lot of things are really working out."

She drew back. Smiling, she looked up at him as if she were tempted to kiss him. Would have, if not for the three little boys playing in the adjacent room.

Later, he promised himself.

They would make up for lost time. And when they did, she would understand how much she meant to him.

As she gazed up at him, a wealth of feelings was in her eyes. He realized he had never seen her looking so happy. "Oh, by the way." She snapped her fingers. "I almost forgot. It's show-and-tell at the preschool this morning."

"They have that for two-year-olds?"

Lulu slipped out of the loose circle of his arms. She grabbed the three insulated lunch sacks they'd purchased for the boys, then opened up the fridge, removed three drinks and three premade PB&J sandwiches. Before he could get there to assist, she closed the door with a sexy swivel of her hip.

"Half the kids in their group are nearly three," she said.

"Oh. Right." Knowing they needed individual packs of graham crackers and dried fruit the boys were convinced was candy, Sam got those out of the pantry and added them to the bags. Noting what a good team they made, he went to get the school backpacks, too.

"Anyway." Lulu paused to match the lunch bags to the right backpacks. Finished, she and Sam zipped them all shut. "I talked to the kids yesterday after school, while you were out talking to your foreman, about what they were going to bring today to show their classmates."

Motioning for him to follow, she strode into the adjacent playroom. "Boys! Remember? It's show-and-tell today. So, do you want to get the toys you picked out?"

Three little heads tilted. They looked up at her, seeming slightly puzzled.

Sam sympathized. For a two-year-old, what happened yesterday might as well have been eons ago. They were usually so "in the moment."

Looking sweet and maternal, Lulu knelt to their level. Gently, she reminded them, "Ethan, you were going to take your stuffed panda bear. Andrew, you were going to take your Frisbee. And, Theo, you were going to take the wall you made with your snap-together building set."

The triplets turned to each other, once again communicating visually the way only multiples could. "No," they said firmly in unison.

All three went over to their beloved Saint Bernard,

who was sprawled out on the floor, as per usual, watching over them.

"Take Beauty!" they chorused.

"Ah, guys," Sam said reluctantly, hunkering down. He hated disappointing them. "I'm sorry," he informed them as kindly as he could. "But that's not possible."

"Take Beauty!" they shouted again.

Uh-oh, Sam thought, catching Lulu's warily astonished expression. They were headed for meltdown territory.

Wondering if there were any exceptions to be made, Sam tilted his head. "Are they permitted to bring pets into the preschool?" he asked Lulu.

Her cheeks pink with distress, she shrugged. "I don't know. Let me call and ask."

Sam stayed with the kids and got them involved in helping straighten their toys. A few minutes later, Lulu returned. "I spoke with their teacher, Miss Cece. Apparently, it is possible, as long as the pet is up to date on all their vaccinations, is good with kids and the visit is brief."

"How much advance notice do they need?"

"If you've got the right vet records, today is good."

"I do."

Lulu's grin widened. Looking extremely happy they hadn't had to disappoint the boys, she declared, "Well then, kids, looks like your best friend is going to school with you today."

"Yay!" The boys clapped and danced with excitement.

She made another phone call, confirming the visit. Because Beauty was so big and couldn't arrive until midmorning, Sam agreed to follow later and drive his dog separately. Anticipating they might need extra help, Lulu pledged to stay on in the classroom as a volunteer.

When the time came, Sam headed into town. He got there a little early, so he walked Beauty up and down the shady town streets. Pausing to give her water from her travel bowl and making sure she had time to take care of necessities. Finally, Lulu texted that they were ready.

Aware he was almost as excited as the kids, Sam entered the school, stopped by the front office to check in and say hello and then headed back down the hall.

The two-year-olds were buzzing with excitement. Their eyes widened when they saw the extremely gentle brown-and-white dog that stood twice as high as them.

Confessed dog lover Cece Taylor welcomed them into the classroom. The fifty-five-year-old educator directed Sam to take his pet to the open space next to the bulletin board. The rest of the kids sat cross-legged in a semicircle on the carpet.

"Okay, Theo, Andrew, Ethan," Miss Cece said. "Do you boys want to come up here and show us your dog and tell us about her?"

The boys stood importantly. Little chests puffed out, they walked up to Beauty.

"And who is this?" Miss Cece prompted.

"Beauty. Doggy," Theo explained.

"Soft. Pet." Ethan demonstrated how to stroke her fur.

"No ride," Andrew explained gravely, pointing at her back.

Miss Cece flashed an inquisitive look their way.

Sam told the assembled group, "Andrew is telling us we don't ever try to ride the doggy like a horse. Because that's not good. We can pet Beauty, though, because she really likes that."

Enthralled, the kids took this in.

"Are there any questions?" Miss Cece asked.

One of the older little girls in the class raised her hand. When called on, she pointed at Lulu. "Who is that?" she asked.

"And that?" Another child jumped in to point at Sam.

Sam bit down on an oath. A land mine. One that none of the adults in the room had expected. Luckily, the triplets were taking the queries in stride. All three boys grinned proudly.

Theo walked over to Lulu, who was seated on a small chair next to Beauty. He took her face in his hands. Gazed happily into her eyes. "Lulu. *Mommy*," he declared.

Was he calling Lulu Mommy? Sam wondered, barely suppressing a sharp inhalation of surprise and delight.

Andrew walked over to Sam. He motioned for Sam to bend down. When Sam did, Andrew took Sam's face in his hands. "Sam. *Daddy*," he said clearly.

Sam felt himself begin to mist up. He wasn't the only one, either. Lulu's eyes were moist with unshed tears, too.

Ethan walked over to stand between Lulu and Sam. He put one hand on each of them and then walked over to Beauty. He took the big dog's face in his hands. "Family," he said reverently, before taking another big breath and puffing out his little chest.

Andrew and Theo echoed the sentiment. Her lower lip trembling, barely stifling a sob, Lulu flashed a smile as wide as Texas. Tears streaming down her face, she engulfed all three little boys, then Beauty and then Sam, in hug after hug. "That's right, boys, Beauty, Sam and I are all part of your family now," she said huskily.

Not sure when he'd ever felt such joy, Sam swallowed the knot in his throat and embraced them all. The boys had been right. They were a family, and a darned good one. He swallowed around the lump in his throat and held them close.

Hours later, Lulu still felt herself welling up from time to time. To her satisfaction, Sam seemed overwhelmed with happiness, too. In fact, they were brimming with joy as they headed downstairs to finish the dinner dishes.

Lulu picked up where she'd left off an hour earlier. It had become clear their little darlings were in desperate need of their bedtime routine a good forty-five minutes earlier than usual. Which, as it happened, was a good thing, because the cuddling and storybook reading took longer and were rife with more mutual affection than ever.

Sighing contentedly, Lulu began loading the dishwasher. "Whoever said good things come when you least expect them was right."

The fabric of his shirt stretching across his broad shoulders and nicely delineating the muscles in his chest, Sam knelt to pick up green beans and potatoes from the floor. His snug jeans did equally nice things to his lower half.

Gold-flecked eyes twinkling, he slanted her a fond glance. "That was some show-and-tell, wasn't it?" he ruminated softly.

Finished, Lulu wiped down the counters. Sam took out the trash. When he came back, they both stood at the sink and washed their hands. Lulu ripped off a paper towel and handed him one. Now that they finally had a quiet moment alone, she asked what had been nagging at her. "Do you think they were trying to call us Lulu-Mommy and Sam-Daddy, or just explain what our role was in their lives?"

He came closer, gently cupped her face in his large, warm palms. "Both."

Lulu released an uneven breath. "I do love them."

He wrapped his arms around her, inundating her with his steady masculine warmth. "I do, too, sweetheart."

Aware how close she was to falling for him all over

again, she released a reluctant, admiring sigh. "And I think they're beginning to love and trust us."

The question was, when would she and Sam ever love and trust each other as much as they needed to, to have the kind of forever-family she still yearned for? Or would they? Had that window closed? If not for her, for him? And if it had, would it be okay if they were just really great friends and lovers and co-parents to three adorable little boys? Although she knew she was happy as is—wildly happy, in fact—the romantic side of her still wanted more, and that disappointed her. She didn't want to ruin everything by being greedy. They had so very much as it was.

Sam's cell rang. He glanced at the screen. Reluctantly stepped away from her and answered. "Hey, Travis," he said. "Thanks for returning my call."

He had called his attorney? And not mentioned it to her?

Oblivious to her shock, he continued speaking in his husky baritone, "I've got Lulu here with me, too, so I'm going to put you on speakerphone." Sam hit the button and set his cell on the counter in front of them.

Lulu and Travis exchanged greetings. Then Sam said, "We were wondering if there had been news about the background check yet."

Lulu tensed.

Travis replied, "I just talked with the private investigator. He's still tracking something down."

Oh no, Lulu thought.

Sam reached over to take her hand. Gave it a reassuring squeeze. "Any idea what he's looking at?" Sam asked his attorney.

Matter-of-factly, Travis replied, "Liz and I never discuss anything with our clients until we receive the final report. Otherwise, people can get upset for no reason other than records somewhere that weren't complete, or some such."

Sam wrapped his arm around Lulu's shoulders and drew her against his side. "Makes sense," he said. Seeming to understand her silence for the apprehension that it was, he continued, "I'm sure everything will be fine."

Maybe…or maybe not, Lulu thought, worried her and Sam's reckless actions in the past could come back to haunt them now.

"That's our assumption, too," Travis said. "Although…" his voice took on a teasing lilt "…Liz and I did hear what happened in preschool, Lulu-Mommy and Sam-Daddy."

Recalling, Sam and Lulu chuckled in tandem. It was all she could do not to tear up again. "It was definitely a moment," she said proudly.

"A moment that's apparently all over the school," Travis continued. "And since our kids are enrolled there, too, Liz heard about it when she went to pick our girls up. I have to tell you, stuff like that is really going to help your petition to adopt."

"Let's hope so," Lulu said.

It certainly helped her heart.

Hugging her close, Sam drawled, "Speaking of our plans to adopt. Any idea when we *can* expect the report from the investigator?"

"Early next week," his attorney said.

"Okay. Thanks, Travis." Sam ended the call. Satisfaction turned up the corners of his lips. "When we clear that hurdle, we'll be one step closer," he vowed.

Lulu bit her lip, still not so sure. "You really think we're going to be in the clear?" she asked nervously. "That no one will ever know what happened when we were in Tennessee?"

He rocked forward on the toes of his boots. "How could they? For there to be a record of it, there had to be follow-through on our part." His gaze drifted over her. "And we didn't...so there should be absolutely nothing standing in our way."

"And we'll be able to move forward with the adoption! Oh, Sam, it's really going to happen, isn't it?" Lulu threw her arms around his neck. "We're all going to be together! We're going to be a family."

"We really are. In the meantime, I'm thinking I'd like a shower." He fit his lips to hers and kissed her seductively. "Want to join me?"

She splayed her hands across his chest. Felt his heart beat in tandem with hers. "You're serious."

"As can be." He kissed her again, leisurely.

"Then so am I." She kissed him back, then took him by the hand and led him upstairs.

The master bath featured an old claw-foot tub that had been nicely refinished, two sinks and a large modern shower. They stripped down, each helping the other, and climbed in. And although it wasn't the first time they had showered together, it was the first time since they had gotten back together, and definitely the most exciting. Water sluiced down upon them from the rainfall shower fixture above.

They lathered each other from head to toe, taking their time, then stood together under the spray to rinse. Then kissed, fiercely and evocatively, until they were both trembling and groaning for more.

He turned her so she was facing the tile, and he slipped in behind her. One hand explored her breasts, the other moved across her tummy and downward. "So soft and sweet," he murmured against her ear.

She arched her throat, to give him better access. "So hot and hard…"

He laughed and brought her back around to face him. Moved her against the wall. And then they were kissing again, barely stopping to come up for air. Quivering with sensation, she felt her body surrendering all the more.

Sam exited the shower just long enough to get a condom, roll it on. He sank onto the bench built into the shower wall, then pulled her down so she was straddling his lap.

She was wet and open. He seemed intent on giving her what she needed. Kissing her deeply. Finding her with his fingertips, possessing her body and soul, until she felt his desire in every kiss and caress.

He loved her as an equal. As a friend. As a lover, and maybe, just maybe, something more. And she adored him, too. Opening herself up to him in a way she never had before. Celebrating the occasion and possessing him as well, with the tenderness and need and singularity of purpose they both deserved.

Afterward, as they cuddled together in bed, Lulu knew this was what it felt like when it was right, when her life was finally on the brink of being complete.

All she had to do was trust in fate. Trust in Sam. And the love that would bring their new little family together.

Chapter Thirteen

The rest of the week passed blissfully, and on Saturday morning, Sam made his famous blueberry pancakes while they all lounged around in their pajamas. Not surprisingly, the boys picked up on the lack of urgency. As if realizing they would normally be rushing around, looking for shoes and getting dressed, Theo cocked his head. "Me. School?"

Sam knelt down so they were eye to eye. He was still in loose-fitting pajama pants and a short-sleeved gray T-shirt. Thick wheat-colored hair rumpled and standing on end, morning-stubble rimming his jaw, he looked slightly on edge. Same as Lulu.

They'd made plans for that afternoon, but this morning it was going to be just the five of them again. That arrangement had not worked out well previously. They were hoping that the boys had been with them long enough that they wouldn't need the distraction of constantly playing with other children to make them happy. That the five of them would be able to feel like the complete family they aspired to be.

Sam smiled down at their little charges. If he was disappointed the boys were already starting to feel restless and on the verge of being unhappy, he did not show it. "Not today, fellas," he said soothingly. "It's Saturday."

Briefly, the boys looked as crestfallen as Sam and Lulu had feared they might be, upon learning there was no school that day. "But we can do other fun things," Sam said cheerfully, rising.

Like what? Lulu wondered. They hadn't discussed this. She moved close enough to feel his body heat. "What did you have in mind?" she asked.

The boys, already bored, wandered back to the play area in the reconfigured family room and began jumping on the sofa.

Keeping one eye on them, to make sure they didn't get too wild, Sam lounged against the counter. "There's a custom backyard play set company over in San Angelo. They've got an air-conditioned sales facility with all the different possibilities set up for kids and their parents to explore. I thought we all might mosey over there and let the boys run around and pick out a swing set for the backyard."

It would sure beat having them jump on and climb all over everything inside the ranch house, Lulu thought. Still… "That sounds like a pretty big investment." Were they getting ahead of themselves? They hadn't even cleared the background check.

Sam glanced over at the boys. They had abandoned the sofa and were now doing somersaults on the rug. He grinned and shook his head in amusement, as the gymnastics turned to a poorly executed game of leapfrog.

He turned back to Lulu. "And a very necessary one, when you think about the fact the closest playground is a good twenty minutes away by car. Convenient to us only when we're already in town."

Winded, the boys collapsed and, lying on their backs, began to talk gibberish among themselves.

Relaxing, Lulu took up a place opposite Sam. She let her gaze drift over the rugged planes of his face. "True."

He looked over at her, as protective as ever. "We're not tempting fate, darlin'." His gaze lingered briefly on her lips before returning to her eyes.

A spiral of heat swept through her, flushing her cheeks. "How did you know that was what I was thinking?" she asked, attempting to keep her mind on the mundane instead of the sizzling chemistry between them.

"That little pleat right here." Sam traced the line between her brows, just above her nose. He caught her around the waist and drew her all the way into his arms. "It always appears when you worry."

Lulu turned her head to check on the boys. Noting they were now calmly playing with their cars and trucks, and that it was safe to give Sam her full attention, she murmured, "I just wish I knew what the PI was still looking into."

"Like Travis said, it's probably nothing to worry about."

She swallowed around the ache in her throat. Aware she thought she'd had it all, one time, only to lose it all, just as swiftly. She released an uneven breath. "But if it is…"

His gaze gentled. "Then we'll fret when the time comes. Right now, we're going to have fun," he promised, a mischievous glint in his eyes. He flattened a soothing palm over her spine. "Otherwise the boys will worry, and we don't want them getting anxious."

She leaned into his reassuring touch, unable to help but think what a good husband and father he would be. "You're right. We don't."

As Sam had predicted, the triplets loved the sales facility. They raced from one sample play yard to another in air-conditioned comfort while Sam and Lulu simultaneously watched over them and checked out the outdoor equipment. The more time went on, the more content she felt.

"You have a beautiful family," the salesman said.

Looking as proud and happy as Lulu felt, Sam wrapped his arm around Lulu's shoulders. Gave her an affectionate squeeze. "We do."

Was this what their weekends would be like when it all did become official? Lulu wondered. Or would they be even better?

She only knew what she hoped.

And what Sam appeared to be counting on, too, she thought, tucking her hand in Sam's.

Together, they went to round up the boys. Eventually, they picked out a sandbox with plenty of room for driving excavators and dump trucks around and an A-frame swing set that held three swings. It came with toddler bucket seats for now, flexible plank-style child seats for later. They agreed that the climbing fort and slide could come later when the boys were big enough to safely handle both.

From there, they went to have dinner with Lulu's brother Matt, and his fiancée, Sara Anderson, and her son.

Although they had napped in the pickup truck, the

boys were tuckered out when they finally arrived home and went through the usual bath time routine.

"Stories!" Theo shouted as they headed for the big leather sofa.

Lulu picked up the stack of favorites, as well as their own homemade book about the changes in the boys' life. With her and Sam sitting cozily side by side and the triplets sprawled across their two laps, they took turns reading through the stack of familiar books. It all felt as comfy and family-oriented as usual, yet when they had finished, the boys looked surprisingly restless. "New. Story," Andrew demanded.

Were they getting bored with the same old tales? Apparently so. Lulu looked at Sam, wanting his input.

"They might have a point," he said, still snuggling close. "Since they do know all the endings."

Aware their bright and lively little boys might need more intellectual stimulation, Lulu suggested, "We could hit the library tomorrow afternoon."

Unfortunately, that did not seem to solve the immediate problem.

Ethan frowned in displeasure. "Story. *Beauty.*"

Not sure what the boys were talking about, although as usual all three seemed to be of the same mind-set, Lulu looked to Sam for help.

Taking her cue, he attempted to clarify. "You want to read a story about a doggy?"

"No. Beauty," Theo insisted vehemently.

"Story. Beauty," Andrew repeated.

Abruptly, it all clicked. "You want us to make our own storybook about Beauty, with pictures of her?" Lulu asked.

"Yay!" the boys shouted in unison.

She and Sam exchanged grins of relief. These were

the kinds of problems they could easily handle. "I think we can do that," she promised. Now that she had experience using the publishing software, it wasn't hard at all.

Pleased their wish was going to be granted, the boys headed to bed. That night, they fell asleep easily.

"I think we're getting a handle on this parenting thing," Lulu mused happily as she and Sam tiptoed from the room.

"I think we're getting a handle on a lot of things," Sam murmured, taking her in his arms and dancing her back toward her bedroom.

Wishing more than ever that the two of them had never called it quits, Lulu asked coyly, "Got something specific in mind, cowboy?"

Lulu was looking at him that way again. The way she once had years ago, every time they were together. The way that said she was his for the taking. But she hadn't been before, and wary of making the same mistake again by assuming too much too soon, he kept to the pace they had agreed upon and the deal they had made.

They were co-parents, first and foremost. Friends. And sometimes lovers.

Although the first time around, they had wanted to get married. Now she saw getting hitched as something to be avoided. He had to remember that.

Take it day by day, moment by moment. Night by night. So he pulled her into his arms. Bent his head to kiss her thoroughly. Showing her all he felt, all they could have, if only she would open up her heart.

Until she moaned deep and low in her throat, arching up against him, and kissed him back with even less restraint than he had shown.

"Beginning to get the idea?" he said. Taking her by the hand, he continued leading her down the hall to her bed.

Eyes glittering with anticipation, she swayed toward him, clearly wanting more. She pressed her lips to his. "Very much so," she whispered.

Prepared to be as relentless as he needed to be in pursuit of her, he drew her flush against him, so she could feel his hardness. He wanted her to know how much she excited him, and he wanted to arouse her, too.

"Because I want you," he ground out against her mouth. "So much…"

She hitched in a breath as they divested each other of their clothes. When they were naked, she murmured, "Oh, Sam, I want you, too…"

He laid her back on the bed, settling between her thighs, sliding lower. Caressing her with the flat of his palms, his fingertips, his lips. Studiously avoiding the part he most wanted to touch. Until she arched and made a soft, helpless sound that sent his desire into overdrive.

She caught his head between her trembling palms. He lifted her against his mouth, circling, retreating, moving up, in. Until at last she fell apart in his arms.

Burning with a need he could no longer deny, he took control of their mesmerizing embrace. Making it as hot and wanton as the kisses she was giving. Finding protection. Lifting and entering her with excruciating slowness and care, making her his in a way that had her surrendering against him. Reveling in the erotic yearning and sweet, hot need. Knowing that this night, this time, she was his, in a way she had never been before. And, if he had his way, always would be.

To Lulu's delight, Sam had plans for their little family Sunday afternoon, as well. Regarding her fondly, he said, "I thought we might drive around the ranch and go see the horses, cattle and cowboys. Then head over to Monroe's Western Wear to get tyke-size cowboy hats and comfy boots and jeans."

"Sounds good to me," she said, returning his affectionate glance. They were feeling more and more like a family with each passing day. So what if they hadn't said they loved each other? She and Sam might not be a traditional couple, but they were a team. And a very good one at that. It was going to have to be enough.

That night, they had dinner with Lulu's brother Cullen, his wife Bridgett and their son Robby. To Lulu's relief, neither her brother nor his new wife inquired into the status of Lulu and Sam's relationship. On the other hand, Beauty, who was back at Hidden Creek and absent from the gathering, was quite the center of focus. The Saint Bernard's name came up a lot while the triplets and eighteen-month-old Robby played with their family dog.

"Beauty. *Play*," Theo explained, petting the top of Riot's head.

"Beauty. *Friend*," Andrew added helpfully.

"Play. *Fun*," Ethan stroked the beagle mix's silky tri-colored fur.

In frustration, Theo turned to Sam and Lulu. "Beauty. Here?" he asked.

Abruptly, Lulu realized what the boys were asking, in their abbreviated way.

"I think they want the two of them to meet," Sam said.

Bridgett smiled. "We can probably make that happen."

And that swiftly, a new canine friendship was arranged.

That evening, the boys listened raptly to the new story about Beauty that Lulu and Sam had pulled together the previous night. They were delighted and insisted on hearing it not one but three times before Lulu finally called a halt.

"More," Andrew demanded earnestly, pointing to the storybook. *"New."*

His two brothers nodded. "Sam-Daddy," Ethan said, affectionately patting Sam's chest.

"Lulu-Mommy," Theo added, snuggling close.

"You want us to make a story about us?" Lulu asked.

The boys responded by getting up to give them great big hugs and smacking kisses. "Yay!" they shouted. More hugs followed. And then they reared back and said the words to both of them that Lulu had never expected to hear, at least not for a very long time.

Wrapping their arms around Lulu's and Sam's necks, in turn, they chorused, *"Me. Love. Sam-Daddy. Lulu-Mommy."*

"You can stop crying now," Sam teased two hours later. He and Lulu were putting the finishing touches on the story about themselves, complete with pictures from their current ranches and of themselves and the boys.

"Oh hush, cowboy! You've been welling up all evening, too."

He grinned, guilty as charged. He folded his arms across his broad chest. Tilting his head, he said thickly, "It was pretty great, wasn't it? To hear them try to tell us they loved us?"

Lulu's happiness increased a million fold. "It sure was."

A brief, contented silence fell. Aware she had never imagined being so happy, she reached over and took his hand. "Oh, Sam, I love them so much."

His eyes glistened once again. Using the leverage of

their entwined hands, he brought her closer. "Me, too. More and more each day."

The joyful tears Lulu had been holding back rolled down her cheeks.

"Ah, darlin'." Sam stroked a hand through her hair and pressed a kiss to her temple.

Her spirits soared as he shifted her onto his lap and went about showing her that the affection in the Thompson-Kirkland-McCabe household did not end with the kids and the family's adorable Saint Bernard.

For the first time in a very long time, Lulu felt her life was really and truly complete. Or at least very, very close to being so. Now, if only they'd get the go-ahead from their attorneys, so they could get the adoption process started!

"You want me to drive the kids to school this morning?" Sam asked her the next morning. Since the triplets had adapted to the new routine, it was no longer necessary for both of them to do the drop-off and pickup. They were now alternating.

But the rest of the day, they were still together. Or at least they had been for the last two and a half weeks. Lulu knew that, too, was going to have to end. They both had work responsibilities to honor. Speaking of which... she hadn't been doing as much as she should with hers.

Lulu bit her lip. Sighed. And felt warmth pool through her as she watched Sam's gaze devour her head to toe.

Trying not to think how much she'd like to spend the morning making love with him, Lulu said, "If you don't mind, I'd like to head over to the Honeybee Ranch this morning and tend my remaining hive."

"No problem," he said, his gold-flecked eyes twinkling. Telling herself he couldn't possibly have known what she was wishing, Lulu said goodbye to everyone, made sure the boys had their backpacks and lunches and then headed out herself.

As she drove onto her property, what had once been her sanctuary felt slightly alien. Definitely overly quiet, now that she no longer had honey to sell and customers coming in.

Even her food truck sat idle inside the locked barn.

It was funny, she thought, suiting up and putting on her beekeeper's hat and veil, how much her life had changed since she had first learned about the orphaned boys and began helping Sam care for them. In fact, she was pretty sure it was her most eventful June ever.

Thanks to the help she had received from her beekeeping friends, the bee colony was making progress. The new queen had been accepted by the hive. The brood combs looked healthy. There were adequate honey and pollen stores.

She added water, then replaced the lid on the hive. Picking up her smoker, she headed for the gate. She was just emerging from the mostly empty apiary when Sam's familiar truck drove up.

Alarmed, because he was supposed to be at his ranch checking on things with his crew, she ripped off her hat, veil and gloves and strode toward him. "Everything okay?" she called out.

Sam opened up the door, his cowboy hat slanted sexily across his brow, a fistful of gorgeous flowers in his hand. "It will be," he drawled, heading for her with a seductive grin, "if you'll agree to go on a date with me."

Chapter Fourteen

Sam watched Lulu walk across the lawn toward him, her honey-brown hair cascading over her shoulders. As she got closer, she stepped out of the white bee suit, revealing a pair of thigh-length shorts and a scoop-necked tank that highlighted her stunning curves and long, lissome legs.

Soft lips curving into a smile that spoke volumes about her sassy attitude, she strolled right up to him. Turquoise eyes sparkling, she tossed out, "Hey, cowboy, didn't you know you're supposed to give a gal some notice before you show up, ready to take her out, looking handsome as can be?"

His heart jackhammered in his chest. "You think I'm handsome?" Still clutching the flowers, he flirted shamelessly.

She let out a slow breath that drew his attention to her full shapely breasts. "Oh, yeah." Poking back the brim of an imaginary cowgirl hat, she wickedly looked him up and down.

Figuring he'd kept his distance long enough, he hooked an arm about her waist and tugged her against him. "Nice to hear," he murmured, pressing the bouquet in her hands.

Their fingers brushed as she accepted the first of many gifts he planned to give her. She wrinkled her nose. "Lots of things are nice to hear." She paused. Their eyes met. Emotion shimmered between them. And once again, he was reminded of all the things they didn't yet have.

Like commitment.

Not for the boys. They had that in spades.

But for each other.

He leaned down to kiss her, giving in to instinct and claiming her as his. When the smoldering caress ended, she pulled away, pouting playfully. "You really should have given me notice."

He shrugged, still way too turned on for the beginning of a daytime date. As was she, if the tautness of her nipples was any indication. He rubbed his thumb down the nape of her neck, felt her quiver in response. "Hey, I love you in a bee suit. And out," he couldn't help but tease.

Her eyes sparkled. "I bet." With a frown, she glanced down at her watch. "Seriously, we've only got two hours before pickup."

Taking her by the hand, he led her toward the porch. "Actually, a little more." Wrapping his arm around her waist, he brought her in close to his side. "I called Kelly yesterday and explained that I hadn't had enough time to do the kind of courting I'd like to do and asked if she and Dan would consider taking the kids this afternoon for a playdate."

Lulu chuckled softly. "I am sure it didn't take much coaxing. They're always willing to help romance along…"

Sam nodded. He held the door for her as Lulu moved inside ahead of him. His gaze drifted over the taut, sexy curves of her derriere. "They said yes. Dan's off today. So it won't be a problem to have them all at their place after school."

Lulu led the way into the kitchen. Perspiration dotted her neck, hairline. She set the flowers down on the island, reached into the fridge and brought out two bottles of ice-cold water. "Nice work."

He accepted his with a thanks. Leaning against the counter opposite her, he matched her drink for thirsty drink. "So what did you want to do?"

Grinning, Lulu wiped her damp lips with the back of her hand, then let the nearly empty bottle fall to her side. "You really want me to answer that?"

He nodded, serious now. "Yes. I do. You've worked so hard to help make my dreams come true."

She furrowed her brow, looking suddenly wary again. "What kind of dreams?"

"Of having a family," he said casually. *And having you back in my life, to stay*, he wanted to add. Leery she would consider that to be pushing her again, or God forbid, taking her for granted, he went on, "I wanted to say thank you."

Lulu reached for a vase. "You're welcome." Looking abruptly way too serious, she slid the bouquet into the neck and added water. Set it in a prominent place on the kitchen counter.

With a bolstering breath, she turned to him again. "Although I should say thank you, too," she said with the careful politeness usually reserved for strangers, "for welcoming me into your home and making my dreams of family come true, too."

Not sure how his attempt to woo her had gone so awry so fast, Sam forced a smile. Yes, they were great co-parents, lovers and friends, but he wanted more. A *lot* more.

"So..." he said, clearing his throat. "Want to do lunch out?" He cast around for anything that might please her. And get this day date back on track.

To his frustration, she was looking as oddly off-her-game as he was.

"A movie?" he proposed. "Shopping?"

That got her. "Shopping? Come on! You hate shopping!"

Didn't he know it. He shrugged, determined to make this her day. Spreading his hands accommodatingly wide, he flashed her a sexy smile. "Your wish is my command today."

Her cheeks lit up with a rosy blush.

He had the feeling she was about to tell him she wanted to make love. But before she could utter another word, her cell phone chimed at the exact same time as his. Lulu started, recalling as swiftly as Sam the last time that had happened. Alarmed, she said, "I hope it's not the school."

It was not.

It was their attorneys.

Lulu knew by what Liz and Travis would not say to them on the phone that their worst fears were being realized, so she went upstairs to hurriedly shower and change into business casual clothes. Then she and Sam drove into town.

Liz and Travis were waiting for them in the conference room. "Why don't you both have a seat?" Liz said.

Sam held Lulu's chair for her, then sat down beside her. As usual, he wasted no time cutting to the chase. "You found something problematic, didn't you?"

Travis grimaced. "Definitely something interesting."

"The two of you are still married," Liz said.

"Still?" Lulu croaked.

Sam asked, "What are you talking about?"

"More to the point, how do you know this?" Lulu demanded, the news hitting her like a gut punch.

Travis looked down at the papers in front of him. "Official state records show you eloped in the Double Knot Wedding Chapel in Memphis, Tennessee, on Monday, March 14, over ten years ago. Alongside another couple, Peter and Theresa Thompson, in a double wedding ceremony."

Lulu gulped. "But our union was never legal," she pointed out, trying to stay calm while Sam sat beside her in stoic silence.

Liz countered, "Ah, actually, it is legal. In fact, it's still valid to this day."

Sam reached over and took her hand in his, much as he had the first time they had been in this room together. "How is that possible?" Lulu asked weakly.

"We never mailed in the certificate of marriage, or the license, to the state of Tennessee," Sam said.

"And for our union to be recorded and legal, we would have had to have done that," Lulu reiterated.

"Well, apparently, the owners of the Double Knot Wedding Chapel did, and your marriage was recorded," Travis said. "And is still valid to this day, near as we can tell. Unless you two got a divorce or an annulment somewhere else? Say, another country?"

"Why would we do that? We didn't know we were married," Sam returned.

Lulu noted her "husband" did not appear anywhere near as upset as she was. She forced herself to settle down. With a dismissive wave of her hand, she told everyone in the room, "It doesn't matter. We'll just explain we were too young, or at least at nineteen I was too young to know what I was doing," she amended hastily, "and get an annulment now."

Again, Liz shook her head. "Sorry. It's been too long. It would have to be a divorce."

Lulu groaned. Talk about a day going all wrong! First, Sam had completely knocked her off guard by impulsively asking her out on a date. And now this! She twisted her hands and asked, "Is it possible we could obtain a divorce, without anyone finding out?"

"You mean like social services or the court?" Travis asked. "No."

Beside her, Sam went into all-business mode. "How does this development affect our proposed petition to adopt?"

Lulu noticed he hadn't said *mistake*.

Liz tapped her pen against the table. "It certainly makes it a great deal more complicated."

Lulu tried to get a grip and adopted Sam's no-nonsense tone. "In what sense?" she asked.

Travis sat back in his chair. "To become guardians, the bar is not that high, if the parents named you in their will. Mostly because guardianship can be terminated rather easily, for any number of reasons. However, adoption is permanent and cannot easily be undone." He cleared his throat. "So when it comes to that process of qualifying, social services and the courts want to see a stable, loving environment for the children. Anything that points to the opposite, like your secret elopement, equally impulsive breakup, and the fact you did not properly follow-through with either an annulment or a divorce and had no idea you were still married, can send up a red flag."

Lulu gulped. "How do we fix this?"

"You could admit you made a mistake, get an amicable divorce and prove you can get along in the aftermath."

Frowning, Sam asked, "How long would all that take?"

Travis made a seesawing gesture. "Potentially months, if not years, to satisfy the court."

Sam leaned forward, gaze narrowing. "And if we stay married, then what kind of detrimental impact will it have on our proposal to adopt?"

"Less of one. But," Liz said firmly, "if you two choose to go that route, you have to show real commitment to each other, as well as the children."

Lulu's anxiety rose. More and more this seemed like an impossible predicament. "How do we do that?" she asked.

Their lawyers exchanged telltale glances, then shrugged. "That is up to the two of you."

At Sam's suggestion, he and Lulu picked up some sandwiches and coffees from the bistro in town, and then retreated to Lulu's ranch to come up with a strategy for dealing with the marital crisis they suddenly found themselves in.

"I can't believe it," Lulu said miserably, burying her face in her hands.

Sam could. He'd always felt married to Lulu in his heart, ever since they said their vows. It was what had made it so hard for him to move on. What Lulu was feeling, though, he had no clue.

"Can't?" he asked before he could stop himself, realizing he had to know where he stood with her. "Or *don't* want to believe it?"

She jumped out of her seat and whirled to face him. Hands on her hips. Like him, she'd barely touched her food. "Would you please stop doing that?" she asked with icy disdain.

The resentment he'd stuffed deep inside rose to the surface. "Stop doing what?" *Wanting you?*

She winced. Looking guilty as all get-out, which of course, she should, since it was her abrupt change of heart, not his, that had ultimately put them in this mess.

She huffed in answer to his question. "Stop bringing up all the angst we felt back then!"

"Can't help it." Within him, anger and irritation surged. "It was a lousy thing to do, insist we get married, along with our friends. And then," he continued, the words coming out along with the hurt, "four days later, tell me the only way we could continue as husband and wife was if we kept it a secret!"

She took another deep breath, suddenly appearing oddly vulnerable. "I wasn't saying permanently!" She gestured broadly, then started to pivot away from him.

Not about to let her run away from him again, he stopped her with a light hand to her shoulder. Turned her slowly back to face him. And finally asked what he'd wanted to know for years. "Why say it at all?"

An emotional silence stretched between them.

He let his hand fall to his side. "You either loved me or you didn't, and apparently you didn't."

"It's more complicated than that, and you know it."

A muscle ticked in his jaw. "Then why, Lulu?" He gritted out. "Why did you run scared?"

Another long, awkward silence fell. "My parents would not have understood."

Aggravated to find her still using that lame excuse, he gave her a chastising glance. "There's no way to know that, because we never gave them a chance to support us."

"It's not like you told anyone in your family!" Lulu

said, just as bitterly. Reminding him she wasn't the only one who had suffered from a hefty dose of pride. She stepped forward and jabbed an accusing finger at his chest. "Since you said we'd either go public with our marriage immediately, or it was all over. And no one would ever have to know!"

Seeing she was about to bolt again, he let out a rough breath and stepped closer. "Can you blame me?"

She tossed her head, silky hair flying in every direction. "For having a 'my way or the highway' approach?" she shot back. "Yes, I can, since marriage is supposed to be a fair and equal partnership."

Her words hit their target. She had a point. He shouldn't be lashing out. He shook his head. "I'm sorry," he said guiltily. "I'm upset." They had been so close to having everything they wanted. And now...

Lulu released a deep breath and grew quiet once again. "We're both upset, Sam." She shoved her hair away from her face. Shook her head in misery. "The big issue is where do we go from here?"

That, at least, was easy, Sam thought. "Isn't it obvious? We stay married."

Lulu's day went from bad to worse in sixty seconds. She stared at the handsome cowboy opposite her, wondering how she had ever imagined the two of them were living in some sort of fairy tale. "Are you serious?"

Looking more resolute than ever, he replied, "We want to adopt the kids. Our best shot at doing that is by being married. And since we already are, why not just leave it as is and go forward as husband and wife?"

How about because we don't love each other? Lulu thought. But not about to reveal the direction of her thoughts, she countered sarcastically, "Just like that?

Presto, change-o, snap our fingers, and we're a happily married couple?"

Even though, if she were honest, she would have to admit that lately she had been feeling as if they were on the verge of being just that.

"Why not? We're already spending time together every day. Sleeping together. Raising three kids together and living under the same roof. Why not just admit that staying married is the best avenue for raising the kids and making them feel safe and secure and loved?"

Because, Lulu thought, *if I do that, then I'm one step away from opening up my heart and admitting the real reason why I've never really been able to get serious about anyone else but you, Sam.* "Because we'd have to tell everyone what we did back then," she blurted out.

Again, he clearly did not see what the problem was. "So?" His gruff response was a direct hit to her carefully constructed defenses.

"It's embarrassing," she whispered, the heat moving from her chest into her face. She threw up her hands and paced. "It makes us look idiotic and reckless."

Sam crossed his arms. Determined, it seemed, to win this argument. His gaze sifted over her before returning ever so slowly to her eyes. "Or wildly in love. I mean, isn't that why people usually elope?"

"Except we weren't wildly in love, Sam." If they had been, they never would have split up and stayed apart for almost a decade. Would they?

He sobered, looking pensive. "Well, what do you want to do, Lulu?" he asked in exasperation. "Split up again and go through the hell of divorce, because even an uncontested one is just that, and then try to adopt?"

Put that way, it did sound unreasonable.

"And what if getting divorced not only ruins our

chances of ever adopting the triplets," he said, in an increasingly rusty voice, "but also casts a bad light on our character and gets them removed from our guardianship, too?"

Lulu swallowed around the lump in her throat. "I couldn't bear that." The thought of losing the triplets was on par with how she had felt losing Sam. Heartbreakingly awful.

Sam compressed his lips. "Well, neither could I."

A stony silence fell.

Lulu weighed the possibilities. Life with Sam and the kids. Life without. There really was no other choice. Not if they didn't want to disappoint literally everyone. "So we're in agreement," she said, trying not to cry. She swallowed hard, aware she had never felt so trapped or miserable. She lifted her gaze to his. "We bite the bullet and stay married for the sake of the kids."

Sam locked eyes with her, looking no happier than she felt. He exhaled grimly, ran a hand through his hair. "I really don't see any other way out of this. Do you?"

Chapter Fifteen

Unfortunately, Lulu did not see any other way out. So they asked Dan and Kelly to keep the kids a little longer and went to see her parents first, figuring they could then leave it to Rachel and Frank to spread the word.

As they sat down together at the kitchen table, Lulu said, "Y'all remember spring break, my sophomore year of college, when I went on a country music tour with some of my best girlfriends?"

Her parents nodded, perplexed, unable to see where this was going.

Hating to disappoint them, Lulu knotted her hands in front of her. "Well, I lied to you," she admitted shamefully. "I *was* in Tennessee. But I was staying with Sam that week, not a group of girls."

Her parents looked at Sam. "I apologize for that," he said with gruff sincerity. "We should have told you the truth."

Her parents paused. "I assume there is a reason you're telling us all this now?" her father said.

Lulu nodded. "There is." She explained how she and Sam had accompanied their friends Peter and Theresa to Tennessee to be the witnesses for their secret wedding ceremony.

Sam reached over and took her hand. Buoyed by the warmth and security of his touch, she plunged on, "I was so caught up in the romance of it all—" *and my incredible, overwhelming feelings for Sam*, she added silently "—that I suggested we make it a double wedding."

Sam lifted a hand. "For the record, I was all too ready to jump in."

"So we eloped, too," Lulu confessed. "And for the rest of our spring break," she admitted wistfully as Sam's hand tightened over hers, "everything was wonderful." For a few heady days, she'd felt all her dreams had come true.

"What happened to change all that?" her dad asked. "And make you break up?"

"When it came time to go home, the reality of what we had done set in for me." Hard.

The memory of that last horrible fight was not a good one. Sam withdrew his hand, sat back.

Tears blurred her vision once again. Embarrassed, she continued, "I knew we'd acted recklessly and I was afraid to tell anyone else what we'd done. And I especially didn't want to disappoint the two of you." Unable to look her "husband" in the eye, she related sadly, "Sam refused to live our marriage in the shadows, so we broke up."

"And got the marriage annulled?" her mother assumed.

"Actually..." Sam went on to explain the confusion

over the paperwork that had followed. "We just found out we're still legally married."

Her parents took a moment to absorb that information. "Which puts us in a little bit of a quandary," Lulu said.

"Little?" her father echoed, finally appearing as upset with her as Lulu had initially expected him to be.

"Okay. It's a pretty big problem," she conceded, chagrined. "But Sam and I are going to figure this out."

"Well." Her mother sighed. "First, I wish you had come to us at the time and told us what was going on, so we could have made sure there were no lingering legal snafus. And supported you. And we *would* have supported you, Lulu, no matter what you thought then. Or think now…"

Her dad, calming down, nodded.

"Second," Rachel said, with a gentle firmness, "as for you being fearful of our opinion, when it comes to your life—" she paused to look long and hard at the two of them "—it only matters what *you* two feel in *your* hearts, not what anyone else thinks." She reached across the table to take Lulu's and Sam's hands. Squeezed. "Furthermore, your family will defend your right to make those choices for yourself, by yourselves, even when we don't approve or understand them."

Her dad covered their enjoined hands with his own. "Your mother and brothers and I want you to be happy, sweetheart. And the same goes for you, Sam." He regarded them both with respect.

"It's up to you to figure out what will make you feel that way and then go for it," Rachel added gently.

Everyone disengaged hands. Another silence fell, even more awkward and fraught with untenable emotions.

"Do you know what you're going to do?" her mom asked finally.

Lulu and Sam looked at each other. "Stay married," they answered in unison.

Sam draped his arm across the back of Lulu's chair and continued with the same steady affability that made him such a good leader. "We think it would provide a more stable environment for the kids."

Frank pushed back his chair and got up to make coffee. Once again, he seemed loaded for bear. "You really think you can make an arrangement like this work?"

Lulu didn't see any choice if they wanted to help the kids. But sensing it would be a mistake to tell her parents that, she answered, "Yes." She hauled in another breath, admitting a little more happily, "Sam and I have recently gotten back together, anyway, so it just makes sense for us to stay married and build on that."

Beside her, Sam seemed calm and accepting of the predicament they found themselves in. Her parents regarded them with equal parts doubt and consideration. Which amped up her own wariness. But to her surprise, Frank and Rachel didn't try to talk them out of it.

"Okay, then," her mom said finally. "But if you're going to stay married—" her regard was stern, unrelenting "—your dad and I want you to be as serious as the institution of marriage requires this time. And do it right by officially and publicly recommitting to each other and saying your vows before all your family and friends. That way, everyone—including and especially the two of you—will know it is not just a whim that can be easily discarded. But an honorable, heartfelt promise you can both be proud of."

"I don't see why you're so upset," Sam said, late into the following week.

Lulu pushed away from her laptop, where she had

been dutifully compiling the expected guest lists for her parents. "Because it's all so unnecessary!" she fumed, stepping out back where the newly installed swings and sandbox sat in the warmth of a perfect summer night.

With the triplets soundly asleep and now snoozing happily through most nights, she should be relaxing and getting to know Sam again. Instead, she was slaving away on the endless To Do lists her parents kept giving her.

She swung around to face Sam, her shoulder knocking into his. "I don't see why we even have to have a wedding, when everyone in the whole county—heck, probably the whole state, thanks to the McCabe-Laramie grapevine!—knows our story."

He reached out to steady her, then lounged beside her against the deck railing. His hands braced on either side of him, he continued to study her face, his expression as inscrutable as his mood the last few days.

Unable to quell the emotions riding roughshod inside her, she challenged softly, "Why do we have to go through the motions of getting married again?" If he'd just told her parents no…

He leaned toward her earnestly. "Because the kids deserve it," he returned with a chivalry that grated on her nerves even more than his calculated calm.

The heat of indignation climbed from her chest, into her face. "They're not old enough to realize—"

"But they will be one day," he countered. "Do we really want them to have to weather not just the tragic loss of their parents and the chaos that ensued regarding their guardianship, but a scandal regarding their adoptive parents, too?"

She curled her hands over his biceps, finding much needed solace in his masculine warmth. "It's not like getting married all over again erases the elopement and paperwork snafu that followed."

He wrapped both arms about her waist. "But it brings closure and a well-respected, time-honored path to the future stability of our family." Tugging her closer still, he reached up to tuck a strand of hair behind her ear. "And proving we are serious about staying together," he continued tenderly, "not just as co-guardians or lovers and friends but as husband and wife, *will* bolster our efforts to adopt."

Abruptly feeling as trapped as she had during their conversation with her parents, she pivoted away and stepped farther into the warm and breezy summer night. Stars sparkled in the black velvet sky overhead. A quarter moon shone bright. "That's assuming we *can* still adopt after all this."

He clamped his lips together, as if he was not going to continue, then did, anyway. "You heard what Liz and Travis said about this." He followed her down into the grass. "We will be able to, we're just going to have to wait a little while and prove we have a solid relationship before submitting our application."

Lulu breathed in the minty scent of his breath. "I get all that," she said grumpily.

His eyes tracked her as she paced restlessly back and forth. "But…?"

She came closer and tipped her chin up at him. "I just don't see why I have to have a wedding dress and a whole big reception complete with a live band and a harpist and a flute and five attendants, when we could just as easily say our I dos in jeans and T-shirts."

He gave her a quelling look. "You really want to give people the impression that this means so little to us we couldn't even bother to get properly dressed?"

Okay, so maybe she was taking her resistance to all the hoopla too far.

"Your attendants are all family, and your sisters-in-laws and your brothers all want to participate in this day. So why not let them be members of the wedding party? Plus, as your mom has pointed out on *numerous* occasions for the last several weeks, you are their *only* daughter. They want the privilege and pleasure of seeing you get married on the ranch, the way you all used to envision, when you were growing up."

Damn, why did he have to be so reasonable when making his points?

Recalling how much she hated arguing with him and coming out the loser, she steered the conversation in another direction. "Your family isn't making such a fuss."

His stoicism took on a tinge of sadness. "That's because we're all scattered all over the world now, since all five of my sisters opted for demanding international jobs. And none of them can get here till the very last moment."

Lulu sensed there was more. "And…?" she prodded gently.

One corner of his lips turned down. "No one's actually said it, but I think it's hard for them, having the first wedding, without either of my parents still here with us on earth."

Lulu drew in a breath, guilt washing over her. She hadn't meant to be so insensitive. "Oh, Sam. I'm so sorry about that."

"It's okay." He squared his broad shoulders, dealing with trouble the way he always did. Head-on. He flashed her a grin. "I think they're still looking down on us from up above. And what they are telling us, Lulu…is that you need to get yourself in gear."

Lulu knew Sam was right.

So she tried.

She went to her final dress fitting. Approved the tuxes Sam had picked out for him and the boys. Went with Sam to taste wedding cake and pick out a band. And sat down with the florist.

But when it came to the last and final thing, she balked.

"I don't want to be married by a minister or say traditional wedding vows."

Sam gave her the long-suffering look that had become way too commonplace during the weeks of wedding prep. He continued getting ready for bed. "How come?"

Because this all still felt like a travesty. Like the romance and the enthralling passion was gone, and now all they had left was the duty of recommitment.

Leery of admitting that out loud, though, for fear of hurting his feelings, Lulu washed off her makeup. "I'd prefer a justice of the peace."

Sam stripped down to his boxers and a T-shirt, then walked into the bathroom. "And why's that?"

Trying not to notice how buff he looked or how much she always seemed to want to make love to him, Lulu layered toothpaste onto her brush. "Because when we got married before, we were too young to know what we were doing."

"And now it's different?" he prompted.

"Yes, totally different. Now that we're old enough to know what we are doing, we are going in with clearer heads and are on the same page about the fact that our nuptials aren't romantically or spiritually motivated." She lounged against the marble counter. "Rather, it's just more of a...an optimal agreement about how we're going to live in the future. So." She drew in a deep breath. "That being the case, it seems like we should use a justice of the peace instead of a minister."

That look again. A very long exhalation. Another heartfelt pause.

"Okay," he said finally. "A justice of the peace it is. What do you want to do about the vows?"

Lulu brushed her teeth, rinsed, spit. As did he. "Maybe we could each write our own."

She expected an argument. Instead, he set his toothbrush back in the holder next to hers and said, "That'll work."

Aware all over again how cozy and right it felt to share space with him like this, Lulu said, "You don't mind?"

"Not at all." Coming close enough to take her in his arms, he gazed down at her lovingly and sifted his hand through her hair. "In fact, I kind of like the idea."

As it turned out, however, Lulu did not enjoy writing her vows to Sam any more than she had liked any of the other wedding preparations. Mostly because she could not figure out what to say. Reciting poetry just wasn't *them*. Everything she wrote sounded either disingenuous or lame. Or both.

Finally, there were just three days left before the big event. And she was nowhere close to having anything to say.

She moaned over her laptop, where she had been continuously typing…and deleting…and typing…and deleting.

Sam sank down on the big leather sofa next to her. With the kids and Beauty asleep upstairs in the nursery, the house was oddly quiet. He draped his arm around her shoulders. "What's wrong, sweetheart?"

Aware this part of her life felt more out of control than ever, Lulu buried her face in her hands. "I'm never going to get my vows written."

Settling closer, he gave her an encouraging squeeze. "Do you want my help?"

Briefly, she turned her head and rested her face against his shoulder. She loved snuggling up to him, especially when her emotions were in turmoil. He made her feel so protected. "No." She sighed. "It has to come from me."

Looking devilishly handsome with the hint of evening beard rimming his face, he bussed the top of her head. "Give it time. It'll come."

Would it? "What if it doesn't?" Lulu lamented, her mood growing ever more troubled. She looked deep into Sam's eyes. "What then?"

They had been down this road before, Sam thought, at the end of their passion-filled Tennessee honeymoon. Then, it had been post-wedding jitters. Was this the pre-wedding jitters?

He hadn't talked her out of making a mistake the last time and heartbreak had ensued. He wouldn't let her run away again.

Tilting her face toward his, he gently stroked her cheek. "There is no rule that says we have to write our own vows, Lulu. We can just go back to the tried and true." Which would be a heck of a lot easier, since he hadn't written his vows yet, either. Although he wasn't stressing out about it.

Lulu shot to her feet. Her eyes were steady but her lower lip trembled. "I can't stand up in front of everyone we love and say traditional vows, Sam."

He rose, too. "Why not?"

Regret glimmered briefly in her gaze. She seemed to think she had failed on some level. "Because they're not true!"

He stepped closer and took her rigid body in his arms. "You'd leave me if I was sick? Or poor?"

She lifted her chin and speared him with an outraged look. "No, of course not," she conceded.

"You don't plan to take me as your lawfully wedded husband?" he asked, his own temper beginning to flare.

As she spoke, her face grew pale, her shoulders even stiffer. She shook her head, determined, it seemed, to think the worst of them. "We're already legally hitched."

He stared at her in frustration. "You don't want to love and cherish me?"

"I…" She sent him a confused glance, making no effort at all to hide her reluctance to further their romance. "You mean love like a friend?" she asked warily.

His heart rate accelerated. "Like a wife loves a husband."

She swallowed, looking miserable all over again. Shoving a hand through her hair, she paced away from him. "See? This is why I don't like this!"

"You've lost me, darlin'." He followed her over to the fireplace. "Don't like what?"

She spun around to face him, the soft swell of her breasts lifting and lowering with every anxious breath she took. "Having to analyze our relationship and spell everything out."

These were not the words of a bride who was blissfully in love. These were the words of a woman who was desperately trying to find a way out of getting hitched. He positioned himself so she had no choice but to look at him. "Our relationship won't stand the test of time, is that what you're saying?"

"Of course we'll be together for the kids' sake. For as long as they need us," she said, her eyes glittering. "But we don't have to go through all this rigmarole to do that,

Sam. We could just continue on, as we have been, as we would have, had we not become aware we were still legally married."

Sam forced himself to show no reaction. He might not want to hear this but he had half expected her to say something similar. "You're saying you want a divorce?"

"No!" Still holding his eyes—even more reluctantly now, he noticed—she gulped. "I'm saying I don't want to go through with this wedding." Tears blurred her eyes, and her lower lip trembled all the more. "If they need us to restate our vows, and honestly I don't see why in the world we need to go to the trouble to do that since our marriage is legal just as it is, then I'd rather just elope again. And make the statement that way."

Sam stood, arms crossed. "Thereby proving what, exactly, Lulu? That we're still the impulsive idiots we were before?"

Huffing out a breath, she went back to her laptop and closed it with more care than necessary. "No," she said. She slid her computer back into its case, zipped it shut. "We would be doing what other couples do when they decide the hoopla is all too much and that life has gotten too crazy. They run off and elope."

He took her by the shoulders and held her in front of him. "We did that, Lulu. It didn't work out so well."

Case held against her chest, she eased away. "I was a lot younger." She stalked into the kitchen.

He watched her set the case down. "True. But still just as skittish when it comes to making an actual commitment."

She opened the fridge. "I'm *completely* committed to the children."

"Just not to me."

She spun back to face him, a riot of color filling her cheeks. "Please don't misinterpret this."

He reached past her to get a beer for himself. His gut tightened as he twisted off the cap. "What other way is there to interpret it, darlin'? You want to stay married to me, so long as you don't have to publicly act like you mean it."

She took a sip of water. He took a swig of beer.

"I'm *living here*, aren't I?"

He grimaced. "As a matter of convenience."

Her gaze narrowing, she set her bottle down with a thud. "Well, that makes sense, because you invited me to *bunk here* as a matter of convenience."

An accusatory silence fell.

She came nearer, her hurt obvious. "I don't understand why you're so upset with me. For once in my life, I don't care what people think about this situation we've found ourselves in. I don't care if my parents are going to be disappointed or mad at me."

There was a time when that would have pleased him immensely, to know that she put their relationship above all else. Now, it felt like a booby prize.

"I only care what *we* think and feel is right for us."

He tore his eyes away from the way her knee-length shorts hugged her hips, her cotton T-shirt her breasts. "Which would be…?"

Noticing her hair was falling out of the clip, she undid the clasp and let her mane fall across her shoulders. "To just skip this whole travesty of a wedding and leave things as is."

"Meaning married."

"Technically." She ran her fingers through the silky strands, pushing them into place, then leaned against the opposite counter, her hands braced on either side of her. "And living together."

He definitely felt burned by her casual attitude. "As co-parents."

"Yes." She caught his hand. "Don't you see, Sam? Everything was great until we found we were still legally hitched."

It had been—and it hadn't. The feel of her smooth fingers in his brought only partial comfort. He tried and failed to summon up what little gallantry he had left. "Just like it was great when we were on a honeymoon." A muscle ticked in his jaw. "But then when we had to go home and tell our families what we had done, it was not so great."

She flushed and shook her head in silent remonstration. "There's no comparison between then and now, Sam," she warned.

"Isn't there?" he asked bitterly. Their glances meshed, held. "You're doing exactly what you did before."

She looked at him, incredulous.

"Recklessly jump all in with me—all the while swearing your devotion—only to jump all out."

Her eyes shone even as her low tone took on a defiant edge. "I won't leave the kids, Sam, if that's what you're worried about."

He knew that. Was even grateful for it.

"But you would be right back out that door if the kids weren't here," he countered, before he could stop himself. "Wouldn't you?"

She stared at him, as if feeling every bit as boxed in— and deeply disappointed—as he felt. Like they needed to take a step back. Give each other time to breathe. Figure out what they really felt. "I don't know how to answer that," she said finally, her chin quivering.

"Sadly, I do." He paused to give her a slow, critical once-over. Wondering all the while how they ever could have deluded themselves into thinking this would work. "We never should have told your parents we would renew our vows. Or fooled ourselves into thinking we could carry off this charade," he said, pain knotting his gut. "And this is what any marriage between us is to you, isn't it, Lulu? A charade?"

Her disillusionment grew. "Given the way this wedding has come about, how could it be anything but?" she asked, her face a polite, bland mask.

She moved closer still, imploring now. "Which is why I can't seem to write my vows no matter how hard I try." She lifted her chin. In control, again. "And why we should cancel it, Sam. So we can go back to the way things were before marriage entered the mix."

It wasn't the legality of the situation that was destroying them. It was her refusal to open up her heart. "I asked you this before but I am going to ask you again. And this time, I want an honest answer." He propped his hands on her shoulders and bore his eyes into hers. "You want a divorce?"

She flinched. "No, of course I don't want a divorce now!"

Now...

Which meant...

Releasing her, his feelings for her erupted in a storm of anger and sorrow. "But you will, won't you?" he concluded bitterly, wishing like hell he had seen this coming. Like their second time around would end any other way. "Maybe not tomorrow. Or the next. But one day..."

She compressed her lips. "You're twisting everything I've said."

He told himself he was immune to her hurt. He had to be. For everyone's sake, one of them needed to be reasonable. "Well, one thing is clear. For us, marriage is and always has been a mistake. We can be co-parents, Lulu, but that is all."

She blinked. "*You're* throwing down the gauntlet and issuing an ultimatum to me? *Again?*"

Not happily.

He shook his head, and with a heavy sigh, said, "No. I'm doing what you've been trying to do, indirectly, for weeks now, Lulu. I'm calling an end to our romantic relationship. This time, for good." Heart aching, he stormed out.

Chapter Sixteen

With a heavy heart, Lulu went to see her parents at their ranch. They took one look at her face and sat her down with them at the kitchen table. "Tell us what's going on," her mom urged gently while her father made them all a pot of coffee.

Pushing away the dreams of what might have been, Lulu knotted her hands in front of her. "Sam and I are still planning to adopt the kids together, but we're not going to have a wedding on Saturday afternoon after all." Lulu swallowed around the lump in her throat. "So it would help me out a lot," she continued, swiping at a tear slipping down her cheek, "if you could help me notify everyone."

"Of course we'll help out, honey." Her dad got out the cream and sugar. Added three mugs to the table. "But...?" He looked at her mom, with the same kind of parental telepathy she and Sam had been sharing.

"…are you sure?" Rachel interjected, handing her a box of tissues.

Wiping away a fresh onslaught of tears, Lulu forced herself to be honest. "I really thought I could do it." Her heart aching, she paused to look her folks in the eye. "Build on everything I feel for Sam and the kids and marry him strictly as a matter of convenience. But—" she felt the hot sting of shame that she ever could have been so shortsighted "—when we started trying to work on our vows, I realized there was no way we could really do this without it all being a lie. And I couldn't base our entire relationship on that. Never mind pretend," she continued thickly, "in front of everyone that it was going to be a real marriage." Her voice trembled. "When I knew in my heart it was all a sham."

"And Sam thinks it's a sham, too?" Her dad brought the carafe over to the table and poured coffee into mugs. Not surprisingly, he was more focused on fixing this problem than consoling her.

Aware she hadn't a clue what Sam was thinking or feeling, Lulu stuttered, "I…ah…"

"Did he actually *say* that it was untruthful for him, too?" her attorney-mom asked, in her cross-examination voice.

"No," Lulu admitted miserably.

"Then what *did* he say?" Rachel persisted.

Sam's angry words still reverberating in her mind, Lulu admitted grimly, "That if I couldn't find some wedding vows that would work for us and go through with the wedding on Saturday, our romantic relationship was off. Permanently this time."

Her dad shook his head in mute remonstration, for once not taking her side. "Honestly, Lulu. Can you blame the guy?"

"Hey!" Lulu scowled, feeling indignant. To calm herself, she stirred cream and sugar into her coffee and lifted the mug to her lips, breathing in the fragrant steam. "He never once said he loved me. Not this time around, anyway…!" So what choice had she had, no matter what her feelings were? A fraud was a fraud! And that was no example to set for the kids, never mind a foundation to base a marriage on.

"So." Her mother sighed in regret. "You don't trust the two of you to be able to sustain a romantic relationship that will go the distance."

Softly, Lulu admitted this was so.

Her mom studied her over the rim of her mug. "Will you be able to be friends?"

Lulu took another sip, and finally said, albeit a little uneasily, "When the dust clears, I think so."

Her dad sat down beside her mom. "What about the children?" he asked.

"We still plan to adopt them."

"Together?" he questioned.

"Yes."

"Living separately," he continued to press, "or under one roof?"

Lulu flushed. Aware that hadn't been completely worked out, but she could assume. "Under one roof, just the way we have been."

Her mom picked up where her dad left off. "And you have faith this arrangement will work."

Lulu replied without hesitation. "Yes."

Rachel's eyes narrowed. "Why?"

Lulu struggled to find the words that would explain what she knew in the deepest recesses of her soul to be true. She looked both her parents in the eye. "Because that part of our life together just works and works really well. And we never ever disappoint each other in that regard."

Her mom's brow furrowed. "And you think not disappointing each other is key."

Lulu lifted a hand. "Of course."

"Oh, honey," Rachel said, getting up to engulf Lulu in a hug. Her dad came around the other side and joined in. "Disappointment is part of life."

They drew back to face her once again. "The more you love someone, the more likely it is that you will disappoint each other from time to time," her dad said gently but firmly.

Her mom nodded. "It's those highs and lows and the ability to weather each storm and come back even stronger, as a couple and a family, that make loving worthwhile."

Thursday morning, Sam had just dropped the kids off at preschool and returned to his ranch, when a caravan of five pickup trucks and SUVs came up the lane.

All five of Lulu's brothers got out and walked toward him. None looked the least bit happy.

Sam bit down on an oath. Great. This was all he needed after the week he'd had. With him and Lulu more or less alternating care of the kids when possible, and doing the polite-strangers dance around each other when it wasn't.

Thus far, they'd manage to keep the boys from picking up on the breech between them, but whenever he and Lulu faced off alone, even for a few minutes, the residual hurt and anger was palpable. To the point they'd more or less taken to completely avoiding each other.

"Told you that you'd be seeing us if you hurt our sister again," Dan drawled.

This would be comical if he hadn't spent the entire night nursing a broken heart.

"I didn't hurt her." Sam pushed the words through his teeth.

Dan adopted a law officer's stance. "Then why is she over at Mom and Dad's ranch, crying her heart out over a potentially canceled wedding?"

Potentially?

Did that mean Lulu was having second thoughts about calling their love affair quits, too? Or just that her folks weren't willing to let her off the hook?

There was no way to tell without speaking to Lulu about it in person.

Sam glared back at the McCabe posse. He curtailed the urge to put his fist through something, anything. "You'll have to ask her that, since she's the one who found it impossible to stand up in front of family and friends and say I do."

"Then what was she going to say?"

"That was the problem. She couldn't figure it out. And was apparently tired of trying."

A contemplative silence fell among the six men.

Chase squinted, his calm, analytical CEO temperament coming to the fore. "I can't believe she would react that way without a very good reason."

Well, she had, Sam thought grimly.

"What aren't either of you telling us?"

A lot of things actually. Like the fact I opened up my heart and soul to her and it still wasn't enough. Or the fact I still don't want a divorce, even though Lulu all but came out and admitted in a roundabout way that her only attraction to me is physical.

Looking very much like the chivalrous ex-soldier he was, Matt rubbed the flat of his hand beneath his jaw. "Are you protecting her?"

Yes, Sam thought, *I am*. Which on the surface wasn't

surprising. Like the McCabes, he had been raised to be a Texas gentleman, too. And gentlemen didn't tell a woman's secrets.

Ever. But this went deeper than that. For the first time, he found himself caring about what people thought. Not about him. But about Lulu. He didn't want anyone thinking less of her because of mistakes they'd both made. So he remained mum.

Jack analyzed the situation with a physician's empathy. "One thing's clear. You're both miserable."

Sam tried not to hang any hope on that. "That's kind of hard to believe since she's been dragging her heels," he scoffed. "And doing everything possible to show her resistance to renewing our marriage vows, for several weeks now."

Matt squinted. "Why would she do that?"

Sam shrugged. "Isn't it obvious? She has a real problem with commitment."

At least to me.

It couldn't be anything else.

The brothers didn't believe that any more than he wanted to. "Is she abandoning the kids, too?" Dan asked.

Sam frowned. "No, of course not. She loves those little guys."

"Then it's just you that's the problem?" Cullen taunted.

Actually, Sam thought, even more miserably, *I don't know what the problem is.* The two of them clicked. They had always clicked. Until it came time to take their love public in an everlasting way. Then she just started putting up roadblocks even he couldn't get past.

"Is there a point to all this?" Sam asked with a great deal more patience than he felt.

The five men nodded.

"The fact Lulu is trying to call the wedding off,"

Chase said finally, "when it's clear how crazy she is about
you, should point you toward some pretty big deficit in
your behavior. And if you're smart—" he paused mean-
ingfully, to let his words sink in "—you'll figure out
what that is. Pronto."

Friday afternoon, Lulu had just finished taking care
of her lone remaining hive when Sam's truck turned into
her ranch. Her heart pounding, because she wasn't sure
she was quite ready to say all the things she needed to
say to him, she drew off her beekeeper's gloves and veil,
stepped outside the apiary gate and began moving toward him.

He walked toward her, too, and as he did, she couldn't
help but admire how good he looked in the usual jeans,
boots, chambray work shirt and stone-colored Resistol
slanted across his brow. As he neared, the masculine de-
termination she so admired glinted in his gold-flecked
eyes.

Her heart thundered in her chest, as her spirits rose
and fell, then rose again.

When she reached him, she stripped off her protective
suit and hung it over the porch railing, feeling suddenly
achingly vulnerable. "I thought we were going to meet
up later," she said with as much feminine cool as she
could muster. When she'd had time to clean up and put on
something besides an old Texas A&M T-shirt and shorts.

He acknowledged this was so with a dip of his head.
"I know what we said before I left to take the kids to
preschool."

"But?" Lulu inhaled the brisk masculine fragrance
of his aftershave.

"I didn't want to waste any more time."

Funny, she didn't, either. But would they be able to work it out? The way they hadn't before?

In that instant, she decided they would.

Taking her by the hand, he led her up the steps to the front porch. Sat down with her in the wooden rocking chairs she'd inherited from her late grandmother and brought his chair around until they were facing each other, knee to knee.

His eyes were full of the things she'd almost been afraid to hope for, his gaze leveled on hers. "I want to start over, Lulu," he continued, his voice a sexy rumble. His hands tightened protectively on hers. "And this time keep working at it, until we get it right." He looked at her with so much tenderness she could barely breathe.

Her heart somersaulted in her chest. She drew in a shuddery breath. "You mean that?" she whispered.

He nodded soberly and hauled in a rough breath. Shaking his head in regret, confessed, "I never should have pressured you into staying married to me. Like it was some kind of social contract or means to an end. Because you're right, Lulu." He stood and pulled her to her feet. Wrapping his arms around her, he brought her even closer, so they were touching in one long, comforting line. "A real marriage is so much more than that. It's about promising your whole heart and soul."

He paused, all the love and commitment she had ever wanted to see shining in his eyes. "It's about vowing to stay together no matter what for the rest of your lives. And that's what I want with you, Lulu," he confessed. "To be with you for the rest of our lives. Because I love you. I've always loved you. And I always will."

Tears of joy and relief blurred her vision. "Oh, Sam," she said, hugging him tight. "I love you, too."

He paused to kiss her, demonstrating the depth of his feelings in a most effective way.

She kissed him back, sweetly and tenderly, letting him know she felt the same.

When they finally drew apart, Lulu confessed raggedly, "But I've made so many mistakes, too."

His gaze holding hers, he listened.

She swallowed around the lump in her throat and pushed on. "The biggest one was not letting you know that I never fell out of love with you. Not at the time we broke up. Not during all those years when we were apart." Her lips curving ruefully, she shifted even closer. "And certainly not the last couple of months."

His hand slid down her spine, soothing, massaging, giving her the courage to finally convey what was in her heart. "Then why didn't you want to say that in your vows to me?"

She drew a shuddery breath and clutched at him, reveling in his heat and his strength. "I was so happy, just living with you and the triplets. I was afraid to upset the status quo. Afraid if I told you how I really felt, only to find that you didn't still love me the way you once had, that it would change things or put too much pressure on us. Somehow ruin things, the way our elopement did."

He sat down again, pulling her onto his lap. "I take the responsibility for that." Regret tightened the corners of his lips. "I knew you weren't ready to marry me at nineteen."

Looking back reluctantly, she remembered his initial hesitation. Realized, too late, it was a warning she should have heeded. "Then why *did* you say yes, when I suggested eloping with Peter and Theresa?" she asked curiously.

His mouth twisted in a rueful line. "It was selfishness.

I was so damn in love with you, and I was graduating college and about to head back to Laramie. I wanted you with me, even if it wasn't the right thing for you. And deep down, you knew we were too young to make that kind of lifelong commitment, too."

"Otherwise I wouldn't have been so afraid and ashamed to tell everyone we'd gotten hitched."

A contemplative silence fell while they both came to terms with the past.

"Even so…" She put her hands across the warm, solid wall of his chest. "I shouldn't have asked you to hide our marriage. Especially when I know now it made you feel like I was ashamed of my feelings for you. I wasn't. I was just afraid of what people would think…that they'd assume I was being reckless and impulsive again." She sighed. "And most of all? I was afraid of disappointing you and ruining everything between us. And *that* I really couldn't take."

"We both made mistakes." The pain in his low tone matched the anguish she'd felt in her heart. "Years ago. And recently, too." He pressed a kiss to her temple, her brow. "I never should have walked out on you when you told me you didn't want to go through with our recommitment ceremony. I should have given you all the time you needed."

Tingles sliding through her head to toe, Lulu called on the perspective she, too, had gained. "I had enough time to figure out what was in my heart."

His brow lifted.

Feeling the thud of his heart beneath her questing fingertips, she confessed in a tone overflowing with soul-deep affection, "You taught me how to love. How to be vulnerable. And how to risk."

He grinned with the shared realization that they'd finally found the happiness they'd both been craving.

"And that being the case…" She recited her feelings in an impromptu version of the vows he'd been wanting her to pen, "I pledge my past, my present and my future to you. I promise to be your wife and take you as my husband forevermore. And—" she hitched in a bolstering breath, looking deep into his eyes "—I promise to do everything I can to make you happy, Samuel Kirkland. To give love and accept it in return. Because I do love you," she finished thickly, knowing she'd never be able to say it enough, "so very, very much…"

Sam's eyes gleamed. "I love you, too, sweetheart," he murmured, bending her backward from the waist and bestowing on her the kind of jubilant kiss couples engaged in at the end of their nuptials.

Grinning, he brought her upright. "And as long as we're speaking about what's in our hearts… I want to thank you for teaching me what love is and making my life so much happier and brighter than I thought it could ever be. For giving us…and the boys…a future." Voice rusty, he went down on one knee. "So, if you'll have me, Lulu McCabe, I vow to love, cherish and protect you for as long as we both shall live." He reached into his pocket and brought out a diamond engagement ring.

"Oh, I'll have you, Sam Kirkland!" Tenderness streaming through her, Lulu drew him to his feet. She gave him another long kiss. "For the rest of my life!"

"You know," Sam teased, when the steamy caress had ended and the ring was on her finger, "our spur of the moment vows were really spectacular."

And heartfelt, Lulu thought. On both sides. "So much so that I kind of feel married again," she teased. Even without the wedding rings.

"Really married," he agreed. Sobering, he went on, "But I still think we should make our union as strong and official as it can be."

And that meant going public with their commitment.

"I'm with you, cowboy." Lulu beamed, excited to tell him the rest. "Luckily for us, there's still a wedding planned for tomorrow at my parent's ranch."

He grinned his sexy, mischievous smile that she loved so much. "You didn't cancel it?"

Lulu wreathed her arms about his shoulders and gazed up at him adoringly. "I couldn't. Not when I still wanted to spend the rest of my life with you so very much."

He sifted a hand through her hair, then drawled happily, "Sounds like we'd better get a move on then, darlin', as I imagine there's still a lot to do."

"We'll handle it," Lulu told him confidently. "And while we're at it, we'll enjoy every moment, every step of the way. Because this time, my love—" she rose on tiptoe to give him another lengthy reunion kiss "—we're doing it right."

Epilogue

One year later

"Mommy, can we take Beauty to court with us?" Ethan asked.

Lulu wasn't surprised the triplets wanted their beloved pet to accompany them. It was going to be an exciting day.

"No, honey." She knelt to help him clip on the tie he had insisted on wearing, because he wanted to be just like Daddy. Who was looking mighty fine, in a dark suit, pale blue shirt and tie.

Sam assisted Andrew with his neckwear. Theo had figured his tie out on his own and didn't need any assistance.

"How come?" Andrew asked, gently petting the top of Beauty's head.

"Dogs aren't allowed in court," Sam explained. "Unless they're service dogs. Like the ones some of Uncle Matt's friends have."

"That wear the special vests," Ethan said. "And help the old soldiers."

"Ex-soldiers, and yes, that's right." Sam grinned.

The boys thought about that for a minute. "Then could we take some of Mommy's bees with us?" Ethan asked.

Sam shook his head. "They need to stay on the Honeybee Ranch."

"So they can make more honey," Andrew said.

"Right." Lulu smiled.

"How many hives do you have?" asked Theo, who was always counting something.

"About three hundred and ten."

Sam had not only created an auxiliary membership that allowed her and other ranchers who did not specialize in cattle to join the Laramie County Cattleman's Association, he had also convinced her she could do more than one thing. So she'd brought the colony back from Wisconsin, nurtured them through the stress of posttravel and added a few more boxes in the spring.

She'd also hired an assistant beekeeper to stay on the property and do a lot of the day-to-day work for her business, so she could concentrate on caring for Sam and the boys, who altogether were quite the handful. Especially now that the triplets had gone from two-word sentences to nonstop chatter and endless questions.

As they prepared to leave, Beauty followed them to the door.

"Ahhh," Ethan pouted. "She's going to be lonely without us!"

"Are you sure we can't take her?" Andrew asked.

"She was in the wedding!"

"That was outside, on Grandma and Grandpa's ranch, and she had special permission to be there."

"Yes, but she was really good."

She had been. As had the boys. And it had been a glorious day, full of the promise of a lifetime of love ahead.

Sam got out a dog biscuit for each boy to give the Saint Bernard. "She'll be waiting for us when we get back," he said.

"And we're going to have a huge party!" Andrew spread his hands wide.

"Yes, we are," Lulu promised.

All the McCabes were going to be there in court to witness the big day. And all of Sam's sisters, as well.

Outside the courtroom in the marble-floored hallway, Lulu and Sam paused to speak to the boys. "This is very important," Lulu said gently.

"So you all need to be on your best behavior," Sam continued. "Do you understand?"

The boys nodded.

Sam and Lulu escorted them into the courtroom and took a seat at the table. The clerk announced the adoption procedure.

Hearing their names, all three boys jumped up onto the seats of their chairs, unable to contain themselves.

Andrew yelled, "Do we take this Mommy? Yes!"

Ethan shouted, too. "Do we take this Daddy? Yes!"

Theo clapped his hands. "You may kiss!"

The courtroom full of family erupted in a flood of laughter and tears. Sam and Lulu shot to their feet, too. Together, they lovingly contained their three little charges.

"Sorry, Your Honor," Sam said with as much solemnity as he could manage, "they have wedding and adoption formalities mixed up."

"Well." The judge cleared her throat, looking a little teary-eyed, too. "It's understandable. The depth of commitment is the same."

It absolutely was, Lulu thought.

"So, if y'all think we can continue…?"

Sam and Lulu bent and whispered a new set of instructions to the boys. They nodded solemnly, raised their hands and when called upon, said, "Sorry, Your Honors. We're going to be quiet until we're *allowed* to cheer."

And they were.

Afterward, they gathered outside the courtroom in the hallway. Hugs and congratulations were exchanged all around.

Hours later, when their company was gone and the kids were finally asleep in their beds, Sam and Lulu met up on the back deck for a glass of champagne in the starlight.

He clinked glasses with her and smiled victoriously. "We did it."

She linked arms with him, sipped. "We sure did."

They took a moment to ruminate on all they had accomplished in coming together. Sam slanted her a deadpan glance. "Think we'll ever get that honeymoon?" he teased.

"Oh, maybe twenty years from now," Lulu joked.

They both laughed.

"Seriously." She rose up on tiptoe and kissed him, sweetly and tenderly. With a contented sigh, she drew back just enough to be able to see his face. "It feels like we've been on one since we got back together."

Bliss flowed between them.

Sam gave her waist an affectionate squeeze. His gold-flecked eyes sparkling with joy, he mimed writing in the sky. "Hashtag. Best Life Ever."

* * * * *